MW01287267

MEN OF THE
N #5 ORTH
THE WARRIOR

Copyright © 2018
By Elin Peer
All rights reserved.
No part of this book may be reproduced in any form without written permission from the author, excepting brief quotations embodied in articles and reviews.
ISBN: 9781980638735
The Warrior – Men of the North #5
First Edition
The characters and events portrayed in this book are fictitious. Any similarity to real persons or organizations is coincidental and not intended by the author.
Recommended for mature readers due to adult content.
Cover Art by Kellie Dennis: bookcoverbydesign.co.uk
Editing: www.martinohearn.com

Books in this series

For the best reading experience and to avoid spoilers this is the recommended order to read the books.

To be alerted for new book releases sign up to my list at **www.elinpeer.com** and receive a free e-book as a welcome gift.

PLEASE NOTE

This book is intended for mature readers only, as it contains a few graphic scenes and some inappropriate language.
All characters are fictional and any likeness to a living person or organization is coincidental

DEDICATION

To YOU.

Because the thought that somewhere, someone is
reading my book makes me smile.

Elin

CHAPTER 1
Straight Talk

Laura

"Women are equal to men in all areas." My sensei spoke in a soft tone, but her aura of authority made the small woman's words stand out as a universal fact.

I shook my head. "Not where I come from. In the Northlands women are limited. We don't work or hold powerful positions. We women are nothing but prized possessions of strong and powerful men."

"And yet you wish to return there." Lennie's dark eyes expressed that it puzzled her. We were sitting opposite each other on the floor after we'd just practiced a round of aikido.

I leaned back. "Someone has to change things in the Northlands. That's why I'm going back."

"To do what exactly?"

"To fight for equal rights for men and women. I'm not trying to turn the Northlands into the Motherlands, but there has to be a middle way."

Lennie wasn't a very expressive woman; her face remained almost impassive. Her tone, however, was one of concern. "How do you know your husband won't mistreat you? You could end up in a worse situation than before you left."

"Magni never mistreated me," I pointed out. "He acted like any other husband would in our culture. I always considered myself lucky that he was my champion."

"But he didn't let you work and you said he refused to teach you how to fight, even though you claim he's the best in the world. If you go back, he might oppress you again."

Resting my palms on the floor behind me, I leaned back. "I won't let that happen. I'm much stronger now."

Lennie looked thoughtful. "He won't make it easy for you."

"I know." I looked down, well aware that Lennie was right. Magni was used to getting his way and he wouldn't like me standing up to him one bit. "If you worry that much, you could teach me some jiu-jitsu or Krav Maga."

"No."

"Why not?"

"I told you, Laura. We don't practice those sports anymore. They are aimed at causing harm to your opponent. Aikido on the other hand will give you the ability to defend yourself without causing injury to your attackers."

"But what if I wish to injure my opponent?"

Lennie's lips disappeared in a thin line as if my words disturbed her. "I didn't teach you to fight for you to turn violent. Use what I've taught you to turn your attacker's momentum against them. And be careful when you do the forearm return move. Your attacker can easily be brought off balance and may break his wrist in the process."

"Got it." I didn't tell her that I had no problem breaking a man's wrist if he attacked me. Motlanders were pacifistic by nature and Lennie would never understand the culture I'd been raised in. "What's wrong?" I asked when I sensed there was something she wanted to say.

Lennie looked down at her hands and took time before she spoke. "Laura. These past six months, you've grown stronger both physically and mentally. I have never seen anyone become so skilled at fighting in such a short time."

"*But?* You can say it, Sensei. I know Motlanders don't like to criticize, but we Northlanders prefer straight talk."

Lennie met my eyes. "I worry about you."

"Why?"

2

"Because you are missing some fundamental communication skills. Nobody can blame you, of course. It's not your fault that you grew up in the Northlands and haven't been exposed to many emotionally intelligent people."

I lowered my brow. "People aren't dumb in the Northlands."

"I never said they were. It's just that you have pointed out yourself that expressing emotions, and developing empathy, isn't as valued in the Northlands as it is here. I worry about what will happen if you go back too soon. Who will teach you to set your boundaries and communicate in a healthy way?"

"If someone doesn't respect my boundaries, I can kick their butt."

Lennie wasn't amused. "The point of teaching you to fight was to empower you to rise above any drama and conflict in your life."

"I know that was your goal, but to be honest, I like a little drama once in a while. Magni throws some explosive tantrums, but often they morph into amazing sex between us."

Lennie wrinkled her nose. "That sounds horrifying."

It was always weird talking about sex with Motlanders since in general they didn't see the point of it. To the majority of them, sex-bots were considered a more hygienic solution to fulfilling any physical need.

"It's not horrifying at all. I wish you'd try sex for yourself."

Lennie had told me that there were sex clubs for naturephiles who had a fetish for the human experience. I'd been curious to see it for myself, but Lennie didn't see the point when I admitted that I wasn't interested in having sex with anyone. Using strong words for a Motlander, she had let me know that the poor naturephiles weren't there for my amusement.

Lennie tilted her head to one side as if she needed to get a clear view to see if I had a hole in my head or something. "I'm not interested in sex, and may I remind you that you complained about Magni being domineering and controlling."

"That's true. He orders me around as if I was one of his soldiers. It's fine in the bedroom, but outside it's driving me crazy."

Lennie made circles on her knee with her index finger. "Why would you go back to a man like that when you can stay here with us?"

I drew in a deep breath, and released the air in a slow exhalation. "The Northlands is home to me and I miss it. Not just Magni, but my friends and family too." Tapping my lower lip, with a thoughtful expression I pondered out loud. "My dilemma is how do I change the most stubborn man in the world?"

"I can't help you with that." She placed a hand on my knee. "Laura."

"Yes?"

"Promise me that if he mistreats you, you'll come back here."

I lit up. "That could work. I'll tell Magni that unless he treats me as an equal, I'll move to the Motherlands permanently. He won't like that."

"Ultimatums should be avoided," Lennie said in a soft voice. "Are you sure you wish to threaten him like that?

I pushed up from the floor with determination and dusted off my hands. "It's the only leverage I have. Cross your fingers that it's going to be enough."

CHAPTER 2
Seeing Magni Again

Laura

The earthquake was the first one of catastrophic proportions in more than a century. We had experienced smaller ones, but none so powerful as the one that hit us ten minutes after I arrived at the border.

Before it happened, I'd been consumed with wanting to look strong, powerful, and unaffected by the sight of Magni. Or at least not let him see how wobbly my legs were.

Magni stood tall and fierce on a stage with officials from the Motherlands and Northlands. He wore his usual scowl and the battle scars that spoke of his heroism as the commander of the armed forces and leader of the Huntsmen, an elite unit of the finest warriors the world had ever seen.

Magni's brother, Khan Aurelius, the ruler of the Northlands, was making a speech and I gave a double take when the hundreds of women in front of the stage cheered and raised posters with slogans like "No more borders," "I'll marry an Nman," "Take me home with you," "Nmen or no one," and "The doctor is mine!"

I knew the last sign was referring to Finn MacCumhail, whom the Motlanders lovingly called *the doctor*. Finn was Magni's best friend and one of the five Nmen who had spent the past ten days in the Motherlands. Yesterday I'd met with him when he tried to convince me to come home, and I'd seen for myself what a celebrity Finn had become.

The ceremony today was an official end to the visit of the five Nmen and a signal to the whole world that the integration process between our nations had begun.

It didn't take Magni long to see me as I leaned against his sleek red drone. We shared a moment of brief eye contact before I looked away with my heart hammering in my chest. The intense fire that burned in his blue eyes only confirmed what I already knew; Magni was furious with me.

I swallowed hard, expecting him to charge over here and confront me with my betrayal. To be fair, Magni had every right to be angry with me. Leaving him six months ago with only a note to explain that I'd gone to the Motherlands, a place beyond his reach, had been a shitty thing to do. If he'd done something similar I'd be furious with him as well.

Still, I didn't regret it. As a female, my world had been limited in the Northlands and my time here had opened my eyes to the woman I wanted to be.

Magni's hands pressed into fists and his eyes were locked on me. It had to take willpower for him to stand still until his brother's speech was over. It was a testament to the fact that Magni was raised to put his country first. He didn't move.

Six months ago, I would have been standing by Magni's side as his quiet, obedient wife, but much had changed in that time. My time here had opened my eyes to the freedom I had been denied as a woman born in the Northlands. In the Motherlands, women didn't need a male protector. They didn't depend on men for their survival, and they were free to work and live independent lives.

Not only had studying martial arts taught me how to fight and defend myself, it had also given me a new self-confidence that showed in the way I walked, and held my head high.

My pounding heart told me I would need every ounce of that newfound strength and confidence when facing Magni. I had angered him in the past, but this time I had humiliated him, and hurt his pride. There wasn't much worse you could do to an Nman, and my husband had every right to punish me. Still, I couldn't bow my head to him. If I did, we would fall back into the unwanted roles of the domineering husband and the obedient wife. If my time in the Motherlands had taught me anything, it was that women were as powerful as men.

This would be my chance to redefine our relationship and show him what a strong woman I had become.

A small shake of the ground was followed by a low rumbling sound that made me look to the crowd of people. They seemed unaffected, so I stayed where I was. When the second more violent shake followed, chaos broke out. People were screaming and running in different directions as the earthquake continued.

Five women ran toward the tree line, and it made me wave for them to turn around. "Run for the drones," I shouted while running toward them. Relief filled me when the woman closest to me changed her course.

The next minutes were a blur of losing my balance and falling to the ground. As a Northlander, I was taller and stronger than most Motlanders and it was in my blood to step up in a crisis situation. I got back up every time I fell and kept directing panicked people to the drones.

"Stop!" I shouted when a woman climbed a tree. "Get away from the tree." My voice was overshadowed by the cracking sounds from the earth, the sirens from the border drones, and the screams of fear all around us.

Watching in horror, I saw trees fall in front of me, uprooted as if Mother Nature was spitting out used toothpicks.

I sprinted to the woman and imitated the most authoritarian man I knew when I shouted like Magni. "Get the fuck down from that tree, right now."

Clinging to one of the lowest branches, the woman's eyes were teary with fright. "I can't," she cried out. "I'm too scared."

Using my strength and height, I helped her down but we weren't quick enough. A large branch fell on top of us, scratching our hands and faces. She took the worst of it and suffered a violent nosebleed.

It wasn't until the earthquake died down that I heard my name being shouted.

"Over here," I called back.

A minute later Magni and Finn came into sight. Without words, Magni jumped over fallen tree trunks to get to me, and cleared away thick branches as if they were nothing but twigs. It was impossible not to appreciate the sight of my husband's agility and strength. He was impressive and masculine compared to the feminine Motlander men that I'd been surrounded by these past six months.

When Magni squatted down in front of me, I jerked back a little, fighting my instinct to hug him fiercely and tell him how much I'd missed him.

"Are you okay – what happened to you?" His hands were all over me when he scanned me for injuries. "Are you hurt?" He was gentle when he lifted my hands.

No wonder he was so worried. My fingers were smeared in blood, but it wasn't all my own. I didn't have any severe injuries, just the shock from experiencing the chaos of the earthquake.

It was tempting to let Magni take over and keep me safe. But I was no longer that helpless woman he had known.

"I'm fine." If I looked into Magni's worried eyes, I would crack, so I focused on Finn instead. "I saw some women run for the trees and tried to warn them to stay clear. This woman was hit in her head."

Finn was quick to take over and assist the bleeding woman, while Magni pulled me in for a tight hug.

"I've been so fucking worried about you."

"I'm okay," I whispered. *Ahh*, the smell of Magni filled my nostrils and had me thinking back to nights of passion between us. I lifted my hands to hug him back but stopped when he narrowed his eyes and ordered, "Now, promise me that you'll never do something like that again."

This was the Magni I knew. Bossy and always ordering me around. I steadied myself, hardening my jaw.

"Laura." Magni gave my shoulders a shake. "Promise me!"

I kept quiet. With my lips pressed together, I refused to look at him. Any time now he would blow up in one of his temper tantrums. This time I wouldn't give in. I was a free woman and no man would ever control me again!

Finn saved me by asking us to help him with the injured in the area. For a while we worked side by side with Finn giving orders. When he told Magni to carry a woman with a twisted ankle and her friend who had injured her knee in a fall, Magni hesitated and looked from the women to me and back again. "Are you sure you want me to touch you?" he asked the women in a skeptical tone.

According to the laws of the Northlands no man could touch a woman without the permission of her protector. With only around one hundred women to ten million men in the Northlands those laws were necessary to protect us females. These Motlander women however, were not used to rules like that, and the closest woman, who had short spiky hair, lit up.

"I would love to be carried by you."

Magni's frown lines deepened when his eyes fell to her shirt that said, *Give me an Nman for every day of the week.*

Still not touching her, he turned to me. "Laura, are you okay with me carrying these two women to their drones?"

Warmth spread inside of me that Magni would ask for my permission. It made me feel like an equal.

"You have my permission," I said with a small nod, although I didn't like the way the two women exchanged a small giggle.

Magni moved closer to the first woman and helped her to her feet. With a nod to her shirt, he said, "Clearly you don't know much about our culture."

"What do you mean?" she asked.

"Your t-shirt. There's no way you could have seven Nmen. The first would kill the others for touching you."

"Really? They would fight over me?" She looked giddy when he placed her over his shoulder, his arm hooked around her knee and his hand holding on to her wrist in a fireman's carry.

The woman gave her friend a smile and placed her hands on Magni's back to steady herself – or to feel his muscles.

"Is it true, would they really fight over us?" the friend who sat on the ground asked Finn.

He nodded. "Yes, we Nmen are very protective of our women."

"That's so sexy," the woman on Magni's back cooed.

I would have sworn I didn't have jealousy in me. But seeing another woman flirt with my husband was a new experience, and when she nuzzled his broad shoulders, it made me want to yank her spiky hair.

"Hey, keep those hands to yourself, I'm a married man," Magni told the woman and began the climb across tree trunks to get her back to her other friends.

"Laura." Magni had stopped and was looking back at me.

"What?"

"Stay with Finn," he ordered. "Don't go anywhere!"

This time I forgave him for being bossy. His words to the woman had eased my jealousy, and I appreciated his telling her off.

People who had escaped the earthquake in drones returned for their friends. Khan, his wife Pearl, and members of the Council of the Motherlands gathered in deep conversation. With the border wall partly collapsed, it wasn't hard to figure out what had them so upset.

Magni was ordering people around, telling them to fill up the drones and return home. The few who had injuries were directed to Finn. With everyone eager to make sure their loved ones were safe, the area soon emptied, leaving only the swarm of border drones flying back and forth along the destroyed wall, blaring out alerts that anyone crossing the border wall unauthorized would be detained.

"It's a miracle that no one was killed," Finn said as we walked back toward Magni's drone.

"It'll be worse in the cities where there are more buildings," I pointed out.

Finn stopped cold with his face frozen in a grimace.

"What's wrong?" I asked.

Worried about his friend Athena, a priestess he'd stayed with for a part of his stay in the Motherlands, Finn insisted that we call her. When she didn't respond, he turned to Magni with panic in his eyes. "I need to borrow your drone."

"What? No."

"Athena might be hurt, and I can't go home until I know she's safe. I need to see her," he exclaimed.

"Can't it wait until I get Laura back home?" Magni argued.

"No, it can't *fucking* wait," Finn shouted. "Athena lives alone and chances are that there is no one with her."

Magni frowned. "But I thought you didn't like Athena..."

Finn cut him off, shouting, "I need your fucking drone."

11

Magni was torn but in the end, he threw his hands in the air. "All right, then take it. But you'd better not wreck it."

Finn didn't say goodbye. He just sprinted for the drone and took off.

"Fuuuck!" Magni groaned, his hands on his hips and his eyes to the sky where his large drone disappeared fast.

I used my hand to shield my eyes from the sun. "It was the right thing to do."

Magni didn't reply but lifted his wristband, calling for another drone to pick us up before he walked toward the gates of the border. "Let's go," he ordered over his shoulder. "I'm taking you home."

CHAPTER 3
Physical Needs

Magni

This was my chance to set things straight with Laura. Now that she was back, I would discipline her and make sure she never ran away again.

"Make sure we aren't disturbed," I told my lieutenant, who was waiting for me when Laura and I got back to the Gray Mansion.

"But sir, Lord Khan just asked me to tell you to come to his office." Excitement shone from the young soldier's eyes as Franklin fell into step next to me. "The ruler returned twenty minutes ago and he's waiting for you. Now that the border collapsed we're all waiting for orders to attack." Franklin was part of my elite unit, the Huntsmen, and always eager to serve.

"I already talked to Lord Khan at the border. He doesn't want us to attack at this point." I walked right past him with my hand locked around Laura's wrist. "Tell my brother I'll see him when I'm done with my wife."

"Understood, sir."

Laura and I didn't talk as we ascended the curved staircase. Nor did we look at each other. The closer we came to our suite, the more my heart was racing. For six months, I had dreamed of this moment. My grip around Laura's wrist tightened when I opened the door. She had to know that I would punish her for being disobedient.

"You're hurting me," she complained and jerked her hand back.

I gave her a light shove into our suite and closed the door behind us. "I don't care if your hand hurts. You fucking humiliated me."

Laura walked over to the window, keeping her back to me. "I know." Her words were low-pitched.

"Do you have any idea how many fights I've been in because of you?"

Her head turned and she frowned. "What do you mean?"

"You turned me from one of the most respected men in the country to the loser whose wife ran away from him. I couldn't go out without men ridiculing me and calling me insulting names." I pulled up my sleeve. "See that long scar?"

"Someone stabbed you?"

"Uh-huh. I was piss drunk or the fucker wouldn't have gotten close enough to cut me. But the point is that you made my life hell."

"I'm sorry."

"You're sorry?" My body was tense from the resentment I held against her.

"It was an impulsive decision."

"You left me!"

"I know. But it wasn't to get away from you. It was to experience the freedom of the Motherlands."

I locked the door and stalked toward her. "Are you talking about you learning martial arts?"

"Yes. That and walking around freely."

With a hand, I spun Laura around to face me. "Did you sleep with anyone?"

"No." Her tone was offended and her blue eyes didn't blink. "Of course not."

I narrowed my eyes. "Are you sure?"

Laura cocked her head to one side. "Have you *seen* Motlander men?"

"What about them?" I asked and backed her up against the wall. When she tried to move out of my way, my palms flew to the wall, trapping her.

To my surprise, Laura didn't cower. She met my eyes and lifted her chin.

"I'm not scared of you, and I'm not the same woman you knew."

"Is that right?"

Her hands pushed at my chest, but I moved closer, taking in the scent of her. "New shampoo?" I asked in a low voice, my fingers trailing down her body, and my nose almost touching her forehead.

"Different perfume too." She licked her lips, her voice raspy.

She smelled nice, but I wanted her the way I remembered and ordered, "Go back to the old ones."

"That's not up to you."

Her words provoked me; I was done playing nice. In a fast movement, I cupped her face and gave her a punishing kiss to show her I was in control.

"What the fuck!" My hand flew to my mouth and I took a step back. "You bit my tongue."

"From now on, you'll ask me permission before you kiss me."

I shook my head with a smirk. "You've spent too long in the Motherlands. You're my wife, Laura. I don't need your fucking permission to kiss you."

"That's where you're wrong." In an agile movement, she moved away from me. "I'm not your property and you don't own me."

My eyebrows flew up. "Don't tell me you've turned into one of *them*."

"All I'm asking is that you'll treat me as an equal."

"But you're a woman."

Laura gave a deep exhalation and rolled her eyes.

"Treat you as an equal. What does that even mean?" I asked.

"It means that you'll respect my opinion and let me make decisions for myself."

I snorted. "You don't want equality. That's a fantasy gone wrong in the Motherlands."

"This is hopeless. You're never going to change, are you, Magni?"

"Why the fuck would I change?" I reached for her but she was quick to move away.

"I'm not going to be your submissive wife anymore."

This time I snatched her up and carried her to the bed. "That's what you think." I placed her across my knees, and my palm hit her behind.

Laura squirmed. "Stop it, Magni."

"Oh, you deserve a good spanking, and you know it."

This wasn't my first time spanking my woman and after the initial squirming, she took it well.

"From now on, you'll do as you're told." My voice was gruff from all the emotions I put into that spanking. The fear I had carried around for six months, worrying night and day that something bad could have happened to Laura. The frustration of breaking into the Motherlands twice and not finding her either time. The anger from my brother when I broke the peace treaty between the Northlands and the Motherlands by kidnapping a woman and holding her hostage to get back Laura in exchange.

I didn't hold back when I spanked her while thinking about the time I sneaked in to the Motherlands with my friend Alexander Boulder. The two of us had to dress as locals to fit in. I would never forget the humiliating sight of my reflection in the mirror: clean-shaven and with fucking ribbons in my hair.

When I was done spanking her, Laura pushed up from my lap, brushed herself off, and looked at me with her shoulders squared. "I allowed you to spank me this time, but only because I feel bad about leaving you the way I did." She pointed her index finger at me. "I'm warning you, though. This was the last time you put your hands on me without my permis..."

I pulled her back down on my lap before she could finish that sentence, and spanked her some more. When I was done, she was panting and my hand was buzzing from the blood rushing to it. "Stay!" I ordered her when she raised her head to push up again. My hand moved down her soft pants between her legs. If her dilated pupils hadn't been enough to tell me she was aroused, the wetness between her legs gave it away. "Tell me you missed me."

Laura's face and neck were crimson in color, her mouth was a little open, and she gave a small moan when I let two fingers circle her clit. "Tell me, Laura."

She drew in a deep breath, not breaking eye contact with me when she admitted, "I missed *this*."

"The spankings?"

"The sex."

My strong hands lifted her to sit on my lap and I kissed her with a deep hunger. My thoughts spilled over and I mumbled into her mouth, "I'm going to fuck you so hard."

Laura responded by pulling up my shirt, and the way her hands roamed over my muscles, with appreciation, made me want her even more. If only all the fools who had accused me of being so lousy in bed that my woman ran away from me could see us now.

Her eyes were hooded and her voice sultry. "I missed *this* a lot."

"Good, because we have a lot of catching up to do. Hold on to me!"

Laura raised an eyebrow. "Say please."

I snorted. "As if."

She squeezed her thighs around my hips, holding herself up with her arms around my neck, when I stood up from the bed. "This doesn't change anything. I'm still not going back to being your obedient wife," she whispered with her lips puffy from our violent kissing.

With both hands free, I had no trouble ripping her soft pants and throwing the torn fabric to the floor. I half expected her to protest my ruining her clothing, but judging from Laura's hungry kisses, it only aroused her.

I kicked off my shoes and stepped out of my pants. Laura was impatient and scratched my shoulders with her nails while placing kisses on the tattoo on my neck. At least our dry spell had increased her appetite for me. I grabbed her ass with both hands and positioned her just right. She felt wet and slick against my crown.

"Who do you belong to?" I asked while looking into her eyes.

"I belong to myself. I'm a free woman."

I growled. "Wrong! You're my wife." I should have put her over my lap again, but the tip of my erection was sliding inside her and my reptile brain took over. It had been too fucking long since I'd been inside her, and the overwhelming feeling of pleasure that ran like jolts of electricity from my scalp, down my spine, and all the way to my toes made me almost lose my balance.

"Fucking hell!" My voice was hoarse when I leaned my head back and closed my eyes.

"Ahhh," she moaned.

"Oh yeah?" My eyes were only slits but I could still see the most beautiful woman in the world leaning her head back and smiling. Laura's ginger-red hair was longer than it had been when she left. Her large blue eyes weren't as naïve and youthful as I remembered them, but she was still absolute perfection to me.

"Don't ever forget that this ass belongs to me." I pressed my fingers into her creamy flesh and made circles on my hips, making sure to give her every inch of me.

Laura leaned her head to one side, exposing her neck. I marked her with my kisses and bites.

We were still in a bubble of sex when a knock on the door sounded. "Go away," I shouted and put her down on the bed, enjoying the sight of my woman on all fours in front of me.

"But Commander, your brother..." Franklin called from outside the door.

My tone was hard and non-negotiable. "Unless the mansion is under attack I'm not available." I hadn't been inside my wife for six months and Khan would just have to wait.

My hands followed the curves of Laura's firm round ass, and I bent over to plant my teeth in her soft skin. She looked over her shoulder, giving me an inviting smile. "What are you waiting for?"

I growled low, letting her know that I was in charge and that I didn't appreciate her challenging me. Picking up a handful of her hair, I tugged hard enough for Laura to crane her neck back. With my other hand digging into her hip, I had her just where I wanted her. At my mercy.

After she'd denied me her body for six months, I wasn't in the forgiving mood. I took her hard and punishingly, her body under attack from my seven-foot-tall, three-hundred-and-forty pound, muscled body.

"Ahh, Magni, yes, yes..."

My palm smacked her behind again and she arched her back.

This wasn't about her pleasure. It wasn't even about mine. It was a sign of dominance and I was making a point.

I smacked her behind again and pushed in and out at high speed. "I'll fucking take you when I want you, do you understand?"

Laura gave me a sly smile. "As long as you respect a 'no'."

Another knock on the door had me cursing out loud and closing my eyes. My anger with Laura was blinding me. She had lived too long among the Momsies who ruled the world and oppressed their men. It was time to show Laura that she had returned to the Northlands, where the last real men lived. I took pride in my masculinity and would never allow a woman to get control over me.

"That's it, Magni, harder. Oh, I missed the sex."

Harder? Here I was afraid I was hurting her and she wanted it harder? Annoyance and confusion made me press her into the mattress, covering her with my body and pinning her arms. Laura would hardly be able to breathe in this position but it was the ultimate way for me to show her who was on top.

I moaned and pushed in balls deep, biting her neck without breaking her skin. It was raw and animalistic, like a strong lion breaking in a disobedient lover.

Laura stilled under me with a long moan, and then her insides cramped around my cock. I hadn't tried to make her come, and part of me didn't want her to. She didn't deserve an orgasm.

"Fuck, Laura." I sounded pained when I came in an explosive orgasm of my own.

A third knock on the door sounded in the far distance and after a few seconds of heavy breathing on top of my wife, I got up.

Franklin didn't move a brow when I opened the door with no clothes on. "I'll be right down."

"Yes, Commander." He spun around and left.

Closing the door, I picked up the rest of my clothing that was spread around on the floor.

"I have to go talk to Khan. Stay here until I get back."

Laura rolled to her side, propping herself up on an elbow. The curve from her hip down to her slim waist had me staring for a few seconds. She was so god damn

20

gorgeous. I picked up my shoes and went to sit on the bed next to her.

"How long will you be gone?" she asked.

I wondered why she didn't cover herself like she used to do. Not that she had anything to be ashamed of, but the changes in her disturbed me.

"I don't know."

"Magni, I know communication has never been our strength, but we need to talk."

"Later." I fastened the second shoe and turned to her. "Take a bath and order some food or something. I'll want a lot more of you when I return, so fuel up."

Laura shrugged. "We'll see. It was really nice having sex with you again. Maybe I could go for a second round later."

I narrowed my eyes and pushed her onto her back, my mouth on her tit, sucking hard enough to leave a mark. "Lose the attitude. You can tell yourself you have a choice, but the sooner you remember the duties of a good wife, the better for the both of us."

Laura laughed. "The sooner you understand those days are gone, the better for the both of us. This is the year 2437 and I'm your equal."

"I don't have time to discuss this now." With a huff of annoyance, I moved to the door. "Be here when I come back."

"You forgot to say *please*."

I shook my head. "No, Laura. It's not a request. It's a fucking order."

CHAPTER 4
Mila

Laura

I had been attracted to Magni for as long as I could remember. With his brooding personality and incredible strength, he was the essence of a true alpha Nman. Every fairy tale that I had read as a child had been about heroes like Magni who protected their women and saved them from danger. He was an intimidating champion and could silence men with a single scowl.

Our first night after I returned from the Motherlands was fiery and passionate. Magni wasn't a talker, but the way he had sex with me said it all. He was angry and punished me in the most delicious way.

Lying in bed next to his large body, I listened to his deep breathing and thought about the conversation I had with my sister, April, yesterday.

"I almost regret calling you if you're just going to yell at me. Here I thought you'd be happy that I was back," I complained.

"Of course I'm happy. It was just a selfish and foolish thing that you did. Ramses has been going through so much shit because of you. Everyone's mocking him – saying that he has to keep an eye on me and make sure I don't run away like my twin." April spoke in a hushed voice as if afraid her husband would hear her. *"He's very angry with you and so am I. For six months I haven't heard from you. How could you do that to me, your own sister?"*

"I'm sorry, April. I didn't mean to hurt you."

"Laila Michelle is angry with you too."

I sighed. Laila was my best friend and we'd grown up together. Unlike my sister, who lived on the East Coast, Laila Michelle lived close by and we used to see each other almost every day before I'd left.

"She gave birth to her twins while you were gone and I went over to see them. Laila Michelle cried a lot and kept saying that she really needed you to be there." April's tone was blameful. "You didn't think about that, did you?"

"April, I didn't exactly plan to go. It was a spontaneous thing and I never intended to hurt anyone. I love Laila Michelle and I love you. That's why I came back."

April's tone was softer when she spoke. "We've all been so worried about you. Especially Magni. He kept contacting me hoping that I'd heard from you. You should have seen him, Laura. He didn't eat, sleep, or function for a long time."

"I know. He says that he got in a lot of fights too."

"He has had the worst of it. Promise me that you'll be the best wife you can be after this. You owe him for what you did. Whatever he wants, you'll give it to him, right?"

I closed my eyes. "I don't want to be a good little wife, April. I want to work, speak up, and have an opinion. Men and women should be equals."

My sister had always been traditional, but it still shocked me when she hissed at me, "You've become a radical like those Momsies. If you bring more shame to me, I'll never speak to you again."

"What is that supposed to mean?"

"I don't want to be known as the twin sister of the feminist who ridiculed her husband and brought shame to our family name."

"Don't tell me you're happy being bossed around by Ramses."

"He's a good man, Laura, and he protects me."

"In the Motherlands women don't depend on men."

"I don't want to hear about the Motherlands. Those women are masculine and extreme in their opinions. I've heard they remove the testicles of their baby boys."

"That's a lie."

"How do you know? Did you see the men's testicles over there?"

"No."

"They are not our friends, Laura."

"I met some nice people that I would call friends."

April scoffed. "That's ridiculous. You know they oppress us, and they are plotting to capture some of our men and show them off like freaks in a circus."

"What? Where do you get this stuff from? Finn and four others just visited the Motherlands and people were nice to them."

"Sure, they smile for the cameras. But we all know they see us as freaks and consider us less evolved than them."

"Have you ever spoken to a Motlander, April?"

"No, but I can tell you this much. They're the freaks with their tiny bodies and the men looking like peacocks with all their make-up. We should catch a few of them and have people point fingers and laugh. See how they would like it."

Shaking my head, I sighed. "No one is going to point fingers at anyone. The Motlanders are nice people."

"Sounds like you like them better than you like us, your family and kin."

I rubbed my face and turned on my side, pushing the thoughts of my conversation with April out of my head. At least Laila Michelle had been more forgiving when I'd called her, and I couldn't wait to see her and her twins.

Magni grunted in his sleep and kicked his duvet off. The man was always warm like he had a furnace inside of him. I had never taken the initiative in sex between us but seeing him sprawled naked next to me, I couldn't keep my hands to myself. He was pure perfection with his ribbed muscles, and the tattoos I knew so well. His lips were

24

parted a little, and his chest rose and fell with his deep breathing. When my finger trailed down over his chest he turned his head muttering something under his breath. My curiosity was heightened when he repeated it. "I love."

I wanted to shake him awake and ask him to tell me to my face that he loved me, but the next words he spoke made me jerk back. Did he just say, "I love Mila"?

My heart was racing with the possibility that Magni had fallen in love with another woman.

"Mila," he repeated.

In my mind I imagined that one of the women he'd carried yesterday had introduced herself as Mila, and now he was dreaming of her. Jealousy twisted a knife in my belly when a mild smile spread on his handsome face.

With a possessive need for Magni to want *me*, I slid my hand down his chest and belly, following the trail of dark hair leading to one of my favorite parts of his body. Using my hand, I massaged him and it only took a few seconds for him to grow erect. He stirred in his sleep and stretched. If he could use sex to claim me, I could do the same to him. With burning jealousy, I straddled him and slid down over his erection.

Magni blinked his eyes open, yawning and rubbing his eyes with an expression of surprise and disbelief. "What are you doing?"

I raised an eyebrow, signaling that it was obvious what I was doing, and moved my hips to take him deeper.

"Ahh, nice. I see you have consented to my terms," he said and placed both arms behind his head, as if he was going to enjoy the show.

"What terms?" I asked, supporting myself on his strong chest, while rotating my hips and enjoying him stretching my insides.

"That we don't need to ask for permission."

I stilled.

25

The smirk on his face made me want to punch him. He said, "I don't recall you asking me for my permission to use my body. I assume that means you agree I don't need your permission either."

I hadn't considered that when I impulsively straddled him, and he had a point.

"Hey, where are you going?" He caught me when I moved back. "You can't start something like that and not finish it."

"I shouldn't have done it. I wasn't thinking."

"Look at me, Laura." With a finger under my chin, Magni forced me to meet his eyes. "Do you know how hot it is to wake up and find my wife riding me?"

"No."

"You have my permission to do it as often as you'd like."

"Who is Mila?" It flew out of me, and I pulled free from his hands.

"Who told you about Mila?"

"Answer the question."

"Answer my question first. Who told you about Mila?"

"You did!" My voice was accusatory. "You talked in your dream and all I heard was 'I love Mila'."

Magni frowned. "I said that?"

"Yes. So who is she?"

"Only the cutest, sweetest, most beautiful…"

My annoyed outburst was as surprising to me as it was to him. "Just say it!"

"Wow, I've never seen you jealous." Magni chuckled.

"Do you love this Mila?"

"Not in a romantic way."

That confused me even more. "What?"

"I'll take you to meet her later today."

"Why won't you tell me who she is?"

Magni got out of the bed and walked to the bathroom, keeping the door ajar while peeing.

I was still in bed when he returned. "You're not going to tell me, are you?" My voice was full of irritation.

"Give a man a minute to enjoy his wife being jealous." Magni looked smug. "Mila is a ten-year-old girl from the Motherlands who lives on Boulder's Island. It's a secret, so you can't tell anyone."

I dropped my chin. "A girl from the Motherlands, living here? How is that possible?" My heart was beating so fast it almost hurt. "What did you *do*, Magni?"

"Hey, don't look at me like that. I didn't hurt the girl. All I did was kidnap a priestess."

"*You kidnapped a priestess*?" My voice was loud and shrill. "When? Where is she?" I spun around, my eyes searching the suite again.

"Calm down. She's the woman Finn went to see in the Motherlands. Her name is Athena."

"I'm confused. Tell me everything."

Scratching his chest, Magni began explaining. "I sneaked into the Motherlands to find you and when I couldn't, I figured I could take a hostage and ask the Council to return you in exchange."

My hands flew to my hair. "Why didn't anyone tell me this?"

"I thought they did."

"No. Do you seriously believe I would have let an innocent suffer because of me?"

"She was only here for five days."

"And then you let her go?"

Magni scrunched his face. "Of course not. What do you think I am? A softie?"

"Did she escape then?"

He snorted. "No, Athena didn't escape. Pearl took her place, and I'm pretty sure it's been all over the news in the Motherlands. How can you not know this? Pearl came to see you, remember?"

"Yes, but she never told me about the hostage situation. She said that she and Khan had met during some negotiations and that they fell in love."

"Maybe she didn't want you to feel bad about causing others pain."

"That would make sense." I nodded. "I feel like a fool for not knowing all of this, but to be honest, I stayed away from any news sources."

"Why?"

"First of all, the news in the Motherlands is a waste of time. There are no juicy stories about violent episodes or rebels trying to overrun the Council."

"Then what do they show?"

"Mostly inspirational stories, tips on gardening, self-help advice, and some videos with pets that do silly things."

Magni rolled his eyes. "Figures."

"I guess I also avoided seeing the news because I didn't want to be reminded of home in case something came up."

"Sounds like you've been living under a rock, Laura."

"Pretty much." I massaged my temples, a headache brewing. "I can't wrap my head around the fact that you kidnapped an innocent woman."

"Yeah, you almost started a war. Did you think I wouldn't try to get you back?"

Guilt gnawed at me. I had been impulsive and taken off without realizing the consequences it could have on others. "I had no idea you would get that desperate." My head hung low in shame.

"It's not all bad," Magni said and lifted my chin. "Pearl is a major pain in my ass, but she and Khan have created an experimental school with kids from both sides of the border. Mila is one of the students."

"A school with girls?" My eyes widened. "But girls don't go to school here in the Northlands. We're home schooled."

"I know, but these are Motlander girls. There's eight of them and two boys."

"Ten children from the Motherlands?"

"Uh-huh."

I blinked my eyes, trying to catch up on all this new information. "I can't believe it."

"I know, it's crazy how much has happened, and now with the border down, we have a chance to conquer the world. It's fucking time men take back power."

His words upset me. "You would attack a neighbor country that's already suffering?"

Magni looked at me with disdain. "What better time to strike than when your enemy is weak? It's a fucking miracle that we didn't suffer much from the earthquake. I take that as a sign that some higher power is on our side."

"The people in the Motherlands aren't our enemies. They're peaceful people."

"Who rule the world and keep us isolated up here," Magni pointed out in a hard voice.

"I thought you liked the Northlands," I said.

"Sure, but I would like to see more of the world. Wouldn't you?" His laugh was hollow. "Oh, I almost forgot. You *did* see more of the world."

"Tell me about Mila," I said to change the subject.

Magni's eyes softened. "Mila is pure and innocent. She looks like an angel and has the cutest dimples."

"Wow."

"Yeah, and you know what the most amazing thing is?"

"What?"

He pounded a palm to his chest. "She asked me to be her dad."

"What do you mean?"

"Boulder and Christina adopted one of the Motlander girls and since Mila's mom died, she asked me to adopt her."

"Why?"

Magni's head turned and he frowned at me. "Because unlike you, she wants me to protect and care for her."

I swallowed hard and looked down.

"It's a shame that the Council of the Motherlands would never allow me to adopt Mila. They don't like Nmen much in general, and after I kidnapped Athena, they hate me."

"But they let Boulder adopt a child?"

Magni shrugged. "Only because he's married to a Motlander and because the girl's mother agreed."

"I see."

Magni's wristband vibrated and he looked down. "We'll have to continue this talk later. Khan wants me to join him for a strategy session before the negotiations with the Motherlands."

"What negotiations?"

He got up and turned to face me. It was hard to keep my eyes from wandering down his magnificent body.

"Khan is all about integrating our countries and he's willing to hold back our troops from attacking the Motherlands."

"That's good."

"I disagree. But anyway, Khan believes he can get the Council to give us what we want in exchange for holding our men back from the border. My troops have been patrolling our side of the wall all night."

"And what is it that you and Khan want?"

Magni moved to the bathroom. "We want men back in power, of course."

"You're not talking about men on the Motherland Council, are you?"

"For a start." With a hand on the door, he gave me a speculative glance. "I've got a long list in my head, but first I'm taking a shower. You want to join me?"

"Only if you promise not to hurt any Motlanders."

Magni raised an eyebrow and there was a hint of a rare smile on his lips. "What are you now? The protector of Motlanders?"

"I have friends there, and I'm not letting you attack them."

"How noble of you to care so much, but you forget that I don't take orders from women."

I took his words as a challenge. Getting up from the bed, I moved closer with my head high and my movements feminine and graceful. My confidence was fueled by the way his eyes ran up and down my naked body and his Adam's apple bobbed in his throat. Magni might think he was in control, but he had done desperate things to get me back. I had much more power than he wanted me to know.

"Promise me that you'll never kidnap an innocent woman again."

"Promise that you'll never run away again."

I nodded my head. "Deal. If I ever leave I'll talk to you about it first."

"Good girl. And you know what my answer will be."

I gave him a mocking smile. "Hopefully something like 'As my equal you are free to make your own decisions. I'll support you in whatever you do.'"

"Hmm… more like, I'll support you in being my wife who does as she's told." He took a few steps and turned on the water.

I shrugged. "Clearly, we still have some work in front of us."

Magni stepped into the shower, closed his eyes, and lifted his face to the spray. With one hand, I confirmed what I suspected; the water was too hot for me.

"It's boiling. Make it colder."

Magni complied and adjusted the water before he moved a bit to make room for me.

Stepping close to him with my back to the water, I leaned my head back with a smug smile. "So you *do* take orders from a woman."

He tucked a strand of my hair behind my ear. "No, but I listen to requests."

"Magni, you're impossibly old-fashioned." My hands trailed over a scar on his shoulder. "At least your body compensates a bit."

His lips tugged upward. "Is that right?"

"You have my permission to make love to me."

He laughed and it made him look almost boyish. "Make love to you? Sure, if that's what you want to call me fucking you hard against the wall."

CHAPTER 5
My Chance

Laura

When Pearl came to fetch me saying that Magni wanted me in the strategy meeting, I didn't believe her for one second. Still, I was excited to get close to the decision-making process for once. Both Athena and Pearl were there, and it was fascinating to see Pearl conduct herself like she belonged at the table. She didn't keep quiet when the men spoke, but freely offered her opinion as an equal. I would have expected Khan to silence Pearl, but instead he listened and valued her opinion. At one point, Khan also spoke directly to Athena, involving her in his plans to get as much from the Motherlands as possible in the upcoming negotiations.

I found the priestess fascinating. Like me, Athena had red hair, but hers was much darker in color and with the intricate tattoos on her forehead, and the green dress she wore on her petite shape, she looked like a forest fairy to me. I wanted to apologize to her for causing Magni to kidnap her. I still couldn't believe he had done something that awful. However, now wasn't the time to bring it up. All I could do was smile at her when she looked over. Warmth spread inside me when Athena smiled back. Her eyes shone with wisdom and kindness, and there wasn't a trace of resentment to be seen.

Khan pointed to Athena. "You will come with us to the negotiation meeting, and when I ask for the seventy-five percent men on the Council you will speak against me. It will make them feel like you're on their side and that you're not being controlled by me." He leaned forward.

"However, when I ask for the thousand Nmen living in the Motherlands over the next five years, you'll support the idea. Do you understand?"

Athena was smart enough to get that what Khan needed was enough good news to calm our people. The men of the North were ready to storm the Motherlands and take back the power that had been denied men for centuries. If Khan failed to negotiate a lucrative deal for the Northlands, he was in danger of being lynched by our people.

I didn't say a word as I sat, listening to them put together a long list of demands. When it grew too unrealistic, I couldn't keep my mouth shut any longer. "There is no way the Council can give you everything on that list," I pointed out.

Magni pinned me with his eyes, his brows drawn closely together, and his tone dripping with annoyance. "They'd better, if they don't want us to invade."

Empowered by the equality I had just witnessed between Pearl and Khan, I squared my shoulders. "I'm sorry to break this to you, but the women in the Motherlands aren't submissive by nature, and they'll have no problem standing up to you." I raised my chin to underline that statement.

Magni's scowl deepened and he leaned across the table. "Don't worry, honey, I love a good challenge."

God, the man was insufferable, and magnificent at the same time. A tingling sensation spread in my lower regions. Magni would never be soft or weak like the men I had gotten to know in the Motherlands. With him I could push and fight. He would stand his ground. Women from the Motherlands would no doubt find his rude domineering manner a turn-off.

On me, however, it had the opposite effect. Annoyed with myself, I crossed my legs and narrowed my eyes, reassuring myself that aroused or not, I'd never go back to being the weak woman I'd been before I left. Whatever it took, I would find a way to show Magni that I meant business. If Khan had learned to respect and appreciate Pearl, then I wouldn't settle for anything less.

"Okay, let me summarize the top priorities on my list then." Khan read from the list that hung projected above the table for everyone to see.

"1: Complete equality on the Council of the Motherlands within the next ten years. If we land on twenty-five percent that's a good start.

"2: Permanent residency in the Motherlands for one thousand Nmen over the next five years.

"3: Free entry to the Northlands for every female who wishes to live here."

"Yes," Pearl nodded her head. "This is where you should be willing to compromise. The Council is going to want the women to have rights. Tell them that you're willing to let the women work, and that they will be allowed to choose their own partners."

"I still say we should have tournaments," Magni exclaimed.

I nodded in agreement. No woman should be denied the chance to see men fight for her. We women of the North spent our childhood and youth dreaming of the day we would get to see our future husband heroically fight for our hand in marriage. Why wouldn't Pearl want the women to experience that?

Pearl continued talking. "We should offer to create a system where every male looking for a female can register. That way the women can make an informed choice."

"That would never work," Magni objected. "What if the women choose some weaklings that can't protect them? With tournaments, at least we know that the husband is strong and capable."

Athena coughed.

"What?" Magni asked her as if she had argued against him.

"Nothing, I'm just excited that the Motlander women might nurture some of the less violent traits in you Nmen. It should be interesting to see the men impress women with more than just their muscles."

I almost laughed at Athena's words. The concept of weaker men marrying women would turn everything upside down in the Northlands. But then again, maybe that would fit my agenda of equality in general.

Magni glared at Athena and crossed his arms. "Yeah, I'm sure you'd like to see us write love poems and jump around and do ballet and shit, but if I were you, I wouldn't hold my breath."

I spoke up. "Love poems sounds nice. An Nman expressing his feelings would be very refreshing."

Magni's foot was tapping under the table and when he met my eyes there was a promise of another spanking for provoking him in public. Another surge of excitement shot through me from the sizzling energy between us. I was annoyed with him. And I was drawn to him. *Argh*... folding my hands under the table, I pressed my nails into my palm to distract myself. Magni made me lose my focus. He made me forget everything I'd learned in the Motherlands about female empowerment. I was slipping back to adoring him, and wanting to make him happy.

Yesterday when I returned to meet Magni again, I'd been so convinced that I was strong enough to stand my ground. Now, I was beginning to doubt myself.

My nails dug deeper into my skin. *I want him to respect me and treat me as an equal.*

As if sent from above, the perfect opportunity to earn his respect presented itself right after the meeting when we all stood in the entrance hall of the Gray Mansion. It was a conversation between Finn and Khan that caught my ear.

36

"I thought you said all the men who had tried to cross the border had been captured," Finn said.

Khan crossed his arms. "Of course I would say that in public. I was trying to stop other men from doing the same."

"Wait, what was that?" I walked over to the group of men. "I thought I heard you say that some men crossed the border without being captured."

Khan exchanged a glance with Magni before he answered. "I'm afraid so. The Council has provided photos from the border drones, asking us to identify the men."

"How many are we talking about?" I asked in a hard voice. My protective instincts flaring up just thinking about the kind people I'd come to care for in the Motherlands being hurt.

"Not many. If the latest numbers that we received this morning are accurate, they caught two hundred and thirty-five men who tried to cross the border unauthorized."

"And how many didn't they catch?"

Khan hesitated before he answered. "Nineteen got away from them, and twelve of them have us concerned. It'll be all right. I'm going to offer the Council to send in the Huntsmen to locate and arrest the Nmen. We'll bring them back here before they do any harm and bring shame to our name."

"I told you," Pearl brushed her hair back in frustration, "the Council will never allow you to send in soldiers. They will insist on solving this problem themselves."

Magni spoke up in his deep voice. "Your mediators aren't equipped to deal with men like that. They could be armed, and I've seen their profiles. At least five of them are dangerous criminals with violent backgrounds."

Athena gasped. "Why would you allow anyone who is dangerous to walk around?"

"These men took their punishment already. Unless they're given a life sentence they're allowed back out when they've served their time," Khan explained.

This was my chance to make a difference and earn Magni's respect. Flicking my long ginger-red hair back and straightening my back, I declared, "If the Motherlands won't allow any of our male warriors to go, then I'll do it. I'm the best female warrior that we have."

Alexander Boulder snorted. "A female warrior – ha, that's a good one."

That provoked me. I had worked my ass off to learn how to fight these six months, and my sensei had praised me for my speed and strength. Pushing my chest out, I narrowed my eyes. "You won't be laughing when I track those fuckers down and bring them back here."

Everyone grew silent just staring at me in disbelief for a few seconds.

"You're serious?" Pearl asked.

"Why not? I'm not letting the Motherlands deal with those twisted Nmen by themselves." I would prove to Magni that I was anything but weak and helpless.

"You're not going anywhere," Magni said in a no-bullshit tone of voice. "You're staying right here where I can keep you safe."

I hardened my jaw, ignoring my hammering heart. "That's not up to you! None of your Huntsmen will be allowed in, and I'm going."

Magni cut me off "The fuck you are. You just got back and the two of us have things to discuss."

"I know, but you're too busy cleaning up this border mayhem for us to talk anyway. You'll deal with it on this side, and I'll track down and bring those men back before they hurt innocent people."

"No!" Magni said in a non-negotiable way, his brows lowered and his stance intimidating.

I couldn't back down now, or he would succeed in bringing back the old dynamic between us, with him being in complete power. "Yes!" I exclaimed and placed my hands on my hips to stop them from shaking.

"Laura dear," Pearl said softly. "This is a job for the most skilled mediators in the Motherlands; I doubt they will let you put yourself in danger."

I raised my chin, signaling that I wasn't backing down. "We'll see about that. I want to give back after everything the Motherlands have done for me, and they'll be fools not to take my offer." I held out my hand to Khan. "Give me every file you have on those shitheads, and I'll find them."

Khan didn't have a chance to answer before Magni grabbed me and pulled me aside. "Have you lost your damn mind?" he hissed.

"No. I can do this."

"I won't let you! What kind of protector do you take me for?"

"I'm not asking for your permission. I can take care of myself."

"By storming after violent men bigger and stronger than yourself, I don't think so." His voice grew low as he spoke through clenched teeth. "I'll lock you up in our suite before I let you go after them."

I scoffed. "If you do that, I'll find some way to escape again, and believe me I won't be returning to you, *ever*!"

"Then I'd better make sure to lock the door." Despite my protesting, Magni picked me up on his shoulder and walked up the stairs. Behind me Athena and Pearl were pleading for the other men to help me, but I didn't want to be rescued. I wanted to fight my own battles, even if I had to use dirty tricks. Not knowing what else to do, I planted my teeth in Magni's neck, making him growl and spank my behind, hard.

"Put her down," Khan commanded in a loud booming voice. Magni stiffened and the distraction that it caused gave me a chance to wriggle out of his hold and run back to the group.

The two women quickly moved in to shield me, and Athena stroked my back in a soothing manner.

Magni stood halfway up the staircase looking at me with fury on his face, before he turned around, and ran up three steps at a time.

"Laura, Magni is right," Khan said and rocked back on his heels with a deep frown. "Chasing down criminals is no job for a woman."

Pearl shook her head at Khan before taking my hands. "Don't listen to him, Laura," she said in a soft voice and turned her head to Khan. "When will you accept that women are as capable as men?"

"When will you accept that when it comes to handling violent Nmen, they aren't?" he said in a sharp tone.

Pearl wasn't intimidated. "You're forgetting that women were police officers and soldiers before the Toxic War."

"And you're forgetting that they had training," Khan pointed out. "Laura doesn't."

That wasn't true, and although I had been taught to look down when addressing our ruler, Lord Khan, I was so agitated that I looked straight at him. "I'm the best-qualified person for the task. I'm not afraid of Nmen and I have fight training now."

Khan took a step closer, pinning me with his dark intelligent eyes. "If you aren't afraid of those men, then you're the least qualified person for the task. I'm not sending a fool on a suicide mission."

"I'll be cautious. I'm not stupid."

"If Laura wants to do this, we should respect her choice," Pearl said and stepped toward Khan when he pivoted around and dragged his hands through his hair.

"Laura." Athena had a worried expression on her face when she looked deep into my eyes. "You have the

40

strength to do this, but I wonder if you're doing it for the right reasons."

"I want to help!"

"Yes, but if you're trying to prove the point that women are strong, there are better ways."

Maybe there were, but I needed something extreme to make Magni take me seriously.

The sound of running footsteps had us all looking up the stairs to see Magni return. He carried a small arsenal of weapons, and Athena gave a loud scream. "He's going to kill Laura."

Magni stopped cold, and then his face distorted in a grimace of anger. "What the fuck are you talking about, Priestess? I took a vow to protect Laura with my life," he snarled. "And just for the record, I don't need no fucking weapons to kill a person."

Walking the last five steps with his eyes glued on me, Magni spoke, "If you're determined to chase those motherfuckers, then I'm going with you."

"That's impossible," Pearl exclaimed. "After you crossed the border, unauthorized, twice and kidnapped Athena, you have become public enemy number one. They would never allow you to pass the border."

"They just did," Magni argued. "I was at the ceremony when the earthquake happened."

Khan spoke up. "You have no idea how long it took for Pearl to convince them to let you come. Both she and I had to make solemn promises that we guaranteed you would return with us to the Northlands, and that you wouldn't be trouble while we were there."

"Public enemy number one, huh!" Magni scrunched his face.

"I understand your frustration, brother, I know it's against your nature to leave Laura unprotected, but you can't leave your post now. There's too much going on here and I need you to stay."

41

Magni groaned and turned to me, his eyes expressive with deep worry. "If I can't stop you, then at least I can make sure that you're wearing the right protection, and that you bring solid weapons." He held out a one-piece suit in a see-through material that I recognized as Proteco.

"Remember the video that I made for you?" he asked in a gruff voice. "The one where I promised you that I would teach you to fight if you came home?"

I nodded.

"Well, I had this made for you, so you wouldn't get hurt while training. There's no better protective gear than this and you can wear it under your clothes."

I took the one-piece and looked it over. "I've seen vests and gloves, but never a full body suit. This must have cost you a fortune."

"As I said," Magni mumbled, "I had it especially made for you."

I was touched by his thoughtfulness and for a second I wanted to reciprocate his kindness by telling him I would stay. But I knew Magni, and he hated indecisiveness and people who didn't follow through on their promises. If I wanted his respect, I'd have to earn it the hard way. "Thank you," I said and held the suit to my chest.

Magni gave a small nod, his brows drawn close together. "I wish you could wear leather on top, but if you want to blend in, I guess that's out of the question." He looked down at the weapons. "They might come in handy for you if those motherfuckers won't cooperate."

I was in a bubble with only Magni and me, and didn't notice the others until Khan called out to Magni as they walked off. "Come join the rest of us in my office when you're done. The negotiations will begin in half an hour."

"Understood," Magni muttered without taking his eyes off me.

"You can take Laura to the border afterward," Khan added.

All I could see was the way my husband's body was tensed up like a tragedy was about to happen.

"Tell me you'll stay," he said, low.

I lowered my gaze to the floor, summoning the strength to follow through on this insane quest I'd volunteered for.

"Laura?" His hand grabbed the back on my neck and he leaned his forehead against mine. "Why are you doing this to me?"

"Because I have to."

"You don't have to do shit, and you know it." His grip tightened before he let go and moved back.

"I'm not asking you to understand, just to accept that I make my own decisions now. I'm not the child you once knew. I'm a woman."

Magni rubbed his forehead. "Where is this coming from? When did I treat you as a child?"

"You always did. You never cared for my opinion or saw me as an equal."

He made sounds of frustration but no real words.

"Would you prefer that I get a ride to the border from one of your men?"

"No, I'll take you myself."

"Then I'll wait for you to finish the negotiations meeting with the Motherlands." I moved toward the staircase.

"Laura."

"Yes?" I stopped and looked back.

"While you wait, search for your sanity, will you? Going after those men is crazy."

"Maybe, but I'm going anyway," I said and walked away from him, my hands folded into fists to hide how much they were shaking.

CHAPTER 6
Letting Go

Magni

My large beast of a hybrid had never flown as slow as when I took Laura to the border.

My head was spinning with ways to make her stay, but locking her up or spanking her into submission would only alienate her and we were already on shaky ground. More than once, I stopped myself before asking my most burning question: "Are you going to divorce me?"

It was my worst nightmare, but asking could potentially put thoughts in her head, something I wasn't willing to risk. All her talk about her newfound freedom in the Motherlands had me nervous that she would want to move there for good.

The negotiations meeting with the Council had been a farce, and I hadn't been able to control my temper when some of the Council members from the Motherlands claimed that men couldn't be trusted with power. They didn't even blink when they said males were power hungry by nature and that history showed we were incapable of maintaining peace.

Of course, my aggressive shouting at them didn't convince them otherwise. But it wasn't in my blood to take insults without standing up for myself. Not even from small Momsies who blinked when they heard the word fuck.

I was still upset that Khan had asked me to step outside when the Motlanders threatened to leave the negotiations if I remained in the room. He should have

45

never bowed to their demands. Fucking tree-hugging vegans who lived to oppress men.

"You don't like Pearl much, do you?" Laura asked me from her seat next to me. The millions of needle trees beneath us gave a feeling of flying over a green ocean.

"No, I don't like Pearl."

"Because Khan listens to her more than he listens to you now?"

My head swung to her. "Who told you that?"

The serious expression on her face didn't take away from how pretty she looked with the braid that ran like a hairband from one ear to the other. "No one. I saw it for myself at the strategy meeting. The two of them are close."

"It's just a phase. Newlyweds are always engrossed in each other. He'll grow bored of her soon enough and things will return to normal. Don't forget that I'm still the second in command in the Northlands. Khan depends on me to rule the country."

"What if he doesn't grow bored with her?"

I kept my eyes straight ahead, not wanting to entertain that thought. Changing the subject, I asked. "Did you talk to your sister?"

"Yes, and I talked to Laila Michelle too. Did you see her twins?"

"Yeah, once. They were only a few weeks old then and I mostly saw two bundles of blankets."

"I missed out on a lot," Laura breathed and played with a blue wristband.

"Uh-huh. Laila Michelle and April were both upset with you for leaving, you know?"

"Yes, they told me. April gave me a hard time, and Laila Michelle got upset when I called her just now to cancel seeing her and her twins today. She agrees with you that it's not a woman's job to chase criminals."

"Are you even sure the Motlanders will let you back inside their country?" It was no secret that I hoped they wouldn't.

"It should be fine, I have papers from the Council."

I wanted to land my hybrid in front of the border as much as I wanted to walk barefoot on lava, but in the end I had to. "Are you wearing your protective suit under your clothes?"

"No, but I brought it."

"Put it on."

"As soon as I go chasing the men, I will."

"I'm not letting you cross that border without you putting on your protective gear. The men could be hiding anywhere and grab you, Laura."

"I doubt they're lurking around close to the border. Besides, we're only talking about nineteen men. On this side there's millions of them."

Narrowing my eyes, I spoke in a firm tone. "On this side of the border I'm here to protect you. As soon as you cross that fucking wall, you're on your own. Put the suit on, Laura!"

"All right." Laura frowned and was annoyed with my being bossy, but she complied. It was hard to restrain myself from touching her when she was stripped down to only her underwear, but if I had sex with her now, I wouldn't be able to let her go.

I might not be the kind of man who showered her with loving words. But if Laura knew me at all, she would understand how deep my love for her was to let her do this. It was a violation of everything I stood for to let my woman put herself in danger. Never in my life had I compromised my own needs to this extent. I doubted she understood the magnitude of what she was asking of me.

If only she loved me half as much as I loved her. Then she wouldn't leave me here to worry about her again.

"Satisfied?" she asked when she was dressed again.

47

"Yes. And the weapons?"

She showed me the four weapons I'd given her, and then I walked her to the border.

"Tell me you're going to be all right." Laura was twenty years old, but in my eyes she was innocent and I couldn't bear the thought that something bad might happen to her.

"Don't go, Laura." Desperation made me add a word that I had only used a few times in my life. "Please." It was the closest thing I'd ever come to begging, but Laura still didn't budge.

"I'll be back soon, Magni. Don't worry."

I snorted because we both knew I'd be worrying non-stop.

"At least *try* not to worry. I'll be fine and when I'm done we can talk about our relationship."

Laura's words made my heart beat fast, like a war drum. "Yeah, I guess," I managed to say but my worst fear was poking up its ugly head. What if she never came back or she came back asking for a divorce because she wanted to live in the Motherlands?

It was counterintuitive to watch Laura walk away from me. For six months, I'd sworn that if I ever saw her again, I would never let her go. And here I stood less than a day after getting her back, watching her move out of my reach one more time. Every protective instinct in me wanted to pull her back to safety. But unless I wanted to hide her in a room somewhere, it was impossible.

To the very last second, I hoped for a miracle. Maybe they would reject her or she would change her mind. But all I got was a smile over her shoulder and a wave from her hand before she disappeared out of my sight.

I wanted to scream out my fear and anger, and blow up every one of the small border drones that hovered above the wall – keeping a camera pointed in my direction. On my way back I flew along the wall, seeing the destruction that the earthquake had caused. Workers

48

were repairing the wall with the help of robots and my soldiers were patrolling on our side of the wall – something that Khan had insisted would show goodwill with the Council and make it easier for us during negotiations.

When I saw a group of men sneaking around at the border I channeled all my anger at them. If I couldn't cross, they sure as hell couldn't either. My woman was on the other side of that wall, and the sooner she found the fuckers who had already crossed over, the sooner I could have her back. There was no way I would let the number of men she needed to chase down grow. Setting down my hybrid I stepped out, taking a wide stance, shouting at the men to turn around. There were three of them and after exchanging a quick look they all attacked me at once. It was just what I had hoped for.

CHAPTER 7
Skilled Mediator

Laura

Pearl had arranged for me to be picked up at the border and taken to meet her mother Isobel, who was temporarily staying in a house thirty minutes from the border. Isobel was in her fifties and the dark circles under her eyes made her look like she hadn't slept since the earthquake. She was the chairwoman for the Council of the Motherlands and even in her sleep-deprived state, she had an aura of sophistication around her.

"Laura, thank you for coming back to us in this stressful time. It's so kind of you to offer your help. May peace surround you." She stood up from her comfortable chair when I entered the room. Besides some long cracks in the ceiling and one window being covered, the room didn't look too bad.

"May peace surround you too." Since Isobel looked like she was about to drop, I gestured for her to sit down.

"We just finished the negotiations an hour ago, and I've been briefing the rest of the Council members since then."

"How did it go?" I asked and sat down on a stool across from her.

Isobel looked out the window, her eyes glazing over. "The immediate threat of war has been avoided, but the price we paid terrifies me."

"What do you mean?"

She refocused and tilted her head. "Laura, we could use your knowledge on how to deal with the men of the North. Don't think I'm not aware that they have a large

50

advantage with my daughter being Khan's adviser. If we hadn't had Athena talk Khan out of having seventy-five percent males on the Council..." She shook her head and closed her eyes. "The thought of *one* male on the council frightens me."

"Khan isn't a bad ruler," I said in an attempt to comfort her.

Isobel's eyebrows arched up. "Khan is a dictator who doesn't want to hear about democracy, but at least there will be two rulers in the Northlands."

"Excuse me?"

Leaning back in her chair, Isobel sighed. "Khan insisted on males on the Council. I suppose that we're better off including Motlander males on our own terms. The alternative at this moment is to risk being invaded by Nmen who would close down the Council altogether. From now on we'll have to pick boys to be trained as Council members. Potentially we could have fifty percent males on the council in as little as ten to twenty years. When that happens, Khan has to appoint Pearl his co-ruler."

I jerked back. "But what about Magni? He's the second in command. I don't think he'd ever agree to that."

"I don't know how Khan will explain it to him." Isobel's voice lowered and her face fell into a sad expression. "My heart goes out to you, dear Laura. I don't like to be negative and say upsetting things about your husband. But with the anger Magni displayed in the meeting today, I don't blame you for running away in the first place. That man is truly frightening. At least you don't have to worry about him now. You never have to see him again. Feel free to build your life here with us."

I shifted my balance from one foot to the other. "I'm not trying to get away from Magni. I mean, sure he's got a temper, but he's also caring and good to me."

51

Isobel lowered her eyebrows. "Interesting. I've heard about this phenomenon. You're not the first woman to defend her abuser."

"What do you mean abuser? Magni never abused me."

"Then I must be misinformed. I was told he admitted to hitting you."

"Spanking me, not hitting me."

Isobel moved in her chair. "I don't understand. What is the difference?"

I shrugged, not knowing how to explain something that I'd never questioned. "To me there's a difference. If Magni hit me across the face, I would be furious with him. The spanking is just something men do. My father did it to my mother, my sister's husband does it to her. My best friend Laila Michelle gets spanked by her husband too. It's not a big deal and it doesn't hurt much."

Isobel reached for my hand. "It's never okay for another person to lay a hand on you. *Never*."

"Then why are you touching me?"

Her eyes dropped to our hands. "No, I meant, it's never okay for someone to hurt you."

"Magni doesn't *hurt* me."

There was pity in Isobel's eyes. "It's okay, Laura. In time you'll come to see things more clearly." She moved back again, holding a hand to her forehead. "And to think that we just agreed to Motlander women being allowed to enter relationships with Northmen. Pearl insisted that Khan doesn't hit her, but from what you just told me it sounds like he's an anomaly and Magni is the standard." Her chest heaved in a deep intake of air that she exhaled with some noise. "May our women who join the Nmen forgive us for not protecting them from their own stupidity."

I forgave Isobel for the insult to my people since she was overtired and stressed out with all the changes happening.

"Pearl told you why I've come back, right?" I asked.

"Yes, yes," Isobel straightened up. "And we could use your help chasing the bad men who escaped us at the border. The good news is that four of them have already been captured. The last fifteen we're still chasing and we have leads on some of them."

"Good."

"Under normal circumstances we wouldn't allow someone without mediator training to do this kind of work, but nothing about this situation is normal, so we'll make an exception. The only thing is that I'll need you to leave your weapons here. Pearl told me you're carrying lethal weapons and we don't allow those."

"But I need them in case the men are armed."

"We don't kill people in the Motherlands." She pointed to a table in front of us. "You can put your weapons there and I'll make sure they are returned to Magni."

"No," I exclaimed, "that will only make him worry more."

"All right, then we'll just lock them up for now. For your safety and for practical purposes, however, we're teaming you up with one of our most skilled mediators. His name is Hans and he will make sure to supply you with a numb gun and a net gun. That should be sufficient."

"I don't need a partner."

"Whenever there is a physical threat involved, our mediators always work in teams. We've already established four other teams working on finding the last fifteen Nmen. You and Hans will make up the fifth team, and you have nothing to worry about. He has years of experience and comes with the highest recommendations from his previous area. If it comes to a confrontation, Hans will defend you."

"I can fend for myself."

"Of course you can." Isobel looked up when a knock on the door was followed by a woman entering with a bowl and a glass of water in her hands.

"Sweet Isobel, you really must eat something."

"Ah, yes." Isobel swung her hand to the plump woman and looked at me. "Meet Linda, who has been a wonderful host to me since the earthquake."

"I'm Laura," I said politely.

"I know. Isobel told me about you, and I'm sorry to intrude upon your meeting. It's just that Isobel is putting everyone before herself. She hasn't slept more than an hour, so I'm being a mother hen and making sure she at least eats a little."

"That's good."

"Would you like something to eat as well?" she asked me.

"No thank you, I'm fine."

As Isobel began to eat what looked like a vegetable soup, Linda dried her hands on her pants and gave me a smile. "Hans is eager to meet you, should I ask him to come in?"

As if summoned, a man smaller than me came into the room. He had long dirty-blond hair that was braided, and an awful lot of make-up on. "Did someone call my name?"

"Hello," I said and accepted his outstretched hands in a formal greeting. "I understand that we're teaming up to go after the missing Nmen."

"That's what I'm told." Hans' eyes darted around the room. "It's a good thing that I'm here. I have a lot of experience with large brutal Nmen."

"Really?" My eyebrows rose up.

"Hans was assigned to be Finn's personal mediator while he was here," Isobel explained before taking another spoonful of soup.

"Ah, I see. But I wouldn't call Finn large or brutal. He's one of the nicest men I know, and he can't be more than

54

six-two since he's only about four or five inches taller than me."

Hans couldn't be more than five-five and leaned his head back. "Yes, well, but you're very tall for a woman."

"I'm a woman of the North. We're all tall, just like our men."

"All I'm saying is that I'm experienced in dealing with Nmen, so you're in good hands."

"Great." I pointed to the door. "Should we get going? We've got work to do, right?"

"Yes, of course." With a look of importance, Hans addressed Isobel: "We'll report back to you as soon as we catch the criminals."

She gave him a tired smile. "Thank you, I appreciate it."

As soon as we were outside, Hans steered me toward a scratched-up drone. "Were you happy that Finn found you while he was here?"

"I guess so, why?"

"I should mention that I was the one who located you for him," Hans said. "Finn didn't think I could do it, since others had tried and failed."

I got the reference to Magni and frowned.

"I'm only telling you to make you understand that I'm very skilled and can get results others can't."

"Good for you," I said unimpressed. If this toad thought diminishing Magni's attempt to find me would make us friends, he was wrong.

"I should also tell you that Finn wanted me to give him your address and I flat-out refused." Hans' hand cut through the air to underline his point. "I stood up to him and made it clear that I would never pressure you to meet with him."

"Really? You stood up to Finn?"

Hans shrugged. "It wasn't hard. Finn has the deepest respect for me, and I would say he and I became very close while he was here."

I doubted that was true, but kept my answer civil. "Good to know. Now can we look at the leads and get going?"

After climbing inside the small drone, Hans used his wristband to project a list of names for me to see. The Nmen were rated according to level of danger and Hans pointed to the bottom of the list. "Let start with Luke."

Luke wasn't one of the five Khan had deemed dangerous. He had no criminal record, so I pointed to the top of the list instead. "No, let's go after Devlin; he's a nasty piece of shit who spent time in jail after stabbing some guy in a bar once. Definitely not someone we want running around in the Motherlands."

Hans' fingers fiddled with his lower lip. "Maybe we could pick someone else to begin with."

"Are you scared?" I asked.

"No, of course not. It's just that you're not a trained mediator, and I would like to see you in action before we go after the worst criminals. I'll need to know how much you have to lean on me."

I looked Hans over. The guy slumped in his seat and after knowing him for less than ten minutes, my guess was that he had spent more time on his make-up this morning than he'd spend on fight training in his entire life.

"All right, then let's start with that guy in the middle of the list, Jonathan. According to my sources he's a thief with questionable morals. But he only has a few fights to boast of."

Hans frowned. "Who in their right mind would boast about fighting?"

"It's a saying. Do you have any leads on him?"

56

Hans searched his information. "Yes. Someone reported a break-in in New Munich and the thief was described as having a large scar that fits his description."

"Then let's go."

"Are you sure you don't want to start from the bottom of the list?" Hans asked with a hopeful tone. "With this being your first time tracking down criminals, we should start out slow. At mediator training they always encouraged caution."

"I'm sure," I said. "And caution isn't really my thing."

Hans' smile was stiff. "Right. It's the same for me. Some people call me a daredevil."

I suppressed a laugh. "Well, come on then, Daredevil. Let's find Jonathan, shall we?"

CHAPTER 8
Flirting

Laura

Our drone looked tiny when it landed next to a larger aid-drone in the city of New Munich. Rescue workers were handing out blankets, food, and water to people affected by the earthquake.

Some of the Motlanders in line looked at Hans and me with hopeful eyes. That made me wish we had brought something to distribute.

It took us a while to locate the woman who had reported the sight of an Nman. She was one of the lucky ones whose house hadn't suffered much damage.

"Can you tell us what happened?" Hans asked with a serious tone.

"I saw a man behind my house and at first I didn't think anything of it." The small woman was in her sixties and spoke in a soft voice. "There are so many strangers in town these days. Still, I should have recognized his jacket as Jeremy's right away. I'm afraid my mind has been rattled with the shock of the earthquake. It wasn't until I got inside and saw Jeremy's closet open that I got suspicious."

"Who is Jeremy?"

"My son. He's traveling for work at the moment, so I knew it wasn't him that had opened the closet." She shivered. "It was shocking to realize that someone had been inside our house, but then I remembered seeing Jeremy's jacket on a man outside and I ran to find the culprit."

"And did you?"

"Yes, he was speaking to Karen Marie over by the dog park."

"Is Karen Marie a friend of yours?"

The woman nodded. "We're all friends here."

"Did you confront the man?" Hans asked with surprise.

"I didn't get a chance to. You have to understand that at the time I thought he was desperate because he'd lost his house. If I'd known he was an Nman, I would have reported him right away." She folded her arms. "He took off when I came close. I only saw him from the side, but he had a large scar on his neck and jawline."

"Did the man look like this?" Hans showed her the picture we had of Jonathan.

She wrinkled her forehead. "Do you have a picture of him without the beard?"

"No, I'm afraid not."

She studied the picture. "It's hard to say. I only got a glimpse of him from the side, but it could be him."

"Was the man you saw shaved?"

"Yes, he was." She looked speculative. "Do you think he shaved at our house?"

"I can't tell. Would you mind us looking around to be sure he's not hiding somewhere?" I asked.

Her eyes softened in a grateful smile. "That would be very kind of you. The thought that a real Nman has been here is scary. If you could make sure he's gone I would appreciate it."

"Good idea. Laura," Hans said with a nod, "you search, while I ask some more questions."

If I had wanted a chance to prove that I didn't need a man to hide behind, I'd hit the jackpot with Hans. No Nman would have let me search the house for a potential criminal by myself. Hans on the other hand seemed comfortable with hiding behind me instead of going first.

I was disappointed that Jonathan hadn't hidden in the house since I wanted to prove myself and catch him.

Our next lead was Karen Marie, who turned out to be a woman in her late twenties with pretty red lips.

"When the man approached me, I thought he was looking for shelter," she explained when we asked her what happened. "He had a nice smile and I expressed my sympathy for him and all the people who lost their homes."

"Did anything strike you as unusual with him?" I asked.

"Yes. He complimented my hair and said that I smelled nice." She tilted her head. "That wasn't the strange thing, though. It was the way he kept looking at my breasts. At first, I figured I had a spot on my clothes, so I asked him if something was wrong." Karen Marie placed a hand on her collarbone and leaned back. "I knew something wasn't right with him from the way he answered me."

"Why? What did he say?"

She frowned. "He said that I had really nice *tits*."

"Did you feel threatened by him?"

She shook her head. "Not at the time, but now that I know he was an Nman, I can't stop thinking that he could have raped or kidnapped me. Except he had kind eyes."

"Not all Nmen are violent. Most treasure women," I said in defense of my people.

Karen Marie looked thoughtful. "The more I think about it, the more I'm convinced he was trying to flirt with me in a clumsy way."

"Flirt with you?" I had read enough old-time love novels to know what it meant. But I had no experience with flirting myself. With women being won in tournaments in the Northlands, flirting with unmarried males wasn't done. "What do you mean he flirted with you?" I asked.

"It's something people used to do in the olden days as a way of showing sexual interest. I read about it in a book once." Karen Marie was distracted when a group of women called out to her as they passed by.

"Do people flirt here?" I asked Hans, who stood next to me.

"I'm not familiar with the expression, but let me do some research." Hans used his wristband to call up information while I continued questioning the witness.

"Did you see what direction Jonathan took off in?"

"That way, but it all happened so fast. And then I learned he had stolen the jacket he was wearing. I'm ashamed I didn't react to his scar or his height. That and his broad shoulders should have alerted me from the beginning." Her tone was apologetic. "It's just that I've never met an Nman and I didn't expect one to turn up here in New Munich."

"It's fine. We'll find him and make sure he's taken back home," I assured her before we left.

Not knowing what else to do, Hans and I flew over the area hoping to spot Jonathan from the air. "Hey, Hans, would you mind helping? You're not even looking."

"He could have gone anywhere," Hans pointed out. "Besides, it's hard to tell people's height from the air, and we're too high up to see his scar." He smacked his tongue and lifted his shoulders in a shrug. "We'll have to wait for a new lead on him and when we get it, I was thinking we could use a secret weapon against him."

"What kind of weapon?"

"I'm talking about the flirting thing." Hans pointed to the files projected above the wristband. "I've been studying the ancient art of flirting and I think I could teach you."

"Excuse me?"

"You could lure Jonathan in with flirting and when you have him distracted, I could come in and catch him."

I thought about it. "It's not a bad idea. We know he likes tits."

Hans lowered his brows. "We would say breasts here."

My lips pursed up. "Yeah, well, I'm a Northlander."

Hans lifted a finger. "Ah, but Jonathan can't know that. You'll have to pretend to be a sweet Motlander."

I sat through twenty minutes of Hans teaching me how to flirt.

"According to my research, it's all about seduction. There are certain facial expressions that draw men in. Like this one." Hans hooded his eyes, pursed his lips, and jerked his nose up and down in some comical movement.

"What are you doing? You look like you're about to sneeze."

"I learned it from a video. You might want to slide your tongue over your lower lip like this too." Hans looked ridiculous and so did I when I tried to imitate him.

"How can this possibly be sexy?" I asked when Hans explained about pointing my chin toward my shoulder and batting my eyelids.

"Just give it a chance."

"He's going to think I have an eye infection and a sore neck or something. Nobody acts this way."

"Do you want to help catch the Nmen or not?"

"Yes."

"Then practice flirting. Look, it's not that hard." Hans showed me all the techniques he had learned, and while I practiced the unnatural facial expressions he continued to research. "Here's an old article that describes how people used to flirt in pre-war times. Listen to this: 'The best flirting was conducted through body language and not verbal communication. Females would giggle and smile, twirl their ponytails, give the guy a "come-hither" look, and drop their school books.'"

"What's a come-hither look? And why was it considered sexy to be clumsy?" I asked with confusion.

Hans frowned. "I'm not sure. Let's see if there's something else we can use. Oh, here's one with bullet points."

"What does it say?" I leaned closer.

"It says men found it attractive when a woman would circle the rim of her glass of wine, twirl a pen, massage her shoulder or neck, continuously cross and uncross her legs, flip her hair, tuck it behind her ears, play with her bangs, or whip strands of her hair in circles."

"Huh." I raised my eyebrows. "Men were strange back then."

"Uh-huh." Hans kept reading.

Magni would think I was disturbed if I behaved like that. A woman who giggled, and couldn't sit still but had to play with her glass and pen, while crossing and uncrossing her legs and touching her hair constantly, would be considered strange today.

I scrunched my face. "That flirting stuff doesn't sound attractive at all."

"You have to do it right. I'll find some videos for you to study."

"And men? Did they flirt too?" I asked.

"Yes, but in a different way."

"Tell me."

Hans searched around before he said, "Here's something about male flirting techniques. Holy Mother Nature, if a modern man did this..." He gave a small chuckle and shook his head. "Listen to this: 'A man would stand to try to make himself look taller and more erect. He might even put his hands on his hips to appear bigger to become the "alpha male" among his group of friends. He would use his physique to signal he's the leader of the pack." Hans laughed.

"What's funny about that?" I asked. "In the Northlands we like alpha males who show leadership and take charge."

63

"But don't you find it two-dimensional? I mean if that's all he has to offer, it would be pathetic, right?"

I wasn't sure what he meant by two-dimensional, but I didn't like him calling our men pathetic. "Our men have raw masculine power and they take what they want. We find that arousing."

"Arousing?" Hans tasted the words as if unfamiliar to him. "Are you saying you like a man to take you by force?"

"As long as it's consensual."

"But it can't be both."

"Yes, it can."

There was a flash of pity in his eyes before Hans focused on the research again. "According to this, men saw themselves as hunters and they would go to bars to get the thrill of the chase. It talks about eye contact being the most important part, and that men would find excuses to touch a woman."

"Touch her how?" I asked with my eyebrows drawn close.

He shrugged. "It doesn't say. But listen, 'A man would make sure his body language was open to show his interest.'"

I spread my arms out wide. "Like this?"

"Maybe. Your guess is as good as mine."

"Don't I look like a fool sitting with my arms spread out this way?"

"Huh, yeah, but maybe try to bend your arms like you're about to hug him. It looks friendlier than holding out your arms like you're about to stop him from passing you."

"Like this?"

Hans tilted his head to one side. "I don't know, maybe it wouldn't look so awkward if you smiled a bit more."

I flashed my teeth in an exaggerated smile, still holding my arms out as to hug. Flirting was the weirdest thing ever.

"Oh here's an interesting point," Hans said with excitement. "The dating ritual often involved the woman playing hard to get by rejecting the man. This served to entice and satisfy his hunting instinct. Even though modern people don't follow the mating rituals of the past, we still experience a mild form of flirting. When making new friends, we smile more than usual, lean in, and imitate each other's body language in a synchronized and unconscious way. It's the ultimate flattery and shows an interest in becoming good friends."

"Hmm," I mumbled and leaned back in my seat, crossing my legs.

Hans leaned back in his seat too, giving me a wide smile, and mirrored me when he crossed his legs as well.

CHAPTER 9
Biology

Magni

Finn's happy whistling warned me before he opened the door to my suite.

"Are your hands broken?" I asked and continued putting on my boots without looking at him.

"My hands are fine."

"Then why didn't you knock?"

Finn grinned. "Because I like to surprise you."

That made me look up and raise an eyebrow. "Let me give you a tip then. If you're trying to sneak up on someone, don't whistle."

"I wasn't aware that I was whistling."

"That's because you live in a fucking bubble lately."

Resting his arms on the back of my large comfortable chair, Finn looked down on me sitting on the stool in front of it. "I remember you being happy when you first got married too."

I kept my eyes down and fastened the boots, not appreciating his bringing up Laura.

"Look, Magni," Finn said. "I know it's hard for you with Laura being in the Motherlands and you being here, but you're my best friend and I want you to be happy for me and Athena."

Taking my time before I answered, I stood up and grabbed my leather jacket from the chair. "I am very happy for you – I already told you that."

"Are you heading back to the border?" Finn asked, his eyes sliding over my uniform.

"Yeah, someone has to do it while you and my brother are playing house with your wives. I'm told they still need about three weeks to have the wall completely rebuilt."

Finn nodded and looked down at my scratched-up knuckles. "Maybe you should take a break from all the fighting or at least wear your Proteco gloves to protect your hands."

"Thank you for your concern," I said without explaining to him that the physical pain of fighting was a welcome distraction from the emotional pain I was in.

"Hey, at least the Motlanders caught another of the Nmen this morning," Finn said.

I gave a snort. "Since when do you call them Motlanders? We've always referred to them as Momsies."

"Since I married one of them. Did you hear what I said about them catching another of the Nmen?"

"Yeah, I heard. But there's still three left. I don't understand why it's taking so long to locate the men. They should stick out like piss on snow."

"Maybe they would have caught them under normal circumstances, but with the earthquake so many things have changed and people are taking in strangers. That makes it easier for the men to hide as homeless."

"You're right. But it's been ten days and I want Laura to come back home."

"Did you talk to her?"

"Yeah, a few times. They teamed her up with a man who Laura tells me is their best. I sure hope she's right and that he'll keep her safe. By the way, Finn, Laura mentioned that you know him. His name is Hans."

Finn took a step back. "Laura is with Hans?"

"Yes."

"Fuck."

"What?" I narrowed my eyes. "Please tell me he's not a threat to her in any way."

"No, no." Finn waved his hand and shook his head. "Hans is pretty harmless. But Laura shouldn't depend on him to save her, that's for sure."

My hands flew to my hair. "Why the fuck would they set her up with a man who can't protect her?"

"Hans is an opportunistic ass-licker."

"What do you mean?"

"He talks a big talk, but he's as soft as they come." Finn picked up a vase and scratched the gold leaf on it, before he put it down again. "Just tell Laura to watch her back, because he sure as hell won't have it."

My face was growing redder by the second.

"Relax, Magni, they only need to find three more. She could be home by tomorrow."

"I wish."

"You've got to stay positive, man."

"You know me, I'm always positive." My voice was flat. "A fucking ray of sunshine."

"That you are, my friend." Finn smacked my shoulder. "But I didn't come here to bathe in your sunshine. I came with the result of the test."

I squeezed my jacket tight in my hand. "You mean the paternity test you did on me and Mila?"

Four days ago, a test had shown that Finn was the biological father of Tristan, a boy who had grown up in the Motherlands. It had been nothing short of a miracle that the two of them ever met, and now I was hopeful that Mila might be my kid too.

"Here you go." Finn handed me a paper. "I went to the school yesterday and Mila kept asking me when you were coming."

Opening the paper, I stared at the result. "I'll go right now."

Finn patted my shoulder with a smile. "You do that, my friend, and while you're there, could you give Tristan a message from me? Just tell him that the papers came and

68

that I'm officially allowed to live in the Motherlands now. We'll be leaving tomorrow."

"Tomorrow?" A knot formed in my stomach. Finn was my best friend, and I hated that he was moving to the Motherlands where I couldn't visit him.

"Are you sure about this?" I asked him. "They're not going to like you there. They hate us Nmen."

"No, they don't. They just hate *you*." He grinned in Finn's typical relaxed way. "That's what you get for kidnapping one of their priestesses."

"Hey, you should be thanking me. If I hadn't, you two wouldn't be married today."

"You're right, but honestly, Magni, I know you dislike the Motlanders, but you've got to give them a chance. They are good people. Even Khan is starting to warm up to them."

I snorted again. "You and Khan are blinded by the sex, that's all. But I'm not. I'll be here to remind you of the four hundred years that the Momsies have been oppressing men and keeping all power to themselves. I'll never forgive them for isolating us in a far corner of the world while they get all the warm sand beaches. I fucking hate the cold up here."

"It's not healthy for you to carry all that anger and bitterness toward them. Athena and Pearl didn't live four hundred years ago, and you can't hold it against this generation of Motlanders. At least they're open to dialogue and integrating our countries."

I rolled my eyes. "Is that you or your wife talking?"

Finn shrugged. "So what if I picked up a bit from her? She's helped me a lot. Maybe she can help you too. Athena is easy to talk to and she knows about emotions and stuff."

"I don't think so," I said in a dismissive tone. "I'm not a talker and you know it."

"But maybe she could teach you not to be so guarded."

"Unless Athena can get rid of that fucking wall, I'm not interested in her help."

"Fine. But just for the record, I've been to a beach in the Motherlands and so have Marco and Archer. Don't forget that things *are* happening."

"Hoo-fucking-ray!" I moved to the door, my fist itching to hit something. "Things are happening alright. But from where I'm standing it's all shit. My wife is gone and tomorrow you'll be gone too. In fact, you know what; if you see Laura over there, the two of you can have a party together. Forgive me for not being able to join you, but as you know there will be a big fucking wall *separating us.*" I hissed the last words and slammed the door behind me before I spewed more of the anger that filled me every time I thought of the Motherlands. That country had meant only humiliation and pain to me. And now it would steal away both my wife and my best friend. I fucking hated it!

When I took off in my drone, I was tempted to go straight for the border in the hopes of finding some fool who thought he might cross unseen. I could use a target for my frustration, but the paper in my hand made me fly to the only oasis I knew these days. The experimental school where Mila lived.

It only took me fifteen minutes to fly there and the minute I landed several of the kids came running.

"Hey, Magni," Raven, one of the Motlander children, called out to me. "Are you here to teach us fighting?"

"No, not today." I tousled her black curly hair and she smiled up at me. Raven had beautiful dark chocolate skin and was the opposite in looks to her good friend Mila, who was blond and waited for me with a beaming smile on her face.

"I missed you," Mila exclaimed and although her mentors, Archer and Kya, had told me not to show her

70

favoritism in front of the others, I couldn't help picking the girl up in my arms.

"I missed you too."

Mila flashed those cute dimples of hers and it instantly soothed my soul.

"Wanna go with me to the lake?" I asked her.

"Can I come too?" Raven was bouncing from side to side with excitement.

"I have something I need to talk to Mila about. But next time you can come with us for sure." I set down Mila, who was half my size. "Raven, do me a favor and tell the adults that I'm taking Mila to the lake. We'll be back in half an hour."

"Okay," Raven agreed and ran back to the school with the other students who had come to greet me.

"You came at a perfect time," Mila said as we walked away from the buildings. "We were about to have science, and it's so boring."

"Are you kidding me, science is fun."

"Fun?"

"Science is where you do experiments and explosions. It was my favorite subject in school, except for fighting of course."

"We've never done any explosions."

"Then ask Archer to step it up. Science isn't supposed to be boring."

Mila nodded with a thoughtful expression. "I'll tell him you said that."

"So, what's new at the school?" I asked and Mila was happy to entertain me with the newest gossip about pranks and crushes.

"Has anyone been mean to you?" I asked.

"No. I think they're afraid you'll hurt them. Nero is still mad at me for the time you hung him upside down in the tree."

"He can be mad all he wants to, as long as he doesn't touch you or tease you. If he does, you'll tell me, right?"

Mila nodded, but something told me she didn't agree with my methods, and that she might be hiding something.

"What aren't you telling me, sweetheart?"

"Nothing," she said but the way she bit her lower lip revealed that she was hiding something for sure.

"Mila, sweetheart, do you know that one of my talents is to get people to tell the truth?"

"How?" she asked and looked up at me with large eyes.

"With little girls like you, I tickle them until they pee their pants."

She wrinkled her nose. "That's disgusting."

"Yes, and it smells bad too, so you better tell me."

Mila took my hand and I melted a little. "If I tell you, will you promise not to get upset?"

"Hmm."

"It's a secret, so I can only tell you if you promise not to tell anyone."

"Hey, I'm the unofficial world champion of secrets."

She tilted her head, as if considering if that was a real thing. "Okay, but if you freak out I'll never trust you again. It's a big secret and I've been keeping it for more than a week."

"Now you have me curious."

She waited until we reached the water. It was November and too cold to sit still for a long time, but we picked up stones and made ripples in the water as we threw them in.

"I saw Solo kiss Willow again." Mila's eyes were wide open and her voice almost a whisper. "But if you cut his hair or get angry with him again, I'll be very upset with you, and you know why?"

"Why?" I asked, annoyed that Solo hadn't learned his lesson the first time I caught him kissing Willow.

"Because Willow loves him. She told me so herself, and she's going to marry him when they're older. They made a pact."

I was quiet when I threw another stone in the water.

"You don't believe me?" Mila asked beside me.

"Yeah, I believe you." I bit the inside of my cheek.

"What's wrong?" Mila asked and took my hand again.

"Nothing. I was just reminded about a time when a young girl made a similar promise to me."

"I want to hear that story."

"Maybe later. First I have something to tell you."

"Is it about the test?" she asked and squeezed my hand.

"Yes, I got the answer this morning, and I'm not your biological father."

Mila's head fell down and her shoulders drooped. Her long blond hair covered most of her pretty face, but I could tell her mouth was quivering.

"I'm disappointed too, sweetie, but it doesn't change anything. If I could choose a daughter, I'd pick you any day and you can call me dad as much as you'd like."

"But how come Tristan gets to be Finn's real son when I don't get to be your daughter? We look just as much alike as they do."

Her indignation and tearful eyes made me caress her hair in a soothing manner, swallowing down my own disappointment.

"I have blue eyes like you and you said it yourself, you have dimples like me. So why can't I be your flesh and blood?"

"I really wanted you to, darling." I hugged her and she continued crying in my arms. I'd never been good with tears or emotions and felt powerless in that moment.

"Maybe you should consider yourself lucky. If you were my biological daughter, you'd probably be mean and scream at people, like I do."

73

She took a moment before she spoke. "Sometimes I get mad." Mila dried away her tears.

"Really? I've never seen you mad."

"I got mad when Storm took my dessert last week."

My left eyebrow flew up. "Storm did what?"

Mila's hand covered her mouth. "I shouldn't have told you that. Please don't hang him in a tree. The boys are already scared of talking to me after you threatened them never to touch or kiss me."

"Good." I gave a satisfied nod. "They should be."

"But I want to be kissed like Willow, one day."

"You will when you marry," I assured her. "And if you let me, I'll make sure only the strongest and fittest males fight for you in a tournament."

"Did you fight for Laura?"

I gestured for us to walk back when I saw that Mila was shivering a little from the cold.

"Here." I pulled out gloves from my inner pocket and gave them to her. They were far too big but she still smiled and thanked me.

"Yes, I fought for Laura. She's much younger than me so I waited a long time for her to be ready for marriage."

"But what about the girl who promised to marry you? Wasn't she disappointed when you married Laura?"

"No, because it was Laura who made me that promise."

"Like Willow and Solo?" Mila's sweet voice rose in excitement.

"No, it was nothing like that. There was no kissing and no pact. Just a promise from a little angel to me, a big sweaty warrior who thought Laura was the cutest thing I'd ever seen.

"Was she prettier than me?"

I looked up at the sky. "The first time I saw Laura, she stood out to me as if she was the only bright and colorful person in a black-and-white picture. She was so vibrant and fascinating with her red-colored hair that I couldn't take my eyes of her.

"How old was she?"

"About your age."

"Ten?"

"Almost. I think she was still nine at the time. I had never spoken to a female child before and one day when I was teaching Khan some fighting techniques, she walked in out of nowhere." Memories made my lips purse upward. "I was horrified to see a girl walking around unprotected and asked her where her father was. It turned out her parents were having tea with my parents in a different part of the Gray Mansion. She had gotten lost while looking for the bathroom."

"Then what did you do?"

"I took her back, of course, and before we entered the door she pulled at my hand to stop me, and then she asked me if I would marry her when she got older."

"How old were you?"

"Old enough to know she wasn't serious."

"And how old is that?"

I smiled at Mila. "I was around eighteen."

Mila wrinkled her nose. "That old?"

"Yeah, ancient almost." We shared a grin. "And I was even older the next time I saw her."

"When was that?"

"When she was twelve and we were at a funeral. As I saw her long red hair in the sea of people, I knew it had to be Laura."

"Did you talk to her?"

"No, but I circled around the room to get a better view and was confused that the little girl I remembered had grown so much."

"Did Laura see you?" Mila asked, soaking up my every word.

"I don't know."

"Why didn't you talk to her? You really should have talked to her."

"I didn't think she would remember me and you forget that it's not the Motherlands, where all males can talk to females. In the Northlands we watch from a distance. I couldn't have walked over and talked to her even if I wanted to. It would have scared her and upset her family. The truth is that it was rare for girls to be out among that big a crowd to begin with, and I promise you that every male in that room noticed Laura and her twin sister."

"Because they were pretty?"

"That, and because at that time girls were married when they were fifteen. Laura and her sister were only three years from being ready. All the young men were weighing their chances of being the lucky man who won them as brides."

Mila gave a grimace. "But they were just children."

"I know, and I wanted to beat up all the men that looked at the girls like they wanted to kiss them."

"Didn't you want to kiss Laura?"

"She was too young for me to think about kissing her. I wanted to protect her from marrying the wrong man."

"Couldn't you have reminded her that she promised to marry you?" Mila asked with big eyes.

I shook my head. "It doesn't work like that, Mila. She has to pick one out of the five champions who win the tournament."

"Are Laura and her twin identical?" Mila asked.

"No."

"Is Laura prettier than her sister?"

"Yes. To me Laura was always the prettiest girl in the country. Her sister is more serious and reserved by nature."

Mila tilted her head next to me. "I wish I could ask Laura if she saw you at that funeral."

"Chances are that she doesn't remember the funeral at all."

"Can't we call her?" Mila ran a few quick steps to get in front of me and walked backward. "Tristan says they opened up direct communication over the border now. I know you said she's back in the Motherlands, but you've spoken to her, haven't you?"

"Uh-huh."

"So call her up right now. I want to ask her about the funeral."

"She's busy chasing bad guys."

"Maybe she's on a break. I really want you to call her," Mila begged.

I held up a palm. "You have to get back to class. I'll call Laura tonight and tell you what she said."

"Promise?"

"Yes."

"And will you tell me the rest of the story about you and her the next time you come?"

"If you want me to."

"I do, and I also want you to tell me about..."

Before Mila could finish the sentence, I took a large step, snatched her from the ground, and turned her around in the air so she hung upside down. It had her howling with laughter when I continued to walk on with her dangling from my arms, teasing her. "Why are you down there? Normal girls have their heads up and their feet down."

All that came from her were fits of laughter.

Mila was my antidote to depression. It was weird how a ten-year-old girl was better at making me talk than anyone else I knew. With her, I never had to square my shoulders or raise my voice. The truth was that I liked who I became around her.

The only person who had seen glimpses of that side of me was Laura. But with her I always had to be careful that she didn't see me as weak or soft.

When I said goodbye to Mila that day, she repeated her request. "Promise to call Laura and ask her about the funeral. I want to know if she saw you there."

"I promise, I'll ask her."

CHAPTER 10

Fight at a Funeral

Magni

Honoring my promise to Mila, I called Laura around eleven that night.

She sounded tired when she answered. "Hey."

"Why haven't you called me?" I kicked off my shoes and threw myself on my couch.

"You know what would be really nice for a change, Magni."

"What?"

"If you didn't start every conversation with a complaint."

"It's a fair question. You know I worry."

She yawned. "I fell asleep, that's why."

I wrinkled my forehead. "Do you get enough sleep?"

"I was working on it, but then you called and woke me up."

"Who's complaining now? At least *I* care about you."

She was quiet.

"Hello?" I bent my knee to pull off my sock when her words made me stop and listen.

"It's not that I don't care about you, Magni."

My heart ran a victory round and I wanted her to say more. When she didn't, I repeated her words. "You care?"

"Yes."

I wanted Laura to elaborate, but she didn't.

"I went to see Mila today. We talked about you."

"Oh yeah?"

"Laura, do you remember being at a funeral when you were about twelve years old?"

"Hmm, yes, I remember."

"Mila wants me to ask you if you saw me there." I closed my eyes, remembering the way Laura had been glued to her sister and looked shy with all eyes on her. With my eyes closed and her voice clear in my ear, I pretended she was next to me.

"Yes, I saw you," she breathed.

"Are you just saying that?"

"No, Magni. I remember because people would step aside when you walked through the room. I thought it was because you were the son of the ruler, but then I saw Lord Khan come in and it was the opposite. People flocked to him."

I rubbed the bridge of my nose. "Yeah, I'm afraid you married the socially awkward brother. People don't like me much."

"That's your version, but I would say that it's you who don't like people much."

I sighed. "You're right, I'm not a people person."

"Your soldiers adore you."

That made me roll my eyes. "They respect me, Laura, that's all."

"Either way, I saw you at the funeral and I asked my father about you. He said you were a strong warrior and that you and Khan were the closest thing to princes that we had in the Northlands."

"Jesus." I scratched my beard.

"I already knew who you were because I had visited you at the castle when I was nine."

"The Gray Mansion isn't a castle."

"It was to me." She paused. "Magni, do you remember taking care of me that night when I spied on you and Khan."

"You spied on us? You told me you were lost."

There was a smile in Laura's voice. "So you *do* remember me?"

"Of course I do, I might be older than you, but I'm not senile yet. But what did you mean that you spied on us?"

"I only told you I was lost because I didn't want to get in trouble. My sister was sick at home, and I was bored listening to the adults. That's why I went out to explore the mansion by myself."

I gave a hollow laugh. "I'm seeing a pattern here. You ditched me and went to explore the Motherlands. Was I boring too?"

"No. It had nothing to do with you. I told you I was curious and that it was a spontaneous decision to leave."

"Sure felt personal." I didn't want to fight tonight, so I changed the subject.

"Did you know Tarzan?"

"Who?"

"The man we buried at the funeral."

"No, I didn't know him, he was an old friend of my father. It's a horrible thing to say, but I was excited for the opportunity to get out of the house and see people. I was happy when I spotted you there."

"I doubt it. You didn't look at me once."

"I did. And I saw you get into a fight."

"Ahh, yes, *that.*" I rested my arm across my face.

"My sister and I watched from the window when you took the fight outside. He was a mean-looking man, and I was so scared he was going to kill you."

"Please," I snorted. "That midget didn't stand a chance. He was all fat and no muscles."

"Nevertheless, April and I were very impressed with your skills, and disappointed that you left after that."

"It wasn't my choice. My father was furious with me for getting in a fight at a funeral."

"Do you remember what the fight was about?"

I sighed. "Yes, I do."

Laura waited and when I didn't elaborate, she asked. "Wanna share?"

I sighed again. "I overheard the fucker make a crude comment about you and your sister. It pissed me off because you were too young to be spoken about like that."

"What did he say?"

"Trust me, it doesn't deserve to be repeated. The man was a pig."

"In that case, thank you for defending our honor."

I found her gratitude unnecessary and yawned. "Any decent man would have done the same. Now, give me an update on the men you're chasing."

"We still have three more to catch. Jonathan, Devlin, and Luke are still missing."

"Be careful with Devlin. I fought him some months ago and the guy is good with a knife."

"Don't tell me he's the guy responsible for the scar you showed me on your arm?"

"I'm afraid so."

"I'll be careful, and if I get a chance to kick him hard, I'll do it for you."

I frowned. "I don't need you to kick people for me. I'd rather you kept away from him. The man is no joke, Laura. He's a big motherfucker."

"Even big guys have fragile balls," Laura said with bravado. "And I'm fired up after we caught another one this morning."

"Who did you catch?"

"Kessler. The sad part was that he'd already violated a woman before we found him."

"Did he rape her?"

"From what I heard, yes."

I made a deep sound in the back of my throat from disgust. "Tell them to send the fucker back to us. I'll make sure I'm part of the welcome reception when he gets here. We'll castrate the son of a bitch before we kill him. I don't tolerate rapists!"

"I won't tell them that, it might make them hesitate to send him back. Motlanders don't believe in a death penalty or torture."

A line formed between my eyebrows. "Not even for a rapist?"

"No. They believe in rehabilitation."

"That's crazy. The world will be a better place without scum like Kessler. If he raped a woman, he should die."

"I agree, but it's late, Magni, I need to get some sleep." Laura yawned. "Thank you for checking in on me."

I miss you. It was on my tongue but wouldn't come out. "Yeah, I'm tired too. We'll talk tomorrow," I said, playing it cool.

"Good night, Magni."

"Night."

I hated the silence and lay awake for a long time, thinking back to the first time I'd known I wanted to marry Laura.

CHAPTER 11
Chasing Bad Men

Laura

The first thing on my mind when I woke up was my conversation with Magni last night. I didn't remember us talking much before I took off to the Motherlands. Back then, he would order me around, and I would listen when he complained about this or that. I had always doubted he knew much about me, since he never asked many questions or seemed to care.

That's why it had touched me that he had cared enough about me, when I was a girl, to beat up a man for making inappropriate comments about me and my sister.

What Magni didn't know was that I'd idolized him since that day. April and I had watched the fight and I'd been more than upset when my twin sister showed an interest in him. I let the memories take me back to the funeral.

"Look at him, isn't he the best fighter you've ever seen?" April breathed in awe. With her eyes glued to him she whispered, *"I think Magni is short for magnificent."*

I agreed and placed my hand on the window, watching him punch the other man in his face with rage.

"Told you he was a fantastic fighter," my father commented behind us. *"Now, that man would be a catch for one of you."*

"I'll marry him," April whispered and squeezed my hand.

"No, I saw him first. He's mine," I said and jerked my hand back. *"You can't have him."*

My father's deep chuckle only upset me. This was a serious matter, and he was laughing.

84

"Sorry, girls, but that young man would win any tournament he enters. He'll be married before it's your turn."

Closing my eyes, I prayed for a miracle, telling God that I'd eat all my vegetables and be nice to my sister, if only he would make Magni notice me.

But God wasn't in the mood to grant wishes for twelve-year-old girls. After an impressive roundhouse kick that sent his opponent to the ground, Magni brushed his hair back and leaned down to say something to the man on the ground, before he straightened up again. Adjusting his clothes, he glared at the circle of spectators as if waiting for one of them to step forward and challenge him. When no one did, Magni walked to his father and brother, and after a few words with them, he left.

I willed him to turn around and see me in the window, but he never did.

"Laura, are you up?" Hans called through the door, interrupting my memories.

"Almost," I called back and swung my legs over the side of the bed. "Did you hear anything about Jonathan?" For eleven days we had chased the annoying Nman, who kept escaping us, leaving a trail of burglaries and frightened Motlanders in his wake. We had caught other Northlanders, but I wanted Jonathan since he was the first we had set out to catch.

"Yeah, he's been seen again. We should hurry."

I got in front of the mirror and braided my hair in Motlander style, something I'd learned to do while I had trained with my sensei. The style wasn't as complicated as the intricate braids used in the Northlands. My sister and I had learned them to perfection from early childhood and this easy waterfall braid took me less than two minutes to do. In general, Motlander women wore their hair casual and didn't use much make-up, while their men used colors, beads, or yarn to make their braids stand out.

"Here." Hans handed me a green drink when I came out from the bedroom. "It's got a ton of antioxidants and some beneficial seaweed."

I sniffed at the drink and tried not to wrinkle my nose.

"Cheers," he said and lifted his own glass. "Here's to catching our guy today."

"Let's do it." I emptied the glass in five seconds and ran my tongue over my teeth to make sure I didn't have any green stuff stuck somewhere.

Hans took my glass back and gave me a nod. "You look pretty today. But remember, talk as little as possible. You have a different accent when you say certain words.

"Jonathan won't hear my accent," I said and adjusted my tight long-sleeved shirt that made my breasts stand out. "He'll be busy looking at my boobs."

Hans took a step back and studied me with a serious expression. "Yes, you do have that sensual glow that some men like."

"But not you?" I asked out of curiosity.

He gave me a sweet smile. "I think you're very beautiful in a sort of Amazonian way."

"What's that supposed to mean?"

"You're very tall and strong, and you seem intrigued by violence rather than disturbed by it. Did I tell you I'm very well read too? In Greek mythology, there was a group of woman warriors known as the Amazons. They were daughters of some god that I can't remember the name of. But the point is they were brutal and obsessed with war."

"Are you calling me brutal?" I said, pretending to be offended.

Hans looked like a puppy who had just been struck. "No, of course not. I didn't mean it in a bad way. My apologies if I insulted you."

"It's okay, Hans. I can live with you not being attracted to me."

"I never said I wasn't attracted to you. You're so different and fascinating from anyone else I've ever met. I just never thought you'd be interested in a man like me."

The truth spilled out of me. "I assumed you were gay."

Hans' hand flew to his chest. "Gay? No, I don't have any preference."

"Well, it's irrelevant anyway since I'm married," I pointed out.

"Yes, of course." Hans lowered his gaze. For a second his eyes lingered on my breasts before he looked away and changed the subject. "Are you nervous about today?"

"More excited than nervous. I want it to work."

"Did you practice the flirting like we talked about?"

"A little."

"Good. I know you can do this, Laura. There's no need for violence when we can outsmart the Nmen."

"You're only saying that because you don't know how to fight." The last three of the Nmen we had captured had tried to escape and every time, I'd chased them down. The first had ended in a net, cussing and threatening. The second had been old and easy to take down, but the third almost had me in a chokehold before I managed to get my legs around his neck and squeeze. The only reason I won that fight was because my opponent underestimated me.

"Cross your fingers that Jonathan is still here," Hans said when we arrived at the town where a man with a description like Jonathan's had been reported for inappropriate communication twice. Thank God his lack of tactful manners stood out and left a trail of upset women behind him.

Motlander men would never come on to women the way Jonathan did. I was a bit amused when I read through the reports of improper communication. I could tell Jonathan was trying hard, and used words that were mild in the Northlands. But telling a woman she had a gorgeous ass wasn't seen as a compliment here.

I sat in the café where he'd been spotted twice. For three hours, I'd sipped tea, hoping Jonathan would show up. When a tall man walked in, I could hardly control my beating heart. From the sheer size of the man, it had to be Jonathan.

According to his file, our target was thirty-one years old and six-foot-three. He had a significant scar on his neck and jaw, which had been caused by an aggressive dog when he was a teenager.

With the large scarf the man was wearing, there was no way to identify him by the scar on his neck. It didn't matter, though. The minute his gaze lowered to my breasts it lingered and he licked his lips. That's when I knew it was him for sure.

Hans was sitting at another table; we exchanged a nod of understanding. He batted his lashes as a signal for me to use all the flirting we had studied together.

The plan was for Hans to look normal, but he pursed his lips and made those funny little jerks with his nose as a silent reminder for me to put on my charm. How anyone could find that expression sexy was beyond me and I refused to do it.

Curious, I kept an eye on Jonathan. It was November and his jacket was dusted with a bit of snow. With his eyes darting around the café he removed his jacket but kept his scarf on.

Three times he caught me looking at him. Each time, I held eye contact for a second before I looked away. The last time I smiled, and let my finger circle the rim of my teacup.

It worked like magic, just like the instructions had predicted it would, and Jonathan took the bait and came over. "Is this seat taken?"

"No." I gestured for him to join me. "May peace surround you."

"May peace surround you too."

88

"What's your name?" I asked.

"Marvin." He gave me a charming smile. "What's yours?"

Leaning forward, I placed my elbow on the table, and rested my chin in my hand. "Take a guess. What name would fit me?" My tone was light and playful like I had learned from the videos.

"Angel would suit you."

"That's sweet of you to say, but that's not my name."

Jonathan was struggling to keep his eyes away from my breasts.

"How about Beauty?"

"Nope, that's not my name either." My smile widened and I gave one of the giggles I'd learned about. "Did anyone ever tell you that you look like one of those sexy Nmen?"

Jonathan stiffened.

"I'm sorry, I didn't mean to be rude. It's just that my friends and I think they're amazing."

I almost pitied Jonathan when his eyes softened and his shoulders relaxed a little. "Really? What do you like so much about the Nmen?"

"Oh, you know, they're just tall and strong, like you. What's your secret? It's rare to see someone with your physique."

He shrugged. "I'm an active man, that's all."

I caught Hans gesturing for me to open my arms like we had read about. *Open body language,* he mimed.

With a smile plastered on my face, I spread my arms out as if I was about to hug an invisible friend. I felt like an idiot, and Jonathan watched me with confusion on his face, the table between us.

"Are you okay?" he asked.

"Yeah, I was just stretching," I lied and pulled my arms back. Moving on to cover my failure, I raised my hand to flip my hair back. That's when I realized I'd made a huge mistake. Several of the videos had emphasized the power of hair in a flirting situation. I couldn't flick and twirl it when it was braided.

Working fast, I undid my braid and let my long red hair cascade down my shoulders. At first, Jonathan sat as if hypnotized, but when I got my finger twisted in a knot from twirling my hair he frowned.

"Do you need help?"

"No." I pulled harder and got my finger out. Going over the flirting instructions in my head, I crossed and uncrossed my legs and bit my lower lip while angling my head in a seductive manner. It was a wonder that Jonathan didn't flee the table thinking that I was manic or something, but he stayed and leaned forward with his eyes on my breasts.

According to Hans the right pace was important when flirting, but Jonathan had proven he was direct and I was eager to get this thing over with.

"I like how big your hands are; can I see them?"

"Sure." With a smug smile he placed his hands on the table, palms down.

I leaned forward, letting the full weight of my breasts rest on the table to make sure he had all the distraction he needed. "I'm fascinated with large hands. Would you mind if I touched yours?"

"Touch all you want." Jonathan's eyes were glued to the part of my body he wanted to touch more than my hands. His breathing picked up, and he didn't notice how my one hand made circles on the back of his hand, while the other pulled out a set of immobilizers from my bag next to my teacup.

"What part of the body is your favorite?" I asked while hiding the immobilizer inside my palm.

"Boobs, I really like boobs," Jonathan said and I gave him points for meeting my eyes for a brief moment.

"Do you prefer to touch them or just look at them?" I asked and tilted my head.

90

Jonathan bit his lower lip and blinked with his full attention focused on my chest. "I like to touch them."

"Then I suggest you sign up for the new register. You know, the one that matches Nmen and Motlander women."

It took him a second to understand what I'd said. With a look of surprise he lifted his eyes to meet mine. By the time he pulled his hands back, I'd already placed the locks loosely around his thumbs and his sudden movement activated the tightening mechanism.

"What the fuck?" We both looked down to his hands, where his thumbs were linked together. "What did you do?"

"Jonathan, it's time to go home." My voice was calm and low. "The other mediator wanted to use a net gun, but I don't think that will be necessary, will it?"

He got up, his eyes darting around the room.

"You can run, but I'm warning you; there's a mediator with a net gun pointed straight at you."

He inhaled deeply and released his breath. "Fuck."

"I have a new numb gun that I'm curious to test out, so if you want to run, go for it."

He slumped down in his chair again. "I should have known you were too good to be true."

"Look at the bright side. You got an adventure that you can brag about back home. And you got to ogle me for a few minutes."

"You do have really nice tits."

I lowered my brow. "I'll do you a favor, Jonathan."

"What?"

"I won't mention that you said that when I speak to my husband tonight."

"Who's your husband?"

"Magni Aurelius."

Jonathan leaned his head back. "Ahh, you're the one who ran away from him." There was a smirk on his face when he looked at me again. "Yeah, we all heard about *that*."

The way Jonathan's eyes fell back to my breasts, with his smirk growing wider, made me lose all sympathy for him.

"You know, if I was your husband, I guarantee you wouldn't have left. I could satisfy you."

Under the table my right hand clenched into a fist, but I made my voice sultry. "Promises, promises."

He locked eyes with me. "You know what they say. Big hands, big dicks. I could show you a really good time."

I looked down as if considering his offer.

"What happens in the Motherlands stays in the Motherlands," Jonathan coaxed. "You've been gone for a long time. Don't you miss sex? I'm telling you I'm strong and virile."

"Oh, I'm sure your body is perfect to satisfy me, but are you sure you're up for it?"

Jonathan's eyes shone with excitement. "Just say when and where."

"You'll still have to go back to the Northlands, but I guess you could satisfy me on the way there."

"Consider it done." He stood up. "I wasn't having much fun here anyway. I miss my friends, beer, and a good steak."

"You thought the women would be all over you, didn't you?"

He nodded. "Yeah, pretty much."

"I have a drone right outside, if you're ready to go back."

"I'm ready."

"Follow me then."

I winked at Hans when I passed him on my way out with Jonathan's jacket over my arm.

The Nman followed me closely and got into the drone with me.

"Do you want the honors?" I asked and smiled when he instructed the drone to take us to the border.

"Please stay seated, be responsible, and use the seat belt," a female voice instructed us.

Jonathan was almost desperate when the drone refused to take off before we were buckled in. "This country is for safety sissies."

"Are you ready for the fun part?" I asked in a teasing voice when we lifted from the ground.

His eyes were hooded with lust when he nodded. "We'll have to set down the machine somewhere so we can get out of these seat belts." He looked around. "It's a shame these drones are so fucking small –we'll have to be creative."

"Jonathan, would you mind taking off your shirt for me?"

"I like how eager you are to see muscles again." He grinned. "Tired of weak Momsimen, are you?"

I smiled. "You have no idea."

"Take the thumb locks off me, will you?"

"Of course, but first I want to see that strong body you bragged about."

With his thumbs still locked together he pulled his shirt over his head. It left him blinded long enough for me to pull out the numb gun from my bag.

"So what do you think?" he asked and lifted his arms to get the shirt out of his eyes.

It happened so fast – his eyes meeting mine and his smile falling when he saw the gun in my hands.

The shot had a low sound to it, but the impact was powerful. Like two heavy logs, Jonathan's arms fell down and his body slumped back in the seat.

We sat close enough for me to lean over and pull Jonathan's shirt back down. His body was numbed, but he could move his eyes.

93

"Here's a tip for you. Never insult Magni in my presence. The next time you hear people gossip about my husband, tell them from me that Magni is a fucking genius in bed."

Jonathan couldn't respond with anything more than incoherent sounds.

"Change of destination," I instructed the drone. "Take us back to the place of departure." The drone changed direction and a few minutes later it landed in front of the café again, where Hans waited for us.

"What happened to him?" he asked when I opened the door.

I shrugged. "Jonathan agreed it was time to go home. When I told him how eager I was to try out my new numb gun, he said that he would be happy to satisfy me and that he had the perfect body for it." I patted Jonathan's cheek with a smug smile and looked at Hans. "It was very kind of him to volunteer, don't you think?"

Hans gave Jonathan an incredulous stare, like he couldn't believe anyone would be that stupid.

I sat back in my seat. "Yes, really, Nmen are tough like that; isn't that right, Jonathan?"

Climbing in, Hans took one of the two empty seats. "I have good news too. Luke has been captured, so we're down to Devlin."

"Excellent. Let's hand over this guy and go find Devlin. I can't wait to go home and spend some quality time in bed with my man." The last comment was a kick at Jonathan, who had made the mistake of dishing Magni in front of me.

Hans coughed.

"Oh, don't be so shocked, Hans, you know we Northlanders have sex. You should try it."

His answer surprised me. "Maybe I will."

I sat back with a bad taste in my mouth. Numbing Jonathan hadn't been enough to make him pay for that insensitive comment about Magni. The gossip about my

94

husband being a bad lover was so unfair. I hated that anyone would think that way about Magni when the truth was that the sex was the best part between us.

Pride and honor meant everything to Magni, and it was becoming clear what my absence had put him through. No wonder he had been so furious with me if smirks and insults had met him everywhere he went.

As soon as we found Devlin, I would return to the Northlands and receive the respect from Magni that I longed for. Once he respected me, we could have what Pearl and Khan had. We could be equals, and everyone would see that Magni and I were strong together.

I smiled a little just thinking about the perfect scenario in my head, not knowing that a very different and less rosy scenario was waiting for me in my near future.

CHAPTER 12
Equality

Magni

"How can you look so unaffected?" Khan panted next to me. "We've been running for more than an hour."

I gave him a sideways glance. "You're getting out of shape if running for an hour is hard on you."

"This isn't running. This is sprinting."

I slowed down a little. "We're almost there."

Five minutes later we arrived back at the Gray Mansion and while I stretched a little, Khan stood with his head down and his hands on his knees. A cloud of warm moistness filled the cold air from his heavy breathing.

"Maybe you should take it easy. You're getting older after all, and we don't want you to have a heart attack," I teased.

Last week Pearl had insisted on our celebrating Khan's thirty-fifth birthday. Christina, Athena, Kya, and Pearl had shown us all how their traditional celebrations involved eating sweets, receiving gifts, and singing songs. We men played along, until we got to the singing part.

To us Nmen, singing involved being drunk. I knew some great crude songs, but they were best sung with beer in one hand and an arm flung around the neck of a friend.

Singing songs about peace and prosperity would hurt my testicles, so I drew a line. The rest of the men followed my example.

Khan looked up. "Did you just call me old? Fuck you."

"You know I'll do almost anything for you, brother, but fucking you isn't on that list."

Khan rolled his eyes and walked up the wide stone staircase. "You know what I meant."

"You want to take a few rounds in the ring?" I asked him. "It's been a while since we've been sparring."

"I don't have time today, and it's a shame that you have energy for that."

"Why?"

Khan straightened up. "Because the whole reason I suggested we should go running was that I wanted you to be tired and calm when I told you something that you might find upsetting."

I let Khan walk inside before me. The house felt like a sauna compared to the outside temperature.

"What is it?"

Khan looked around the large foyer and pointed toward his office. "Let's take this in private."

My footsteps were heavy when I followed him. I didn't need more bad news. I'd already sent Finn off this morning to live in the Motherlands and Laura still hadn't come back. What I needed was some good news.

"Sit down." Khan gestured to a chair in front of his desk and closed the door behind him. "There's something I haven't told you about the negotiations with the Motherlands."

I followed him with my eyes when he sat down opposite me at the desk.

"You know I told you how the Motherlands were forced to accept our demand for equality on the Council within the next twenty years?"

"Yeah, you said it might happen in ten years if all goes well."

"True, but you should know that the Council had a condition."

"What condition?"

"When the Council reaches full equality, we in the Northlands must follow suit."

"I don't understand."

"Pearl will be my co-ruler."

Jerking back in my chair, I held up a hand. "Wait a minute. Is this for real?"

Khan had a serious expression on his face, his elbows resting on the side of his chair, and his hands folded in front of him."

"It's an official title only. I'll still be the ruler. I've already told Pearl that I don't intend to consult her on everything."

"But you already do!" I exclaimed and slammed my palms on the armrests of my chair.

"I don't blame you for being upset about this. But it's a long way in the future and until then you'll remain the second in command."

I got up from my seat, my eyes narrowed into slits. "I would rather die than take orders from a Momsie."

Khan exhaled deeply. "I was afraid you'd feel that way."

My voice was booming as blood rushed through my veins, fueled with the injustice of being overruled in such a humiliating way. "We never used to have women present when important discussions were being made. Now you can't take a piss without consulting Pearl first."

Khan picked up a marble cube from his desk and turned it in his hands while keeping his eyes fixed on me. "How about you go have a beer with a friend and digest the information before we discuss it further?"

"What friend? Finn moved to the Motherlands a few hours ago. Boulder is hovering over his pregnant wife."

"You have other friends."

I snorted and spread my arms out, looking around the room. "Where? I don't see anyone. I used to be close to you, but that was before you turned into Pearl's puppet."

Khan scowled. "I'm not her puppet."

"You can't even see that you've been brainwashed by the enemy."

Slamming the cube down on the table, Khan shouted. "Pearl is *not* our enemy!"

When I stormed out of his office, Khan was right on my heels, shouting after me, "I didn't give you permission to leave."

I ignored him and steered right in the direction of the office he had made for Pearl only a few doors away. She was sitting in her chair facing the door when I entered.

"The game is up, lady!"

Pearl tilted her head. "Hello, Magni. I assume Khan told you about the Council's demand for equality in both countries."

I sputtered, "He did, and I see your fingerprint all over this scheme. You're like a fucking trickster, distracting my brother with a magic trick, while emptying his pockets with your other hand."

Khan positioned himself between us.

"What are you accusing me of stealing?" Pearl asked in a calm voice that stood in sharp contrast to my agitated state of mind.

"His sanity, his free will, basically our country," I sneered. "Once you have power you'll change everything."

"Change can be good."

I pointed an accusing finger at her. "I'm on to you, woman. You plan to make the Northlands a democracy. Admit it."

Pearl nodded. "I'm a believer in democracy. You're right about that."

I spun to Khan. "Ha! There you have it. We kill men for treacherous talk about democracy, yet you want to make her your equal? Over my dead body."

"You're overreacting. All of this is in the future, and we should be focusing on the fact that men will be back in power in the Motherlands for the first time in four hundred years."

"Momsimen." I wrinkled my nose. "I want *us* to be in power. The last real men who don't cower to women or apologize for being males. What you have negotiated is young boys being stripped of their male pride and emasculated by women before they are allowed to be part of the Council. And you're willing to give up half of your power of the Northlands for it."

"Magni, masculinity is much more than war and fighting," Pearl said. "Our men are strong and proud too."

I took a step forward, provoked by her words. "Did you just say *our men*? At least you're not hiding whose side you're on."

My towering over Pearl was too much for Khan, who pushed me back. "Don't touch her."

I widened my eyes. "Are you completely blind? Don't you see what's going on here?"

Khan lowered his brows and took a strong stance between Pearl and me.

Deep sadness over seeing my brother tricked by the enemy made me want to rip Pearl's office apart. I lashed out and shoved a pile of books on the floor in a threatening way. "You're a fucking fool, Khan."

Khan's nostrils were flaring and he spoke in a low menacing voice. "Step the fuck back. If you touch Pearl, I'll *kill* you."

His words hit me like a physical blow. "You would kill me? So I guess that's it huh? You choose her over me?"

"Don't make me!"

"How the fuck am I supposed to protect you from your own stupidity?" I shouted at him. "If our father was here he would tell you that she's a poisonous snake who's got her fangs in you. You just don't see it."

Khan's face scrunched up into a grimace of rage, and he pushed hard at my chest. "Get the fuck out of my sight."

I was just about to turn around when Pearl spoke up in a matter-of-fact tone. "When you two are done shouting, I would like us to talk about it like sane people."

I pointed at her. "I'm not letting you brainwash me the way you have him."

She ignored my insult. "You're allowed to be disappointed and angry. I know many Councilwomen are in shock about the decision to have males on the Council. If they were as expressive as you are, they would be shouting and fuming too."

"I'm not going to fall for your mental tricks." I narrowed my eyes again. "You sit there, pretending to be nice, but I'm not falling for it. I see what you're doing."

Pearl folded her hands in her lap. "I would love to know what it is you see me doing. Will you come back tomorrow when you're calm and sit down with me to talk things through?"

Khan spoke in a deep voice. "You're not talking with Magni without me here."

"Why?" I looked at Khan. "Are you scared I'll give your wife the spanking you aren't man enough to give her?"

His fist hit my jaw so fast, I didn't have time to blink. "No one touches my wife."

My respect for Khan was wearing thin. I'd been raised to know my place as the second in command. Our father had always emphasized that Khan and I were strongest together. For years, I had backed down in confrontations between us and swallowed my pride.

My fist clenched, and I took a step back, afraid that I wouldn't be able to control myself if I stayed in the room. Khan was five years older than me, but I had been physically superior since my early teen years.

"I'm warning you," I said in a low ominous tone. "If she has her way, our days as free men are numbered."

When I turned and left, Khan didn't answer or come after me. He stayed with Pearl.

CHAPTER 13
Don't Come Back

Laura

I was abruptly woken by someone shaking me.

"Laura, wake up. It's me," Hans whispered.

"What are you doing here?" I asked in a drowsy voice and blinked my eyes open.

Hans had turned on a night lamp and was sitting on the bed. "Your invitation has me unable to sleep."

"What invitation?"

"You know, your suggestion that we should have sex?"

I rubbed my eyes, unsure if this was some kind of nightmare. "I don't follow."

Hans smiled and slid a finger down my arm. It made me jerk back. I wasn't used to men touching me. My father would have cut his fingers off, and Magni would have beaten him for touching me without permission.

"I'm sorry," he said and tucked his hand in his lap. "Do you prefer to be the aggressive one?"

I shook my head to get my mind to work. "What? You have to be delusional if you think I invited you to have sex with me."

He tilted his head. "Ah, I see. Is this where I pursue you and you pretend not to want me?"

"Huh?"

Hans narrowed his eyes, thinking, and then he pushed me back with decisiveness using both hands on my shoulders.

"What are you doing?" I protested while pushing back. But Hans kept fumbling around on top of me, trying to kiss me.

I punched him square in his face, making him cry out in pain. "Get off of me." I bucked and kicked him to the floor, where Hans curled up with his hands covering his nose, making whimpering sounds.

With every hotel fully booked because of the earthquake we'd been staying with people that had volunteered through a public system to take strangers in for a night. Hans slept on a couch while I'd been in a guest room.

"Shhh," I shushed him. "Be quiet, you're waking up the whole house.

Hans scrambled to sit up, his fingers dabbing at his nostrils to check for blood.

"Don't look so offended," I told him. "You were way out of line, and you only got what you deserved."

"But all the signals were there," he defended himself.

"What signals?"

"You've made several sexual references today and you told me I should try sex."

I rolled my eyes. "I didn't say you should try sex with *me*."

"Oh…" Hans got up and dusted himself off with a pout. "I see that I've misread the situation, but there was no need to assault me like that. I could report you for your aggressive behavior, you know?"

I got out of bed to stare him down.

Hans cleared his throat and moved to the door. "Don't worry, I'm a big enough person to forgive you."

Looking down my nose at him, I spoke in a sharp tone. "Goodnight, Hans."

"Goodnight."

When he finally closed the door behind him, my shoulders relaxed and I went back to bed. With restless energy, I tossed and turned for what felt like hours, wondering how in the world Hans could have gotten the impression that I wanted to have sex with him. At least I was certain he would never make that mistake again.

I'd only dozed off a little when Magni called me around three a.m. It alarmed me that he would call me at this time of the night and sitting up straight, I answered, "Magni, what's wrong?"

"Laura, it's me." Magni's voice was slurred and the hologram above my wrist was too dark for me to see his face.

"Are you drunk?"

"Pretty drunk."

"Magni, what's going on?" I turned on the light, not liking the sadness in his voice.

"I'm calling you to say goodbye."

"You're calling me to say goodbye?" I repeated, since his speech was so slurred he was hard to understand.

"That's right."

"Where are you going?"

"Maybe Alaska… or the moon. Not sure yet."

I rubbed my eyes again and sat up in my bed. "Magni, what's going on?"

"I'm a joke."

"What? Did you say you're Joe?"

"A *joke*." This time he pronounced the word slowly. "Don't come back, Laura, you're better off without me."

I sighed. "How much did you have to drink?"

"A little woman is going to outrank me. Can you imagine me taking orders from a Momsie?" He gave a hard laugh. "I'd rather die than have Pearl boss me around."

"Is Finn with you?"

"Nope, he's on your side of the wall. I'm all alone over here."

"You're not alone."

"Very alone. You left. Finn left. Khan hates me."

"Why would Khan hate you?"

"Because he's bedaz… bedazzled."

104

"What are you talking about? How about you get some sleep?" I suggested.

"Don't have time."

"Why not?"

"There's an asshole staring at me. We're going to fight."

"Magni, no!" I got up and paced the floor, my heart beating so fast that it hurt in my chest. "Why would you fight anyone when you're this drunk?"

"He talked shit about you. I don't toler... tolerate that."

"I know, but I need you to ignore it tonight."

"Can't do that, babe. I already said I'd kick his head up his ass. You should see how ugly the fucker is. Something's seriously wrong with his head. He's got four eyes."

"Hey, enough with the chit-chat," someone yelled in the background.

"Shhh, I'm talking to my wife."

My mind was spinning with a way to get Magni out of the hole he had dug for himself. "If you promise me not to fight him, I'll come home."

"Don't come," he mumbled. "You don't want me anyway."

"Magni, where are you?"

He didn't answer but shouted at someone. "Hey, shithead, don't touch my beer."

"Magni, meet me back at the suite. I'll leave right now," I said in a frantic voice.

"No, I mean it, Laura. Khan has lost his mind and Pearl is run... running the country. It's all shit here!"

"That's the alcohol talking. Put the bottle down and go home."

A gruff male voice sounded in the background. "Hey, asshole, time to dance."

"Magni... *Magni, don't.*" I gave a yelp of frustration when the connection between us was cut. Eight times I called him, but I got no answer.

Not knowing what else to do, I called Finn.

"Magni called me. He's drunk and getting himself killed in a fight right now. You need to help him," I pleaded.

Finn's voice was rusty from sleep. "Don't worry. Magni's been in drunken fights before. He'll be fine."

"You didn't hear how drunk he was. I could hardly understand what he was saying."

Finn yawned. "Trust me, killing Magni will take an army."

"Or one knife placed in the right spot. Finn, he's not immortal."

"All right, you've got a point." He yawned again. "I'll get someone to pick him up."

"But all I know is that he's in a bar somewhere."

"I have a pretty good idea where he might be. Don't worry about it, Laura. Magni is strong, and tomorrow he'll have a headache and regret the whole thing."

I made a pained sound. "He never used to do anything like this."

Finn sighed. "What can I say? Things changed when you ran away."

Guilt gnawed at me again. "I never meant to hurt him. I wasn't trying to get away from Magni. I just wanted to see the Motherlands for myself. If I'd known how bad things were at home..." Tears were pressing and my voice grew thick. "It's all my fault."

"Laura, please don't cry."

I couldn't help it. Self-blame and fear for Magni had my tears running freely.

"Oh, crap, Athena, I think Laura is crying."

"She's crying?" I could hear Athena's soft voice.

"Look, you handle Laura while I call the guys and get them to pick up Magni before he kills someone."

"Sweetie." Athena's pleasant voice sounded clearer now. "Talk to me."

"I messed up and now Magni might die because of me."

106

"Finn is doing what he can. He says Magni will be fine. You'll see him again."

"I don't know. Magni doesn't want me to come back. He called to tell me goodbye."

"Oh, honey, you don't believe that's what he wants, do you?"

"I told him I'd come back home, but he said I shouldn't. I wish I knew what he was really thinking, but he's so closed off to me."

"Laura, you're young and it will take time for the two of you to grow together. That's normal."

"It's not normal for him to get so drunk he can barely talk. Why would he do that?"

"What does your gut tell you?" Athena asked. "Why do you think he's getting drunk?"

Tears were still falling. "Because he's angry with me."

"You see anger. I see hurt."

I dried my nose and whispered. "I guess."

"And why is he hurting?" she asked.

"He said it's because Pearl will outrank him."

"That might be one of the reasons, but according to Finn, Magni's drinking binges started when you left. Why do you think that is?"

"Because people mocked him."

"No. That's why he fights. It's not why he drinks."

"Then you tell me, Athena, because I can't read his mind."

Athena made a sound of sympathy. "You don't have to read his mind, dear. You have to read his heart. What did he lose when you left?"

"Me."

"Yes, but what did you represent to him?"

I was losing my patience with Athena. "You keep asking me questions, but I don't know the answers – all I know is that I'm his wife."

"Yes, but I'm looking for the word 'purpose.' Being your husband and protector gave him purpose."

"Purpose." I sighed. "Yeah, I suppose so."

"He's drinking to forget his pain. To not feel so lost for a night."

I dried my nose again. "How do you know him so well, Athena?"

"Darling, I don't know Magni. But I know people."

"But Magni isn't like other men."

"Why not?"

"He's stronger."

"Only physically. Mentally he's fragile. Tonight shows that very clearly."

The thought of Magni being fragile had me frowning. "I always thought of him as special."

"He *is* special," she said. "I've never met anyone like him. Magni reminds me of the wind."

Talking to Motlanders sometimes made me feel like we spoke two different languages. They spoke in metaphors and used references no Northlander ever would.

"Magni is a strong force of nature. And you know, sweetie, there's nothing wrong with being powerful if the power is channeled into something constructive. A strong wind, for instance, can be harvested and light up entire cities with its energy. But sometimes the wind takes a destructive path, turning into tornados that can tear the city apart."

"You're calling Magni a tornado?"

"What he does with his power only time will tell. I would like to see him use it for good, but right now I see Magni as unbalanced and ungrounded. That's what makes him fragile."

I was listening to Athena with deep frown lines on my forehead.

She continued, "He can't use his physical strength to fight the enemy within him."

"You're talking about him being a hot-head, but I have no idea why he's like that." I brushed tears away.

"Neither do I. My guess is that Magni has never learned how to express his emotions. Maybe he was ridiculed for crying as a child. Maybe he was always second because of his brother the future ruler. Maybe he is boiling over on the inside. Maybe throwing a fit is learned behavior, since his father did the same and got respect for it. Maybe he experienced people being afraid of him and felt a surge of power. Who knows, Laura?"

"Athena, please just tell me what I need to do."

"That's not my place."

"But I'm not sure if I should stay here or go home." I sat down on the bed.

"Then meditate until you get your answer," she suggested and sounded like my sensei. It annoyed me that Motlanders thought everything could be fixed with meditation.

"I can't sit still. I need to do something to help him," I said and got up to pace the floor again.

"In that case you have your answer."

"But what if I get home and he rejects me?"

"Laura." Athena's voice dropped. "You're the warrior who didn't think twice about going after a group of violent men to protect the innocent. If you can do that, you can face anything."

It's not the same thing, I thought, but was grateful that Athena was taking time in the middle of the night to talk to me.

"Thank you, and tell Finn to call me as soon as he knows anything."

"I will, dear," Athena promised before we ended the call.

Tiptoeing through the house, I woke Hans up in a hushed voice. "Listen, something happened at home, and I'll have to return."

"What, *now*?" Hans pushed up on his elbows and I gestured for him not to get up.

"You can go back to sleep. I'll take the drone and send it back to you. If you get a lead on Devlin, call me."

He frowned. "Just tell me the truth. Are you leaving because of what happened between us?"

I wanted to roll my eyes. But maybe I was being too hard on Hans. It wasn't his fault that he couldn't read my signals and that he had made a mistake. "No, I'm not leaving because of you."

"Are you sure?"

"Yes, I'm sure; there's a situation at home that needs my attention, but I'll be back, I promise."

CHAPTER 14
Friends

Magni

A breeze of cold air made me pull my covers higher. Cracking an eye open, I saw Boulder opening the window.

"What are you doing?" My voice was rusty from sleep. "You're letting out the heat. Close the door and the window."

Boulder sat down on the edge of the windowsill and looked at me. "I'm letting in some fresh air. It stinks like a brewery in here." He was wearing a thick jacket and crossed his arms. "Wanna tell me what happened last night? I thought you'd stopped that shit months ago."

Flashbacks from last night had me groaning and rubbing my face.

"Do you remember telling Laura not to come back?"

"Close the fucking door," I mumbled and reached for my clothes. This time Boulder complied.

"I might have said some stupid stuff to her," I admitted. "I was upset."

"She thought you were getting yourself killed."

I pulled a thick sweater over my head. "Why?"

"Because you told her you were about to fight some random jerk who had talked trash about her. According to Laura, she had to guess half of what you said in your drunken state. She was convinced you wouldn't be able to fight."

"The guy was drunk too."

"I know, I saw him."

After putting on my socks, pants, and boots, I looked at Boulder. "Wait a minute. When did you talk to Laura?"

"She called Finn, who called me. That's why Archer and I showed up and brought you back here."

Running a hand through my shoulder-length hair, I gathered it on top in a messy bun. The sides were shaved short, and I loved the convenience of this hairdo.

"I'm hungry," I said and reached for a tooth cleaner. The small rice-kernel-sized device began polishing and cleaning while I looked myself in the small mirror and groaned. My jaw was yellow and when I touched the skin it hurt.

"Laura is here."

My hand froze mid-air and I slowly turned my head to look at Boulder. "What did you say?"

"Laura came early this morning. She's up at the school."

My blurry brain kicked into gear. "Why didn't you tell me?"

"I just did."

I flew out of the cabin with Boulder next to me. "Is she okay?"

"Laura is fine, she's been waiting for you to wake up. We figured you needed time to sleep."

My wristband told me it was half past ten in the morning, and I cursed softly. By now my Huntsmen would be wondering why they hadn't heard from me.

"Did you tell Khan about my visit to the bar last night?"

"No."

"Good, I'd rather he didn't hear about it."

"He told me about you two arguing yesterday. You shouldn't have gone after Pearl like that."

I spun around and grabbed Boulder's jacket. "She's manipulating him and he can't see it."

"You're upset about the Council's demand for her to be Khan's co-ruler." Boulder pushed me back in a gentle way. "I get that."

"It'll be over my dead body," I swore.

112

He frowned. "Don't fucking say that."

I narrowed my eyes. "I'd rather die a free man than be tamed by a Momsie like Khan and you."

"What the hell is that supposed to mean?" Boulder's face scrunched up. "If anything, Christina makes me a better man."

"Yeah, but you have to admit that Pearl is like a spider waiting to bite the head off her mate."

"That's crazy talk. The Pearl I know is kind, wise, and generous. Khan used to be unpredictable and moody. I'd say she's been a good influence on him."

"The woman is manipulative and dangerous," I claimed. "You just wait until our people learn that the Council has Khan by his balls, making a woman our ruler."

"I agree that most won't like it at first, but these are times of change, and many welcome it."

"Do you?"

Boulder shrugged.

"Do you?" I repeated.

"I think Pearl is a good influence on Khan."

"You can't mean that."

Boulder shifted his balance from one foot to the other. "I know you hate the Motlander women, but we have a lot to learn from them."

I snorted. "Like what?"

Boulder looked around. "It's hard to explain, but Christina asks me questions that no one else does. She connects me to a part of me that I hardly knew myself."

My eyebrows drew close. "What part?"

"How I feel about things and what's going on inside of me. It's like I've been sailing my whole life on this amazing ocean where the coolest things were happening under the surface. She's encouraging me to jump in the water with her and go explore."

My head hurt, I was thirsty and hungry, and the last thing I needed was to lose another friend to the enemy.

"You're as bad as Khan. Who the hell talks about their emotions and feelings?"

Boulder and I had reached the kitchen inside the school and I went straight for the coffee. "You're even talking in metaphors like the Momsies now." I shook my head and mumbled under my breath. "Fucking ocean talk."

"You understood what I meant."

"Yeah. I understood, but it's fucking depressing to hear my last friend left here talk like a sissy."

"I'm not a sissy, and I'm not your last friend here."

I threw up my hands. "Finn left, remember?"

Boulder bumped my shoulder with his own to get to the coffee. "I think Archer would be offended to hear that, since he helped drag your ass back here last night."

"Archer did?"

"Uh-huh." Boulder sipped on his coffee. "It's funny with you, Magni. I've known you for more than ten years and all those years I've seen men circle you, trying to become your friend. Great men look up to you and admire you, but you never let any of them in."

I shrugged. "Trust doesn't come easy to me, that's all."

Boulder scoffed. "That's an understatement."

"Besides, I have Finn and you."

"Yeah, but you don't talk to us about things."

I put down my coffee cup and found some leftover breakfast to eat. "Of course I talk to you. We're talking right now, aren't we?"

"Sure, we talk about politics, sports, and how annoying Khan is, but we don't talk about all the stuff that's under the surface."

Rolling my eyes, I stuffed a piece of apple in my mouth. "I'm not jumping into the fucking ocean with you."

"Why not, are you scared of what you might find?"

I scoffed. "I'm just smart enough to stay in the boat. You might have seahorses and mermaids under your surface, but I guarantee that my ocean is full of sharks and rip currents that will drag me down."

"And here I thought you were fearless," Boulder challenged.

I snorted and stuffed more food into my mouth.

Right then, Archer walked in. "Could you two keep it down? The kids are meditating in the other room."

"Is Laura with them?" I asked Archer, who snatched a roll from my plate and took a bite.

"She went to the lake with Kya. They should be back soon."

"Hey Archer, can I ask you something?" Boulder said.

"Sure."

"Would you consider me your friend?"

"Sure. Why?"

"How about Magni? Would you consider him your friend?"

Archer looked from Boulder to me with a thoughtful expression. "Sort of."

"What makes you hesitate?"

Archer scratched his arm. "I don't know."

"Is it because you're not sure if Magni sees you as a friend?"

"I guess."

"He does!" Boulder lifted his cup. "And he's very grateful that we saved his ass last night."

"No problem." Archer smiled. "Gotta get back to the class."

When the door closed, I frowned at Boulder. "I can speak for myself."

"You haven't made a new friend in ten years; it was time."

"I don't need you to find me friends."

"He was already your friend, you just couldn't see it."

The sound of voices from outside made me look out the window to see Kya and Laura walking back to the school.

"How are you feeling?" Laura asked when I walked outside to meet her.

"Fine." My mind was analyzing every little signal from her. She didn't look hurt, but she avoided eye contact and seemed guarded.

"Hey, Magni," Kya greeted me and smiled at Laura. "I'll see you later."

I waited for Kya to enter the school before I spoke. "You came back."

Laura met my eyes briefly before she looked down. "I did."

"Are you staying?"

"No."

Boulder had talked about an inner ocean and in that moment, I was sucked down under by a huge wave. "Laura." My voice was ashy and it hurt to speak. I couldn't remember our conversation from yesterday but I knew I'd been in a bad state. Laura wasn't like Christina or Pearl. She wasn't interested in my feelings or emotions. Northlander women wanted their mates to be strong and tough. Not whining in a drunken state. "You didn't have to call Finn," I managed to say despite the huge knot in my throat.

"I had to do *something*."

It was another stab to my gut. My woman shouldn't feel that she had to save me. I was the protector, not her.

"I would have been fine." It came out harsher than I intended it to.

For a few seconds, we stood opposite each other in a tense silence until the door opened behind us and the children came out.

"Hey Magni, are you gonna work with us today?" Storm, one of the boys, asked. He stood in a large group of boys that all looked hopeful.

"Don't you boys have school?"

"It's Saturday, and we already did the morning run, breakfast, and meditation. Now we're free to have fun."

I had forgotten what day it was and drew in a long breath. "Maybe I can spar with you boys later. Right now I have to talk to my wife." I met Laura's eyes and saw them widen when a pair of small hands snaked around my waist from behind.

Only one child would hug me like that. "Mila, come meet my wife, Laura," I said and twisted my body to reach for her. I had forgotten how shy Mila used to be when she first arrived at the school. With Laura being a stranger, Mila had reverted to being shy. Looking down, and staying close to me, she kept her hands around my waist.

"It's okay, I met the children this morning." Laura smiled at Mila. "Magni told me nice things about you."

Mila looked up at me and I nodded at her to go on.

"I've heard about you too," she said in a soft voice. "And I asked Magni to call you so I could hear your voice."

Laura gave Mila a small smile. "You did?"

"Yes, I wanted to know if you saw him at the funeral when he was in love with you."

"I wasn't in love with her," I corrected Mila. "Laura was a child back then."

"But you *liked* her," Mila insisted.

"It's getting cold out here. Maybe we should go inside." I didn't wait for them to agree but walked back in.

"Laura, can I show you my favorite part of the school?" Mila asked behind me.

"I would love that."

Other children moved around us and one of the boys bumped into Laura.

"Hey, watch it," I warned him with fire in my eyes.

117

"I'm sorry." Hunter held up both hands and hurried away.

"Take the running outside," Kya instructed. "Marco, Archer, and the other boys went to play soccer. Anyone is welcome to join them. How about you, Raven? You like soccer."

The room emptied out as most left to either watch or play soccer.

"This is my favorite part," Mila said and pointed to a door that seemed to be the broom closet.

"Why?" Laura asked.

"It's where the instruments are." She opened the door and we could see different musical instruments in boxes. "We used to have them out here, but some of the students can't keep their hands off them, and it's distracting."

"Which instrument do you play?"

"I sing."

"Oh." Laura smiled.

Mila pulled out a box. "I love to play with the pitch box."

"What does it do?" Laura reached out to see the box with her hands.

"It gives singing lessons. I have to follow a song and if I'm off key, the box shows it. If I remember all lines and sing the song in a perfect pitch, I go on to the next level." Mila's dimples came out when she smiled. "I'm the only one who's at level thirty-one."

"Wow, that's great. Maybe you can demonstrate how it works," Laura suggested.

Mila moved closer to me and I placed my hand around her. "It's okay, Mila, you don't have to be shy with Laura – she can't sing for shit. She'll be impressed with your voice."

Laura crossed her arms. "Says the man who makes people's ears bleed when he sings in the shower."

"I hum in a low baritone," I corrected her and squeezed Mila closer. "So you see, honey, it really won't take much to impress the both of us."

"Okay." Mila took the box from Laura and pointed to the cozy corner. "You can sit there."

I arranged my seven-foot body on the floor next to Laura, who picked a large orange pillow to sit on.

"Magni, you should use that pillow. It's my favorite." Mila gestured to a heart-shaped fluffy one in purple.

"Nah, I'm good," I said and shook my head.

But Mila wanted me to be comfortable and brought it to me. "Feel how soft it is."

Laura studied me when I took the pillow. She might think me a softie for caving but there was no way I could reject Mila's kindness. I took the fluffy pillow and sat on it. Good thing my body was large enough to cover most of the damn thing.

When Mila began singing, Laura gave me a look that said, *I didn't expect this.* The girl had a beautiful voice and the machine showed that she was right on pitch.

"Do you want to try it?" Mila asked Laura when she was done.

Laura tilted her head and looked at me. "I'll do it, if Magni does it."

"Will you?" Mila's eyes became pleading. "It would be so much fun."

"Sorry, hon, but my singing voice is best when I'm drunk."

"What's that?"

Laura was quick to explain. "Here in the Northlands there's something called alcohol. People who drink it become silly and irrational. Sometimes they think they have amazing singing voices when they don't. Other times they think fighting someone is a great idea even if they see double."

119

"That's right," I pitched in. "You wouldn't know about it since alcohol is forbidden in the Motherlands. Just like most other fun things are forbidden there."

"I had a lot of fun back home," Mila pointed out.

"Yeah, but that was before you knew what it's like in the Northlands. I'm sure if given the choice, you'd want to live here, *right*?"

Mila bit her lip.

"I mean, you wouldn't leave your husband to live in the Motherlands, would you?" I didn't look at Laura, but the comment was aimed at her.

"I don't know." Mila looked down. "Maybe if he wasn't nice to me."

I frowned. "Oh, I'd make fucking sure he was nice to you, sweetheart."

Mila came to sit in front of us, her body leaning against my knee, and she reached for my hand. I burst with pride, hoping that Laura noticed the girl's adoration of me.

"I've been thinking about what you said." Mila spoke softly. "About you arranging a tournament for me when I'm older."

"What about it?" I asked. "It's the only way to be sure you get a worthy husband."

"But what if he hits me?"

I frowned again. "Why would he hit you?" Her words triggered me and the thought of any man laying a hand on my little princess had me disliking the idea of her ever marrying.

"It's just something I heard – rumors that Archer once hit Kya's behind." She looked down and fiddled with her hands.

"I know, sweetie, but that was just a spanking."

Mila's eyes were large and full of concern, so I explained. "Spanking is not the same as hitting. It's less painful and doesn't leave marks."

120

"But you said husbands are supposed to protect their wives. Then why would they hurt them? I don't understand why Archer couldn't just be nice to Kya. You would never be that mean to Laura, would you, Daddy?"

This conversation had me sweating. "Ehm... no, of course not," I said, hoping Laura wouldn't reveal the truth.

Mila leaned in to hug me. "I knew it. Then I want my husband to be just like you when I grow up."

I patted her hair. Her comment should have made me square my shoulders in pride. But Laura and I both knew that I had always considered it a husband's responsibility to discipline his wife. If Mila understood that I'd spanked Laura several times, my little pacifistic princess would be disappointed with me.

When Laura spoke up, I held my breath. "If you decide to stay and have a tournament, Mila, I'm sure Magni will explain to your champion that the best kind of marriage is one where both parties respect each other. He would never allow anyone to make you feel like your opinion doesn't matter or that you're not equal to your husband."

Laura was beating me at my own game, and I cleared my throat. "I don't know about that. Men and women aren't equal in the Northlands."

"Why not?" Mila asked.

"Because men are born leaders. It's their role to take charge and be in control. You wouldn't want to marry a wuss, would you?"

"No, I guess not." Mila looked at Laura. "If you could do it again, would you have a tournament?"

Laura took time to think about it. "Ever since I was a little girl, I dreamed of my tournament. It's a very special day for a Northlander woman when thousands of men fight for her. My answer would be a big yes."

"But would you have chosen Magni again?"

I sucked in a deep breath and quickly said, "Laura, you don't need to answer that." Mila adored me and I didn't want Laura to tell the girl what a disappointment I'd been as a husband. "Thank you for the beautiful song. It's time for me to go and show the kids how to play soccer."

Mila smiled. "They say you play unfair and that you cheat."

I got up and stretched my arms in a yawn. "I would never cheat."

"You picked Plato up from the ground so he couldn't reach the ball with his feet."

"So?"

"You can't do that." Mila insisted. "You have to play by the rules."

I grinned and pulled her up from the floor. "I should have known you could never be my biological daughter. There's no way I would have produced such a wonderful rule follower."

Mila grinned up at me and turned to Laura. "Will you come and play soccer with us?"

"Sure. But I'm warning you, Mila, I'm no rule follower either."

Mila shrugged. "It's okay. Northlanders never are."

CHAPTER 15
Fight Me

Laura

I loved being at the school. When I was a child this hadn't been a possibility, and my circle of friends had been very limited.

Seeing girls and boys interact was surreal, and my heart was in my chest when I watched them play soccer.

Some of the girls were fast runners and didn't hold back. I was especially impressed with a girl called Raven. With her tongue between her teeth, she took on boys twice her size, colliding with them to get the ball. Every time there was physical contact my eyes flew to the men watching. I was sure the boys would be in trouble for touching her, but nothing happened.

If any male had been that rough with me as a child, they wouldn't be around to tell it.

Mila was cheering for Magni and the others, and it occurred to me that she jumped with excitement every time someone made a goal.

"Which side are you cheering for?" I asked.

"Both sides."

"But you have to pick one side."

Mila tilted her head. "Just because you like one team doesn't mean you have to dislike the other. I love to see how happy they get when they score."

I shook my head and smiled. "Mila, you just like everybody, don't you?"

She moved closer and whispered, "No."

That had me curious, since she seemed like the sweetest person in the world. "Who don't you like?"

Mila spoke low enough for only me to hear. "Nicki's mom. She did bad things to Nicki and that's why Nicki doesn't see her mom anymore."

"Who's Nicki?"

"She's the girl who just made a goal."

"Oh, the one who made it in the wrong end?"

Mila nodded. "It was a great goal, though."

"Yeah, except her opponents got the point."

She shrugged. "I don't care much for the points and I don't care for Nicki's mom either. She was mean and I don't like people who hurt others."

"I feel the same way."

Mila turned all her attention on me. "Then why do you hurt Magni?"

Her words slammed me in my chest. "What do you mean?"

"You make him cry on the inside."

"That's not a thing."

"Yes, it is. The boys here don't cry on the outside, they cry on the inside. You can see it when you look into their eyes. They are hurting."

"Magni is no *boy*."

Mila gave me a puzzled expression, so I added. "I mean, he's not a very emotional man. He would never cry and he's horrible at expressing his feelings."

"That doesn't mean he doesn't have them."

Blinking my eyes, I took in her words. Of course, Magni had feelings; I just didn't know the depth of them since he didn't talk to me about how he felt.

I watched him play soccer with the kids for a while. The players were keeping warm by running around, but after freezing for half an hour, I headed back to the school building.

Almost there, the sound of heavy footsteps made me look over my shoulder to see Magni run to me.

"Where are you going?" he asked with cheeks red from the cold.

"I wanted to get some hot tea to warm up."

"How long are you staying this time?"

"I'm not sure. Hans is going to contact me when there's a new lead for Devlin." We went inside to the kitchen, where I moved around to boil water while Magni sat on the counter watching me. When I blew warm air on my hands, he reached out and pulled me into his arms.

"Let me warm you."

"Thank you."

"Put your hands under my shirt."

He didn't wince when my ice-cold hands slid up to his belly, soaking up the heat that emanated from him.

His chin rested on the top of my head and his arms were wrapped around me. "I wish you would stay here," he muttered.

"Then why did you ask me not to come back?"

"What?"

"Yesterday. You called me to say goodbye."

Magni groaned.

"Honestly, Magni, I didn't know if you meant it or not."

"Did you miss the part about me being drunk?"

"No, but you know what they say: alcohol is a truth serum."

"Whoever said that hasn't been drunk. I've heard men boast that they can lift a drone, but I've yet to see them actually do it."

I changed the subject. "Why didn't you tell Mila the truth? You shouldn't have lied to her about never spanking me."

Magni's hold around me tightened. "You don't understand. Mila adores me. I don't want to spoil that by telling her about things she doesn't understand yet. It's not her fault that she was born as a Momsie. It will take time to open her mind to our way of living."

"She's a sweet girl and it's obvious that she loves you."

Magni pulled back enough to see my face. "Love is a big word."

"Not for Motlanders." I moved back a little. "Thank you, I'm warm now."

Magni watched me prepare my cup of tea without either of us saying a word.

"Do you want one?" I asked and turned my head to see him deep in thought. "Magni, I asked you if you want a cup of tea."

He shook his head.

"What are you thinking about? You look so serious."

"You, going back to the Motherlands."

"We still need to bring Devlin back."

"Can't you leave him to the Momsies to catch? They've done pretty well so far."

"Only because I helped them catch several of the nineteen criminals on the list. None of the Motlanders could have fought Diego like I did."

Magni pushed off from the counter and came to stand next to me. "What do you mean you fought him? You told me they all surrendered."

His closeness and intensity made me lean back. "They did, but only after they were pacified. Most of them tried to get away and the worst one was Diego de la Vega."

Magni's forehead was furrowed with deep frown lines. "What happened?"

My mouth felt dry from the tension emanating off Magni. I licked my lips and searched for a way to tell him. "It was only Hans and me that day, and, well, things didn't go according to plan. Diego pushed me back and tried to escape. Both Hans and I fired our net guns, but we missed. That's why I took up the chase."

Magni's jaw tightened and he scoffed. "Net guns. Why didn't you use the weapons I gave you? The wolf gun would have toasted his ass."

126

Telling Magni that Isobel had those weapons would only make him worry more, so I didn't. "I'm a really good fighter, Magni. You would have been impressed with me."

His ears were growing redder by the second and it made me so nervous that I kept talking when I should have stopped. "I even managed to get out of Diego's choke hold and put immobilizers on him. Hans was very impressed by that."

Magni's eyes bulged and his voice rose. "The asshole had you in a choke hold?"

"Yes, but it was only for a few seconds."

Magni crossed his arms and took a strong stance as if he was a wall designed to keep me in. "That's it, you're not going back there. Diego was child's play compared to what Devlin will be."

My tea spilled over when I set down the cup with a solid bump. "Don't start with me, Magni."

"How the hell am I supposed to protect you when you don't listen to me?"

"I can do this."

The way Magni pressed his lips together made him look like he was suppressing a scream. With a groan he leaned his head back as if the answer on *how to make your wife listen* was written on the ceiling.

"Magni, trust me, I can take Devlin down."

"Show me, Laura. I wanna see how you'd take a man my size down."

"He's smaller than you. According to his file, Devlin is only six-five."

"Which means he's got eight inches on you and a hell of a lot more muscle. Not to mention fight training. How the fuck do you expect me to be okay with you going after him?"

I mirrored him, crossing my arms and pushing my jaw out. "I'm not asking for your permission."

A silent power struggle took place between us until Magni muttered, "If you're so damn sure of yourself, then show me how you'd immobilize me."

I crossed my arms. "That's not fair. Devlin isn't the best fighter in the world; you are."

"My point exactly. If you can take me down, I'll trust that you can take care of yourself."

My voice rose a bit. "No one can take you down."

"At least try."

"No, Magni, I'm not going to humiliate myself in a fight with you."

Magni spun around, throwing his hands in the air with loud sounds of frustration. That's when I made a fast move and kicked his feet out from under him.

With wind milling arms, he knocked over a chair on his way down and landed on his ass with a hard "thump." The look of surprise on his face was priceless and had me smiling with satisfaction.

"Huh, looks like taking you down wasn't so hard after all. Told you I was good."

In a fluid movement Magni got back up and brushed his pants off with annoyance. "Nice one, but what are you going to do when he gets back up? You'll need a lot more than a surprise attack if you want to beat someone like Devlin."

"Then teach me."

"Laura, this isn't some superhero movie. Size and strength matters in a fight and unlike you, Devlin has been training since he was a child. Be realistic for a moment."

With stubbornness, I repeated, "Teach me."

"I would rather you stayed here."

"You once said that you admire people who stick to their promises. I'm committed to help track the fuckers down and I'm sticking to it."

He sighed and hung his head for a second before meeting my eyes with resolve. "In that case, let me teach

128

you a few things before you go." He held up a finger. "But I'm warning you, Laura. If you whine we'll stop."

"I never whine."

"You'd better not."

CHAPTER 16
Getting Physical

Laura

"Let's go again!"

I got ready for what had to be Magni's hundredth attack on me.

"You still need to be faster, Laura."

My arms were heavy as lead from the endless times I had defended myself the way he had shown me. We had trained more than two hours outside the school. In the beginning students had been around to watch and cheer for me, but the cold had made even Mila retreat to the school building by now. My fingers were freezing and I couldn't feel my toes. But with Magni's comment that he hated whiners, I was determined not to complain.

"Show me what to do if he chokes you," Magni instructed and took his position. Lennie, the sensei whom I'd trained with in the Motherlands, had been smaller than me. It was a completely different ball game to practice with someone as big and strong as Magni, and I was worn out.

"Laura, you're not trying. You have to practice until you've got it right."

I squeezed my lips tight together, biting back the words that wanted out. Couldn't he see that I was an exhausted ice cube?

"At least show me again how you would defend yourself if Devlin has a knife." Magni pulled a stick from his back pocket that he had used as a prop earlier. He didn't show any signs of fatigue or being cold.

My defense was too weak, and Magni pressed the stick against my throat. "Learn or lose, Laura!"

Swallowing my pride, I asked in desperation, "Can we stop now?"

Magni didn't look happy about it, but he waved a hand toward the school building. "Let's go warm you up with a hot shower."

"How come you aren't cold?"

"I've been training outside all year round since I was a child," he said on the way to the school. "Trust me, this is nothing. I've been on survival camps in three feet of snow. *That* was cold."

We showered separately and although it helped, I was cold again the minute I stepped back out of the shower.

"The cabin will be nice and warm," Magni said when he saw me come out from the girl's shower room with my arms wrapped around myself. The short walk from the school building to his cabin felt like a long hike. As soon as we were inside the cabin, I grabbed the blankets from the bed and pulled them tight around me.

I was surprised that my teeth didn't clatter when I began to talk. "I couldn't feel my toes when I got in the shower. It's a bit better now, but I'm still cold."

"Take a seat." Pressing on my shoulders, Magni gestured for me to sit down on the bed. "Let's get you out of these boots."

If I hadn't been so miserable from the cold, I would've enjoyed seeing Magni kneel down in front of me and remove my boots with great care.

"Sorry if my feet stink, I didn't have any clean socks to put on."

Magni's strong hands were massaging my left foot. "You're fine. In my line of business, I see, hear, and smell things that would make most people sick. Trust me, smelly feet is not even on the list of things that disgust me."

"So they *do* smell?"

Magni lifted my foot to his nose.

"Noo, don't do that," I said with embarrassment.

A smile tugged at the edge of his mouth. "I'll let you smell my socks and we can compare."

"You don't need to touch them."

"Laura, stop talking about your feet, you're fine." He moved on to massage my right foot while I sat under the blankets.

"You know, it's kind of depressing that Mila seems to understand things about you that I don't."

"Hmm."

"She said some pretty profound things."

"Yeah, she's a smart kid."

I angled my head. "Do you ever wonder if we missed out on something? Growing up here, I mean."

Magni shrugged. "I know we missed out on sandy beaches, but I think it's worth it to avoid all the stupid rules they have in the Motherlands."

Leaning back on the bed, I supported my weight on my elbows. "I don't like all their rules either, but sometimes when I speak to Motlanders, I feel like they understand a lot more about people than we do. Athena has all these ideas about why you drink and fight."

"What would she know about it?" Magni scoffed. "I doubt she's ever been in a fight or been drunk in her whole life."

"No. But she's a smart lady."

Magni snorted. "Athena wouldn't last a day in my world."

"Finn loves her," I pointed out. "And he respects her."

"Why are we talking about them?"

I sighed. "I'm just saying that I wish we were better at talking about how we feel."

Magni stopped massaging my foot and gave me a scrutinizing look. "I'm not good at talking."

132

"My point exactly." Leaning forward, I met him nose to nose. "I'm not good at it either, but I want to be."

"Why? So you can dig around in my head?" Magni narrowed his eyes. "I don't recommend it."

"I wish you weren't so closed off to me."

His eyes hardened. "And I wish you could accept me for who I am."

"But that's the problem, Magni. I don't know who you are. How could I when you won't show it to me?" My voice was shaking with emotion. "You are everything I dreamed my husband would be. You're strong, brave, and handsome."

"*But?*"

"But that's just the wrapping. I can't read you, or figure out what's going on inside your head."

Magni put my feet down and stood up. "Then you're not listening. How many times have I told you not to go back to the Motherlands? That's what's on my fucking mind."

I stood up too, but still had to lean my head back to meet his eyes. "Why? You say it's because you're afraid I'll be hurt. But I have a feeling that the real reason you don't want me to go back is because it's embarrassing to you that your wife has a life of her own."

Magni crossed his arms and lowered his brow, but kept quiet.

"I never liked it when you bossed me around, but it was all I ever knew. My entire life men have been telling me what to do. You have no idea what that's like. I was always told that it was a sign of protectiveness, until Christina pointed out to me that it's really possessiveness."

"Bullshit!" Magni boomed. "You love it when I'm in charge. It turns you on."

"In bed, yes, but not outside the bedroom."

Magni snorted again. "I'm a domineering person, Laura, deal with it. Besides, Christina wouldn't have known possessive from protective when she made that comment. Why don't you ask her now? I guarantee you that with her being pregnant, Boulder is more protective than ever. Ask her if she still sees it as possessiveness."

"Boulder loves Christina. He even *tells* her so."

"Ah, I see. That's what this is about, isn't it? You want me to shower you with flowery love poems and shit. I'm not that guy, Laura."

Standing opposite my husband, I asked the question that I was most afraid of hearing the answer to. "Are you saying you don't love me?"

"I'm saying I don't like this conversation. I'm not good at talking about my emotions." He turned his back on me, pacing the small cabin.

"Then practice until you get it right – isn't that what you just told me?"

"This isn't fight training. It's different."

"If a ten-year-old can master talking about emotions, then we can learn it too."

"I don't *want* to learn," Magni objected.

I narrowed my eyes and slammed him with his own words again. "Learn or lose!"

Magni paled and he spoke slowly in a low voice. "Is that a threat? You're going to leave me, aren't you?"

My heart was hammering in my chest from the tension between us. "I don't want to leave you, but I've told you that things need to change between us."

"For fuck's sake, Laura, don't you see that it already has? I just spent two hours teaching you how to fight. When have I ever done that?"

"I appreciate that, but I want *more*. I want the closeness that Khan and Pearl have. The mutual respect. It's clear to see how much they love and admire each other."

134

Magni raked his hands through his hair in frustration. "We are not *them*! You keep talking about what *you* want, but what about what *I* want? I don't recall ever hearing you say that you love *me* either."

I opened my mouth to say something in my defense, but he was right.

Holding up a hand, Magni spoke before I had a chance to respond. "It's okay, Laura. I never expected you to love me, and I respect you for not lying to my face."

"Magni, I…" Words failed me. How could he not know how I felt about him?

Magni's eyes were fixed on my hair when he spoke the next words. "It's a shame that our marriage was such a disappointment to you that you'd choose to leave. For what it's worth, I was always proud to be your husband."

"Until I ran away," I whispered as my head fell.

He didn't confirm it, but with a finger under my chin, he lifted my head.

If I were a Momsie, I would've told him that I loved him a long time ago, but those words weren't spoken often among us Northlanders, and he already held too much power over me.

What I couldn't say in words, I told him in my own way. Placing one hand on his strong chest, and sliding the other around his nape, I lifted up on my tiptoes and kissed him.

Magni closed his eyes, and my hand on his chest lifted when he drew in a deep intake of air.

I kissed him again, and this time he spread his lips, inviting me to deepen our kiss. Warmth spread in my body when his arms snaked around my waist, pulling me close against him. He followed up with that sexy sound deep in his throat that only Magni could make. It ignited an electric current that ran from the top of my spine all the way down to set off a fire between my thighs.

For two people who couldn't communicate well outside of the bedroom, at least we were compatible in this part of our relationship. There was an equal amount of desire and frustration.

"I should punish you for leaving me again," Magni mumbled against my neck.

A slow smile spread on my lips, "Are you going to?"

Magni's hand tugged my head backward when he pulled my hair, looking deep into my eyes. "I want to."

Excitement shone from my hooded eyes, but I didn't speak.

"You would like that, wouldn't you?" he muttered.

I smiled.

"Why the hell do you have to make things so difficult?" Magni asked in a low gruff voice.

I didn't have an answer for him but I complied when he ordered, "Take off your clothes."

Magni communicated with burning eyes, hungry kisses, strong hands, and short commands. The rougher the better for me. And Magni was an expert at rough.

His hair was still wet from the shower when I reached up to play with it. With a grunt Magni pinned my hands to stay in control. It didn't keep me from kissing him, and we battled for control a bit with him biting and suckling on my lower lip, giving me the perfect mix of pleasure and pain.

Using his strong hands, he pushed me down on the bed, pressing my legs apart with his knees. His expert fingers made sure I was wet and ready before he pushed inside of me. I closed my eyes and gave a deep moan, loving the sensation of being filled by him.

Magni encapsulated me with his body and after feeling like a giant among the Motlander women, it was wonderful to feel small in his arms. With a smile on my lips, I moved my right arm, silently signaling that I wanted him to let go of my wrist. Magni released my arm and allowed my hand to travel over his bulgy biceps and muscular shoulders. Every part of his body was delicious and toned.

"You feel amazing," I whispered against his ear, biting at his earlobe.

Magni's only response was an increase in his pace of sliding in and out of me.

"What position is your favorite?" My voice was still a whisper but my eyes were full of mischief. I had fantasized about Magni while we had been separated, and more than once I'd wondered what position he preferred.

"Every position that involves having sex with you," he answered in a breathy voice.

"I like it when you take me from behind, and when I ride you."

As if my words were a challenge, Magni took me in every position possible. After my second orgasm, I was exhausted, but Magni wasn't done. "Get on your hands and knees."

The bed was rocking and when my moans became too loud he covered my mouth with his large hand, pulling me up and back against his chest. Our bodies were covered with a sheen of perspiration. The cabin was like a sauna, and I could hardly breathe when his arm locked around my chest and he bit my shoulder in a sign of dominance.

Only a low growl came from him but he might as well have said the words "You're mine."

Closing my eyes, I rotated my hips, wanting him to do it again. Magni read my signals and lifted my hair away to bite my neck without breaking the skin.

"Come inside me," I panted.

His heavy breathing and the way he intensified the pace told me he was close.

"Yes, yes… that's it, Magni. Come in me."

Leaning back on his haunches, Magni brought me with him to a shared orgasm. Pressing himself as far inside of me as he could, he emptied every drop of warm semen while calling out my name. "Lauraaa, fuck yes, Laura."

I leaned my head back on his shoulder, panting from exhaustion.

"My leg is cramping." Without letting go of me, Magni changed our position to spoon on the bed. He was still inside of me, but stretching his leg and flexing his foot. I tried to move forward to give him space, but he held on to me. "No, stay."

We lay together and I reached for his hand and intertwined our fingers. Magni kissed my shoulder and buried his head in my hair. I blamed it on the lack of sleep from the night before that we fell asleep at seven thirty – connected, sated, and in each other's arms.

If only things could have stayed that way, but eight hours later, I woke up to an incoming call from Hans.

"I'm sorry, I know it's three in the morning, but I have news."

"Did they find Devlin?" My voice was hopeful, as I wanted to stay in bed with Magni.

"No, but we have a solid lead. There's a village about half an hour from the border where some mysterious activity indicates Devlin might be holding a woman hostage."

"What do you mean?" I whispered with a knot in my chest.

"We don't know what's going on for sure. Except the woman has been buying more food than usual and she has been acting strange. She lives in a one-person unit and neighbors have heard bizarre noises lately. One team investigated the reports more than a week ago, but the woman denied anything was wrong."

"But the reports keep coming?" I guessed.

"Yes. The other teams are hours away, but some of us are aiming to meet up in the village around six a.m. to arrest him. Will you meet us there? It's not far from the border."

"Yes. Send a drone and the address, will you?"

"I'll do that and I'll see you in a few hours."

"Okay," I whispered and ended the call.

It was tempting to let Magni sleep and avoid the potential fight that was bound to happen when I asked for a lift to the border. But tempting or not, I had promised him never to leave him with a note again, so I gave his shoulder a gentle push. "Magni, wake up."

"I *am* awake."

"Then why were you snoring?"

He turned on some light. "To see if you would sneak away again."

"You don't trust me." It was a statement more than a question.

"I used to."

With a deep sigh, I got up and dressed. "Can you take me to the border?"

"Do I have a choice?"

"I can wake Marco or Archer and ask them to do it."

Magni began to dress. "Remember what I told you. Don't let Devlin get close to you. No need to play a hero, and don't hesitate to blast the motherfucker to hell if he as much as points a weapon at you.

"Uh-huh." I made sure to pack my bag with the safety equipment.

"Look at me, Laura."

I turned to him and saw deep frown lines on his face.

"What did I just tell you?"

"To not be a hero and not get too close."

"Yes, and kill him if necessary."

I nodded without telling him that I had no intention of killing anyone.

"And if he sneaks up on you, knee him in his crotch. You don't have the strength to fight him off without dirty tricks, so castrate that scumbag if you get the chance."

"Got it!"

"Do you have everything?" Magni nodded to the bag.

"Yes." I closed it, praying that he wouldn't ask to see the weapons he'd given me.

"Do you want to eat something before you leave?"

"No."

"Do you want to take a shower?"

"I'm already fully dressed."

"Right, but maybe you should have a cup of coffee or tea at least."

"Magni, you're trying to stall for time, but it won't make a difference. I'm meeting the others in a few hours and I want to get going."

We put on our jackets in silence and walked side by side to the drone. Frost on the grass gave sound to our footsteps, but no words were said between us.

Only when we were at the border did Magni speak. "What can I do to make you stay?"

"If all goes well, I'll be back later tonight."

"Until you decide to leave again." His remark was dry and bitter.

"Magni, I know we have a lot to discuss…"

He cut me off, his voice shaky. "Promise me that this is the last time I'm taking you to this fucking border."

"I don't want to fight with you."

"Then *promise* me," he said between gritted teeth.

"We'll talk about it when I'm back."

"Laura, you're killing me," Magni exclaimed and backed up a step. Light from the drone fell on his face, and looking into his blue eyes, I saw deep sadness. Mila's words resounded in my mind: *Magni cries on the inside.*

"Do you have your safety gear?"

"Yes."

"Weapons?"

"I'll be fine. Magni, try not to worry about me."

His nostrils expanded and he heaved in air like he was in physical pain.

"I'll call you later."

A vein on Magni's temple popped out, and I figured the way he buried both hands in the pocket of his jacket was his way of keeping from dragging me back to the drone.

"I'll see you later." I only took three steps before I turned around and went back to hug him goodbye.

Magni was stiff and only gave me a brief squeeze. Maybe giving me a tight hug would have made it harder for him to let go.

"Be careful," he whispered against my hair.

"I will."

Once we landed, there were a hundred and three steps from his drone to the border. I know, because I counted them to distract myself from the overwhelming need to turn around and see if Magni was watching me.

When I reached the crossing, I couldn't stop myself from looking back. Magni stood on the hilltop in front of his drone, his hands in his pockets, his eyes on me.

Catching Devlin will prove to Magni and everyone else that I'm a force to be reckoned with. I have to do this!

After waving one last time at him, I crossed the border, determined to keep my promise. If I'd known how my encounter with Devlin would go later that day, I wouldn't have left the Northlands.

CHAPTER 17
Devlin

Laura

As promised, Hans had made sure a drone waited for me as soon as I crossed into the Motherlands. Half an hour later, I arrived at the village where Devlin was believed to be keeping a woman hostage. It was only four in the morning, and none of the other team members had arrived yet.

I chose to land the drone outside the rural village and walk to the house. That's when it hit me that it had been a mistake to get here early. Standing for two hours looking at a dark house, until Hans and the other mediators arrived, wasn't a solid plan. I debated whether to go back to the drone and wait there, or to investigate by myself. Isobel had the weapons that Magni had given me, and I'd left the non-lethal Motlander weapons with Hans. Still, a tiptoe walk around the perimeter of the house didn't sound too dangerous, and it could prove useful later on when we had to come up with a plan on how to surround the house.

I made sure to be quiet, and kept the light from my wristband turned to the ground only.

The house was small and very old. It was hard for me to see what it was made of, but I guessed it to be GOTO blocks like most old houses here. My sensei had lived in a house like this, and she had told me that GOTO was short for *Gift of the Ocean*, a program that transformed plastic trash into building blocks. Some of these houses had been built more than two hundred years ago and were routinely renovated and upgraded. They didn't use GOTO

142

blocks to build anymore since they had run out of plastic trash long ago. That's why it made sense to treasure these old houses. With everything from the old world either buried or destroyed after the war, the houses had become a historic part of the Motherlands.

Looking over my shoulder to be sure no one was around, I tripped over a shovel standing against the wall of the house. It spooked the hell out of me when it made a jarring noise as it fell down on some empty flowerpots. Thinking fast, I hunched down close to the wall, covering the light from my wristband with my other arm. I held my breath and didn't move a muscle.

A dog barked in the distance and I thought I heard a voice from inside the house. For what felt like ten minutes, I listened for movement, but no one came and my pulse calmed down enough for me to stand up and move along. Quiet as a mouse, I tiptoed around the next corner and froze to the spot. A faint light shone from a window, and my first thought was to retreat to the drone to wait for the others.

I had only taken a few steps before I heard sounds that made the hair on my neck and arms stand up. Turning my head, I listened. My brain registered what those sounds were, but I didn't want to believe it.

Folding my hands into fists and closing my eyes, I swallowed hard and took a long inhalation of the cold night air.

Muffled screams and low groans sounded again, awakening the bravest part of me. Telling myself that I was a Northlander and that we always rose to the occasion, I walked back and rose up on my toes to look in through the window.

The room was dimly lit, but I saw enough to understand that an innocent Motlander woman was being brutally raped by a large man who could only be Devlin.

143

My hand flew to my mouth, and my eyes grew wide when I watched the poor woman being pressed into the mattress. Her hands were tied down to the bed, making it impossible for her to fight him off. With Devlin covering her mouth with one hand and strangling her with the other, she was suffocating.

My stomach was in an uproar and I felt like vomiting. This was exactly what Motlanders had always accused Northlanders of being: rapists and monsters.

One of the escaped Nmen had already raped an innocent woman and now Devlin was doing the same.

The woman's eyes were rolling back in her head, her legs kicking. The motherfucker was killing her and I was the only one around to interfere.

What would Magni do?

The answer was obvious. *Magni would storm in there and break Devlin's neck to save the woman.*

There was no time to wait for backup. I had to act now!

Needing a weapon, I ran back to the side of the house and picked up the shovel before I sprinted to the front entrance.

The door was locked.

"Fuck!" I muttered under my breath and stepped back.

If I'd learned anything in these past six months living in the Motherlands, it was that Motlanders were trusting people who didn't lock their doors. I had once asked my sensei about it, and she'd joked that it didn't matter since the GOBO doors were so easy to break down that a lock wouldn't hold anyone out anyway.

I considered testing to see if she was right, but knocking down the door would alert Devlin that I was coming.

My hands flew to the small keyboard on the side of the door and taking a chance, I pressed 1-2-3-4. Nothing happened. I tried 9-8-7-6 and then I saw the house number on a sign just above the box. No one would use

144

that obvious a number, but I had to test it. With frantic movements my fingers took a long shot and pressed 1-0-2-4. I held my breath when a green light lit up and the door clicked. I would have to have a serious talk about safety with the woman living here, but first I had to save her life.

The sounds from the bedroom overpowered the low creaking sound from the door as I entered. Holding out the shovel in front of me, I steered towards the dim light coming from underneath a door to my right.

My palms grew sweaty when I heard squeaking sounds from the bed and skin pounding against skin.

"You feel that? You like having a real man between your legs?" Devlin's deep voice was raw and panting. "Told you I'd fuck you hard if you didn't do as I asked you to."

It felt like my heart was trying to beat its way through my spine to get the hell out of that house, but I kept thinking about Magni. A month after we got married, we'd witnessed a crash at a drone race. We'd been on a balcony with Khan as guests of honor when two of the drones nearly collided and one of them spun out of control and crashed. Khan was shouting for people to get back in case the drone exploded, while Magni crawled over the balcony and jumped down, making his way through an audience that was in panic. I had watched in horror as he ran straight to the drone, kicked in a window, and pulled the pilot out. Magni always stormed ahead when others ran away, and if he were here right now, he wouldn't retreat. Tightening my grip around the shaft of the shovel, I moved closer with what would have been graceful cat-like movements if my legs hadn't been stiff from fear.

With my hand on the doorknob, I counted down from three in my head.

3. 2. 1.

Boom. With my heart in my throat, I slammed the door open.

My brain registered the scenario in front of me with Devlin still on top of the poor tied-up woman, now with her knees on his shoulder. My hands clamped around the long shaft of the shovel, pulling it back to swing it full force against the back of Devlin's head.

He turned his head just as the shovel made impact and was knocked on his side with a howl of pain.

My blood pumped with the speed of fury, and tunnel vision made me focus only on the disgusting monster in front of me. Taking advantage of his initial shock, I used the shovel to strike him again and again. He held up his arms to protect himself and shouted incoherently at me, but I couldn't hear a thing for the noise in my ears.

I hit him as hard as I could on his back, arms, shoulder, neck, and hands. This disgusting man represented all my childhood nightmares of being taken by an evil man, like my father always warned about.

I channeled all my fear and rage at him with a hard kick.

"No." The scream came from the woman and I scrunched up my face in disbelief. Motlanders were peaceful by nature, but she should be happy for me to punish this creep for raping her.

Devlin was quick to take advantage of my momentary confusion and ripped the shovel from me.

I tried to kick him again, but he blocked and got up to fight back.

"Where the fuck did you come from?" he sneered at me. "Did you really think you stood a chance against an Nman?"

I didn't tell him I was a Northlander myself because I was too busy reacting to his attack. Even with the things Magni had taught me, Devlin was too strong and fast for me. My strategy had always been to keep my distance but within seconds he was breathing into my face, with a hand squeezing around my neck.

146

I turned my head and closed my eyes, as if surrendering. It made him ease his grip a little.

Magni had told me that Devlin would underestimate me, and he'd been right. His words for me to *castrate that scumbag* if I got the chance made me hammer my knee up into Devlin's naked crotch.

Shoving me hard against the wall, he fell to his knees and buckled over in pain.

"No," the woman cried out from the bed, yanking the ropes that had her tied to the bed. "Don't hurt him."

"I'm saving you." My hands were already untying the knots to free her.

To my surprise, she ran to Devlin asking him if he was all right.

Blue in the face, he couldn't respond.

"You didn't have to hurt him. What did he ever do to you?" She asked with a blameful stare at me.

"*Me?*" I shook my head. "He was raping *you*."

"Breathe, babe, just breathe," she instructed him, while stroking his back up and down.

My hands went to my hair, and my eyes widened in a *what the fuck* expression. Nothing made sense.

"He had you tied down."

She ignored me, focusing only on the man on the floor.

Looking to the bed, I assured myself that the ropes were still there. They weren't just in my head. And then I saw it.

"What is this?" I asked and took a few steps to pick up the sign leaning against the wall. It said,

> *I'd take an Nman N-E day.*
> *The border is bad.*
> *Nmen are good.*

"For fuck's sake," I muttered and turned to her. "You are one of *those women*?"

She only spared me a quick glimpse. "I don't know what you're referring to or who you are, but I want you out of my house."

I pointed an accusing finger at her. "He wasn't holding you hostage, was he? You've been hiding Devlin all this time."

"So what if I have? It still doesn't give you the right to go and beat him up."

Devlin groaned, and I wasn't sure if it was because of the physical pain or the humiliation of his woman seeing him get beaten up by a woman.

"You don't understand," I said. "Devlin is a criminal. He's been in prison."

"Yes, he told me."

"And you still allowed him inside your house?" I couldn't fathom the stupidity of this woman.

"He never hurt me," she insisted, and that made me pick up one of the ropes and hold it out to her in an accusatory manner.

"How can you say that? He had you tied down and I saw him strangling you."

Her eyes were shooting daggers at me. "I'm a naturephile, okay? We like role plays, and I don't have to explain my fantasies to you."

"Your fantasies?" My tone was incredulous.

Devlin lifted his face; a large red mark from where the shovel had hit him was already showing. "It was just a role-play," he explained in a strained voice.

"It didn't look like play to me. It looked like you were raping her."

"I was *pretending*." He gave me a hard stare. "Julia knows I would never hurt her."

I rubbed my face, as if I could somehow wash away what I had seen. "This makes no sense to me."

Julia found a robe to cover her naked body, and faced me. "I was up at the border when the earthquake

148

happened. That's when I met Devlin. It was a spontaneous decision to bring him here." She brought him his clothes and I looked away as he dressed himself.

"Didn't it occur to you that he might be dangerous?"

"No. People say mean things about the Nmen all the time, but it's just rumors and lies. My friends and I have read every article about the women who have married men from the North. They all tell how wonderful their men really are."

I was shocked at how naïve she was.

"Because they married good men. This piece of shit..." I pointed to Devlin, "...stabbed a man to death and went to prison for it."

"He only stabbed the man because they were both intoxicated and the man attacked him. Devlin was only trying to protect himself."

"Oh yeah?" I looked down at Devlin. "And is that why you stabbed my husband too?"

"Your husband?"

"Magni Aurelius. He's got a scar on his arm because of you."

"Fuck that, it wasn't my fault." Devlin frowned. "Look, fighting Magni is no joke. That guy is legendary and when I met him I was heading over to tell him what an admirer I am. If I'd known what a foul mood he'd be in, I would have kept my distance. I bumped into him by accident and he got so mad that he slammed me up against a wall. Your husband is crazy, and if I hadn't pulled my knife, he'd have smashed my head in."

"He was going through a tough time, that's all," I defended Magni.

"No shit. I heard that you left him. I would be going crazy too."

Julia spoke up. "Devlin and I love each other."

I lowered my brow. "You've only known each other for three weeks."

Devlin pulled her into his arms and they both looked at me. "Julia is right," he said. "We can't get enough of each other. It was love at first sight."

My jaw dropped at the sincerity in his voice. I'd been chasing this man for three weeks, thinking he was violent, brutal, and a danger to the Motlanders. And then it turns out that he was in a consensual relationship with a woman who saw him as a gift from heaven. It was mind-boggling to me that Devlin could declare his love for Julia without hesitation. How could it be so easy for him to say when Magni couldn't get those words over his lips?

Clearing my throat, I addressed him. "You'll need to go back to the Northlands."

"I'm not going anywhere unless I can take Julia with me." He tightened his grip around her, and she reciprocated by clinging to him with her arms around his waist.

"I'm sorry but it's not up to me." I could tell him to apply to become a permanent resident here, but there was no way the Council would allow someone with a criminal past to move here.

"If you try to split us apart, we'll do something drastic," Julia declared.

"Look, I'll give you time to say goodbye, but there's no way I can let you stay with her."

Devlin sighed. "You could pretend that you didn't find me here."

I shook my head. "Others are coming."

"Then you could let me and Julia leave together. I could take her back to the Northlands."

"Devlin, it wouldn't work. Julia will have to apply to marry you the official way."

"But how long will that take?" she asked with a pout.

"I don't know." For a moment I took in the two lovers. My mind had a hard time catching up from seeing what I had perceived as his raping her to the image of the two of

150

them standing in each other's arms. "I suggest you take time to say goodbye. I'll be waiting outside."

Leaving the house, I chose a strategic position that would allow me to see if they tried to escape out a window.

My head was about to explode with all the impressions from what had just happened. But I kept my promise to Magni, and called him up.

As soon as his hologram appeared above my wrist, I blurted out what I was most proud of. "I found Devlin, and I took him down."

Magni looked worried. "Where is he now?"

"He's still in the house saying goodbye to Julia. She's the woman he lived with these past three weeks. Turns out she was one of those women from the border. She's been hiding him, and you'll never guess what I walked in on."

"What?"

"They were having sex."

"You saw them?"

"I thought he was raping her. Otherwise I would've never gone in by myself."

Magni's expression hardened. "You went in by yourself? Where are the others?"

"They are on their way."

"Tell me *everything*!"

I started from the beginning and told him what had happened.

"Why the fuck would you use a shovel instead of one of your guns?"

I closed my eyes, realizing my mistake. "Because I didn't have my weapons. Isobel took them from me when I first arrived here. It's illegal to carry lethal weapons in the Motherlands."

His eyes bulged. "She left you defenseless?"

"No, they gave me a numb gun and the net gun. Except I didn't have them on me."

151

Magni's face was growing redder by the second. "Are you telling me that you went in there completely unarmed?"

"You would've done the same thing."

"That's different."

"I did the job. Why can't you just be proud of me?"

Magni let out a sigh of frustration. "And you think Devlin is just going to go with you like that?"

"He's nothing like you described. He told me that they love each other."

Magni snorted. "He's a horny Nman. Of course he would say that."

That comment pissed me off. "You weren't there, and from my experience saying *I love you* doesn't come easy to Nmen."

Magni ignored my comment. "As soon as the others arrive, leave the fucker to them and come back here. Do you hear me, Laura?"

Rationally, I knew Magni had been worried about me and that he wanted me back where he could keep me safe. But the way he ordered me around in his usual bossy manner triggered my need for him to treat me as an equal.

"I think I may visit some of my friends while I'm here."

"Laura." He spoke my name as a warning. "I want you home, *now*!"

"Why? Are you horny?" I tilted my head. "No, I guess not, since if that was the case you would have no problem telling me that you loved me, right?"

A deep groan escaped Magni. "*Laura.*"

My hands were shaking and my throat hurt from suppressing my scream of frustration. Why was love so effortless for others when it was so difficult and complicated for Magni and me?

"You're coming home *right now*."

"No. I warned you not to boss me around. I'll come back when *I'm* ready."

Magni was biting down on his fist with his cheeks bloated from the scream he held back.

"I just proved to you that I can take care of myself. I'm done waiting for you to treat me like an equal. I'm a warrior like you."

Magni's snort was the last straw that made me lose my temper and hiss, "You know what, I've had it with you. You treat me like a helpless child, and I'm sick of it."

"What the fuck is that supposed to mean? I didn't treat you like a child a few hours ago when I fucked you, did I?

"No, but I can't be with you just because the sex is amazing. At least here in the Motherlands, people respect and appreciate me." I spoke fast and with an accusatory tone. "If you can't give that to me, I'd rather stay here."

Magni was furious and hissed, "You're coming back here, right now. That's a fucking order."

My voice grew shrill. "No, I'm not! And you don't get to order me around anymore. I've tried to reason with you, but you won't listen."

"You're *not* staying in the Motherlands," he shouted.

"Yes, I am." I had chased down Devlin and the other men and deserved Magni's respect. His dismissal of what I'd done was offensive and infuriating.

"If you stay, don't bother coming back. I'm not joking, Laura, I'm done with this shit. Make a choice. Me or the Motherlands."

My anger clouded my brain and I didn't even hesitate. "Goodbye, Magni."

"Laura," he called out, but with my body trembling from hurt, and my mind clouded with disappointment, I disconnected the call.

CHAPTER 18
Betrayal

Magni

What I had feared all along was happening. Laura wasn't coming back to me. Now that the escaped Nmen had all been captured, she had no official excuse to stay in the Motherlands. Everyone would know that she had made her choice and that our marriage was over.

I was pacing my office at the Gray Mansion, my fingers itching with the need to throw something. My brother wasn't the only fool blinded by his woman; I was one too.

Like an idiot, I had taken Laura to the border myself, trusting that after a night of amazing sex she would come back to me. How wrong I had been!

Laura didn't want what I had to offer, and why would she? My life was unraveling, with my pride in tatters and my wife and brother turned against me.

The intense pain in my chest made me wonder for a moment if I was having a heart attack. I slumped down in a chair, hoping to slow down my pulse and get my thoughts under control.

She's gone!

Laura is gone!

The thoughts were on a loop, sinking in like a dull bread knife cutting through a loaf of bread.

She's not coming back.

I won't see Laura again.

Closing my eyes, I could smell the scent of her hair from when I held her in my arms last night.

I knew this would happen.

I fucking knew this would happen.

A knock on the door made me straighten up and take a deep breath. "Come in."

Franklin, my lieutenant, walked through the door. "Commander, you said you wanted to know if there was any suspicious behavior from your brother's wife."

"Yes."

"Half an hour ago she left for the Motherlands."

"Was Khan with her?"

"No. One of the security officers took her."

"Why? What the hell is she going to do in the Motherlands at five in the morning?"

"The security officer did not know. He is scheduled to pick her up again at six a.m."

I tapped my index finger against my upper lip. "She wants to be back before anyone notices that she left in the first place."

"Yes, Commander, it looks that way."

"Thank you for informing me. Reassign the security officer; I will be picking up Pearl myself."

"Yes, sir, understood."

"And Franklin," I said when he was by the door. "Don't tell Khan about this."

"What if he asks me where you are?"

"I'm not asking you to lie to your ruler. But unless he asks you, you'll keep quiet."

With a brief nod, Franklin left my office.

I might not be able to control my own wife, but I wouldn't look the other way while Pearl sabotaged Khan and our country.

At six a.m., I was at the border to pick up Pearl.

She paled when she saw me – a sure sign that she was up to no good.

"Good morning," I said and opened the door to the drone for her. "I was up early anyway, so I figured I might as well come get you."

As Pearl watched me with her chin raised; a few loose tendrils from her long blond hair blew around her face in the morning breeze. From the first time I'd met Pearl, the elegant regality she carried herself with had annoyed me.

"How nice of you," she said in a polite tone that didn't match how stiff she was when she got into the military drone that I'd taken in order to be incognito.

As soon as we were in the air, I started my interrogation. "What kind of errands do you run in the Motherlands at this time of day?"

"I would rather not say."

"So, you admit that you're hiding something?"

"I have a right to privacy."

"No, you don't. My job is to have my brother's back and right now I suspect treason. You'd better start talking, lady."

Pearl gave me a stern look. "Magni, there's really no need to be dramatic. I love Khan and I would never do anything to hurt him."

"People do stupid things with good intentions all the time," I said in a flat tone. "Tell me what you were doing in the Motherlands."

"I'm sorry, but that is confidential."

I gave a low snort. "You forget that I still outrank you. Tell me what the fuck you were doing in the Motherlands."

"No." Pearl turned her head, signaling that she was done with this conversation.

First Laura disobeyed me, and now Pearl was doing the same. It was infuriating and enough to give a man a headache.

Crossing my arms, I gave my most intimidating scowl. "Look at me, Pearl."

In a slow and graceful movement, she turned her head and looked at me with no fear.

"I am done playing your games. Either you tell me what you were doing in the Motherlands or I will take you to an interrogation cell."

"I doubt Khan is going to be happy when he hears that you threatened me."

I shrugged. "Just doing my job."

"Are you sure? It feels personal." She sighed. "I'm sorry that you feel like I come between you and your brother. That's not my intention, and I see that you're both hurting. For the sake of keeping peace between you, I will tell you this much. I had a doctor's appointment in the Motherlands."

"Why? Are you sick?"

"No."

"Then why did you go and see a doctor? We have doctors here."

"I went to see a gynecologist?"

"A what?"

"A doctor specializing in females," Pearl explained. "I know you have doctors here in the Northlands, but none as specialized as the ones we have in the Motherlands when it comes to female health."

"It could just be a cover story for you meeting with the Council to discuss ways of infiltrating the Northlands. I don't trust you. Give me the address and the name of this doctor."

Pearl shook her head. "Why? It's not like you can go and check it out for yourself."

"I don't need to, I have contacts."

"Would it help if I showed you the pills that the doctor gave me?" She pulled two oval-shaped boxes out of her bag and held them out to me.

"What is this?"

"Medicine."

I gave her a look of annoyance. "I can see that, but what does it do? You just said you're not sick."

157

"It's mostly vitamins."

I had interrogated people for years, and every instinct I had told me that Pearl was hiding something significant. Reading the label, I searched for clues, worrying that these might be some kind of poison that she would give to Khan. "I'm going to have to take these."

"You can't do that, I need those."

"I need to run a test and see that they aren't some kind of poison."

"Why would my doctor give me poison? Magni, you're making no sense at all."

"I'm just making sure you're not slipping some sort of poison into Khan's beer, that's all."

Pearl's jaw dropped, and her voice was shaky when she spoke. "You think that I am conspiring to murder Khan?"

"You wouldn't be the first one."

Her blue eyes were full of shock and kept blinking. "I can't believe you would think that of me. Are you so blinded by paranoia that you can't see my love for your brother?"

"Words are cheap. I've learned not to trust anyone."

Pearl tilted her head and gave me a look of deep sympathy. "It's a sad thing to see someone as cynical as you. I know your father was a hard man, and it can't have been easy to be the younger brother, always destined to be number two."

I raised an eyebrow in warning, but Pearl didn't take the hint.

"Your father wanted you to be the ruler, didn't he? You were the stronger, and a warrior superior to Khan."

"Khan is an excellent fighter."

"But not as good as you are."

If Pearl thought I was going to fall for her flattery, she was wrong. "No one is as good as me."

158

"And yet you're always in the shadow of your brother. How does that feel?"

"Nice try, but I already told you that I'm not going to fall for your manipulative mind games."

"You're not used to people showing an interest in you, are you?"

"I'm not in the habit of sharing personal information, that's for sure."

"And yet you expect me to share personal information with you. You can't ask for something that you're not willing to give."

I studied the woman in front of me. Her eyes shone with intelligence, and unlike the hundreds of people I had interrogated in the past, she didn't lash out in defense or anger. I'd never seen Pearl being anything but calm and collected. Right now she was setting up boundaries, but she did it in a nonconfrontational manner. I cleared my throat. "People who have nothing to hide, hide nothing. It's possible that you're not lying to me, but you're not telling the truth either."

"Only because the secret I carry is one I wish to share with Khan before anyone else."

"You're pregnant!" The thought struck like lightning, bypassing every filter I had.

From the way Pearl's face stiffened, and her eyes widened, I knew that I had guessed right.

"Fuck!" I closed my eyes and folded my hands into fists. There was no way in hell Khan would give up on Pearl now when she was carrying his child. The power she had over him would only increase.

"Can't you be happy for us?" she asked in a soft voice.

I couldn't explain to her that her pregnancy was just another reminder of what a failure I was as a man and a husband. Laura and I had been married for close to two years, and I hadn't succeeded in getting her pregnant in that time. Khan and Pearl had been married for three months and she was already knocked up. So was Christina, my friend Boulder's wife, and Kya, the woman teacher at the school. I should be happy that we had a baby boom in the Northlands, but it pained me deep inside that I was left on the outside, watching other people's happiness while I had never been more alone.

I landed the drone at the Gray Mansion, and got out at the same time as Pearl did. On purpose, I walked in the direction opposite hers, but she called out to me.

"You don't have to be afraid of Khan. I won't tell him that you were mean to me."

"Go ahead and tell him. He should know I'm just doing my job." My voice sounded flat and dead.

"I worry about you." Pearl sounded sincere, but I didn't need her sympathy or pity.

"Don't," I grunted and walked on.

CHAPTER 19
Pissing Contest

Laura

I knocked on the door when I entered Julia's house for the second time. She and Devlin were still in the bedroom, sitting on the bed and holding hands. Her eyes were red-rimmed from crying and he looked like he had just been swimming two miles in cold water.

"The others will be here within a few minutes," I said. "Maybe it's better if we just pretend that I never came in here and saw what I saw." I frowned. "I know you said that you were just playing out some sort of fantasy, but I would have to explain that it looked like rape to me. It's a bad word to have in your report. You know, in case you want the Council to approve Julia joining you in the Northlands."

Devlin and Julia exchanged a concerned look. She was tucked against him and his hand kept stroking up and down her arm. "We would appreciate it if you didn't mention the part about the role playing," he muttered.

I pointed my index finger straight at Devlin. "Don't try to run when we come in. I won't hesitate to shoot your ass with a numb gun, and I have to be honest with you, it's kind of a buzz to see a big-ass guy like you go down and be powerless."

He snorted. "Don't you think I would've run by now if I was going to escape?"

"I'm just saying, don't run!" I turned around to walk out. "Oh, and you should both act surprised. Pretend that you've never seen me, okay?"

They both nodded when I left.

161

It was still dark when Hans and the other two mediators arrived.

"We should surround the house." Hans spoke with a look of importance. "And then one of us will approach the door and come up with some story about being lost and thirsty. That way she will let us into the house and we can look around."

Cheryl, one of the mediators, wrung her hands. "I like the part of your plan where we surround the house, but maybe we could adjust the part about telling a story." She was too polite to remind Hans that lying wasn't the way of the Motlanders.

It took them almost ten minutes of polite discussion before they agreed to simply ask the woman living there if she had seen Devlin.

"We should agree on who of us should knock on the door," Cheryl said. "I suggest we send two people, in case he gets violent."

The fourth mediator, who had introduced herself as Lizzie, was scrolling through files on her wristband. "Procedure says that it should be the two most experienced mediators. According to this, Hans is the most skilled among us."

Hans's voice sounded a bit shrill. "If someone else would like to go first, that would be fine with me. I don't want to take all the glory or the excitement."

I didn't blame them for being frightened. We had all heard horrible stories about Devlin, and they didn't know that he was sitting in the house holding hands with his girlfriend.

I raised a hand. "I don't mind going."

"Good." Hans looked at the other two women. "And who else wants to go?"

They both looked down, and an awkward silence filled the early morning.

162

"I think maybe we should wait for more backup," Hans suggested.

"We *are* the backup," I pointed out. "Didn't you tell me that you're the best mediator there is?"

"I am." Hans shifted his balance from one foot to the other, straightening up.

"Then let's go."

"I'll take the left corner," Cheryl said and pointed to Lizzie. "Why don't you take the right?"

Hans looked terrified as we walked shoulder to shoulder, side by side to the house. When I knocked on the door, he pulled back enough for me to be in front. It hit me hard how hypocritical I was when I rolled my eyes at Hans' lack of male pride. I had just been fighting with Magni for being too bossy and protective of me, and here I was resenting Hans for hiding behind a woman in the face of danger.

Julia opened the door. Her eyes were puffy from crying.

"Sorry to bother you this early, but we're looking for a man named Devlin."

Her lips quivered again and her hands dried away more tears.

Behind me Hans leaned closer, and whispered to Julia, "We are here to save you."

"May we come in?" I asked.

Julia nodded and left the door open as she walked back in to the living room.

Hans pushed me forward, keeping his position behind me.

"Good morning," I said to Devlin, who sat fully dressed on the sofa. "Are you Devlin Hyde?"

"Yes."

I opened my mouth to speak but Hans peeked out behind me and beat me to it.

"We're here to escort you back to the Northlands."

Devlin had a grimace of disgust on his face as he watched Hans cower behind me. "If you have something to say to me then come out and face me like a man."

Hans took a small step to the side, now visible to Devlin. "I said, we're here to escort you back to the Northlands." The net gun that he was holding in his hands was shaking because of his hands' trembling.

Devlin turned to look at Julia. "I see what you mean, babe. If that's what Motlander men act like then I don't blame you for not feeling turned on by any of them."

"We will need you to stay calm while I place these immobilizers on you." I held up the thumb lock, and took a step closer.

"No," Hans screamed. "He is a murderer – do not get any closer."

"What the fuck are you talking about?" Devlin sputtered.

"We know you killed a man, and that you went to prison for it."

"It was a drunken bar fight. He died because he attacked me. It was self-defense."

"That's easy for you to say, but we're not taking any chances. Toss the immobilizers over and let him put them on himself," Hans instructed in a high-pitched voice as he dried perspiration from his forehead.

Devlin caught the thumb lock that I threw to him, and turned it around in the air. "Do you honestly think that this small thing would immobilize me?" He smirked. "If I wanted to escape, I could kill you two with my hands tied behind my back.

Hans looked like he was about to pee his pants in fear. "We have backup," he said while waving the net gun at Devlin.

I understood what Hans couldn't possibly understand. Devlin's pride was humiliated from my attack on him earlier. He wanted Julia to think he was the biggest alpha and he was throwing around big talk to impress her.

"I know you could," I said softly. "We've read your files and know that you are a fierce warrior."

"That's right." He pushed his chest out.

"You'll forgive us for being scared of you, but we need you to put on the thumb lock."

The edges around Devlin's eyes softened a bit. Maybe he understood what I was trying to do.

"Julia, honey, would you mind putting this stupid thing on me?"

Hans, who was still under the impression that Julia had been a hostage, warned her. "Don't go near him, he has no power over you anymore."

She ignored Hans and walked over to plant a big kiss on Devlin's lips.

Hans reacted with the same amount of disbelief that I had. "What is going on here?"

Julia explained how they had met at the border and she had invited Devlin to come and stay with her.

"But he's an Nman," Hans protested.

"I know." Julia put on the thumb lock, effectively tying Devlin's arms behind his back.

"Could you write in your report that I went voluntarily?" Devlin asked me. "Maybe that will help when Julia applies to come and live with me."

"You want to live in the Northlands?" Hans asked in a high-pitched tone of disbelief. "With him?"

"What's so hard to believe about that?" Devlin asked. "Women like strong men. Maybe if you removed all that makeup and packed some muscle on that boyish body of yours, women would like you too."

"I'll have you know that I am very fashionable," Hans defended himself. "The majority of women in this country would find someone like you grotesque and primitive."

"Not me," Julia assured Devlin. "I think you're amazing."

The two of them exchanged a heated glare.

"Ahh, yes," Hans said in a dry voice. "There are a few confused women who seem to have lost their common sense. I suppose you are one of them, and I would strongly recommend that you spend some time in a place of reflection."

I'd had enough of the pissing contest between Hans and Devlin. "We'll need you to follow us outside."

Julia was crying when we walked Devlin outside to one of the drones. Images of her being taken by force this morning had me frowning to myself. I stayed behind with Hans to take a report from her.

"How come you were dressed and awake at six a.m.?" Hans asked like he was some detective unraveling a mystery.

"Devlin is a light sleeper. He thought he heard a noise outside, but it was only a dog barking."

"Then why didn't you go back to sleep?"

"We made love instead." Julia narrowed her eyes, showing she was tired and annoyed from Hans' endless questions. "After that, we were hungry and got out of bed."

When Hans kept pushing her to let us take her to a place of reflection, I intervened.

"If she doesn't want to go, she shouldn't have to."

He pulled me aside. "Laura, you don't understand. Something is wrong with her. I was looking around just now and found a sign in her bedroom. She has a fetish."

"A fetish?"

"An Nman fetish."

My lips pursed upward. "Is that a thing?"

"Yes, the press has been reporting about it, and Julia has a clear case of it. She's a *romantic*." He said the word as if it was a terminal diagnosis.

I shook my head. "Some of us like big rough men. Get over it, Hans. It's not a sickness, it's a preference."

He was brooding when we left Julia. "I'll make sure Isobel gets our full report."

"Good, will you tell her to return Magni's weapons to him?"

"Yes."

"Why do you look so disappointed, Hans? We found all the Northlanders. You should be excited about that."

"I don't think you realize how disturbing it is for some of us to see women throwing themselves at Nmen."

"What do you mean?"

"For generations we have been everything women wanted us to be. Gentle, kind, nonthreatening, pretty, and understanding. I suppose you could say we Motlander men suffer from a collective guilt complex. But how could we not? For four hundred years we've been held accountable for what happened in that awful war when power-hungry men destroyed our planet. We have done everything in our power not to show those unwanted masculine traits and to make it up to women." Hans' words were fast and agitated. "So how do you think it makes me feel when you and Julia make it sound like someone as primitive and ugly as Devlin is more attractive than me?"

"Devlin isn't ugly."

Hans held his hands to his face. "Did you see his untrimmed beard? His skin had no glow and his pores on his nose were the size of golf balls."

"I agree Devlin is a bit rough around the edges, but so are most men in the Northlands. Magni included."

"And you *like* that?"

"I like that he takes pride in being a man, and I think you should too."

"I would rather die than look as unkempt as he did."

167

"No one said that being a man means that you have to be unkempt. I'm sure there are women who appreciate a man who takes good care of himself."

"Appreciate, yes, but I've never seen a woman fawn over a man the way Julia just did. Might I remind you that you kicked me out of your bed?"

I ignored his pout. "It's nothing personal. I can honestly say that I haven't met a single man in the Motherlands who tempted me in the slightest."

"Me included."

"Yes. There's no spark between the genders here. No polarity or excitement. It's all friendliness and hugs and kisses."

"Would you prefer that we were *coming on* to you?" Hans chuckled with disdain, as if the thought in itself was beneath him. "Modern men have evolved, you know. We are no longer cavemen dragging home women by their hair."

I sighed. "Women are attracted to men with high levels of testosterone. It's biology, Hans." It wouldn't matter if I stood here until the sun went down. Hans and I would never agree on what made a man attractive. "I need to go now, and you have a report to write."

"Are you going back to *him*?"

"To Magni?"

"Yes."

I scratched my collarbone. "I'm visiting a friend first and then I'll make up my mind."

There was a look of disappointment on Hans' face. "I didn't take you for a weak woman."

"Excuse me?"

"Strong women would never let themselves be controlled by a man."

His words hit a nerve. "I have to go."

"I hope to see you again," Hans called out behind me as I walked away at a fast pace.

I lifted my hand to signal that I had heard him, but I didn't tell him I hoped to see him again. That would've been a lie.

CHAPTER 20
Purpose

Magni

Franklin caught up to me when I walked into the mansion. "I should warn you, Commander, Khan knows that you picked up Pearl at the border and he's not happy about it."

I grunted. "How does he know?"

"I'm not sure but I have a theory. I think he is having both of you tracked and he's getting alerts when you two are in close proximity. He knows you can be hard on Pearl and he doesn't like it. Khan wants to see you right away."

I didn't look at Franklin when I threw a few things into a bag. "Yeah, well, I'm not in the mood for a fucking lecture. You can tell Lord Khan that I'll be on the East Coast."

"For how long, Commander?"

"I don't know."

Franklin frowned. "What about the situation at the border?"

"What about it?"

"Should we continue to patrol?"

"Yes, those are my orders and you'll make sure they are carried out until Khan or I tell you otherwise."

"Understood, sir."

Franklin stood in the doorway when I passed him and smacked his shoulder. "I'll be in touch, Lieutenant."

For a moment I considered swinging by the school to say goodbye to Mila, but the black cloud above my head was weighing me down too much.

Laura didn't want me, Khan didn't appreciate me, and I didn't have much to offer anyone anyway.

There was nothing for me here, and nowhere to go. If we hadn't been so fucking isolated up here in the Northlands, I would've found some desert island with a warm beach to get away from it all.

My sleek red drone took me to the East Coast in a few hours. Erika, my mom, currently lived in a grand mansion with my father's best friend Mr. Zobel. They had both lost their spouses and it seemed natural that they would marry, but Khan and I didn't like him much. Mr. Zobel had always been a harmless snob who sucked up to our dad when he was still alive. With our mom being a beautiful woman, Khan and I both felt she could do better. As her protectors, we had allowed her to live with him in the hope that she would grow tired of him.

It didn't surprise me that my mother and Mr. Zobel were both home when I arrived unannounced. They lived in a golden cage and almost never went anywhere.

"What a lovely surprise," my mother chirped with a happy smile. "You should've told me you were coming, I would've had the kitchen bake that pumpkin bread you love so much."

"Don't worry about it."

"How long are you staying? Are you well? You don't look too well. Did something happen?" My mother was fussing over me, stroking my chin and shoulder.

"I'm fine," I lied.

"And Khan? How is he?"

"Yeah, Mom, everyone is fine. I'm here to see you, not talk about me."

"Oh, darling, that's so kind of you." She lit up. "I could show you the green room. I got one of the rose bushes to bloom, which is very rare this time of year. I'm really quite proud of it, and it has the prettiest pink color you can imagine."

"Sure, Mom, I would love to see it."

Erika hooked her arm under my elbow and looked up at me with a bright smile. It was nice to see how happy my presence made her, and at the same time it made me feel bad that I visited so seldom.

"Zobel will be delighted that you are here. You *are* staying for dinner, aren't you?"

"Yes."

"Wonderful."

We walked through the mansion, one room more opulent than the other.

"Don't you just love this house?" My mother pointed to the vaulted ceiling. "It's a replica of ancient paintings from the Renaissance. Zobel has a rare antique art book that he bought for a high price. I can show it to you if you want to see."

"Maybe later."

For the next forty minutes, my mother small-talked about flowers, sun exposure, greenhouse temperatures, quality of soil. I nodded, listened, and leaned in to smell the rose that she was so proud of.

"It's beautiful."

She smiled with pride. "Thank you."

"Mom, can I ask a question?"

"Of course, darling."

"Why do you say Zobel and not his first name?"

She looked thoughtful. "I suppose it's because I've known him for thirty-five years as Mr. Zobel."

"Didn't he tell you to use his first name?"

"If he did, I don't recall it."

"Are you still thinking about marrying him?"

A flash of sadness disappeared behind a façade of false bravado, as Erika took a seat. "He's a nice man, and marrying the richest man in the country isn't the worst that could happen to a woman."

I sat down beside her. "Mom, you make it sound like you want Zobel for his money. It's not like the alternative

172

is living in a shack. Khan and I would take care of you. You know that, right?"

She patted my cheek just like she had when I was a small boy. "I know. But I don't want to be a burden to you two."

I wanted to tell her that she was going to be a grandmother soon, and that Khan could probably use her help to make sure his child wasn't indoctrinated by Pearl. But if the situation had been reversed, and it was Laura who was pregnant, I would've wanted to share the good news myself. I also couldn't risk that my mother might call Khan to congratulate him before Pearl got around to telling him herself.

Just then Zobel walked in, greeting me with his loud voice and open arms. "Welcome to my humble abode."

The man lived on the biggest estate in the country, and there was nothing humble about him or his golden palace.

I stood up to shake his hand and on purpose I avoided asking him how he was. The last time I'd asked, he had gone on and on about his painful arthritis, his lazy workers in the factories he owned, and his mistrust of his tailor.

"I was just telling my mother that we miss her, and that we wished she would visit us more often," I said.

He gave a fake smile. "It's such a long journey, and Erika prefers it here."

I ignored his comment and looked straight at my mother. "So many things are happening at home. You're missing out on a lot."

My mother looked down.

"What do you say we go get a brandy?" Mr. Zobel suggested and patted my shoulder in a jovial manner. "We know all about what is going on at the Gray Mansion. Your mother and I have watched all the news about the situation with the Motherlands." While we walked Mr.

Zobel shook his head. "I can't say that we are happy about it."

My mother was behind us and I turned my head to look at her. "You saw Khan's plea for people to stay calm and stay out of the Motherlands?"

"Yes, we did," she confirmed with a serious expression.

Mr. Zobel placed his hand on my shoulder. "Your father would be rolling in his grave, Magni. All this talk about being good neighbors to the Motlanders..." He paused when we entered one of the many rooms in his house, gesturing for me to take a seat in what had to be the ugliest couch I had ever seen. While he poured brandy into crystal glasses, I looked at the yellow fabric with the little birds and couldn't decide what I disliked the most: the yellow couch or the mint-green cushions with prints of candy on them. If Finn were here, he would have been pointing out the obvious: the chocolate print had the color and shape of turds.

"What was Khan thinking, missing an opportunity like this?" Zobel came closer, handing me one of the glasses. "There's no better time to attack your enemy than when they are weak."

I shrugged. "That's what I said, but Khan wouldn't listen, and with a Motlander as his wife it was a tough choice for him."

Zobel gave a sideways glance to my mother. "Erika, dear, would you mind getting that book on medicine I bought at the latest auction? I want to show it to Magni. It's in the library."

"Of course." My mother nodded her head and smiled at me. "I'll also see if I can find the book on art that I told you about."

As soon as she had left, Mr. Zobel drew me closer with a hand on my arm. "She's going to be searching for a while. That book isn't in the library. It was a ploy to get you alone so you can tell me the truth, what is going on? We hear rumors of Khan being controlled by his wife."

"Pearl is a strong woman with a lot of influence over him," I admitted.

Being almost a head shorter than me, Mr. Zobel was looking up with a speculative expression on his face. "Can't you reason with him?"

"I tried."

"And he thinks our people are just going to stand by and watch him take our enemy's side?"

I shrugged with a sigh. "You know Khan, he's strategic and never does anything without a plan. He has managed to get things through that no one before him has ever done. Within the next ten years, there will be males on the Motlander Council. Finn is now living in the Motherlands with his wife, Athena. None of that would've been possible if Khan hadn't negotiated it."

Mr. Zobel didn't look impressed. "Why take crumbs when you could eat the whole cake?" he asked in a low voice. "Your father wouldn't have hesitated, and neither would you if you had been the ruler."

I frowned.

Mr. Zobel looked down, rocking back and forth on his heels. "I never told you this, but your father once said that he wished you had been his firstborn."

"I know, he said the same thing to Khan and me when he was in a bad mood." It wasn't something I liked to think about.

"Magni, I've known you since you were a baby and I'm soon going to marry your mother. I feel like that puts me in a close position to you and I would like for us to be honest with each other."

"I'm always honest."

"That you are, but the subject I'd like to discuss with you is sensitive in nature. Can I trust you?" He rubbed the long narrow beard that went to his chest.

"Is this about my mom?"

"No, it's about you."

His serious demeanor made me fire my next question at him. "You've heard rumors, haven't you?" Of course they would be talking about Laura leaving me.

"More like speculations and whispers."

"About me?"

"Yes. Are you happy with Khan?"

"Fuck no." My answer was honest. "He won't listen to reason and most days I want to punch him back to the way he was before he met Pearl."

Mr. Zobel's lips pursed. "Have you considered what good you could do for our country if you were to take your brother's place?"

I stiffened. "What are you talking about?

Mr. Zobel looked to the door, making sure no one was near. "I'm a wealthy and influential man," he said in a low and conspiratorial voice. "Your father always praised you for your strength and loyalty to our country. People are questioning where Khan's loyalty lies, and whispers are growing louder. Many agree that things would be better with you as the ruler."

"I doubt that our people want me as their ruler."

"Of course they do. Not even that stunt your wife pulled on you can take away that you are by far the most natural-born leader we have. Men have taken a few jabs at you, but can you blame them? For years you've been untouchable and superior to everyone else. It's no secret that the only reason Khan is still in power is because he has you to fight his battles. I'm not the first one to question why he is the ruler and not you."

My mind was trying to understand the ramifications of what he was saying.

"I'm sure you can depend on your wife coming back to you as soon as you take the throne." He smirked. "Women are drawn to men with power and money. They always have been."

An hour ago I had felt lost. Now Mr. Zobel was offering me a chance to redeem myself and show that I still had purpose.

"The question is, Magni, are you ready to do what it takes?"

"Are you asking me if I'm ready to kill Khan?"

Mr. Zobel's eyes shone with excitement. "Well, are you?"

Folding my hands behind my back, I asked, "You really think that the people would rather have me as a ruler than Khan?"

Mr. Zobel nodded. "I'm sure of it."

"How do you know?"

He took a long sip of his brandy, and took his time before he spoke in a confidential whisper. "People are concerned about the integration process with the Motherlands. What happens to our freedom if we become part of the Motherlands? No one is complaining about all the women that have moved here, of course, but we want to make sure that we influence them and not the other way around."

"I see."

"With you being married to a Northlander, you wouldn't be as easily swayed as Khan has been."

"Right."

"It's a delicate matter, of course, but I consider myself close enough to you to bring it up. I am to be your new father, after all."

"Have you spoken to anyone else about this?"

Again he looked to the door, which told me that he hadn't spoken to my mother about it.

"It has come up in conversation."

"Who can we count on for support if we do this?"

In a whisper he gave me names of rich and influential people.

"And if I don't do it? Do you have someone else in mind to take Khan's place?"

Keeping his eyes on the golden liquid, Mr. Zobel swung the brandy around in his glass. "We would prefer it to be you."

"And what is it that you want of me?"

"There are still holes in the border wall. We should invade."

"The Motherlands are not defenseless."

"No, but with the destruction from the earthquake they are weaker now than ever before." Mr. Zobel grasped my shoulder and looked into my eyes. "Now is the time to strike and bring those bitches down."

I gave a loud exhalation. "I hear what you're saying."

The old man nodded with enthusiasm. "We'll need to act fast before that damn wall is rebuilt. I say we should invite some friends over for a game of cards tonight."

"Can we trust these *card players* to keep quiet?" I asked.

Mr. Zobel expressed a small scoff and whispered. "With a subject of treason, I guarantee that they won't be talking. But you have to give me your word that we can count on you to deal with your brother."

I raised an eyebrow. "Don't worry, I'll set up a meeting with him and get him one on one."

"Maybe you could make it look like an accident." Mr. Zobel looked out the window with a thoughtful expression. "A fight between brothers gone wrong. We could make sure the news spread it as a tragedy and not a coup." He looked back at me. "Yes, that's a good plan, and once you're in power, you'll run the country with an iron fist just like your father did."

"Before I do anything, I think it's only fair that the card players who want me in power should express their loyalty to me."

He patted my shoulder. "Consider it done, my son."

My body felt light and I smiled a little. This morning I had felt lost and sad. Now Mr. Zobel had shown me that there was a need for me after all. I had a purpose again.

CHAPTER 21
At the Core

Laura

Athena was surprised when I showed up at her house.

"Laura, what a lovely surprise." She smiled and came to take my hands. "If you're looking for Finn, he's not here. He's picking Tristan up."

"That's okay, I came to see you." I looked up at her peculiar house. "Why does your house have wings?"

She smiled and looked up too. "It's called a Dutch mill. All priestesses live in one."

"Why?"

"It's a long story. Basically, it represents energy and since all humans are connected by energy, the mill is a sign of unity."

I frowned. "I thought your house had been destroyed; that's what Magni said."

"The roof collapsed, but thanks to good neighbors it was repaired two days before we arrived back here."

"Wow, you must really mean a lot to your neighbors."

"I would like to think so." Athena waved for me to enter her house. "My house is small and nothing like what you're used to at the Gray Mansion, but it's cozy and I like it here." None of the five chairs around her dining table matched. Her couch looked worn and old, and the artwork on the wall could've been made by children. Athena slipped out of her shoes and curled up on the couch with a throw-over blanket. "It's cold today."

"At least it's not raining anymore," I said and took a seat on the other end of the couch.

"Here you go." She lifted the soft blanket. "It's big enough to cover both of us."

I had only met Athena once and spoken to her by wristband, and yet sitting on her couch with our feet touching under the blanket didn't feel awkward.

"Are you happy to be back in the Motherlands?" I asked.

"I am. Finn and I spent all day yesterday cleaning. Luckily the water damage wasn't too bad. My friend Jameson, who lives about ten minutes from here, made sure to cover up the hole in the roof a few days after the earthquake. I helped him and his family in the past, and he said it was his way of returning the favor. Jameson's also the one who helped fix the roof before we returned."

"Sounds like you have good friends."

"I do. It's something to be grateful for." She patted the couch. "My old sofa didn't survive, but I found this one in a donation center. It's comfortable, don't you think?"

"Yes, it's very soft."

Athena looked at the open kitchen and back to me. "Oh my, forgive me for being a bad hostess. I should offer you some tea or food." She sighed. "It's just that I've been on my feet all morning, and my leg is still giving me grief from the injury. Do you mind if I rest for ten minutes before I make you something?"

"Oh no, you don't have to worry about it. I didn't come to drink tea, I came to talk to you."

"I'm honored. Is it about Magni?"

"Yes."

Athena looked serious. "As far as I heard he wasn't harmed in that bar fight."

"No, he wasn't. I don't think he even remembers fighting."

"I'm sensing the bar fight is not what you're here to talk about."

Biting my lip, I sat for a second before I blurted it out. "I want what you have with Finn, and what Pearl has with Khan."

Athena tilted her head. "And what is that?"

"Love." With a determined expression I began to explain. "Finn and Khan listen to you and Pearl. There is a mutual respect between you."

"That's true."

"I've told Magni that I want that, but he's so stubborn and rigid. It's like hitting my head against a wall."

"Laura, it's dangerous to compare yourself to others. You never see the full picture."

"But I see enough to know that there is equality between you."

"Finn can be challenging too, and I'm sure that if you asked Pearl, she would say the same thing about Khan. But I agree with you that Magni is inflexible in his view on women."

I threw up my hands. "Thank you. I'm so glad you're on my side."

Athena frowned. "There aren't sides in a partnership, Laura, you're supposed to be a unity."

"A unity? The man can't even express how he feels about me."

"Do you have doubts about his feelings for you?"

"Yes and no. On the one side, I know Magni is loyal to the bone and would protect me with his life. On the other side, I'm not sure it has anything to do with me as a person, but just the fact that I am his wife."

"You think he loves the idea of a wife more than you as a person?"

"Sometimes. And then when we have sex, I feel connected to him and convinced that he cares about me. It's all a guessing game with him. I just wish that he would say that he loves me."

Athena leaned forward and took my hand, her thumb stroking back and forth across my knuckles. "What does he say when you tell him you love him? He must say something."

"I haven't said those words."

"You haven't?"

"No."

"Why not?"

I lifted my shoulders in a small shrug. "Because he should say it first; he's the man."

Athena began chuckling.

"What is so funny?"

"What is funny is you sitting here, accusing Magni of being a traditionalist who doesn't want to meet your need for equality. When in reality, you're a traditionalist yourself."

"What do you mean I'm a traditionalist?"

"You have fixed ideas about your roles in the marriage; you just admitted it when you said Magni has to go first because he's the man. What kind of strange rule is that?"

"I don't know. It just feels right."

"What else does he have to do first?"

"Well, this may sound silly to you, but if there is any sort of danger I would expect him to protect me. I mean, I want to be able to protect myself and all, but if I was with Magni it would be strange if he were to hide behind me."

Athena smiled. "It should be safe to assume that you don't have to worry about that with him. He's very protective of you."

"And I like that. I just don't like it when he gets bossy."

"Ahh, the old tale of balance."

"Magni is always telling me what to do." I affected a deep mocking voice. "'Laura, it's cold outside, you should put on gloves. Laura, did you drink enough? It's important to stay hydrated. Laura, I want you to go to bed now, your body needs to be well rested or your immune system will suffer.'" I rolled my eyes. "It's like that all day, every day."

Athena's chest rose in a deep intake of air. "Sounds to me like Magni is telling you all day, every day, that he loves you."

My eyebrows drew close together.

"There are many ways to say I love you. You and Magni both have to practice communicating. You can't only listen to the words, Laura. He's speaking to you through his actions, his touch, and if you think about it every one of those bossy orders, as you call them, is an expression of love for you."

I must've looked confused, because Athena elaborated.

"Maybe you would feel different if he said, 'Laura dear, I can't stand the thought of you freezing, so please remember your gloves.' Or, 'Laura darling, your well-being is of my greatest concern and I just want to make sure that you're getting enough water and sleep.'"

I played with the tip of my braid. "Athena, I doubt that's how he thinks."

"Only Magni can tell you how he thinks. But if you can't see the good intentions behind his requests, then you need to look again. It's like he's shouting I love you without actually saying the words."

I scratched my shoulder. "I've never thought about it that way."

"What do you think would happen if you showed him the same interest and care?"

"I don't know."

"Then maybe you should try it. My guess is that it would make him feel loved by you."

Thinking hard, I played with my wristband for a while. "You really think I should tell him that I love him?"

"That depends."

"On what?"

"On whether or not you really love him."

"I do. It's just that he makes it hard. Like today, when I called to tell him that I had captured the last of the Nmen who escaped after the wall collapsed. Magni didn't praise me for being a badass or anything. He just ordered me to come home right away. It's like he thinks that now that I'm done chasing bad guys we can go back to the way things were."

"And you don't want that?"

"No. I want to be his equal. Not some sweet submissive wife he can just order around." I paused. "I understand what you said about his concern being an expression of love, but Athena, you don't know him. He can be overwhelming at times."

Athena's eyebrows rose in perfect arches. "You are talking to the woman whom he kidnapped. Believe me, I agree with you that Magni can be overwhelming."

I closed my eyes. "I still can't believe he would do that, and I'm so sorry that happened to you. I blame myself."

"You're not responsible for his actions. I'd like to think it was a desperate act of love."

I leaned my right elbow on the back of the couch, and rested my face in my hand. "It blows my mind that you don't hate him for what he did to you."

"Oh, I'm no saint. I've had a few moments of intense dislike, and I'm still no fan of Magni's."

"But you don't hate him."

"Of course not. Hate is a heavy burden to bear; I don't wish that for anyone. Besides, I'm sure Magni has a few redeeming qualities or else Finn wouldn't be his friend.

"Magni *loves* Finn," I said.

"How do you know?"

"Oh, it's obvious when you see them together. Finn is one of the few who can make Magni laugh, and he is fiercely protective of Finn."

"Interesting how you've interpreted Magni's protectiveness towards Finn as love, yet when he's protective of you it's bossiness. Setting your boundaries is important, Laura, and I would encourage you to stand your ground on issues that are important to you."

I rubbed my nose, taking in her words.

Athena had a knowing smile on her lips. "How old are you, Laura?"

"Twenty."

"That's old enough to stop feeling entitled."

Jerking back, I protested, "I don't feel entitled."

"That's good, because people who are waiting for others to give them love are missing something profound."

"And what's that?"

"The love was always there. Love is the core of your true self. No one can take that away from you. You need to change your words from 'I *want* love' to 'I *am* love.'"

I narrowed my eyes in a skeptical expression. "I am love?"

"Yes, you are. We all are."

"I don't know about that, but I do know that I've been waiting to hear Magni say those words to me for a long time."

"Maybe he's waiting to hear them from you too."

I rubbed the bridge of my nose again. "You think so?"

"Laura, never be afraid to show what's in your heart."

"But what if he doesn't say the words back to me?"

Athena drew in a deep breath. "You are not telling him that you love him in an attempt to make him say it back to you. You are telling him that you love him because that's what is in your heart. If he reciprocates the feeling and wants to share that with you, great. If not, it will never take away from the gift of love that you gave him."

I gave a small head shake. "Sometimes you Motlanders are a bit much, you know that, right?"

"Yes, Finn tells me the same thing." Athena lifted her head and looked out the window with a smile. "Huh, speaking of the sun…"

Finn's drone landed in front of the house.

"Where I'm from, we say talk about the devil."

She smiled at me. "Yes, that sounds very Northlandish."

We watched Finn and his son Tristan get out of the drone and walk to the house. They brought in a blast of cold air when they walked through the door.

"Hurry, close the door – I'm freezing." Athena tucked the throw-over all the way up to her chin.

Finn removed his jacket and threw it over one of the chairs. "What a surprise. I didn't expect to find you here, Laura."

"Finn, honestly, how many times do I have to tell you to hang your jacket?"

Finn silenced Athena with a loud kiss on her lips. "Ah, the joy of having a wife to remind me of senseless things. I always knew I was missing out."

Tristan sat down on the coffee table in front of us. "Guess what?" His eyes were shining with excitement. "The most amazing thing just happened."

Finn moved a cup out of the way, and sat down on the coffee table next to Tristan. "Tell them."

"You do know that we have chairs in this house, right?" Athena pointed out. "Please don't break it."

Finn looked down at the solid table. "This ugly thing would survive a zombie invasion."

"Anyway." Tristan took back the conversation. "Archer called Finn and you know how he has a friend who designs and builds drones and hybrids?"

"Yes, I remember Archer mentioning that."

Tristan could hardly contain his excitement. His heels were lifting up and down, making his knees bop. "The guy's name is Wrestler and he has agreed to meet with me.

187

He might have a spot for me as his apprentice when I turn eighteen."

Athena gave Finn a worried glance before she looked at Tristan. "You're only fifteen. It's going to take years before you're done with school. And how would you convince your mom to let you go and live in the Northlands?"

"I would be an adult then. My mom wouldn't have a choice."

Athena wrung her hands. "I worry that Randa Christine is going to be angry with me."

Finn swung a dismissive hand in the air. "Don't worry about his mom; if this is Tristan's path in life, it will happen. Isn't that what you told me?"

"Yes, but..." Athena trailed off.

Finn gave her a mischievous grin. "Sweetie, life is too short for buts, unless it's your butt and it's naked."

Athena laughed and shrugged at me. "He can't help it. On the outside he's a thirty-two-year-old man, but on the inside he's sixteen."

Finn got up and went to pick up a fist-sized figurine that he brought back. "Let me remind you that you said laughing is a spiritual practice, and that I'm a spiritual gangster." He handed the figurine to me. "Look at how happy that guy is. He's like me, and Athena says he had millions of followers."

"I never said you were like the Buddha."

"Yeah, you did, remember how you said that he used humor and laughter too?"

"I would follow you," Tristan piped up and was rewarded by his father, who pulled him in for a sideways hug.

"There you have it. My first follower."

Athena crossed her arms and lowered her brow. "I hate to burst your bubble of self-importance, Finn, but organized religion is banned in the Motherlands."

"I don't think it counts as a religion if he only has one follower," I pointed out with a smile.

"It would be more like a really cool cult." Finn tapped his chin. "We would need to find some catchy name for it."

"How about Finnibun and his single follower?" Athena suggested with a saccharine smile.

I laughed. "You call him Finnibun?" It was so much fun to see how Athena could get away with teasing Finn.

"It's an internal joke between us," she explained. "It turns him on."

Tristan rolled his eyes and smacked his tongue against his palate. "Do you mind?"

"Did you just roll your eyes?" Athena asked with disbelief. "I shouldn't be surprised, with you hanging out with the Northlander boys."

"Do it again," Finn elbowed Tristan who repeated his eye roll in an exaggerated way that made Finn laugh out loud. "You rolled your eyes so far back it looked like you were channeling spirits. I swear, this cult of ours just got way cooler – are you sure you don't want to join us?" he asked me.

"I couldn't. That would ruin the name of Finnibun and his *one* follower."

Tristan stood up from the table pointing at Finn. "If you start referring to yourself as Finnibun, I'm out."

I shrugged. "So much for your cult, Finn."

Tristan was going through the kitchen cabinets. "I'm hungry, Athena. Do you have anything to eat?"

"Not much. People are hoarding so there wasn't much in the store."

Finn spread his arms and held his palms upward. "Don't worry, honey, holy people like me can turn stone into bread and rain into beer, just like Jesus."

"You didn't go to church much as a child, did you?" I asked.

Finn didn't have a chance to answer before Tristan interrupted. "You have churches in the Northlands?"

"We do, and we learn about God and Jesus in school. If Finn had paid attention, he would know that Jesus turned water into wine and fed thousands of people with a few loaves of bread and some fish."

Tristan gave a skeptical frown. "How is that possible?"

"It's not," Athena said in a flat tone.

"Don't listen to her; we holy people perform miracles all the time."

"In that case, would you mind performing some miracles around here?"

"I would be happy to, honey, but we Nmen specialize in beer and meat, and since you don't like either I'm not going to waste a miracle on a nonbeliever like you. I'll save them for my cult members."

"How about a cup of tea for me and Laura then? Do you think your abilities would cover that?"

"No problem." Finn got up and moved to the kitchen. "I *could* get the water to boil just by looking at it, but sometimes it freaks people out when I do that, so today I'll just do it the old-fashioned way."

"Uh-huh." I gave him a smile.

"When is the interview with Archer's friend?" Athena asked Tristan.

"Tomorrow morning."

Her eyes widened. "But we just got back here two days ago."

Tristan nodded. "I know. I feel guilty about leaving here again so soon, but you've seen our family unit. The house is nowhere ready to move back in to, and they are all cramped together at Martin's mom's house."

"But they miss you, Tristan." Athena sounded sad.

"At least I got to spend all day with my family yesterday. Even my mom can see that I'm better off staying with you and Finn until our house is rebuilt. You

190

would have been proud of me, Athena, I've given the twins more hugs in one day than I have their entire lives," Tristan claimed.

"That's good, I'm happy to hear it." Athena looked to Finn. "Did you give Charlotte the toy back like we talked about?"

"I did. She was very happy to see it again. I told her she could still donate it at a later point, if she wants to."

"What toy are you talking about?" I asked.

Athena explained. "Charlotte is five years old and Tristan's younger sister. When she heard that children in the Northlands don't have toys, she was kind enough to give her favorite toy to Finn. She wanted him to bring it to a child in the Northlands which is really nice, but now that most of her toys have been lost in the earthquake it seemed the right thing to give it back to her."

"Kids in the Northlands do have toys," I pointed out. "At least my brothers and I did, but I guess if you grow up in a school like Finn, it might be different."

"Talking about school..." Tristan lit up. "Solo, Storm, and Hunter are going to be surprised when I get back tonight."

Athena's shoulders sank. "Tonight?"

Tristan gave her a sympathetic glance. "If you don't want to come, Finn and I could go by ourselves."

"That's a bad idea." Finn turned and looked at her. "I don't want us to split up." The love that shone from him made me even more certain that I wanted what Athena and Finn had. They were so relaxed around each other, but then Athena was incredibly wise, and Finn had always been easy-going and fun.

"I wish Magni and I were more like you two," I blurted out.

Finn spun and looked at me. "That's funny."

"Why?"

"Because I've spent my whole life looking up to Magni wishing I was like him."

"You have?"

"He has," Athena confirmed. "It's one of the things we have had the most discussions about."

"Everybody looks up to Magni." Tristan had found an apple and was talking while chewing. "I don't know a single boy at the school who doesn't want to be him when they grow up."

Finn gave a mock expression of disappointment. "I thought you wanted to be like me."

Tristan looked conflicted. "I do."

"But?"

"It's just that... Well, have you seen Magni fight?"

"Yeah, I've seen him fight all right. I've taken punches from him since I was your age."

"He's so fast, and one time, when he and Archer were sparring they kept going until Kya screamed at them to stop. Archer is a phenomenal fighter, but he almost collapsed with exhaustion, while Magni just asked if anyone else wanted to spar with him."

"Yup, he's always been like that. A machine."

"But that's the fucking problem, Finn," I said and threw my hands up in the air. "Sometimes he's more machine than man. I wish he would show more emotions." I stopped talking when I sensed all three of them staring at me.

"Uh-oh, someone has to go outside," Tristan said in a singsong voice, pointing at me while looking at Athena.

"What do you mean I have to go outside?" I asked them.

"Athena always makes me go outside when I used the F word." Finn scrunched up his face. "She might look sweet and all, but trust me, Athena can be coldhearted. I've been standing outside in the snow waiting for her forgiveness, just for using the F word."

192

Athena nodded. "What can I say, I don't like it when people swear in my house."

With a mischievous grin, Finn looked from Laura to me. "Lucky for you, Laura, this is now my house too, and I don't give a flying fuck about people swearing in my house."

"Finn." Athena's eyes bulged. "Not in front of Tristan."

"He's *my* son, and he just spent two weeks in the Northlands. I'm pretty sure he's gotten used to people swearing by now."

Tristan confirmed it. "You should've heard the boys, Athena, they knew some awesome words."

She gave a sigh of resignation. "There is nothing awesome about people swearing. It's a low level of communication and it's offensive."

Finn smacked his tongue. "Nonsense. It's fun and colorful. Like spices on food."

Athena turned to look at me. "Do you see what I mean? Told you Finn could be challenging."

Finn laughed, and brought two cups of tea for us. "Sorry, darling, you're not going to find any sympathy from Laura on this subject. She's one of us; raised to use the full scope of the English vocabulary. A little swearing doesn't offend her."

"It really doesn't," I agreed and took my cup of tea.

Athena picked up her cup too. "That would make me the challenging one then, I suppose, because it really does hurt my ears."

"Do you want me to kiss them better?" Finn teased.

"No thank you. I just want my tea."

"Okay, but drink up because we have to leave soon." Finn turned to Tristan. "Did you tell your mom that we might be gone a few days?"

Tristan nodded. "I'm on it."

"Laura, we could give you a ride. My hybrid is a lot faster than the drone you arrived in."

I looked down, plucking invisible dust from the blanket. "I'm not sure that I'm ready to go back yet."

"Why not?" Finn asked.

"Magni and I had a big fight."

"So what? I have fights with him all the time."

"I got really mad at him, and I said some mean things."

"Don't worry about it. You won't find anyone more loyal than Magni. He might be pissed at you, but he still wants you to come back."

"Are you sure about that?"

"A thousand percent."

Athena smiled at me over the rim of her teacup. "Not so long ago, you stood up to Magni calling yourself a warrior. You were brave enough to volunteer to chase down dangerous men before they hurt innocent people. I can't imagine someone as courageous as you would be scared of going back to face Magni, just because you had a fight with him."

"Of course I'm not scared," I lied, but the truth was that I was terrified that I had pushed Magni too far this time.

Finn clapped his hands together with a self-satisfied expression. "Great, then it's settled. You're coming back with us."

CHAPTER 22
Bitches

Magni

We were nine men in the room, eight of them older than me and friends of my father. Being rich and influential, these men were used to getting their way.

Some of them I hadn't seen in years, but a few of them had met with me and Khan recently. It was hard to shake their hands when I thought about the way they had sucked up to my brother calling him the best ruler in the history of the Northlands.

With large glasses of whiskey, and the pretense of a card game, we waited until my mother and all the waiters had left the room.

"We all know why we are here," Mr. Zobel began. "Every one of us is concerned about the current political situation, and we want change."

I met the eyes of the eight men sitting around the round table. They looked serious, like me.

"Mr. Zobel tells me that you would prefer me as the ruler. Is that true?" I confronted them.

They all nodded.

"What changes would you like to see? Be specific."

Sheldon Grant, a man around seventy, leaned back and folded his arms across his fat belly. "There's no need to beat around the bush. I'm old and like to be in bed by ten." His comment made the others laugh. "Khan has been sucked in by his new bride. All her talk about humanism and kindness is sickening. Our forefathers refused to be ruled by women and *so shall we*." His last three words were emphasized with his head nodding three times. "I

195

don't want to hear talk about integration. The only way for our two countries to unite would be when the women bow to our male superiority."

"Hear, hear."

Empowered by the others' support, Sheldon kept going. "We are the elite. Not many in this country have married like we have. That means we are the few who can testify to what women are truly like. They have foolish notions, are irresponsible, and have the intellect of children. They should never be allowed to make important decisions for themselves or others." He looked at me. "Your wife is a good example with her thoughtless and selfish behavior."

A nerve in my jaw gave a tic and I fought my instinct to tell him to go fuck himself.

Maximilian, a tall lanky man with a big beard, leaned forward. "Women are only good for one thing and that's breeding and pleasure. When we take over the Motherlands everything will change. My wife died more than five years ago, and I'm ready to take on a whole fucking harem of women." He smirked. "Why limit ourselves when there are millions to choose from?"

Deep laughter filled the room.

"That's right, there's enough for everyone. The Momsies are so bloody soft-spoken that they won't fight back."

I tucked my hands under my armpits and frowned.

"What's wrong? Don't you want a harem of your own?" Maximilian asked. "Everyone knows you got a rotten egg with that girl you married."

My scowl grew deeper and he got nervous. "I'm sorry, I didn't mean to offend you."

"Leave Laura out of this," I muttered in warning.

Mr. Zobel gave a fake chuckle. "What you do with Laura is up to you, as long as you don't allow her to corrupt you like Pearl did with Khan."

196

I nodded and the old man next to me patted my shoulder. "Magni is too much of a man to fall for a woman's tricks. He's always serious and focused on the task ahead. That's what's going to make him a great ruler."

Maximilian raised his glass to me. "As long as you don't mind the rest of us having a great time with the feast of women."

"Suit yourself," I muttered, and one of the men, who had been brown-nosing my brother only two weeks ago, began entertaining everyone with a description of a movie clip he had once seen.

"I'm telling you, all the men sat around a table where a beautiful young woman served as a human tray with delicacies spread out on her breasts, thighs, and belly." He illustrated with his hands. "She lay in the middle with her long hair, looking gorgeous, and saying nothing."

"Perfect!" someone chimed in. "The only time I want to hear my woman speak is when she tells me how lucky she is to have me as her husband." He elbowed the man next to him. "And when she tells me she's pregnant."

Mr. Zobel raised his glass of whiskey. "Let's cheer for the pretty creatures on the other side of that wall. It's time they learn their place. To give them any influence is to piss on our forefathers' graves. We owe everything to those brave men who refused to be ruled by women. I'll be damned if we're going to stand by and watch Khan give away our freedom and power."

The tall, lanky man spoke again. "Khan is thinking with his cock. The same thing happened to me when I first won my wife." He laughed. "I was so fucking horny for her that I let her get away with far too much."

"That's a beginner's mistake," Sheldon said and lifted his own glass. "Women will take advantage of you if you're not careful. They are sneaky like that."

"It's just like a golden retriever I once had." Mr. Zobel was stabbing his index finger down at the table. "I swear

197

that little bitch knew how to play me with her cute adorable eyes."

I kept my face impassive.

"The women wouldn't like it if they knew you were comparing them to dogs," the man to my left pointed out. "I don't have much respect for the Momsies, but my wife and daughter are fine women, and I would challenge anyone who said otherwise." He downed the last of his whiskey.

"I know they are," Mr. Zobel clarified. "But that's because you raised them right. They know and accept that we men are superior in all ways. It's time we showed the Momsies that as well."

"That's right!"

"You said it!"

The men were laughing and nodding in agreement. It made Zobel push out his chest. "They won't like it at first, but eventually they'll learn to spread their legs and be quiet like good girls."

I cut through the bullshit. "Besides a female harem for each of you, what are your expectations?"

"It would be natural that you reward our loyalty by giving us land in the Motherlands."

"And what are you willing to give me?"

"Any support you need."

For another hour, I took mental notes of their demands for more influence, before I pushed my chair back and stood up with my fingertips on the table. "Thank you, gentlemen. I will arrange a meeting with Khan tomorrow, and once that is done, you will hear from me."

Shaking hands with each of the eight men, I saw only greed and ambition in their eyes. I didn't like a single one of them, but I trusted that they had what it took to back up their promises.

CHAPTER 23
Poetry

Laura

Magni wasn't at the school when I arrived with Finn, Athena, and Tristan.

I slept in Magni's cabin thinking about the awful conversation we had after I caught Devlin. If only he had acknowledged a job well done on my side, I wouldn't have gotten so mad that I chose the Motherlands over him. I bet that if I'd been one of his Huntsmen, Magni would have shown me more respect. The bedsheets smelled of him and me, and it brought back memories of the amazing sex we shared before I went to catch Devlin.

Blaming myself for telling Magni that I chose the Motherlands over him, I couldn't sleep. It had been a desperate attempt to stand up for myself, but it wasn't true and I was racking my brain to find a way to take back my words without seeming weak.

Boulder came by the school early Monday morning to drop off Raven, who'd spent the weekend with him and Christina. He told me Magni was on the East Coast and asked if I had talked to him.

"Not yet, but I did tell him I returned." It wasn't true. Earlier that morning, while still in bed, I had dictated messages to Magni but nothing sounded right and I deleted all of them.

I needed a bit more time to get my head straight before I saw him again. After a long-overdue visit with Laila Michelle to see her and her twins, I returned to the school and spent the afternoon with the children. It was easy to see why Magni was so fond of Mila. The girl was adorable and sweet to everyone.

When they had English, she whispered for me to come and sit next to her.

Kya pointed to Nicki. "I'm sorry we ran out of time on Friday, but we're all excited to hear you present what you learned when you explored a question related to the English language."

Nicki came up to stand in front of the class.

"My question was, why do we all speak English and not some other language?" She looked down and because she wasn't wearing shoes, I could tell she was bending her toes. "What I found out was that English was only one out of about seven thousand languages spoken before the war." She looked down at her notes. "English was the third most-spoken language in the world with Mandarin being number one and Spanish being number two."

"What's Mandarin? It sounds like a fruit," Raven commented.

"Mandarin was spoken in a country called China. It was part of Asia and is one of the places that is now uninhabitable. With billions of people killed during the war, English was the language spoken by most survivors. That's why the Council made it the official language in 2061."

"Thank you, Nicki, that was very good." Kya smiled at the girl and clapped her hands. "Now it's time for us to work on our poetry lesson. You're going to either write your own poem or pick one written by a child. Plato and William, did you decide on a poem you wanted to analyze, yet?"

"I found one about beer, is that okay?" Storm asked.

"Ehm, yes, I think so." Kya looked to Marco, one of the two assisting mentors. "Could you take a look at it?"

"Sure."

"And what about you, William?"

"I don't like poetry," the boy complained.

"None of us do," Solomon, the oldest of the boys, said in a loud voice. "It's a waste of time."

"Fighting is a waste of time," Shelly, the other assistant mentor, chimed in. "If you ask me."

Marco looked up. "You don't get to call fight training a waste of time; just because you wouldn't know how to fight off a toddler."

"Fighting a toddler would be easy," Shelly retorted. "I get to practice on you all the time."

Marco raised his right arm and flexed his impressive biceps. "Does a toddler look like this?"

Shelly looked at him and gave a serious nod. "Yes, they have the exact same facial expression when they take a dump."

Mila's dimples came out when the kids and I laughed. "They are always like that," she whispered to me. "It can be very entertaining."

Kya clapped her hands. "Can we focus on the poetry please?"

A few groans were heard but the children settled down and spread out in the high-vaulted schoolroom that had once been an old ruin of a church.

"This is the poem I picked," Mila told me and projected it onto the table. "It was written before the war by a thirteen-year-old girl. My old teacher read it to us last year and I was moved by it." Our heads were close and my eyes ran over the poem.

"A child wrote this?"

"It's better if you read it out loud. Do you want me to read it to you?"

"Yes."

Mila read to me in a low melodic singsong voice. The girl's clear voice in combination with the strong message of the poem made the hair on my arms stand up.

Generation of Mirrors

It's easy to be overwhelmed.

With all the hate and fear,

It's a them and us mentality and threats are all we hear.

The scary talk about nuclear war and end of humanity.

What happened to the adults in this world – don't they see the insanity?

I don't have much power; I'm just a kid after all.

At least that's what I used to think, before I picked up the ball.

Now, I'm determined to make a difference and put a smile on a friend's face.

Remind them they are special and that within *us* – there's a *special* grace.

We are the pure ones, not yet conditioned to think in color or race.

We don't have to be stars or heroes, just a generation of mirrors.

Let others be blinded by the darkness while we reflect only the sun.

That being people who inspire us – people who are young.

People who make a difference – *even if it's just a small one.*

I'm going to point *my* mirror in *their* direction.

To reflect and magnify their light – and I can't wait to see the reaction.

What's going to happen when my friends do the same?

When our whole generation refuse to be blinded by hate and blame.

When we push back the darkness and laugh in its face.

No one can tell me that's not our place.

I know stronger and wiser people have fought and given their lives.

I don't mean no disrespect, but it's time to be strategic and not buy into the lies.

Darkness cannot be fought with violence and hate.
It will only grow stronger and swallow us up in endless debate.
Only light can conquer darkness – even a child like me can see *that much is clear.*
But I can't drive a car or make adults listen – if they don't want to hear.
Still, we're a generation of sun-chasing mirrors, ready to do our part.
And using simple things within our reach, it might not be that hard.
We'll pick up our phones and use social media to make people feel warm.
Think of the contrast it will be to the usual media storm.
Compliment a stranger and make them smile.
A little kindness will go a long mile.
We'll crack jokes and feel the laughter as a healing power.
One that will make our hearts sing and blossom like a flower.
We'll talk about people we admire and respect.
And share what we are grateful for and hopefully – *everyone will feel the effect.*
So, my final question to you is this: will you help make this message clearer,
by only reflecting bright light in *your* mirror?

"What do you think?" Mila whispered. "Isn't it amazing?"

"Wow." My eyebrows lifted. "Are you sure it was written by a child?"

"Yes. She was only thirteen and her name was Pearl, just like our Pearl."

"It's a beautiful poem."

"You can tell that it's very old by the words she uses, but it makes me want to cry that children back then were afraid of nuclear war and the end of humanity."

"Well, with good reason," I pointed out.

Mila looked sad. "I'm happy I didn't live back then. At least now there are no weapons like that."

"True, but we still have plenty of issues to deal with."

A triangle formed between her eyebrows. "Like what?"

"Like finding a way to get rid of the wall between the Northlands and the Motherlands."

"But I thought Pearl and Khan were working on that."

"They are."

"Then you don't have to worry. Pearl is the smartest person I know, and Khan has some good ideas too."

I tilted my head. "You think Pearl is smarter than Khan?"

Mila jerked back a little. "You don't?"

"I don't know. People call Khan a genius."

"They do?"

"Yes."

"Huh, I didn't know that." Mila looked back at the poem. "I guess that's because people here hadn't met a real genius before Shelly arrived."

"Shelly is a genius?" I looked over at the teenager with the bushy eyebrows, unruly hair, and bad skin.

"Yes. She's even smarter than Pearl, but in a different way."

"I see." There was a moment of pride in my chest. I was surrounded by intelligent women and sitting next to a girl who had female role models that I hadn't had access to when I was her age.

"There's plenty of things she sucks at though."

"Who, Shelly?"

"Yes." Mila widened her eyes and nodded her head with exaggeration. "She can't fight *at all*. Her cooking isn't good either, and she is hopeless at drawing. It's like her intelligence wasn't distributed evenly in her brain. In some areas she's a genius, in other areas she's *hopeless*." She whispered the last part.

"Mila, are you analyzing the poem?" Kya asked from the other end of the room.

"I'm sorry. I got a little distracted," Mila admitted and returned to the poem, pointing her finger at a line. "I like this part where it says, 'only light can conquer darkness – even a child like me can see *that much is clear*."

"I like that too."

She tilted her head. "It's nice how she uses the word clear in reference to the light."

"Yeah."

"And I think she's right. If someone is being mean to you it doesn't help to be mean back. Someone has to smile first."

I sucked in a breath, Athena's words playing in my mind about my telling Magni that I loved him instead of waiting for him to say it first.

"You're right, but smiling first can be difficult," I pointed out.

"You think so?" Mila looked thoughtful. "For me it's harder to be mean. It feels bad inside, like I can't breathe right." She held a hand to her chest. "Sometimes I get the same feeling if I see people fighting. It makes me sad."

My hands stroked over her long blond hair. "You're a born pacifist, aren't you?"

"Maybe; I've always loved babies."

"That's good, but you know a pacifist loves everybody, right?"

"I'm not sure what a pacifist is. Is that a person who makes pacifiers?"

I laughed. "No, it's a person who loves peace."

"Oh." She smiled. "Then that's what I want to be when I grow up."

"I'm afraid a pacifist is not a job description, Mila. It's a mindset."

"What a shame. I think I would have been good at it."

"I'm sure you would." With a smile plastered on my face, I looked back at the poem. "I think this is my favorite part, *'We'll talk about people we admire and respect. And share what we are grateful for and hopefully – everyone will feel the effect.'* I wish I was better at that. But it's difficult."

Mila took my hand under the table. "Kya says that difficult isn't the same as impossible. Maybe you just need to practice."

I looked down at our hands and felt honored that the girl showed me trust. "I think Magni needs to practice it too. He's not good at giving compliments."

"What do you mean? He says nice things to me all the time."

My head snapped up. "He does?"

"He loves my dimples, my hair, my singing voice, and he thinks I'm pretty."

"He told you that?"

"Yes," Mila said as if it wasn't a big thing. "I tell him nice things too."

"Like what?"

"That I like his eyes, and his smile."

"Me too."

"I also like it when he picks me up and swings me through the air." With her elbow on the table, Mila rested her chin in her hand and gave a wistful sigh. "I really wanted Magni to be my father."

"He wanted that too, Mila."

She gave me a sideways glance. "He wants to have children with you."

"I know."

"Did you know that he wants to name your boy Mason after the first ruler in the Northlands?"

"No."

206

"Magni likes that name."

This was something my sister and I had talked about since we were little girls and I smiled. "I've always known that if I have a girl I'll name her Aubri."

"That's pretty. And if it's a boy?"

I squeezed her hand. "Sounds like Magni already picked out the name Mason."

Mila and I sat in a small bubble when Kya called for a break. "You have half an hour to play. It's a beautiful day so put on your jackets and go outside."

"Who wants to play hide and seek?" one of the boys called out and Mila's head turned.

"I do."

"Have fun," I said and waved back when she ran out the door to play with the other children.

"She's sweet, isn't she?" Kya came to sit on a desk next to me.

"Adorable. If I ever have a daughter, I would want her to be like Mila."

Kya placed a hand on her belly. "Mila is very interested in my pregnancy. When we told the children, she was the first to ask if she could babysit when the baby is born."

"That's nice."

Finn came in with Athena. He was throwing an apple from hand to hand.

"How did it go?" I asked. "What did Wrestler think of Tristan?"

"It went well, why wouldn't it? Tristan is my son. He can charm anyone."

Athena gave Kya a hug and sat down next to her on the table. "Wrestler said he would think about it. He was a little skeptical when he learned that Tristan has grown up in the Motherlands."

"Wrestler told you that?"

"Yes, he made it a condition that if he takes Tristan on as an apprentice, there will be no more schooling in the

207

Motherlands. Wrestler wants him to study in the Northlands from now on."

"Is that what Tristan wants to do?" I asked.

"Of course it is, he loves it here and..." A loud scream interrupted Finn and made us all jump up. Finn sprinted out the door with Kya on his heels, while Athena and I ran to the window. My heart galloped and I gasped out loud when a boy shouted. "She fell from the roof." He was over by the cabins and even from this distance, I recognized the beautiful long hair on the girl lying as if lifeless on the ground. It was Mila.

CHAPTER 24
The Meeting

Magni

Khan didn't look up when I entered his office. He was focused on a game of chess in front of him, two of his fingers touching a bishop. His brow furrowed in thought.

"Don't you ever get bored of playing yourself?"

He didn't look at me when he answered. "Pearl tricked me with her knight yesterday, and I'm making sure that never happens again."

I took a seat in front of him. "Do you think you can leave your toys until we're done talking?"

With a deep inhalation, Khan lifted his eyes and looked at me with irritation. "Don't fucking test me, Magni. My patience with you is running thin."

"Maybe you need to go and meditate some more with that wife of yours."

"My wife has a name, and you should use it when you go and apologize to her."

"What for?"

"I didn't ask you to pick her up at the border." Khan's nostrils flared. "I asked you to stay the fuck away from her."

"I thought you just now asked me to go to her and apologize. Make up your mind."

"If you threaten or intimidate her one more time, you and I are going to have a serious problem."

I leaned forward, hardening my jaw. "It's my job to have your back, and I don't fucking trust Pearl."

Khan narrowed his eyes. "Maybe she's right about you. You've become paranoid and see danger where there is none."

I jerked back. "You don't think you're in danger?"

"There will always be small-minded people who think they can run this country better than I can." Khan waved his hand dismissively. "Just wait until the women start pouring in with the new matchmaking system. No one will be talking about a revolution then."

"If I apologize to Pearl, it will be because *I want to*, and not because you tell me to. And at this point I don't want to."

Khan slammed his fist down on the table. "I am your ruler, and you *will* take orders from me."

Standing up, I leaned over the table with my palms planted firmly in front of me. "Shut the fuck up."

Khan flew up from his chair. Like two male gorillas we stood opposite each other with hard expressions.

"I'm done with you taking me for granted." Spit flew from my mouth when I hissed at him. "My whole life I've been in your shadow, cleaning up shit for you. I've killed people to keep you and Mom safe, and this is the thanks I get?"

"We each play our role."

"And now those roles have changed. You fucking sold me out. Did you think I would be okay with Pearl outranking me?"

"I already told you. It's a pro forma thing and only in the far future."

"You'd better show me respect and appreciate what I do for you."

"Is there a threat in that statement?" Khan asked through gritted teeth.

"Yeah, I've been thinking. Maybe a small cabin in Alaska would be a nice change. Bear hunting, fishing, and peace and quiet sounds like a fucking good deal compared to politics and a brother who betrays me."

"I didn't betray you." Khan pulled back, his voice calmer. "I get why you're angry, but you have to get over it, and it is not Pearl's fault."

Straightening up my back, I crossed my arms. "You do what you gotta do. I'm going to Alaska to look at cabins."

"What about Laura?"

I scrunched up my face, a knife twisting in my heart. "She chose the Motherlands."

Khan rubbed his forehead and sighed. "I'm sorry to hear that."

"It is what it is," I said refusing to show him how broken I was on the inside. "You'll have to find someone else to do your dirty work. I'm done."

He angled his head and frowned. "Magni, don't."

Ignoring his attempt to reason with me, I continued talking. "I brought Mom back. You need to speak to her."

"Why, what's wrong?"

"Zobel and his friends are conspiring against you, and I didn't want her in his house when the soldiers arrived this morning."

Khan dropped his jaw. "You're not serious?"

"Dead serious."

"I don't believe it."

"No, why would you? You and Pearl already agreed that I'm a paranoid fucker, right? But for all it's worth, it gave me a sense of purpose when I spent two hours interrogating all eight conspirators last night. They told me everything to my face."

"You tortured Mr. Zobel?" Khan's hands flew to his hair.

"The only person who was tortured was me! I had to sit there and listen to their disgusting talk about women. Don't worry, you'll see what I mean when you listen to the

211

recording I got from last night." While talking I used my wristband to transfer the file to him.

He looked confused. "Why would they tell you anything? That makes no sense."

I angled my head. "Because they thought I was in on it."

"What?" Khan looked like he had swallowed a fly. "Why?"

"Because they were eager to invade the Motherlands and wanted to take advantage of the border wall being down. The greedy bastards were eyeing a chance to divide the Motherlands between them and grow their wealth and power."

"Yes, but why you?"

"Isn't it obvious? I've been advocating for us to invade as well and I don't trust Pearl. With the Motlanders rebuilding the wall, time was running out..." I shrugged. "They took a chance on recruiting me, hoping that I was fed up too."

"Who was there?"

For every name I gave him, his ears grew redder and when I played a bit of the recording for him, Khan began pacing his office.

"It's best if Khan's death looks like an accident. The few people who are loyal to him should be given no reason to suspect that it was treason that killed him."

"Was that Sheldon Grant who spoke?" Khan's face was distorted in cold fury. "Those motherfucking traitors. Just wait until I get my hands on them."

I shrugged. "It's all taken care of. This morning, at a quarter to six, I had eight teams simultaneously picking them up."

"Where are they now?"

"The usual place, no special treatment."

"Why didn't you tell me sooner?"

"I'm telling you now."

212

Khan plunked down in his chair. "Who did they want to replace me with? You?"

"Uh-huh. They think that Pearl has too much power over you, and they knew I agreed."

"But not enough to take my place?"

I snorted. "If I wanted to be the ruler of this country, I would've taken you out a long time ago. The job is not for me."

"You never considered it?"

"Sure. But I was fourteen and I grew out of it when I realized how boring the job is. You sit behind a desk all day. I always preferred to be hands-on. Being among my Huntsmen and feeling the adrenaline of a good fight; those were the best days to me."

"I should thank you." Khan looked a bit stiff when he said it. We weren't raised to apologize or give thanks.

"It's okay. Just because you're a gigantic ass doesn't mean I have to be one."

For a moment none of us spoke, and the room filled with an energy that prodded at my emotions. When Laura first left me, I had gone on a drinking binge, and I would never forget Khan for being there for me. We were the two only people who would ever understand what it had been like to grow up as the sons of Marcus Aurelius. The man had been a monster at times, and hardest on Khan. I could remember being frantic for a way to distract my father to spare my brother. Working out and practicing fight techniques had been an obsession of mine. Not because I loved it, but because it was the only thing I knew my father would always take time to watch me do. And as long as he was watching me, he wasn't harassing Khan.

It was Khan who broke the silence. "Alaska, huh?"

"I would prefer a warm beach down south, but I hear those are crawling with Momsies, and you know how I feel about them."

"I don't want you to go. I need you here."

213

I shrugged. "You should have thought about that before you agreed to make Pearl your co-ruler."

Khan opened his mouth looking like he wanted to argue, but then he closed it again with a sigh of resignation.

"Fine, but I want us to tell Mom together."

"Why? I did the hard work. It's only fair that you break the bad news to her. I hate it when she cries."

"She's going to want to hear it from the source."

In the end we went to our mother's suite together. Khan did the talking, and I was the silent brooding son in the background.

"Did you know anything?" Khan asked her.

Erika was fiddling with her hands, her face pale, and her eyes full of tears. "No."

"You never suspected anything?"

She shook her head and sniffled. "I had no idea."

"You know the punishment for treason in this country. Zobel will be executed with the others and their assets will be confiscated."

"Please don't kill him. I'm sure he didn't mean it," Erika begged.

"Mom." Khan sat down beside her. "He wanted me *dead*."

Her voice was thick when she spoke "He was your father's best friend. I've known him for thirty-five years. He would never do something like that."

I was shocked at how naïve she was.

Khan played some of the conversation for her, and several times he looked up at me when blatant treason was discussed. "The evidence is there, Mom. Zobel is a fucking traitor and you need to accept it. He wanted Magni to kill me."

She was miserable and confused, and it dawned on me that I remembered her standing up to my father in my childhood. Where had that feistiness gone?

"Why would you defend him? Do you love him that much?" I asked her.

"I don't love him. But I don't want him to die either."

"Where is your indignation that he wanted to kill your son?" I asked. "How can you not be furious with him?"

She hid her face in her hands, sobbing. "I don't understand what is happening. I trusted him. Why would he do something like that?"

I groaned. "The man has always been a greedy selfish bastard, that's why." Seeing my mom crying made me regret I hadn't strangled Zobel with my own hands. She deserved so much better than him.

Khan leaned in and kissed Erika on the top of her hair. "Mom, it's going to be all right. I'm going to have Pearl come up here and talk to you. She's much better at things like this."

We waited in the room for Pearl to arrive. She and Khan spoke softly by the door as he brought her up to speed.

"Oh no." Pearl drew a hand in front of her mouth, and then she looked to Erika with deep sympathy on her face.

We left the women with Pearl holding her arm around Erika, and speaking low to her.

After closing the door, Khan looked at me and drew a deep sigh. "It's early, but I could use a cold beer before I go deal with those fuckers."

I raised an eyebrow. "Are you sure you don't have to ask for Pearl's permission first?"

"Very funny. You want a beer or not?"

A smile tugged at my lips. "Hell yeah, I want a beer."

CHAPTER 25
Broken

Magni

Khan and I had only emptied half of our beer when Archer called me.

He might as well have dunked my head in a bucket of ice water when he told me the bad news.

"Why the hell was she on the roof?" I exclaimed and stood up.

"What happened." Khan stood up too. "Who was on a roof?"

"Mila."

"Finn was here, and he took care of her. Mila is going to be all right," Archer assured me.

"Are you sure?"

"Yes. She broke her leg and a wrist, but the worst part is her concussion. She's been throwing up and seeing double."

It was like my head was about to explode. "For fuck's sake, Archer. How could you let this happen?"

"They were playing hide and seek. The boys go up there all the time. I guess it was just icy and slippery."

"But this is Mila, she's…" I stopped myself from saying "precious" since that would indicate I didn't care about the boys, which wasn't true.

"Laura is with her but Mila has been asking for you."

"I'm coming." I was just about to hang up when I realized what he had just said. "Wait, Archer, did you just say that Laura is there?"

"Yes, she arrived with Finn last night."

I looked at Khan. "Did you know that Finn and Laura were back?"

"No." He frowned. "Maybe I should leave my desk more often."

Returning my attention to Archer, I said, "Tell Mila that I am on my way."

"Do you want me to come with you?" Khan offered.

I threw my answer over my shoulder. "You go deal with the traitors while I take care of this."

"Okay, but call me with an update. Pearl and I will check in later."

The flight to the school from the Gray Mansion took fifteen minutes on a normal day. Today I was there in ten minutes, including the time it took to sprint from the hybrid to the school building.

Finn waited in the doorway. Holding up both his palms, he gestured for me to slow down. "Easy, Magni, you look like you're ready to murder someone."

"Where is she?"

He pointed. "In there with Laura."

"Archer said she broke her leg and her wrist."

Finn nodded. "I already applied bone accelerator; it's the concussion that worries me."

"How bad is it?"

"Bad enough that I want her under observation for the next twenty-four hours. Laura volunteered to care for Mila."

"Magni." The sound of Mila's voice from the other side of the door pulled me closer. Opening the door to one of the teachers' rooms, I saw Mila lying pale on a bed, with Laura sitting next to her on a chair.

It was suddenly hard to breathe. When Mila reached out her hand for me, my legs carried me forward and I kneeled down next to her, kissing the back of her small hand.

"You're not mad at me, are you?" she whispered.

"No. I just don't like to see you like this. What were you thinking going up on the roof?"

"I needed a place to hide, and Plato said that they would never find us on the roof."

"Plato told you to climb the roof?"

Mila looked sad. "Don't be mad at him. He does it all the time."

"I don't care if he does it all the time, it's too dangerous."

"That's what I said, but he told me nothing would happen."

"He's a fool. Why would you listen to him?"

Mila's eyes teared up. "I didn't want to, but then I remembered what you told me."

"What did I tell you?"

"You said that boys were born to lead and take charge. That's why I followed him."

I lifted my hand and let it fall to my thigh with a deep sigh. The universe was no doubt trying to prove a point to me. My mother's naïveté and lack of critical thinking had shocked me. But maybe it shouldn't have. If she had been told over and over that men were better decision-makers than women, it was no wonder that she had developed a dependency on Zobel.

"I know I said that, Mila, but you're a smart girl, and you should always listen to your instincts. Don't ever put yourself in danger because of a stupid boy."

Her eyes widened. "You shouldn't call anyone stupid."

"Oh, believe me, stupid is the nicest thing I can think of at the moment. There are other words that I would like to call Plato."

Mila lifted a hand to her mouth, her cheeks blowing up and her eyes bulging with urgency.

Laura was quick with a bucket and I held Mila's hair back when she threw up. From the look of it, there wasn't

218

much left in her stomach but bile. I knew from experience how painful it was.

"You can give me the bucket." Finn spoke behind us. "Magni, it might be a good idea to take Mila to your cabin. The kids have been quiet so far, but school is almost out and I would prefer that Mila rests."

"Sure." I handed him the bucket while Laura helped Mila drink a little.

"There are teeth cleaners in that drawer." Finn pointed to a blue dresser along the wall. "She likes the ones with the strawberry flavor."

Laura and I wrapped Mila in the thick duvet before I carried her to my cabin. Her head rested against my shoulder, and I placed a kiss on her hair before I gently laid her down on the bed.

Mila gave me a tired smile. "Laura wants to name your daughter Aubri."

"What daughter?" I looked from Mila to Laura, and down to her belly.

"No, it's not like that. I'm not pregnant or anything," Laura said with blushing cheeks. "Mila just asked me what names I like."

"Audrey." I tasted the name.

"No, it's Aubri with a b, right, Laura?"

Laura nodded. "Yes, that's right, with a b."

"That's a pretty name," I said in a soft voice, and pulled a chair over to sit next to her.

"Laura is okay with naming your boy Mason. She told me that she likes that name."

Laura was sitting on the foot end of the bed, her hand running up and down Mila's good leg on the top of the duvet. There were so many questions in my mind that I couldn't ask Laura in front of Mila. First of all, I was dying to know what Laura was doing here when she had been clear that she chose the Motherlands over me. A part of me wanted to believe she had changed her mind, but if that was the case, why hadn't she told me that she was back? Maybe she had come back to collect her things. The thought alone made me want to throw up in a bucket of my own.

"Close your eyes, and rest. Magni and I will wake you up every hour like Finn instructed. You don't have to worry about anything," Laura said with a soft smile to Mila.

"Laura," Mila whispered. "Will you tell me about the time that Magni fought for you in the tournament? He told me the story, but I would love to hear your version."

Laura and I exchanged a quick glance. "Okay, but I'm not a very good storyteller."

Mila pulled the duvet to her chin. "My mom used to twirl my hair and tell me stories. Sometimes she would sing to me. She had a beautiful singing voice." A few tears escaped Mila's pretty blue eyes.

"I'm sorry you lost your mom." Laura gave Mila's good leg a sympathetic squeeze. "Did Magni tell you that I lost my mom when I was little too?"

Mila nodded. "I was so sad to hear it."

"It's okay. It was a long time ago."

"For me it's worst at night. When Shelly and Kya have the night shift, they let me sleep with them sometimes, and when Magni is here, he holds me and calms me down. One time we went outside to look at stars." Mila turned her head and looked at me. "That was nice, do you remember?"

I lifted Mila's hand and kissed the back of it again. "I'll never forget it."

Laura gave me a surprised look that I didn't know how to interpret. If she thought less of me for being soft around Mila, there was nothing I could do about it. Mila was too important to let that influence me. With my little girl in pain, I would give her all the support she needed.

"I don't feel so good," Mila said in a weak voice.

"Do you need a bucket again?"

"No, but my leg hurts."

Laura took Mila's other hand and spoke with a voice full of sympathy. "It's the bone accelerator working, sweetie. Try to think of the pain as a good thing."

I got up. "Let me get Finn. He should give you some pain reliever."

"Finn already did," Laura informed me. "He gave her the maximum dose. She'll have to wait another two hours for her next dose."

I grunted. "I'll tell him to give her more *now*!"

"Magni." Laura's voice was firm and with my hand on the door handle, I turned to her.

"What?"

"I already asked him and he said that he would if he could. Finn is the doctor and you need to respect that. You just told Mila not to let people pressure her into doing something against her better judgment, and now you want to go and pressure Finn."

My first reaction was to tell Laura not to tell me what to do, but she did have a point, and the last thing Mila needed was Laura and me fighting.

Going back to my seat, I made Mila a promise. "I'll talk to Finn in an hour."

She nodded a thank you, and turned her head to look at Laura. "Will you lie next to me when you tell the story?"

"If you want me to." Laura crawled behind Mila, and with her back to the wall, she propped herself on her elbow and looked at me. "I can take this first shift. I'm just going to tell Mila the story and help her fall asleep."

"You do that, but I'm staying." I'd never heard Laura's side of how she'd experienced the time I won her in a tournament, and now that she was about to tell Mila, I wasn't going anywhere.

With her left hand, Laura began twirling Mila's long blonde hair. "Okay," she said and inhaled deeply, before she started telling.

CHAPTER 26
The Tournament

Laura

"Mila, I don't know how much Magni told you about me. But I grew up on the East Coast with my father, brothers, and my twin sister. My mother died during childbirth when I was eleven. She had given birth to four children, and suffered six miscarriages, when it happened.

"I know marriage isn't normal where you grew up. In the Northlands, however, it's what all girls look forward to. From the time we're little girls, we fantasize about the day men will fight for us and we will choose our champion." I chuckled. "I can't tell you how many hours my sister and I have spent talking about what outfit to wear on our wedding day. It was our favorite subject.

"It used to be that we girls would marry at the age of fifteen, but then our old ruler got ill, and Khan changed it to eighteen. I don't know why, but I was very upset with him for doing that. You see I had my outfit picked out and all." I smiled at how silly it sounded.

"Do you still remember what you were going to wear?" Mila asked.

"Of course. I was going to have my hair up in a beautiful braid, and my father had given me a black pearl necklace that I would wear with this beautiful white velvet dress that he had ordered especially for me." I didn't look at Magni when I spoke; all my talk about clothing had to be boring to him.

"I know why the rules were changed," Magni said.

"Why?" Mila asked.

"I'll tell you later. First, let Laura tell her story."

223

"Because my sister and I were twins, it was an enormous event that attracted thousands of men to participate in the tournament. I suppose they thought the chance of winning would be twice as good as in a normal tournament, but with the large amounts of participants, it was lower. The way it works is that every participant must pay a fee. That money, as well as the entrance fees for the spectators, goes to the prize money."

Mila frowned. "I thought *you* were the prize."

"The five strongest men are presented to the bride, and the champion that she picks gets both her and one million dollars.

"April and I studied the lists of participants, and held our breath when vile and disgusting men were added to the roster of participants. We cheered and danced when handsome and likable men signed up to fight for us. And every day we kept looking for the one name we most wanted to see.

"Whose name was that?" Magni asked with deep frown lines on his forehead.

I smiled. "I'm not giving away any spoilers. This is my story.

"My sister had her eyes on a young man called John from our area. She would get all flustered and nervous when she spoke about him. We used to come up with all these scenarios of how she would marry him and they would have ten children together." I sighed. "We should've known he could never win against that many strong warriors. He was more like a young version of Finn: funny and charming, but not meant to fight."

"Finn isn't a bad fighter. He can stand his own," Magni pointed out before I continued my story.

"That morning when the tournament began, April and I had only slept for a few hours. Knowing that it was our last night together, we held hands and talked all night. We were excited about men fighting over us. At the same time we were devastated that we would be separated, and scared that we wouldn't like the men presented to us. I was crying all morning, because the one man I wanted to fight for me wasn't on the list."

"Was it Magni?" Mila's eyes were wide open.

I nodded and gave her a small smile. "Yes, it was. For as long as I can remember, I was impossible to be around when a new tournament was announced. I would look daily to see if Magni's name would appear on the list of participants. The one time it did, I cried myself to sleep for a week."

"That was for Laila Michelle's tournament," Magni said, low.

"Yes, it was." I looked him in the eye before I returned my focus to Mila. "Laila Michelle is my best friend, and her tournament turned into a tragedy when the boy she was in love with died in a brutal fight. I was a year younger than her, and held her in my arms when she sobbed with grief. The next night, Laila Michelle was presented with five champions and she had to pick one of them."

Magni groaned. "That whole tournament was a farce. We would've done things differently if it were today. To make her pick like that was inhumane."

"True."

"But what happened to Magni? You said he was part of the tournament." Mila turned to look at him. "I bet you were one of the five champions."

I answered before he could. "Magni pulled out before his first fight. Everyone speculated on why he would do that, but all I cared about was the chance that he would fight for me."

"Were you in love with him?" Mila asked.

"I thought he was the strongest and most handsome of them all."

Mila wrinkled her nose at Magni. "That must've been before you got that tattoo up your neck."

225

A smile tugged at his lips. "You don't like my tattoo?"

"Not that one."

"He had the tattoo," I said. "But I thought it made him look fierce. Anyway, you can imagine my horror when my tournament was postponed three years. Magni was nine years older than me and with the new rule, a girl called Evangeline on the West Coast was the last to have her tournament at the age of fifteen, and only because it had already been planned.

"I didn't for one minute think Magni would wait three more years to marry when he could win Evangeline."

"Was she pretty?" Mila whispered.

"Very pretty."

"Prettier than you?"

I gave a nod. "Yes, at least I thought so."

"But he didn't fight for her, did he?"

"No. And I gave the craziest happy-dance scream when I found out." Out of the corner of my eye, I saw Magni shaking his head.

"But I don't understand," Mila rubbed her eyes. "You said Magni's name wasn't on the list of participants for your tournament. Then how did he win you?"

"There had been a mistake. During one of the fights, Laila Michelle came running to me, telling me that she had seen Magni in one of the other arenas. With thousands of participants, there were fights happening simultaneously in five different places. April, Laila Michelle, and I were all euphoric, and I kept telling my sister that I would never forgive her if she picked Magni. I felt he belonged to me because I had seen him first."

Mila interrupted. "Are you talking about the time you were little and walked in on him and Khan fighting? Magni told me about that."

"Yes. I wasn't sure if he remembered that night, but *I* did."

"But Magni *did* remember." Mila looked up at the large man sitting next to her, who gave her a soft smile.

It was striking how much more handsome Magni was when he wasn't scowling. And maybe because my story made me relive the enormous crush I had on him throughout all my teen years, butterflies were now fluttering around in my stomach.

"When all the fighting was over, my sister and I stood in our white dresses, facing nine beat-up warriors, and Magni, who had his knuckles bruised, but otherwise looked fine. My heart was hammering and my hands were shaking, because even though I loved my sister, I didn't trust a hundred percent that she wouldn't pick Magni." I sighed deeply and scrunched up my face at Mila. "And April *did* pick him."

"Noooo." Mila lifted her head. "She didn't."

"The young man she wanted had lost his game, and nine out of the ten champions in front of us looked horrible, with swollen eyes and broken noses."

"But your sister *knew* you wanted to marry Magni."

"Yes, April knew. I suspect she always had a small crush on him too, and that's why she picked him."

"Then what happened?"

"I got mad at her and declared to Khan and everyone in the room that I wanted Magni as well."

Magni gave a small groan. "It was a catfight."

Mila's eyes widened. "You fought over him?"

"There was a little pushing back and forth, but Khan would have none of it, and he announced that it would be up to Magni to pick April or me."

"He picked you." Mila gave a satisfied sigh. "I love this story. Did he kiss you?"

"Yes, we were married right after, and he kissed me in front of everyone."

"It was a good kiss." Magni gave me a small but genuine smile.

227

"That's so romantic."

Mila's comment wiped away Magni's smile, as if the word romantic was an insult.

"Now, enough storytelling. Close your eyes and see if you can fall asleep. Your body needs to heal," I instructed and kept twirling Mila's hair.

Five minutes later, her breathing had slowed down, and she was sleeping.

Magni sat in deep thought on the chair but looked over at me when I asked him a question: "You said you knew why the age of marriage had been changed from fifteen to eighteen."

He scratched his beard. "Officially, it was because of that boy who died at Laila Michelle's tournament. Khan and I agreed that we had to do something to prevent a tragedy like that from happening again. That's why we changed the minimum age of the participating men from sixteen to twenty-one. At the same time, we raised the minimum age of the brides from fifteen to eighteen. Everyone assumed that the two changes were connected, but the truth is that it was because of you."

"Me?"

He sighed. "Yes. I saw you at Laila Michelle's tournament. You were fourteen and everyone was talking about how pretty you and your sister were, and that in less than a year we would all be fighting for you. To me you were a kid and it was sickening to hear them talk about you in a sexual way. I guess ever since that night when you were nine and trusted me to take you back to your parents, I've felt protective of you. That's why I pushed Khan to change the age. My idea was that it would give you enough time to mature and grow into a woman instead of a child. I wanted him to have the same minimum age for women and men, but he refused to raise the age of the brides to twenty-one. The compromise was eighteen."

I raised both eyebrows. "Wow, good thing that you didn't convince him. There would've been a six-year gap with no tournaments. As I recall it, people didn't take the three-year gap very well. Imagine if it had been six years."

Magni looked down at Mila. "I still think it should be twenty-one. No one should marry as young as you did, Laura."

That provoked me. "I was ready!" I said in a firm voice.

"Were you? How can you say that when you ran away? We haven't even been married for two years, and you've already given up." He threw his hands in the air. "You tell Mila a story about wanting me and it sounds wonderful, but the reality is very different, Laura. We both know it."

"I didn't mean what I said about choosing the Motherlands."

Magni bent forward, resting his elbows on his knees, and his eyes on the floor.

"Sometimes you drive me mad with your bossy ways. I was so proud that I had brought down Devlin, and you didn't even praise me for it."

"When do you ever hear me praise *anyone*?"

"I wanted you to be proud of me and respect me as an equal."

Magni snorted and was no longer whispering when he turned his head to me. "Laura, are you sure you want to bring respect into this conversation?"

Avoiding his hard stare, I focused on his shoulder. "I know I haven't been a good wife to you, but I'm here and I'm willing to work on our marriage."

"What marriage? You made your choice."

I paled and met his eyes. "I already told you that I didn't mean what I said yesterday morning. I was just angry at you for ordering me around."

"I don't know what to think anymore, Laura. You come and go as you please and expect me to be okay with it. I listen to your story of how we ended up together and it sounds to me like you were in love with the *idea* of being married to me, more than you were interested in me as a person."

"That's not true; it's you who don't see me as a person. The first year we were married, we never talked. At least not like this."

"I told you, I'm not a talker."

"You're doing pretty well right now."

He groaned. "I've already told Khan that I'm getting myself a fishing cabin in Alaska. I'm done with all of this shit. He and Pearl can rule the country if they want. You can go and live in the Motherlands."

My voice shook a bit. "I don't want to live in the Motherlands."

He shrugged.

"Did you hear me? I don't want to live in the Motherlands. I want to live here in the Northlands with you."

"You wouldn't like Alaska."

"I'm not talking about Alaska."

"Look, Laura, I get it. I represented a young girl's fantasy of a strong hero who lived in a palace. I was the closest thing to a prince you could get. But if I wasn't enough for you with all that fairytale stuff, then I'm sure as hell not going to be enough for you when I live in a small cabin in Alaska."

"Enough about Alaska, Magni."

"I'm serious."

I angled my head and pointed to Mila. "You're going to leave her here wondering why she wasn't enough to make you want to stick around. I'm sure that's not traumatic to a girl who already lost her mother." My tone was sarcastic.

"That's not fair. I'd still visit."

My throat was hurting from all the emotions stuck down there. "Why can't we get along?" I asked.

"Because you're impossible to get along with." His hands closed in fists and this time his eyes centered on my lips.

I had seen that expression before, and always seconds before he kissed me. Only this time we had a sick child between us and he couldn't get an outlet for his frustrations by having sex with me.

"I recognize that expression on your face. If Mila wasn't here, you'd be all over me, wouldn't you?"

"No."

"She's sleeping; you can say it."

He frowned. "Maybe I would, but with a child in the room, that's not fucking happening."

I gave an eye roll. "It wasn't an invitation. I'm just pointing out the obvious. It's always been our pattern, you know?"

"So what? Kissing you is the best way to shut you up."

My eyes were shooting daggers at him. "Are you saying that the only reason you kiss me is to get me to shut up?"

His tone hardened and he lifted his chin in a challenging way. "No. Sometimes I'm just horny."

Disappointment and anger boiled in my stomach, like potent ingredients in a witch's brew. I had come back to the Northlands with the intention of being the bigger person and telling Magni how I felt about him. But the colossal wall he kept around himself was impenetrable. In a state of distress, I threw a comment at him soaked with the poisonous mix from my cauldron. "Too bad you're not more like Devlin. When he got horny he told his woman that he loved her. You don't even give me that much."

"Go back to the Motherlands if you want poetry." His tone was a low sneering sound.

"Telling your wife that you love her has nothing to do with poetry." I shut my mouth when Mila stirred between us, but it was too late and her eyes blinked open.

231

"Are you two fighting?"

"No, we're just discussing something. You have nothing to worry about, dear," I caressed her cheek.

"I thought I heard you talk about poetry."

"That's right, I was telling Magni about the powerful poem you read to me today."

"It's my favorite one." Mila yawned and placed her head against my shoulder. "We should read it to Magni."

"That's a great idea. We'll do that later."

Mila looked up at me as if something clicked with her. "Remember your favorite part from the poem about paying compliments? You should be really proud of yourself, Laura."

"Why?"

"Because you said that giving other people compliments and saying nice things about them was hard for you, and yet you said all those amazing things about Magni. Now he knows that you were in love with him for years before you married him, and that you thought he was the most handsome of all the men."

"A real fucking prince," Magni said low and looked down.

Mila turned her head to him. "What did you say?"

"Nothing."

She yawned again. "Magni, when did you first know that you loved me?"

He looked taken aback. "Ehm, I don't know."

Mila closed her eyes and smiled. "I knew I liked you when we sat under the stars and talked, and you held my hand. I loved you when you had to leave the school and you picked me up and said you would take me with you as a souvenir. You didn't do that to anyone else, and it made me feel special."

"You *are* special," Magni whispered to her. "I told you I think of you as a daughter."

Mila gave him the sweetest smile. "That makes me happy."

Magni's Adam's apple bobbed in his throat, and he leaned over and kissed the top of her hair.

Mila's eyes were hooded when she looked at me and yawned again. "Laura, when did you know that you loved Magni? Was it when he chose you over your sister?"

I took my time before I answered. "No, it was about a month after we got married. I wasn't feeling well, and he brought me a tray of breakfast. Magni had never asked me what I liked in the morning, but he had picked out my favorite things."

Magni moved in his seat. "It didn't take much brainpower to figure out. You picked the same four things for breakfast every day for a month."

I looked into his eyes. "The point is that you noticed."

Mila wasn't done, and asked Magni. "When did you know that you loved Laura?"

Magni scratched his arm. "That's a long story."

"Tell us."

"It's not a good story, and only Khan and Finn know it."

"We won't tell anyone," Mila promised. "You can trust us."

Magni exhaled deeply. "Okay, I'll tell you, but I warn you: you might not like me when you hear the truth."

My heart started racing from the seriousness of his tone. Magni was letting us see what was behind the tall wall he surrounded himself with, and I was scared to breathe and miss a word he said.

CHAPTER 27
Ending an Era

Magni

"Anyone who knew my father feared him. If they didn't, they were fools. He was ruthless, strong, domineering, and often cruel," I told Mila and Laura, who were both on the bed looking at me with their eyes wide open.

"I was my father's favorite son, and it's because of him that I grew to be the best fighter in this country at an early age. My father was relentless, and would push both me and Khan to an extreme. With Khan being his firstborn, it was always worse on him. I suppose my father was like every ruler before him; he wanted to secure his legacy. Khan and I wished there had been more of us sons to share the burden of his impossible expectations.

"Breeding heirs to the throne was of high priority to him and from the moment Khan and I turned eighteen, he obsessed about us marrying and having children of our own.

"Khan didn't show any interest in tournaments. Maybe it was his own way of rebelling, but he paid a heavy price. Our father did everything to pressure him, accused him of being a homosexual and humiliated him at any opportunity.

"It wasn't much better for me, but we both withstood his pressure until I was twenty-three and Khan was twenty-eight. By then our father had become more irrational and unpredictable than ever. He'd started threatening to kill Khan if he didn't follow orders. To take the pressure off Khan, I agreed to fight for Laila Michelle that year." I paused and locked eyes with Laura. "On my way to my first fight, I saw you." In my mind's eye, I remembered the fourteen-year-old version of Laura who had stared at me with such longing.

"The memory of you being nine and telling me to wait for you wouldn't go away. I never confirmed that I would wait, but seeing you that morning did something to me. There was such hurt and disappointment in your eyes, as if we had made a pact and I was letting you down." I shook my head. "I couldn't do that."

Laura and Mila were both staring at me, soaking up every word I said.

"My father went ballistic when I told him I was backing out of the tournament. He ordered Khan to fight instead of me, and when Khan refused, the two of them got in a physical fight." I folded and unfolded my hands, while forcing myself to continue telling about the secret I'd kept for so long.

"Again, our father threatened to kill Khan. At first, I didn't think he was serious because he had threatened to kill him so many times. This time, however, my father pulled out a knife from his boot and jabbed it in Khan's direction. Khan was stunned and didn't move back fast enough when our father slashed the knife again. The second time he cut Khan, his white shirt turned red. I acted on instinct, making a high kick to get the knife away from my father, but that only made him turn on me. When he attacked, I saw red. He'd already tried to kill my brother, and now he was coming for me."

"What did you do?" Mila whispered.

"At first, I defended myself and kept at a distance, trying to talk him down. But he kept shouting about all the ways he would kill us for not following his orders. I made sure that he could never harm us again."

Mila gasped. "You killed your father?"

235

"No, I injured him enough that he wouldn't be a danger to us."

"Was that why he was in his bed for the last three years of his life?" Laura asked.

"Yes, officially he had a heart attack that caused him to fall and injure himself. Only Khan, Finn, and I knew the truth."

"Wow." Laura held a hand to her mouth.

Mila frowned. "What does all that have to do with you loving Laura?"

I blinked a few times. "Ehm, well, because you asked when I knew that I loved her, and it was my loyalty to her that made me rebel against my father and refuse to fight for Laila Michelle."

Mila turned her head to look at Laura. "Is loyalty the same as love?"

Laura's eyebrows drew close. "I'm not sure."

"To me it is," I said. "Words are cheap. I don't need people to tell me they love me. I'd rather that they show it by being loyal and staying with me through thick and thin."

Laura gave me an incredulous look. "Says the man who's talking about moving to Alaska."

"You're moving?" Mila exclaimed with a gasp.

I brushed my hair back. "It's nothing. I shouldn't have told you the story; I'm sorry. How are you feeling, Mila? Still hurting?"

The girl ignored my attempt to change the topic. "Are you moving?"

When I looked down, Mila knew it was true. Her loud sniffle made me look up to see tears well up in her eyes.

"Oh, fuck! Sweetie, I was going to talk to you about it."

The same expression of hurt and disappointment that had been on Laura's face on the morning of Laila Michelle's tournament now met me again.

236

"But you said you would be my dad." Mila's golden hair and teary blue eyes made her look like a sad angel.

"And I meant it."

"Then why did you say that love is loyalty and that it's about staying together through thick and thin? If you move away that must mean you don't love me."

"I *do* love you." It was the first time I spoke those words.

Mila hid in Laura's arms, crying.

"Shit, shit, shit." I got up and paced the small cabin. "Laura, I told you I was bad at talking about emotions. Look how I fucked it up." It came out accusatory, as if it was Laura's fault for making me express my feelings.

"Then make it right," Laura said. "Tell her that you're not going to Alaska."

I wanted to, but I was in way over my head, and did the only thing I knew how to do. Picking up my jacket, I walked out of the cabin, slamming the door, and heading for the forest to clear my head.

I had only made it to the first trees when Finn called out to me. "Hey, wait up."

I didn't slow down, but he caught up anyway. "What's going on?"

"Something is wrong with me." My voice was raw from emotion.

"Wrong? What are you talking about?"

"All I know how to do is break people. Mila is in my cabin sobbing her eyes out because of me."

Finn looked from me to the cabin and back again. "What did you say to her?"

"She knows I'm moving to Alaska."

For a moment Finn just stood there, as if waiting for me to take it back. When I didn't, he laughed.

I punched him hard on his shoulder and walked on. "It's not fucking funny."

"You told Mila you were moving to Alaska?"

"I told Khan and Laura too."

"And they *believed* you?"

"Of course they believed me. I'm not a jokester like you; people take me seriously."

Finn was still laughing. "That's because they don't know you like I do. Have you forgotten about the time we went to Alaska? We froze our asses off in that shed of a cabin, and you swore you would never set foot in that place again."

"I enjoyed the bear hunting," I defended myself.

"Only because you thought it was funny how fucking scared I was of actually meeting a bear."

"Yeah, that was funny."

"Alaska might be okay in the summer, but you wouldn't last a winter up there."

"I'm tough."

"Sure you are, but when was the last time you cooked a meal for yourself?"

"I can cook."

Finn patted my shoulder. "Magni, my friend. I love you, man, but sometimes you think with your ass."

"You love me?"

He held up both palms. "As a brother, so don't get any funny ideas."

"You never told me that."

He shrugged. "I thought it was implied."

"*It was.* So why the hell do you have to go and say it? You've only lived in the Motherlands for a few days, and now you are expressing your *love* for me. If you don't stop that shit, I'm going to call the guys together and we'll do an intervention on you. You'd better not turn into a softie."

"Don't worry, it won't happen again. From now on it will just be implied that *I love you*." He spoke the words clearly and with a smile on his face, provoking me on purpose.

"Stop saying it." I tore my hands through my hair. "I'm almost thirty years old, and I've never heard those words said to my face. And then in one day, I hear them from both you and Mila." I didn't count Laura's talk about loving me because of my breakfast choices. That didn't ring true to me and had to have been a story to please Mila.

"I swear, those damn Momsies are infiltrating us. This love shit is all around now."

"You're right. It's a fucking slippery slope. The L word is like a gateway drug into hugging. We should be outraged."

I spun to look at Finn. His eyes were sparkling with humor and once he started laughing, he couldn't stop.

"It's not funny, Finn."

"Yes, it is."

"I made a mess of things with Mila and Laura."

"That's bad." He stopped laughing. "You might have to bring out the big guns."

"What big guns?"

"The A word."

I lowered my brow. "Asshole?"

"Nope, I mean A as in apology."

Jerking back, I crossed my arms. "You're not serious. Laura would lose all respect for me."

He tilted his head from side to side as if weighing options. "You would think so, but in my experience, apologies have the opposite effect on women. At least with Athena."

"Tsk, you can't compare the two. Athena likes soft men." When Finn frowned, I added. "Not that I'm saying you're a full-on softie yet, but you know what I mean, right?"

"No." Finn placed his hands on his hips and shifted his balance onto one foot. "Care to elaborate on how Athena likes *soft* men?"

239

I groaned and leaned my head back, looking up at the sky. "Fuck, I'm so bad with words."

"No shit."

"Which is why Alaska makes perfect sense. The wildlife won't care if I say the wrong thing. No one's going to be offended or cry up there."

Finn lowered his brow. "I've known you since you were twelve, Magni. You've always been a loner, but isolating yourself is an extreme, even for you." He paused. "And what about your hero complex? Who are you going to save up there?"

I snorted. "I'm no hero."

"Then what do you call someone who keeps saving other people?"

I turned around, walking back toward the cabins.

"I know you don't like to talk about it, but you can't punish yourself forever for what happened to your sister. It *wasn't your fault*." Finn spoke the last three words slow and clear. "What happened to Dina doesn't take away from the fact that you saved me from Mentor Johnson."

My jaw hardened. Finn and I never talked about the monster from our past. I'd been the new student at Finn's school when I noticed something wasn't right. Curiosity and intuition had made me listen through the door to Mentor Johnson's office. What I heard had made my blood boil to the point where I kicked in the door and ended the torture that Finn was suffering at the hands of that fucking sadistic mentor.

"You would've done the same thing," I muttered.

"I would like to think so, but we both know that I am not the only person you've saved. You stood up for Khan against your father, and saved his life. Don't think I don't know how hard that was for you. And what about Laura?"

"What about her?" My tone was harsh because I hated the way Finn saw me as a hero when I was anything but.

"You always protected her."

240

"That's not how she sees it. She thinks I'm bossing her around and being a dick."

"You've been in more fights to protect your woman than any man in this country. You could have married her when she was fifteen, but you wanted to wait for her to grow up. I always thought that was incredibly selfless of you, and that we all paid a price."

"What do you mean, that *you* paid a price?"

"I had to deal with your moodiness. Remember that time when we saw Laura at the football game, just after she had turned seventeen?"

My hands ran through my hair. It was a redundant question. Finn had been there when I stopped dead in my tracks, gaping at the sight of Laura. The girl that I had last seen when she was fourteen had transformed into a breathtaking young woman with curves and a smile to die for. For years, I had felt protective of her because of the short connection we shared when she was nine. But that day I'd felt more than protective of her. I'd felt physically attracted to her too.

"And what about the pilot you saved from the burning drone, or that kid you carried for miles during the survival camp at school?"

"He broke his leg and was slowing us down. Everyone would've done that."

"Maybe. But these examples are just a few of the dozens of times when you sacrificed yourself to help others. You should give yourself credit for it, and stop isolating yourself. You never had social skills, but that's because you push people away, and never practice at it."

I sighed. "I miss the good old days when I could fix my problems by beating up the bad guys."

"Ahh, yes. Those were the days. You beating up bad guys, and me patching them back together. What a team we were."

My eyes glazed over, memories assaulting me of my sister saying those exact same words to me.

CHAPTER 28
Dina's Death

Magni

"What a team we were." Dina's eyes were sparkling with mischief as she caressed my hair, and continued the story from when I was younger. "I distracted the cook and you snatched two of the biggest cookies she had baked."

I laughed. "How old was I?"

"Let's see; you're seven now, and it was two years ago." Dina gave me the schoolteacher look that she often used when she taught me to read or count.

"I was five."

"Yes, and how old was I?"

Math had never been my strong suit and I frowned.

"Use your fingers like I told you to," she instructed. "What is fifteen minus two?"

"But I only have ten fingers."

Dina gave a low melodic chuckle and let me use one of her hands to count.

"You were thirteen then."

"That's right." Tousling my hair, she planted a kiss on my cheek. "You're such a smart kid, Magni."

"Will you sleep here tonight?" I asked with a hopeful tone in my voice. I loved snuggling up with Dina.

She took my hand and moved closer. "I would like that very much."

"Are you excited for tomorrow?"

"Are you?" she asked.

I frowned. "I like to see men fight, but I don't want you to move out."

Dina's expression changed to one of sadness. People always said she and I looked alike. We had inherited our father's blond hair and blue eyes, while Khan took after our mother with his dark coloring. Right now I was playing with her soft golden locks and inhaling the scent of Dina. It represented everything I loved, from warm hugs, bright smiles, to comforting back rubs when I couldn't sleep at night.

"I don't like the thought of moving out either. I'll miss you and Khan."

"And Mom and Dad," I added, thinking she'd forgotten about them.

"I'll miss Mom a lot."

"Are you nervous about picking the right champion?"

She nodded. "Mom says not to expect love, but I want him to treat me well."

Pushing up on my elbow, I looked deep into my sister's eyes. "If your husband isn't nice to you, I'll beat him up for you, I promise."

Everyone would have laughed at a seven-year old threatening to beat up a grown champion, but Dina didn't. Her tears welled up a little and she leaned in to kiss my forehead, engulfing me once again in the comforting scent of her. "Thank you, Magni, I know you will. You've always been good to me."

"That's because we're best friends."

"And we always will be," she promised before we fell asleep.

The next day I watched as many fights as I could. Never had so many men entered to win a bride, but then Dina was no ordinary bride. She was the ruler's daughter, and the potential influence from becoming her husband drew the crowds.

In the evening, I saw her step forward looking like a true princess with her white dress and long blond hair braided

244

by my mother. I thought Dina was the prettiest girl in the world.

The man she chose was very large and when he picked her up and carried her around on his shoulder like a trophy, she smiled and waved at me.

I sized him up, and my immature seven-year-old self whispered to my brother Khan, who sat next to me. "If he's not good to Dina, you'll have to help me kick his ass."

Khan lifted an eyebrow, silently asking me if I was serious.

"I promised her," I emphasized.

Khan looked to Dina and her champion. "I don't think we could beat him, Magni. He's too big."

"If you won't help me, I'll do it by myself."

Khan heaved his chest in a sigh. "Tell you what. If Dina complains, we'll come up with a plan to help her, all right?"

This was so typical of Khan. Always scheming and being strategic, but he was almost five years older than me and my closest ally, so I'd take it.

We never got a chance to come up with a plan. Dina went to the East Coast with her new husband and we never saw her again.

Five days later, my mother gathered me and Khan. With eyes full of tears, she sat us down and told us what had happened. "There was an accident."

"What kind of accident?" Khan asked.

"It's Dina. She fell out a window."

I stiffened and my pulse raced. "Is she okay?"

Erika's shoulders jerked up and down as she hid her face in her hands, crying.

"Mom, is Dina okay?" I had to know.

"She died last night." The words came out in a sob but I heard them and my whole world stopped.

"No," Khan said beside me. "That's not possible. It can't be."

"I'm afraid so. She fell out of an attic window."

I wanted to scream that it was a lie! Dina would have never been that careless. She was smart and knew about danger. She had always watched me like a hawk, warning me not to get too close to cliffs, fires, windows, or anything that could harm me. I could recall being scolded at least five times by her for hanging out the window. There was no way she had fallen by accident.

An iron band tightened around my throat, and I jerked back when my mom reached for me. It was like my body was burning and I couldn't stand her touching me. I wanted to run as fast as I could and find Dina. We would laugh together that she'd pulled a prank like this.

Nothing would happen to Dina. I'd promised her that much.

"What was she doing in the attic?" Khan asked our mom.

"I don't know. Your father has gone to investigate."

The words registered with me, but I refused to believe they were true. This was just another game of hide and seek.

"Magni, stop," my mom called out when I knocked my chair over and stormed out of the room. I sprinted through the house, searching my room, Dina's room, the kitchen, the library, and every one of the places I could remember her hiding in the past. When she wasn't there, I searched the garden. My voice was hoarse from calling out her name, and after hours of searching, I collapsed in the far end of the park where no one would hear me sob.

She was never spoken about again. It was like Dina had never lived.

Except she had lived!

She had sung to me, read to me, kissed away my tears, and held me. She had played with me, been my best friend, and slept in my bed often.

My dad ordered all pictures of her removed to spare my mother the pain of seeing constant reminders. Dina's old room was converted into a bathroom and walk-in closet for one of the guest rooms. The Gray Mansion was purged of evidence that Dina had lived here for fifteen years. The few times I dared bring up Dina's name at dinner, my father flat-out ignored me and changed the subject.

After that, I began questioning if Dina had been real or an imaginary friend from my childhood.

That's when I made a last attempt to find some evidence of my sister's existence, and discovered a picture in my parents' room under my mother's bed.

Dina was younger than I remembered her. A pretty girl around ten or eleven with the long blond hair, blue eyes, and cute dimples that I had loved so much.

I took the picture and slept with it under my pillow for months, brooding over all my unanswered questions and my guilt for not having protected Dina like I'd promised her.

At twelve and a half, I was huge for my age and strong beyond my years. My nine years of intense fight training was showing and my father praised me, saying that the world had never seen a more exceptional talent than me. With my strength and speed, I'd be the best fighter the world had ever seen.

His words empowered me to ask him the question that was burning in my chest.

"Dad, what happened to Dina?"

"I don't know what you're talking about," he said and turned his back on me.

His disrespectful dismissal of Dina's life made me explode. I destroyed everything within my reach and servants fled in fright as glasses and cutlery went flying through the air. My father had to physically restrain me with the help of two from his security unit, and after that, I was sent to live at a school. There was no talking things through. No apologies or explanations. I was a twelve-year-old with a shitload of grief and unanswered questions, who hated the world.

After our father died, I'd searched for pictures of Dina from media events in the past. I only found her wedding photos and they were too painful to keep.

A few years ago, I'd tried talking to my mother about it, but it came across as blaming her, and Erika broke down crying. To this day it still haunted me that I didn't know what Dina had been doing in that attic. Had she been killed or did she die while trying to escape her husband's brutality? In my mind she'd been attempting to climb down from the roof. The thought that she'd committed suicide was too outlandish, since the Dina I knew loved life. There was no way to ask her husband since he died a few weeks after my father's visit to investigate. Rumors said my father arranged it, but it was all speculation.

Finn was one of the few I'd told about Dina. We almost never spoke about her, and for him to bring her up in a conversation like he'd done tonight was rare.

I kicked at the ground in front of the cabin, and stuffed my hands deeper into my pockets. Finn had gone back to the school when I'd asked for a minute to clear my head. I'd been out here for at least fifteen minutes and my head was as chaotic as ever.

Apologize. That had been Finn's advice to me. What he didn't understand was that I would rather face four opponents at once in a physical fight. At least when people were attacking me, I knew how to protect myself.

I cracked my knuckles and rolled my shoulders, while muttering low curse words before I went back into the cabin.

Mila wasn't sobbing anymore, and both she and Laura watched me when I took off my jacket. "Ehm, I thought I should come back and explain myself." I shifted my balance. "I didn't mean to make you cry, Mila. It's just that all this talk about, ehm..." I coughed. "This talk about love is new to me and I'm not very good at it."

They both looked at me, and neither spoke.

"I've never given an apology before, but I hope you know that I don't like it when you cry."

"Are you going to give me an apology?" Mila asked.

I furrowed my eyebrows in confusion. "I thought I just did."

Mila shook her head. "You have to use the words 'I'm sorry' or 'I apologize.' Otherwise it doesn't count."

"Okay." I took a deep breath and spoke on the exhalation. "I apologize."

Mila reached out her hand to me. "I can tell that you have been crying, so I forgive you."

"I never cry!" I said in a gruff voice because I would never admit to that with Laura in the room.

"You cry on the inside." Mila kept her hand outreached as an invitation to sit on the chair next to the bed. I took it and held her hand in mine, just like I had when I made her sob a little while ago.

"If you move away, will you promise me one thing?" she asked.

"Anything."

"Will you take me with you?"

"Sweetie, Alaska isn't a place for children, and you need to stay in school."

Her face fell. "Then won't you please stay, Magni?"

I gave a loud puff. "For now I will."

CHAPTER 29
Town Hall Meeting

Laura

For three days Magni kept his distance. I was sick and tired of not knowing how to act around him. I needed him to sit down and talk to me. To figure out a way for us to live as husband and wife with the respect and love that we both deserved.

He'd asked that I go back to the Gray Mansion, but to remind him that I made my own decisions, I stayed at the school. Magni was gone most of the day and when he came around the school at night, he was more closed off to me than ever. Twice we'd had sex, but both times had felt purely physical and as soon as it was over, he'd turned his back on me. My choosing the Motherlands had not been forgiven or forgotten by him. More than once, I regretted leaving his bed that night I went to catch Devlin. If I'd known Devlin wasn't a danger to anyone, but living with his girlfriend, I would have stayed with Magni that night.

Athena, Finn, and Tristan were still at the school as well. Wrestler had asked to meet Tristan for some testing on Wednesday morning, and the boy was so nervous about getting the apprentice job that he'd begun biting his nails.

On Tuesday evening, the school was packed when Boulder, Christina, Khan, Pearl, and Magni joined us for the poetry night that Kya had arranged.

All the children had either written a poem of their own or picked out a poem written by a child. After dinner we sat for an hour listening and clapping.

Mila read out *Generation of Mirrors*, the beautiful poem she had shared with me, and Raven enjoyed the spotlight with her own poem on farts that had all the boys laughing.

"The last person tonight is you, Solo." Kya smiled to the oldest of the boys at the school. Solomon reminded me of a younger version of Magni: strong, tall, fierce, with blue eyes and blond hair.

"Do I *have* to?" he asked and shot a sideways glance at Willow, who sat a few seats from him.

"Yes, you have to." Archer pointed to a spot at the end of the table where the other children had read out their poems.

"Can't I stay in my seat? Mila got to sit down."

Archer raised an eyebrow. "Unless you have a broken leg like Mila, you don't get to sit. Go, Solo!"

The fourteen-year-old boy made his way to the end of the table and a few of the oldest girls shot long glances in his direction.

He shifted his balance and rubbed his nose. "Ehm, okay, this poem is about light versus darkness. It's called Truth, and this is how it goes."

Darkness:
Turn your back on the light, you'll see me in the shadows.
Let me educate you and open your eyes to the cruel truth of this world.
It will overwhelm you with sadness and make you feel depressed.
I can show you *the* truth.

Light:
Turn your back on the shadows, you'll feel my warm light shine in your face.

Let me educate you and open your eyes to see the beauty of this world.
It will inspire you and make you want to share your happiness with others.
I can show you *the* truth.

Both:
Look up at the sun or down at the shadows.
We both show the truth, because we are the truth.
Depressed or inspired, the choice is yours.
We can show you *a* truth.

Everyone clapped and Kya asked. "That was a very deep poem, Solo. Can you tell us who wrote it?"

"Some kid."

"Do you remember the name of the kid?"

"Nope. But I'm sure it was a girl."

"Okay, but can you tell us what the poem was about?"

"Some shit about looking up or down."

Kya raised a brow. "That's your analysis?"

"Yeah. It's stupid. Lightness and darkness can't talk – it makes no sense."

"Then why did you choose that poem?"

Solo was already on his way back to his seat next to Storm and Tristan when he threw his answer over his shoulder to Kya. "Because it was the shortest of the poems you had us pick from."

The other boys laughed.

Kya didn't give up and drilled a little more. "But what did you think of it?"

Solomon looked back at her. "I think it's a waste of time, and I don't see why I have to learn about that stuff."

Kya's nostrils expanded and she raised her chin like a weapon aiming straight at the disrespectful young man.

"Poetry is like music, Solo. Would you like a world without music?"

"Nooo." He dragged out the word.

"Then there is your answer to why you have to learn about poetry. It's the heartbeat of a culture."

Pearl got up from the table and walked over to place a hand on Kya's shoulder. "Thank you, dear."

Kya's black curls bobbed around her face when she nodded. "My pleasure."

Pearl turned to address the children. "A big thank you for sharing your favorite poems with us. I enjoyed it very much." Holding up her hands, she led a round of applause that we all took part in before she made an announcement. "This is the first time we've all been gathered, and that gives us an excellent opportunity to have our first town hall meeting."

"What's that?" Marco asked and caught a piece of bread that William was throwing at another boy. "William, do you want to be on kitchen duty for a week?" Marco's voice was stern and William was quick to put his hands on the table, signaling that he was done throwing food around.

"A town hall meeting is an opportunity for a community to discuss important matters," Pearl explained. "With all the changes we face here in the Northlands, it would be interesting to hear different perspectives. I suggest we start by talking about how to deal with all the Motlander women who wish to move here."

Magni, who sat next to Khan, leaned forward and spoke in a booming voice. "That's easy. They marry a man and become his wife. End of story."

"I'm afraid it's not that simple. Motlander women are used to having a profession and would like to contribute with their unique talents." Pearl turned from Magni to

Christina and Kya. "I'm sure you worry about what kind of life your daughters might have in the Northlands as well."

Christina nodded and Kya clapped her hands with excitement. "Yes, let's do a town hall meeting. It would be a great way to show the children how democracy works and how important it is for everyone to feel heard. Maybe we could do a vote as a learning experience."

Magni flew up from his seat. "I'm shutting down this madness before it gets any further. The only two people with a vote in this room are Khan and me. We don't need anyone's advice on how to run the Northlands."

"You're not the only two people living in the Northlands. The rest of us have an opinion too," I muttered, low enough that Magni didn't hear me.

"A town hall discussion will offer you and Khan valuable input." Pearl folded her hands in front of her. "What you do with the input is up to you."

Khan leaned back on the bench, supporting his back against the wall. "I told you, Pearl, this isn't how we do things here."

Magni, who was standing next to Khan, looked down on him. "You knew she was going to pull this shit on us?"

"No, but I'm not surprised since Pearl has been talking about town hall meetings for days now. She wants us to tour around the country and listen to people's input."

"Jesus Christ." Magni's outburst had everyone looking at him. "Get your woman under control, brother."

Magni's words provoked me.

"Women aren't supposed to be controlled by their husbands," I said, my pulse drumming like a freight train with too much speed to slow down in time to avoid the disaster.

Magni pinned me with a dirty look that spoke of spankings and scoldings, but my frustration with him was bigger than the lust his heated looks inspired. "I'm with Pearl. Let's hear what everyone has to say."

Pearl gave me a small nod of recognition.

"I'm with Pearl too," Christina pitched in and was hushed by Boulder, who warned her not to get involved. "Of course, I'm getting involved," she told him. "I love town hall meetings."

When Athena, Kya, and Shelly supported the idea, the children began to speak up as well.

"Can we stay and listen?" Rochelle, who was the younger sister of Shelly, asked.

Magni shook his head at Khan. "Aren't you going to say something? First you allow women to have a voice, and now children too?"

Khan looked thoughtful and then he rose in a slow movement. "I'll allow this town hall meeting to take place, but there will be no vote and no children present."

A collective sigh of disappointment was heard from all the children.

"It's okay," Pearl comforted them. "We can do a separate town hall meeting for children only. I would like to be present and if some of you have good ideas, I'll present them to Lord Khan on your behalf."

"It's late anyway," Archer added.

Nero wrinkled his nose. "It's only eight-thirty."

"Goodnight, Nero." Lord Khan gave him a direct glance that made the boy lower his head in respect.

"Can I stay?" Tristan asked. "I'm fifteen and I'm not a student."

Khan looked to Shelly, the assistant mentor, who was still in the room and fifteen too. "Tristan, you and Shelly can stay, but you'll keep quiet unless spoken to."

Solomon stuck out his chest. "I'll be fifteen soon, can I stay too?"

"No." Archer stabbed a finger in Solo's direction. "I'm placing you in charge of getting everyone to bed. Make sure they use their teeth cleaners and stay in their own beds. Lights out at nine-thirty, okay?"

Proud to be trusted with the responsibility, Solomon nodded with a serious expression. "Got it."

A minute later all children had left the dining room. Pearl tilted her head. "Athena, dear, would you like to lead the meeting? I know you've done many town hall meetings in the past."

"No, it's fine. I'll let you do it. It was your idea."

Magni's expression was that of a thundercloud but he had resumed his seat next to Khan.

"With the children out of the room, let's start our first town hall meeting," Pearl began in a soft voice. "Today's agenda will be to discuss visions for our future. Let's begin with ideas on how to deal with the list of almost seven hundred Motlander women and men who are interested in a relationship with an Nman. And by relationship, I should specify that some of the people on the list are interested in friendships with the potential to grow into more.

"By people, you mean women, right?" Marco asked.

"There are twenty-four males on the list too. Twenty-one of them have expressed an interest in a romantic relationship."

The men exchanged glances, but Finn was the only one who commented. "Think of it this way, Motlander males are more feminine than most of the women in the Motherlands anyway."

"Hey, that's offensive," Christina complained. "You make us sound like we're masculine."

Pearl continued. "Let's focus on ideas on how to match the Northlanders with the Motlanders."

"How many Northlanders have signed up so far?" I asked.

"Applicants are still trickling in from both sides of the wall, but so far we have two million and eighty-seven thousand Nmen hoping to find a wife.

A loud whistle came from Archer. "That's a lot."

"Yes, and the number is growing fast. I don't see how we can make the best possible match without interviewing all of them, but that's too time-consuming. The Council is overwhelmed with the disaster relief after the earthquake and they asked if we have suggestions."

Shelly raised her hand.

"What do you suggest, Shelly?"

"Algorithms."

"What do you mean, algorithms?"

"We have millions of men and seven hundred women. We could have all participants fill out a questionnaire and design a program that matches the people with the highest compatibility score."

"How would you do that?" Pearl asked.

Shelly looked up for a second. "Give them a hundred questions about values, habits, and expectations for a marriage and see who matches the best."

Khan took up the flow. "Shelly, I like how you think. It sounds like an easy solution."

Athena's voice was calm and unrushed when she spoke. "You're forgetting something important."

"What?" Pearl looked at her.

"Even if a couple have a high compatibility score there is no guarantee that they have chemistry. Finn and I don't have much in common, but somehow we work in spite of that."

"I have an idea," Marco said. "Let's run Shelly's system and then we'll have the fifty most compatible men fight for each woman."

"No fighting." Pearl's voice was firm.

Shelly raised her hand again and was allowed to speak by Pearl. "If we could figure out what makes it work between people in relationships that are functional, then we can make a system that matches couples using those algorithms."

"You think algorithms can predict chemistry?"

"What do you mean when you say *chemistry*?" Shelly asked with a frown. "Are you suggesting we should do blood tests on people?"

"No, I'm saying that sometimes there's a special attraction between two people. It doesn't have to make sense from a rational point of view, but that person just gets under your skin."

Shelly pulled her sleeves over her hands as if protecting her own skin and frowned. "I don't know about chemistry or attraction, but if we're to make some kind of system, we'd have to find couples that are happy and design the algorithms around them. The problem is to find a sample group large enough. We only have four couples of Nmen and Motlander women."

"Boulder and I are happy," Christina offered.

"So are Khan and I."

"Yes, but we would need a larger number of couples to get an idea of what makes you successful as a couple. Algorithms based on four couples are too random."

Khan cut in. "We'll find some programmers to create a system and maybe you can talk to them about your ideas, Shelly. For now, we'll have to work with what we have."

"Can I ask a quick question?" Marco stood up. "Will there still be prize money for the Nmen who marry?"

"No, of course not. I didn't get a prize when I married Athena either. The prize money is connected to the tournaments."

"There will be no tournaments and no fighting," Pearl pointed out. "The Council has made that a condition."

Marco sat down with disappointment on his face.

Shelly's eyes were on Marco. "I think you had a good idea about giving the women a number of men to choose from. Instead of letting the fifty most compatible men fight for her, maybe we could let them charm her instead."

"Charm her how?" Marco asked with a frown.

"I don't know, and maybe fifty is too large a number, but we could let them record a video of themselves that she can watch."

Tristan raised his hand. "That's a great idea, and then the woman can pick out five or ten men that she finds attractive and wants to meet."

"I like it." Khan nodded. "That's what we'll do."

"Good." Pearl looked at Magni. "Do you agree?"

He uncrossed his arms and tucked his hands in his pockets. "No, I don't agree. I want tournaments, but since we can't have that I guess we'll have to rely on some fucking algorithm."

Pearl gave a satisfied smile.

"Now that Khan and Magni have approved, we can move on to discuss how we take advantage of all the knowledge the women are bringing."

"What knowledge?" Magni asked.

"There are highly educated and resourceful people on the application list. Librarians, architects, environmental workers, programmers, mediators, doctors, nurses, psychologists, and artists of different kinds. They have been told they'll be allowed to work here."

"As long as we can keep them safe," Magni said.

"How do we do that?" Pearl asked.

Heads turned to look at Shelly as if she had the answer to everything.

Self-aware, she tucked her hands under her thighs and hid behind the curtains that her long brown hair provided to hide her blushing cheeks. "How would I know? Safety isn't my specialty."

"I understand you want to plan everything, Pearl, but we'll have to treat each woman's request to work on a case-by-case basis," Finn commented.

"Of course, but wouldn't it be good to at least discuss it?" Pearl argued, but Khan shut her down.

259

"I agree with Finn, and this is enough town hall meeting for one night."

Pearl angled her head. "But there are still so many things for us to discuss."

"Discussions are good. That's how we broaden our minds," Athena added.

Khan answered in a flat tone. "My mind is stretched plenty and I listened to you for half an hour, that's enough." As to underline that the meeting was over, Khan leaned toward Archer. "I want to hear about your plans for the survival camp."

My focus changed to Finn, who was stretching his legs and said, "Hey, Marco, did you sign up for a Motlander wife yet?"

Marco, the only single adult in the room, shook his head. "No. I have my hopes on winning a million dollars like Magni did when he won Laura."

"Magni, did you hear that?" Finn waited for Magni to join the two men. "Marco wants to go your route and fight in a tournament rather than sign up for a Motlander wife."

"Good for you." Magni patted the young man's shoulder. "How old are you again?"

"Twenty."

"Then you have plenty of time. Don't rush into marriage. Especially not with a Motlander."

"What's wrong with us Motlanders?" Shelly asked.

Magni rolled his eyes. "Don't even get me started."

Khan looked up from his conversation with Archer. "I heard that. Careful what you say, Magni. You're surrounded by Motlander women and their husbands."

"So what? Do you think I'm afraid of any of you?"

"All I'm saying is that you'd never allow anyone to be disrespectful to Laura. Don't think we're any different with our wives."

"That's right, and there's four of us to beat some manners into you," Boulder added.

"Make that three," Finn waved a hand dismissively in the air. "You know my policy. I never fight."

"Not even to defend the honor of Athena?" Marco asked with an incredulous glance in Finn's direction.

Finn gave the young man a grin. "Don't get me wrong, if someone physically touched her, I would stab a syringe into their eye. But Athena is a spiritual gangster like me. Mentally, she wears a bulletproof vest and Magni's opinion of her makes no difference to her." Finn looked proud when he nodded to Athena. "Isn't that right, babe?"

Athena gave him a soft reassuring smile in response.

"It would be pointless for any of you men to fight Magni," Pearl said in a matter-of-fact tone. "By being rude to us Motlanders as a group, he's being rude to his own wife too."

Magni stiffened. "Why? What are you talking about? Laura is a *Northlander*," he exclaimed and looked from Pearl to me with confusion.

Flames shot up my neck, and licking my chapped lips I exchanged a panicked glance with Pearl, who shouldn't have dropped that bomb right now.

"I'm so sorry," Pearl breathed. "I thought he knew."

"*Laura.*" The way Magni said my name, in a deep voice, sounded like a warning.

"Ehm." I coughed from the thorns on the words I had to force out. "It's true."

A vein near Magni's temple popped out and his facial color grew crimson red. I had seen him throw tantrums many times, but seeing him too mad to speak was new and terrifying.

With a shaky voice, I explained. "The thing is... I was granted citizenship when I lived in the Motherlands."

Magni's hands were pressed against his thighs in tight fists, his lips formed a grim line, and he looked at me with disgust.

"I'm still a Northlander too," I called after him when he stormed out. "*I'm both*."

The front door to the school slammed hard and the rest of us stood for a few seconds, collectively holding our breaths.

"You shouldn't have told him that," Khan reprimanded Pearl.

"I'm sorry!" she repeated. "It just slipped out."

"Let me go talk to him," Finn suggested and moved to the door.

"No!" Khan took a step forward. "I know Magni and right now he needs time to calm down."

"Why is he so mad about you being a Motlander?" Shelly asked.

I closed my eyes, unable to express in words what I felt on an instinctual level.

Athena answered for me. "Shelly, try to see it from Magni's point of view. He has been raised to see us Motlanders as the enemy. To hear that Laura crossed over to become one of us must have felt like the ultimate betrayal to him."

"I didn't cross over. It was just a formality for me to live there. I've always been a Northlander."

"That's right, and we're not the enemy," Shelly pointed out. "I don't understand what Magni's problem is."

"His problem," Khan said dryly with an undertone of annoyance, "is that Magni's life revolves around his role as the defender of the last free men. He doesn't like the influence you Motlanders have over us, and he doesn't trust you." Khan gave Pearl a sideways glance. "To learn that your wife has been keeping something this big from you, and that the person you consider your adversary knew about it, would be a blow to any of us."

Sympathetic glances met me from the women, and Christina placed an arm around me. "He'll get over it. You know Magni; he's a hothead."

I nodded, but inside I knew this time things were different. Everyone had a breaking point, and my gut told me Magni had reached his.

"Fuck me." Marco ran to the window. "Magni's drone is lifting. He's taking off."

Finn walked over to stand next to Marco, looking at Magni's red drone flying away from us. "Maybe he'll really go to Alaska this time."

I was so used to Finn making fun that it hit me hard how serious he sounded this time. With my eyes large and my body stiff, as if rigor mortis had just set in, I stood with an equal amount of despair and disbelief.

"Don't worry," Boulder said and walked over to stand next to Marco by the window. "He'll be back. As long as Laura is here, he'll always come back."

I recognized the same doubt on Khan's face that I felt myself.

The last pieces of string holding Magni and me together had been brutally snapped just a few minutes ago. For the first time, I felt the painful desperation he must have felt when I left him without a goodbye seven months ago. I sucked in a shallow breath that failed to fill my lungs. The strings that had once bonded us were now suffocating me and I couldn't speak.

"You look sick, Laura. Do you need to sit down?" Pearl and Athena led me to a chair. "You need to take a deep breath, honey, you're pale as a corpse." I tasted the salty taste of tears in the back of my throat and tried to focus on their blurry faces through my wet eyes.

My voice broke and my chest felt like it weighed a thousand pounds when I whispered, "He's gone. I lost Magni!"

The fact that none of the women contradicted me made it sink in deeper. Magni was gone and he wasn't coming back to me.

CHAPTER 30
Alaska

Magni

I had come to Alaska to make the pain stop.

But even though the shitty, small cabin I'd moved into three weeks ago provided cover from the cold, the snow, and the wind, it did nothing to stop the pain of defeat.

My pride was hurting, and my sense of justice was destroyed.

For as long as I could remember, Khan and I had fought to expose anyone who was a threat to the rule of the Northlands. Any talk about democracy was considered treason and the person spewing such poisonous thoughts would be dealt with as a rebel.

So how the fuck did my brother end up marrying a woman like Pearl? Others had died for whispering about change. She spoke the words out loud like a proclamation of doom, and Khan allowed it.

Tramping through the snow, my warm breath stood out in clouds of moisture. I had to turn around soon or find my way back in the darkness.

Hungry and feeling angry with the world, I kept going. The days of breakfast buffets, room service, and delicious dinners prepared by the chefs at the Gray Mansion were gone.

Alaska offered the solitude I'd wanted, but my diet had become meager and unvaried. I'd never thought I'd miss vegetables.

For three weeks I'd survived on melted snow and a deer I shot on my first day here. Now, I was out hunting again, freezing my butt off, and hating life.

For the last three weeks, I'd been going over how everything fell apart from the moment Christina Sanders crossed into the Northlands. In hindsight, we should have sent her back as soon as we learned she was a woman.

I blamed Christina for putting thoughts into Laura's head.

I blamed Laura for running away to the Motherlands and for lying to me about becoming a Motlander.

I blamed Pearl for manipulating my brother into marrying her.

I blamed Khan for being weak and not seeing through Pearl's soft words.

My list was long and right now, I blamed myself that I hadn't gone fishing instead of hunting for meat. The snow was too fucking deep and I hadn't seen any signs of deer or elk today at all.

Turning back, I reached down and scooped a handful of snow into my mouth. It wouldn't do much for my hunger and I'd have to find another way of getting food. People who lived up here had spent the summer stocking up to survive the winter. Only a moron or a desperate man would come here with nothing but his clothes and boots. The last description fit me.

How long have I been out hunting?

My reflex of looking down to my wristband hadn't left me despite the fact that it'd been three weeks since I took my wristband off.

Khan would have been able to track me with it, and I wanted to be left alone. That's why I had parked my drone further south and bought an old drone to take me here.

As I climbed over a fallen tree, my eyes caught something that made me sneak closer to investigate. The roots of the large tree formed a cover and inside it lay a hibernating bear.

My stomach rumbled and I lifted my gun, pointing it at the bear's head.

With my finger on the trigger, I hesitated as a pair of large blue eyes popped into my mind. Mila would be devastated if she could see what I was about to do.

Swallowing hard, I focused on my hunger, but it still didn't feel right to kill a sleeping animal.

Who might be pregnant, a voice that sounded a lot like Mila's pointed out in my mind. It wasn't long ago we had talked about bear cubs and how they were born around the end of January while their moms were still hibernating.

This is such bullshit. Mila might love animals, but she wouldn't want me to die of hunger either.

As if I'd lost my fucking mind, I began talking out loud to myself.

"I can't eat a whole fucking bear and it would be too heavy to drag back to the cabin anyway."

My hunger didn't care for the excuses and to make a point, my stomach gave a loud growl of complaint.

"I could cut off a leg. That should be plenty of meat." Leaning my head back, I looked up to the sky, wondering how long it would take me to cut off the leg. "I don't have time, it's getting dark soon. And what if the blood from the leg attracts wolves? I don't need to become the hunted one."

Lowering my gun, I hissed out, "Fuck!"

I couldn't kill the bear; I would have to find another way of feeding my growling stomach.

The hike back to the cabin should have taken an hour, but without my wristband to guide me, I had to rely on the marks I'd noticed on the way here. It would have been fine, if the snow hadn't started falling so hard that I couldn't see a thing.

Lost, cold, and miserable, I promised myself that if I made it back to the cabin, I'd fly south to buy provisions. The downside to being recognized was nothing compared to the chance of dying alone in the wilderness.

That's why the next morning, I found myself back in the small rural town where I'd left my drone and bought the old one that had taken me to the cabin. *Fresh food and friendly service*, it said on a handmade sign outside the only store in town. I didn't find either, when I entered the shithole of a shed that was half empty and only had canned, frozen, or processed food. Picking up a bag of nuts, I checked the expiration date and put them down again. March 2437 was nine months ago.

"No need to be greedy," the old man who worked here said in a gruff voice when I emptied his shelf of the only eight beers he had out.

"I'm thirsty – do you have more in the back?"

"No."

I could tell a liar when I met one and insisted. "Would you go check?"

His upper lip lifted in a grimace of irritation as he shuffled his feet past me toward a door in the back of the store. I wrinkled my nose at the stench of alcohol and unwashed hair and clothes that reeked from him. Not that I smelled too good myself, but that old fucker was disgusting with his greasy hair, his beer-reddened nose, and the rotten teeth that showed when he spoke to me.

"Don't think I don't know who you are. All high and mighty, coming in here giving orders as if I'm your personal slave or something."

"I only asked if you had more beers."

"More beers, more beers..." he mocked and disappeared behind the door.

Less than five seconds later he returned. "Nope."

"You sure you don't have any more beer?"

"That's right, *your highness*."

Marching past him, I slammed the door open to see for myself. As I suspected, he was lying.

"That beer isn't for sale," he said behind me.

"Why the hell not?"

267

"It's for other customers." He ended the sentence by muttering something under his breath that I didn't hear.

"What did you say?"

With his bent-over posture, the greasy old man turned his back on me and moved away.

In two quick steps, I grabbed his shoulder and swung him around. "Answer me."

"The beer is not for sale. Go back to the palace. I'm sure you people have more than enough."

I narrowed my eyes. "Careful what you say, old man."

He smirked. "Or what? Are you going to kill me? I'm not scared of dying. It would be a fucking relief compared to living this miserable life."

"Your misery isn't my fault."

He scoffed. "Then whose fault is it? Why do you get to have a wife, live in a palace, and own that expensive red drone that you hide behind Elton's house? It's not my fault that I wasn't born with a silver spoon in my fucking ass like you were."

"I won a tournament," I said through gritted teeth and shoved him away from me. "Men have gone from rags to riches plenty of times. If you didn't win that's on *you*. Unless you entered and fought, I don't want to hear your complaints."

"Tournaments cost money and you only end up dead." He flicked his finger up and down to underline his point. "Rich people should be forced to share their money with the rest of us."

"Right. Because you're so fucking great at sharing. Maybe you wouldn't be so poor if you sold your beers instead of drinking them all yourself."

"Fucking royal prince, coming here to lecture me." The old idiot muttered and shuffled his feet again when he moved away from me. "Thinks he's better than us."

"You're damn right I'm better than you. At least I clean my teeth, and I don't talk to myself like a crazy person."

The minute I said it, I remembered talking to myself in the forest. *Shit!*

While tearing food items from his shelves, I lashed out at him. "You're just a bitter old man who's lost touch with reality. Why don't you take some responsibility instead?"

"It's not *my* fault. It's their fault." He pointed out the window as if talking about the whole world, and when he thought I wasn't looking he pulled up a beer from under his counter and emptied it.

"He's just a drunken bastard," I muttered to calm myself down, and frowned when I realized I'd just spoken out loud to myself again.

"You can only buy two of those." The old grease ball sneered when I emptied his stack of dried beef sticks.

"I'm getting all of them." I smacked the items I'd found onto his counter and he rang them up with grunts and low cuss words.

"I dare you to say that louder to my face, old man."

Lucky for him, he had enough self-control to keep his mouth shut.

I left there with enough provisions to last me a week. After loading my things in my drone, I looked over at the store and was tempted to walk back to correct the *fresh food and friendly service* sign to a more honest version saying *food and no service.*

"Fuck, I really need to get my shit together."

A crazy person like that wouldn't rile my feathers on a normal day, so why did I let him get under my skin like that?

The answer was evident, even to me. That crazy, bitter man in the store would be me in thirty years if I stayed here. I was only three weeks into my solitude and I'd already begun talking to myself. If I weren't careful, soon I'd be blaming the whole world for my misery instead of taking responsibility.

I already am, a voice in the back of my head whispered, but I wasn't ready to hear it and pushed it down. After all, I wouldn't be in this bloody situation if it weren't because of Christina, Pearl, Khan, Laura, and all the other people. It was all *their* fault.

CHAPTER 31
Missing Magni

Laura

Pearl kept me busy and I knew why. She didn't want me to sink deeper into my depression over losing Magni. Over the last month I'd practiced functioning like a normal person – talking, eating, and sleeping – while the real Laura lay bleeding in a corner of my soul. I would smile but there was no joy. I would ask questions but there was no real interest. I was playing my role and keeping up a façade for survival.

For a long time, I'd been determined not to be controlled and bossed around by Magni. Now that he was gone, I realized how much easier he had made my life.

With Magni I'd never worried about my safety. His warm body had given me comfort at night, and at day he'd been my protector. Even when he was gone on missions, his eye for detail had made sure that I was protected by his most trusted soldiers.

My façade of bravado was draining, but I kept it up for Mila, who had her own grief and didn't understand why he never called or came to visit her anymore.

The truth was that I was a wreck.

At night I cried into Magni's t-shirt. I tossed and turned, with my mind going over everything that I wished I could take back or do in a different way. My appetite was gone and I blamed myself for losing him. April and Laila Michelle blamed me too. My sister had painted worst case scenarios about never seeing Magni again, and insisted that my best option was to remarry. "Maybe your next husband can control you better," she'd said and the idea of someone else claiming ownership of me, made me sick. I didn't want to remarry. I wanted Magni, but April was stating the obvious. Women didn't live alone in the Northlands, and if Magni didn't come back for me, I would be forced to marry someone else. The thought made my stomach cramp with pain and my head was spinning with plans on how to escape if that happened. Maybe I could go to Alaska and search for Magni. Maybe I could somehow make him care about me again.

"Laura, did you hear me?" Pearl asked and touched my elbow.

I blinked my eyes. "What? Sorry, I just lost my concentration for a second."

"Do you want to take a break? We've been working hard all morning."

"No, it's fine."

Pearl leaned back in her seat and looked out the window. "I know what we should do. Let's get our jackets and take a walk and talk in the park. I could use some fresh air."

A guard followed us at a distance as we strolled through the winter garden.

Linking her arm with mine, Pearl spoke in a concerned tone. "I worry about Khan."

"Oh?"

"He doesn't get more than three or four hours of sleep at night. Magni left a large hole to fill. It would be better if he hadn't left so abruptly. There are rumors among the soldiers."

I nodded. "Yes, I heard. How could they think that Khan would hurt Magni?"

"The timing of Magni's disappearance is just very unfortunate. With the eight traitors arrested for trying to make Magni the ruler, it would look to everyone like Magni has gone missing because Khan felt threatened by him."

"Are things calming down?" I asked.

"No. Khan is busy putting out fires, but to be honest I worry how much longer he can keep up this pace."

"What are you going to do?"

Pearl's eyes were on the path in front of us. "I'm going to do everything I can to show the people that positive change is upon them. I've arranged for the press to document the first meeting between a Motlander applicant and the five most compatible men that she was paired with."

"But Shelly said the matching program isn't ready yet."

"True. We are working with the beta model, but we have to start somewhere, and everyone is growing impatient." Pearl turned her head to look at me with eyes full of worry. "I'm afraid if we don't give them what they want, we could be in danger."

"You think the people will overthrow Khan?"

"I hope not. But when I ask him about it, he always tries to change the subject." She sighed. "He misses Magni."

"We all do. I worry about Mila."

"Yes, me too. Kya told me that you let her sleep with you last week when you stayed at the school."

I nodded. "I know what it's like to lose a mother, and I can't even imagine how she feels now that Magni left without a goodbye. I've told Mila it's not her fault, but you know how children are. She thinks there's something wrong with her."

"Poor girl. And you, how are you holding up?"

"Fine," I lied.

"I'm grateful for the energy you put into the integration projects. Khan and I were talking about naming the first mixed school after you."

"You don't have to do that. I'm so excited that the next generation of Motlander girls will be able to attend normal schools with the boys."

"I wouldn't call them normal schools yet; let's stick with experimental." Pearl tightened her hold upon my arm. "I like your idea about bumping up the Motlanders from the application list who are bringing their children with them. If there are any teachers on the list, they should be prioritized as well. Once we know which Nman they will be matched up with, we'll have a geographic place to locate the schools."

"Pearl, are you still intending to let the public know about the experimental school on Victoria's Island?"

"Yes, we're letting one camera crew in to film and shoot interviews and show how well the children are getting along. I'm hoping it will assuage the people when they see the progress that we're making."

"But aren't you worried about the safety of the children? I mean if people get curious and want to go see it for themselves?"

Pearl waved her hand dismissively. "Don't worry. The location will remain a secret for now."

"Good. And what about Erika? She told me you invited her to help out."

The water fountain in front of us was shut off for the winter. Walking around it, we made a loop and headed back to the mansion. "Working with us helps Erika focus on something else than what happened to Mr. Zobel." Pearl licked her dry lips. "It hasn't distracted her as much as I hoped, though. Erika withdrew her request for Khan to show Mr. Zobel mercy."

I slowed our pace and gave her a puzzled expression. "The man was a traitor who tried to kill Khan. He's not worthy of her mercy."

Pearl gave me a reproachful look. "Laura, you Northlanders can be so hard. I will never approve of the death penalty."

"You're not alone. Many here consider death too easy a way out. They think it would be better to let the criminals rot in a cell."

"That's not what I meant. A society should always try to rehabilitate. No good has ever come from harsh punishments."

I gave her an incredulous look, silently asking *Are you serious?*

Pearl sighed. "Laura, surely you can see that punishing people only pushes them further into the abyss. What they need is to be invited back into the light."

I rolled my eyes. "You Motlanders are so naïve."

"Would you rather have me speak like Erika? Once she recovered from the initial denial of Mr. Zobel's betrayal, she declared that she would kill him *herself.*"

I gave a firm nod. "Of course, and I would be glad to help her."

"*Laura,*" Pearl exclaimed. "Don't say that. You couldn't live with yourself if you took someone's life."

"Yes. I could." My tone was pragmatic. "If they wanted to hurt me and my family, I'd rather kill them first."

Pearl shook her head with a sad expression. "Sometimes it feels like we're decades apart."

I snorted. "Let me guess; you think you're more evolved than us?"

"When you speak like people from medieval times, then yes. An eye for an eye never worked for any society. All it did was blind people."

We'd hit a cultural wall that neither of us knew how to climb. Still hooked at our elbows, we walked back to the mansion in silence.

When we reached the building, a knock on a window made us look up to see Khan waving at us from his office with a serious expression on his face.

Waving back, I commented, "He looks exhausted."

"Told you."

He signaled for us to come inside, and we walked into his office. Khan had lost weight, his olive skin didn't have its usual glow, and he had prominent black circles under his eyes.

"Do you have an update for me?" he asked and kissed Pearl.

"Yes, and I'll give it to you after you've slept."

"I don't have time to sleep, sweetheart." He gave her a tired smile and turned to me. "Laura, could I ask you to check in on my mother? She's not taking Magni's disappearance well and with the loss of Zobel she'll need our support."

"Of course. I promised Mila that I'd come to see her later and that she could sleep with me in Magni's cabin tonight, but I have a little time before that."

"Good. And what did you decide about the first matching?" Khan trailed off and lifted his head when loud voices were heard outside the office.

My ears stiffened as well. "It sounds like someone is fighting."

"Get into the saferoom, *now*!" Khan was quick to press a point on the underside of his desk, and a part of his book cabinet popped out, revealing a room behind it. He was pushing Pearl inside it when the door swung open and four soldiers stormed in.

"Oh, thank God, it's you – what's going on?" Khan asked Lieutenant Franklin, one of Magni's trusted Huntsmen. "We heard fighting – are we under attack?"

Franklin and the other three men surrounded us and raised their weapons.

"What the fuck?" Khan pushed Pearl behind him. Fury raged on his face when Franklin stepped closer and kicked the bookshelf closed.

I didn't think but acted on instinct when I attacked the soldier holding a gun on me. Instinctively, I knew he wouldn't shoot a woman, but I should have known that he

276

was trained for combat. I fought with everything I had learned and quickly got the feeling that he was only defending himself but doing nothing to hurt me.

Twice, I got out of the hold he had on me, and one of the other soldiers got impatient.

"For fuck's sake, Jacob, she's only a woman."

The soldier grabbed at my arm, but I managed to twist my body and reach for a marble cube from Khan's desk that I smacked on his jaw.

He cursed out loud and his hand flew to his face. "Grab her."

Two other soldiers came at me at the same time, and I didn't stand a chance.

"Let go of me," I snarled with adrenaline pumping through my body.

"It's okay, Laura, don't fight," Khan said to calm me, but when I looked over at him, he stood staring into a gun, using his body to shield Pearl.

"What are you doing, Franklin? What is this, a coup?" Khan was focused on the lieutenant in front of him.

"No. It's a rescue mission."

Pearl and I exchanged confused looks.

"Tell us where you're keeping, Magni, and we'll let you go."

"Have you lost your mind?" Khan's voice was seething with anger. "Put that gun down, right now."

Franklin licked his lips and narrowed his eyes. "Can't do that. Here's how it's going to go. Either you tell us where Magni is or we'll search through the mansion."

"Magni isn't here," Pearl said.

"Then where is he?"

"Alaska somewhere."

Franklin shook his head. "That's a lie. Magni wouldn't leave without saying goodbye to us. Did you kill him?"

"No, I didn't kill my brother. He went to Alaska."

"It's the truth," Pearl exclaimed.

"Take a seat, all of you." Franklin waved his gun to a sofa that stood by the window.

"You're making the biggest mistake of your career," Khan warned him, but the young lieutenant didn't let that stop him from giving an order to the other men in the room. "Take the others and search the mansion."

"I'll have to kill you for this, you know that, right?"

"Khan, stop it." Pearl put her hand on his thigh. "Now isn't the time."

I agreed with her, but understood how hard it was for Khan to be passive and do nothing.

"For the last time. Put the gun down!" Khan hissed.

Franklin sat down on the edge of Khan's desk and lowered his gun. "This would all be over a lot sooner if you told us where the Commander is."

Khan's answer came pressed out through his teeth. "For the hundredth time: Magni is in Alaska."

"Then tell us where so we can confirm it."

"I already sent an officer from the security team to locate him and deliver a message to him."

"And?" Franklin asked while I leaned back to see Khan's expression better. This was news to me.

"The officer was able to track down his drone and wristband, but no one in the small town would tell him where Magni had gone from there."

Franklin stood up. "They have to know."

"According to them he bought an old wreck of a drone and took off."

"He talked about a cabin?" I said. "Do you know which cabin that might be?"

"We've already been to a number of cabins. So far no luck."

"Hmm," Franklin scratched his dark beard. "If what you're saying is true, I'll go myself and interrogate the people who sold Magni the drone. My methods are different from those of the security team."

278

"There will be no torture," Pearl exclaimed, with a finger pointed at Franklin.

He straightened his back. "I'll do whatever it takes to get information on the Commander."

Pearl looked baffled. "Why in the world would you risk your career and life to find Magni?"

"The Commander would do the same for us."

One of the three men who'd come in earlier returned. "Nothing so far, sir. He's not being kept in his suite as you suspected. We'll keep searching."

Franklin lifted his chin in a nod. "Why don't you tell them what the Commander did for you last year?"

The man was wearing his uniform, and straightened his back. "The Commander saved my life."

I leaned forward. "What happened?"

"Three other Huntsmen and I were on a mission to stop a group who were believed to be conspiring against Lord Khan. It was a set-up and we were captured." He scratched his shoulder. "The rebels demanded Lord Khan in exchange for us and when we insisted that would never happen, they tortured us. They were mean motherfuckers and had already cut off Newman's ear when Magni came to our rescue. He convinced them that their chances of getting you to come in person were better with him as the hostage than us."

My hand closed in a fist, and my breathing was shallow as I listened.

"They released us, although two of us had to crawl out of there after the severe torture we'd gone through in the few hours they had us."

"They smashed your knees in." Khan nodded as if remembering something.

"Not mine, that was Kennedy's, Lord. With me they broke both my feet."

279

Pearl gasped. "That's horrible." She looked like she was about to cry. "Why would anyone be so cruel to another human being?"

The man frowned. "So I couldn't run or fight," he said in a tone that revealed that he thought it was self-explanatory. "The Commander took our place and saved our lives that night."

"And that's why we're doing the same for him now," Franklin said. "Commander Magni wouldn't hesitate if one of his men was in peril, and we're not stopping either. Not until we find out what happened to him."

"I told you. He's cooling down his anger in Alaska somewhere." Khan leaned his head into his hands, his elbows resting on his knees.

"With all due respect, Lord Khan. The Commander would never stay away this long without getting in contact. It's been a month."

"He had his reasons." A sideways glance from Khan told me that he was blaming me for Magni's impulsive decision.

"It was my fault," I admitted. "We had a fight and he left in anger."

Khan shook his head. "I think we all contributed, but you don't owe them an explanation."

"If he's not in the mansion, we'll go to Alaska to track him down. We'll keep you here all night until we find him."

Khan closed his eyes and leaned his head back. "I don't have time for this shit."

"Maybe the universe is forcing you to take a break."

Khan groaned. "Don't start, Pearl."

"I tried to get you to slow down and you wouldn't. It took a man with a gun to get you to sit down. I doubt it's a coincidence."

Khan was making circles on his temples with both index fingers. "Your loyalty to Magni is admirable, Lieutenant Franklin, but you really didn't think this through, did you? How do you plan to tell Magni that you held a gun to my head and attacked two females in his family, one being his wife?"

Franklin exchanged a glance with the other soldier, but didn't respond.

"What did you think was going to happen after this? We're not hiding the Commander, and since this is not a coup, you have to let us go at some point."

"We would rather suffer the consequences of being wrong about Magni needing our help than live with ourselves if we were right. As I said, the Commander would do the same for us."

"Yeah, he's a real fucking hero." Khan threw his hands up in the air. "Just know this: if Magni was here right now, he would kick your sorry ass for wasting our time like this. And so would I, if I didn't have two women to protect."

Franklin frowned. "We don't wish to hurt any of you, but we're ready to do whatever it takes to find our Commander."

I sat back in the sofa and crossed my legs. "Let's hope you succeed."

CHAPTER 32
Hero in Hiding

Magni

If not for my fucking pride, I would've gone back by now. It had been more than a month, and I missed Laura and Mila like crazy.

They were the first thing on my mind when I woke up and the last thing when I went to sleep. It was a constant state of worrying and longing for them. On my good days I thought about going back and convinced myself they would be happy to see me.

On my bad days, I was sure they were better off without me.

The solitude of Alaska left me alone with nothing but the torture chamber of self-reflection.

Like most of the men I'd ever interrogated during my career, my vanity and pride had refused to cooperate and admit to any blame. Instead, I'd stayed busy, focusing on improving my already great shape with an obsessive determination. I had walked on my hands, done push-ups, climbed trees, and been out hiking every day.

After four weeks of stubborn denial and resistance I'd begun to crack with the humbling realization that I was a giant shithead.

I'd promised Mila that I'd be there for her, and instead I was hiding like a coward.

I cringed to my toes when I thought about my reaction to learning about Laura having citizenship in the Motherlands. Why hadn't I spoken to her about it? How would I live with myself if anything happened to Laura or Mila and I wasn't there to protect them?

For years, people around me had made excuses for me, allowing me to throw tantrums like I was a fucking three-year-old. I was embarrassed to think about all the times I had thrown things around, and verbally abused people.

Two days ago, while dragging myself through deep snow, an epiphany had suddenly struck. I doubted that any of the Motlander women could have been more insightful than I was at that moment. For days I'd been asking myself why the fuck I had to be such a hothead, and then a childhood memory offered me an answer.

"He's only five and he doesn't like potatoes. Can't he eat the other things on his plate?" Dina's eyes were downturned and her hands were trembling a bit. Standing up to our father wasn't easy.

"Stay out of this. Magni is a big boy and he doesn't need his sister to protect him." Our father resumed eating and when he looked up again, I still hadn't touched the mountain of potatoes in front of me. Khan and my mother were quiet and kept their gazes down. When our father was in a certain mood, it was best not to speak or we would set him off in one of his explosive fits of rage.

"Eat the fucking food," he repeated.

I picked up a potato and took a bite, but the damn thing grew in my mouth and I couldn't swallow.

Dina offered me her napkin when my cheeks grew to double size and I was close to throwing up.

With a loud thud, my dad's elbow hit the table as he leaned forward with his eyes narrowed and his knife stabbing through the air. "Did you just spit out your food, boy?"

"I hate potatoes."

"That's too bad, because you're going to eat every one of them, including the part you spit out."

"Marcus," my mom said in a pleading voice.

"Don't!" He gave her a hard stare. "If you think eating potatoes is the worst that will happen to him, you're wrong.

Magni will grow up to be a warrior and he'll endure torture and pain like a real man."

"But he's so little," Dina defended me.

"Eat the fucking potatoes!" My dad's hand flew to my neck and forced my head down to my plate.

It made me see red. I knocked the plate from the dinner table and kicked the chair back to get up.

"I'm not eating them," I shouted and swung my hand across the table, sending my plate, glass, fork, and knife into the wall.

"Magni," my mom screamed and reached for me.

That only made me scream louder, trampling on the potatoes that were now on the floor, and picking one up to throw again.

It was my father's deep laughter that got my attention, and my hand with the potato stalled mid-air.

"That's my boy. Did you ever see such fire and strength in a five-year-old?"

My mom gave a strained smile.

"You're not going to allow any man to mess with you, are you, Magni?" My father was still laughing and used his finger as a hook to reel me in. "Soon, grown men are gonna fear you, my son." His large hand tousled my hair and everyone relaxed again. "You chose his name well, Erika."

My mother smiled. "Yes, he lives up to it."

"Tell me the story about my name again." It was one of my favorites.

"Magni was the son of Thor and the strongest among the Norse Gods," Khan said in a flat tone and rolled his eyes. "We've told you a million times."

I lifted my chin, declaring, "I'm going to be the strongest too."

Even my sister was smiling now. "I know you will, Magni."

I plumped myself down on the small bed in the cabin, pushing the childhood memory away. No wonder I'd

284

become so temperamental, when it had been a source of amusement for my father. Problem was that even though I understood it, I had no clue how to change it.

Closing my eyes, I directed my thoughts to one of my favorite memories instead, bringing back images from my first night with Laura.

"I choose Magni Aurelius." April's words made my body tense up. I hadn't waited this long to marry the wrong sister.

Laura's head turned to her twin and her eyes narrowed a little. She wasn't happy about April's choice.

Khan stood between the two brides and us ten champions. He knew I wanted Laura. We had talked about it many times.

My lips were pressed together and I was breathing through my nose. Why the fuck had he asked April before Laura? No one in the audience would have noticed if he'd made a small error and asked the younger twin before the older. What was an age difference of seven minutes anyway?

Laura was watching the nine champions left to choose from. I wanted her to look at me, but her eyes stopped and rested on the man to my right.

No no no... I wanted to shout for her to pick me, but speaking could get me disqualified.

"I choose..." she began before she trailed off and lowered her eyes.

I'd never used the word please in my life, but at that moment, I chanted it over and over, willing her to pick me.

As if hearing my thoughts, Laura lifted her face and locked eyes with me. Please, please, please pick me, I repeated on the inside, not speaking a word.

"I choose Magni Aurelius too."

At the wedding reception everyone was talking about the cat fight that Khan had to break up between the two sisters. Men gave me nods of respect and envious smiles when they saw my arm around Laura. Both twins were beautiful, but to me Laura was the most incredible woman in the world. Her innocence intrigued me but it was the strength that shone from those pretty blue eyes of hers that had me fucking obsessed with her.

We didn't stay long at the reception. I wanted her for myself and led her to my suite in the Gray Mansion.

"Your new home," I said and let her take in the large room with the fine furniture. "Make yourself comfortable, what is mine is yours."

Laura looked like a lost swan as she stood in her white dress taking in everything around her.

"Here." I handed her the glass of wine that I'd just poured and took one for myself. "Cheers to our new lives as husband and wife."

Her hands trembled a little when she raised the glass and took a sip. "It's very nice here."

"Uh-huh." Every nerve ending on my body was on alert. In my mind we'd consummated our marriage a hundred times, but this was real life. Now that the door was closed and Laura was all mine, I wanted to experience everything I had dreamed of with her. The thought alone was more intoxicating than the wine in our glasses. After so many years of waiting, she had chosen me and soon she'd give herself to me.

"Are you nervous?"

Laura shook her head but the way she licked her lips and kept her gaze on my shoulder revealed that she was.

"I'm not going to hurt you."

"I know," she whispered.

"Are you tired?"

"No, I'm wide awake." She leaned her head back, emptying her glass.

"Do you want more wine?"

"No." Putting her glass down, she lifted her gaze to meet mine. "I'm ready."

"You're ready?" Butterflies spread in my stomach at the resolve in her eyes.

"Yes."

Part of me wanted to ask her what she was ready for, but teasing her wouldn't be fair. Instead I put my own glass down and led her to the bed at an unhurried pace. "You want to consummate our union." It wasn't a question, and I followed up by leaning down to kiss Laura for the first time since the wedding ceremony. God, the sensation of her soft lips on mine was more divine than I could have imagined.

"I have wanted to do this for a long time," I whispered and kissed her again – this time a little harder with my hand snaking around her waist, pulling her closer.

Laura made the sweetest sounds as our kissing grew deeper. She was like the most delicious dessert: every bite an explosion of sweetness on my tongue.

"I want you out of your dress." My voice was raspy with need, and she stiffened a little. "It's okay, I just want to see you."

Laura was compliant when I turned her around and opened her dress in the back. She kept her gaze down when I slid the dress off her shoulders and let it fall to the floor. My experience with women's underwear was nonexistent, and I had to study her bra a little before I undid it.

My hands slid down her back, feeling the creamy skin against my fingertips. Planting small kisses down her spine, I inhaled her feminine scent as if it was a fragrance designed to enslave me.

Every part of me tingled when I slid my fingers inside her panties and pulled the white silk fabric down over her delicious ass. It was like unpacking a gift that I'd waited twenty-nine years for.

Squatting down behind her, I let Laura's underwear fall to the pool of white fabric already by her feet. And then I looked up to see the whole vision of my gorgeous wife, naked with only her long red hair to cover her shoulders.

Laura was leaning on her left leg, her right knee slightly bent and her heel lifted just a bit. She didn't turn, but waited for my next move.

Her ass was magnificent and with my hands I made circles on it, feeling the fleshy part of her hips and buttocks.

"Laura."

"Hmm?" She still didn't turn.

Standing back up, I undressed myself, letting everything drop to the floor. Maybe she had hoped sex would be done in the darkness under the covers, but that wasn't what I wanted.

Turning her around I saw how perfect she was before I met her eyes. "I'm not going to hurt you," I repeated.

Laura's right hand was clenched around her left wrist. Her crimson cheeks made her large blue eyes stand out even more.

"Have you ever seen a naked man?"

She gave a small shake of her head, swallowed hard, and kept her stare fixed on my face.

"I've never seen a naked woman either."

We gave our eyes time to explore each other. My focus lingered on her breasts. They were fuller than I'd expected, and I couldn't wait to feel the weight of them in my hands.

The small sound she made had me look up to see her staring at my very erect cock.

"Do you want to touch it?"

With shallow breaths Laura tore her eyes away and held her position when I stepped a little closer.

I lifted her hands and placed them on my chest. At first, she didn't move them, but when I began touching her shoulders and breasts, she reciprocated.

"Why do men have nipples?" she asked in a low voice. "I always wondered about that."

I gave a small smile and leaned in to kiss her neck and jawline. "Don't you like my nipples?"

"Yes, you're very attractive, it was just a silly thought."

"You think I'm attractive?" My hand fisted into her long hair, pulling her head back a little. My mouth was licking and kissing her neck.

"Uh-huh." Laura's eyes were closed and she sucked in air when I closed the gap between us. My cock pressed against her belly and it gave me chills to feel her skin rubbing against it every time I moved a little.

"I think you're fucking gorgeous."

Laura moaned in reply, and I couldn't stop myself from bending down and lifting her onto my hips.

Her arms wrapped around my neck and we kissed as I carried her to the bed. My head was full of things I wanted to experience with her and the warrior part of me wanted to conquer and howl out my victory. This woman wasn't just the prettiest, she was loyal too.

So many questions were on my tongue, but I didn't ask her if she remembered making me a promise of marriage almost a decade ago. If she had forgotten, I didn't want to know. Loyalty was everything to me and at that moment Laura was the loyal partner I'd waited for my whole life.

She smiled at me when I spread her legs and kissed my way down to her brown curls, eager to taste her.

"What are you doing?" she asked in a raspy voice and gasped when I licked her.

I didn't answer her but tightened my grip around her thighs, holding her in place.

"Oh shit," she moaned, and arched her back.

The taste of her was nothing like I'd expected. I had once read a book that called it sweet honey, but whoever wrote that book either hadn't tasted honey or women. Laura's taste was pleasant, like a female nectar that couldn't be compared to anything I'd ever tasted before. Her moans intensified and she closed her eyes when my tongue circled her clit. She liked it; the research I'd done on sex between men and women had been right on that part.

"Scooch up on the bed," I instructed her and got up on my knees.

Lying on her back with her legs spread, Laura looked like a goddess. Her nervous smile, when I lay down on top of her, made my protective side flame up again.

"Are you okay?" I asked.

"Yes, I'm just not sure what to do."

"You don't have to do anything. I'll take care of you from now on, Laura."

"I meant about the consummation thing. I'm not sure if I'm supposed to do something."

"You can do whatever you like. With me you'll be safe."

Her hand lifted and she played with my hair. Even that small touch had my cock hammering with excitement. When I was around seventeen, I'd overheard my father give advice to a champion before his wedding night. "Don't make the mistake of waiting," he'd said and slammed the man's shoulder. "Establish your rights from the beginning and make sure she understands what you expect of her. You have the rest of your life to get to know each other; the breeding comes first."

I wasn't sure what he had meant when he said that the first time was always going to be bad for the bride, but I would do my best to make it tolerable for Laura.

Holding myself up on my elbows, I positioned myself and started pushing inside her.

Her eyebrows drew inward and she tensed up.

"Relax," I whispered and kissed her again, eagerness tearing me up from the inside.

We looked deep into each other's eyes, and the small nod that Laura gave me made my heart fucking burst with pride. That nod silently told me that she trusted me and that she wanted me to go on.

I pushed in deeper and pulled back a little, only to push in again. Being inside Laura was a thousand times better than having sex with a sex-bot. She was a real woman, with

290

a beauty mark on her arm, and a small scar on her chin that no one would notice unless they were as close to her as I was.

"Ohh." Her small moan made me almost lose my mind. There were so many things I wanted to try with her, but I'd promised myself that the first time between us would be about making her feel safe with me.

"We're going to be doing this a lot," I whispered into her ear and rotated my hips to get deeper inside her.

"I won't mind," she breathed and pressed her fingertips into my shoulder blades.

In my head, I checked off the box of establishing my rights. My woman understood that sex was expected of her and she was submitting herself to me.

Increasing the pace, I put my weight on my left elbow and took her hand. She intertwined our fingers and looked down at my lips with an invitation to kiss her again.

This time, I let my tongue slide inside her mouth and explored the feeling of our first French kiss.

Laura tightened her squeeze on my hand and moaned into my mouth, making my head feel like it was about to explode with pleasure. All my plans about being gentle and taking it slow were forgotten after that. My face grew hotter and perspiration formed on my forehead as I pumped in and out of her with speed and force.

"Get on your knees," I instructed her and pulled out to give her room to turn.

Laura complied, and the mere sight of her on all four in front of me, with her creamy ass welcoming me, made me smile. She was my reward for fighting in the tournament, and with deep satisfaction I pushed inside her from behind.

"Careful," she mumbled when I was a bit rough, boring my fingers into her hips and hammering my cock deep inside her.

My right hand smacked her fleshy cheek, making her jerk and look back at me with a raised eyebrow.

"Stand still and let me take you," I ordered, and her face softened a little.

"That's it, Laura, you're going to make me a good wife, aren't you?"

Her answer came out breathy: "Yes, Magni."

"And are you going to do as I tell you to?" I pushed in to the root of my cock and felt it hammering inside of her.

Laura leaned down on her elbows, making the sexiest arch that made her ass stand out in a perfect shape. "Yes, Magni."

"Good girl," I muttered and fucked my perfect wife until I came in an orgasm that had me groaning out her name.

Lying on the bed in the Alaska cabin, I rolled to a fetal position, trying to ease the pain in my chest. How had Laura gone from being such an obedient wife to becoming a constant challenge?

Even good memories, like my first time with Laura, left me unable to breathe and filled me with regret. I'd lost her and every other good thing in my life.

It was just as well no one could see how fucking pathetic I was, or how wet my pillow was in the mornings from crying in the night. I didn't cry during the day; my pride wouldn't allow it. But being stuck in this fucking cabin, with too much time to think, had forced me to face my demons and I was exhausted from battling them.

Because of my stinking pride, I'd doomed myself to a life in isolation and loneliness. If I stayed here, I would end up like that deranged store owner with nothing but bitterness and anger to keep me company.

This is stupid!

The longing to see Laura again and experience the magic of being close to her made me stand up.

It's too late, she doesn't love you anymore. It's better to stay away than have her pity you.

Pride made me sit down again and kick at the small table in front of me. I fucking hated this cabin and its

292

crappy furniture. I wanted my suite with a nice bathroom and a comfortable bed.

Even if Laura divorces you, it's better to go back than live in this shithole.

I stood up again, pushing my unruly hair back. My stomach was growling for food and the thought of going hunting in the snow was depressing. What I wouldn't give for a shower, some decent food, or a hug from Laura.

I wished that I weren't too fucking proud to go back.

If only pride were a physical opponent I could fight. Tearing the door open, I walked outside in the cold and screamed out my despair. Bending forward, I clenched my fists and emptied my lungs in a soul-wrenching scream that had me almost blue in the head from a lack of oxygen.

Birds lifted from the trees and took flight. For a second I wished I had wings and could escape too.

"I hate you, I hate you." My words were directed at my pride and an eerie laughter from within filled my head.

You're not going anywhere. You would rather rot here, than admit that you were wrong, and we both know it.

"I'm not staying here."

Images of my brother with Pearl as his co-ruler made me groan and pride laughed again.

You'll be Pearl's little errand boy if you go back.

I'd never fought a greater opponent or felt this beaten in my life. Pride was a sadist that taunted me with the power he held over me, pushing at every sore wound.

In return, I focused on Laura, Mila, and the few other people I loved. I would never see them again as long as I stayed here. Falling to my knees, my scream of pain morphed into a sob accompanied by snot and tears.

Pride mocked me: *Real men don't cry, Magni.*

"Shut the fuck up," I hissed. With the amount of pain I was in, I almost expected the snow around me to be red with blood, but pride didn't leave any trace in the white snow. With an evil laugh, Pride whispered back, *Laura chose the Motherlands – you weren't enough.*

"I hate you," I repeated.

I'm just protecting you my friend.

"No."

Stay here where no one can hurt you again.

It took everything I had to push back and ignore all the worst-case scenarios playing in my mind. Sucking in air as a fuel, I got up from the ground. "I'm going back," I declared.

Don't be stupid. You'll be ridiculed.

Dusting snow off my pants, I muttered, "I might be crazy enough to talk to myself, but I'm not stupid enough to stay in this miserable place for the rest of my life."

CHAPTER 33
Late Night Talks

Laura

Mila was sleeping with her head in my lap, and my fingers played with her long blonde hair.

"Do you want me to carry her to her bed?" Marco asked me.

It was only Shelly, Marco, Archer, Kya, and me left at the table and it was late. Mila had come in because of a nightmare, and I'd let her fall asleep in my lap.

"That's nice of you, Marco, but give me a few more minutes with her."

Kya, who sat next to me, caressed Mila's hair and smiled. "You and Mila have grown close."

"I feel closer to Magni when I'm with her, and she's so easy to love."

"Just don't take off like Magni did. Her small heart has suffered enough already."

Sitting on the long bench by the dining table, I leaned my head back against the wall. "Let's not talk about Magni."

Archer frowned. "I can't believe his men would storm the Mansion like that."

Kya looked over at her husband. "Didn't you hear that Laura doesn't want to talk about Magni?"

"But it's not fair that eight of our best Huntsmen are facing life in prison because of that failed attempt to find Magni."

"I thought Khan was planning to kill them. Did he change his mind?" Shelly asked.

"Pearl argued their case until she was blue in the face," I said. "She gets almost hysterical when the subject of the death penalty comes up. She says it's a violation of human rights and it's medieval."

Marco crossed his arms. "Yeah, that's Pearl for you. She'd prefer to sit down and talk things through. Like that ever helped."

"Hey, making people reflect on their actions is a good thing," Kya argued. "And you Nmen kill people for senseless reasons."

"We do not," Marco retorted. "We just don't believe that people can change. Killing them guarantees they'll never make the mistake again."

"Of course people can change, Marco. I'm a good example of that." Shelly looked straight at the young man. "I used to be quiet when I arrived, and now I speak up for myself."

"I suspect you never changed, you just grew bold enough to show your personality." Marco gave a small grin. "At least when you were quiet, we assumed you were nice."

"At least I *have* a personality."

Marco angled his head. "Oh, that's nice, Brainy. But wait, do you remember when I asked for your opinion?" He angled his head. "Yeah, me neither."

"Be nice, Marco," Kya pleaded. "Shelly is leaving in a few days. You might miss each other."

"Maybe for the entertainment value," Shelly said dryly. "People in the Motherlands don't climb poles to solve mathematical questions, and we don't mumble to hide that we can't remember science facts."

"Hey, if you're referring to this morning, I was just tired. I knew the answer." Marco leaned closer to Shelly. "It's basic knowledge that the universe is made up of protons, neutrons, and electrons."

Shelly locked eyes with him. "You forgot morons."

Marco rolled his eyes, turning to Archer, who was laughing like me. "It's such a pity that Shelly won't be marrying an Nman. I would have loved the chance to discipline her."

Kya shook her head. "No one is spanking Shelly."

Marco looked over at the fifteen-year-old girl, who had turned pale. "I'll have to use my imagination then." He held up his palm with a challenging smile.

"You would want to marry me?" Her tone was incredulous.

"If that's what it would take to make your ass red."

We were all expecting some witty comeback from Shelly, but she bit her lower lip and shrank back in her seat. With her face turned downward, she effectively retreated behind the curtain of her long unruly brown hair.

Archer didn't notice the awkwardness of the situation. "Did Khan say how long he'll wait until he sends out search parties for Magni?"

"What happened to a man's free choice? If he wants to live in Alaska, shouldn't he be allowed to?" Marco asked.

"And leave his wife behind without a word?" Kya's hand rested on her belly. "If that's the kind of husband you're going to be, Marco, then it should be you getting that spanking."

Archer flashed his teeth in a grin. "Not all wives are as hardcore as you, Kya."

Marco wrinkled his nose. "Don't tell me you'd let her spank you."

Humor played in Archer's eyes. "She tried once as retribution for me spanking her, but it was more like a tickle."

Marco swung his head to Kya with his eyes wide. "For real?"

She ignored him and looked at me. "Is Khan going to send search parties out?"

"He already did. Someone up in Alaska has to know something. Problem is that the locals aren't talking."

"Why not?"

"Most of them are weirdos who want to be left in peace. There's a strong tradition in that part of the country that if you rat on a neighbor you don't wake up the next day." I shrugged. "Magni isn't the only one hiding."

Archer frowned. "Then Khan could put out a reward. Maybe money would make them more cooperative."

"I asked about that, but Khan refused. He says that if he spreads the news that Magni is alone, it'll only make him a target for his enemies."

"Then what are you going to do?" Kya gave me a worried glance.

I drew in a deep breath and emptied my lungs in a sigh. "There's not much I *can* do. Except wait, pray, and distract myself by coming here and working with Pearl on the integration projects."

"Feel free to repeat the fight session with the girls that you did today. It was empowering for them to see a woman who can fight." Archer smiled.

I sat up straighter and looked at him. "You mean that?"

"Of course. You're very good."

"For a woman," I added with my eyes narrowed.

"I didn't say that. For someone who has trained for less than a year, I'm impressed with your skills. You're fast and precise in your movements. If you want, we could give you more training – expand on the martial arts, you know, and spice it up with some kick-boxing."

My voice rose to a small shriek. "I would love that!" Mila stirred in my lap from my excitement and Archer, Kya, and Marco smiled.

"Good, I know the perfect teacher for you," Archer said. "We'll start tomorrow."

CHAPTER 34
Return

Magni

My hand stroked my red hybrid when I saw it again. The impressive machine had been designed for me a few years ago and had cost me a fortune.

Getting back in the pilot's seat was a little bit like coming home. I looked around to make sure everything was just the way I'd left it a month ago.

Firing up the engine, I put it on automatic drone mode with the Gray Mansion as the destination, while I reached for my wristband to see what messages and calls I'd missed.

While muttering curse words to myself, the lines of worry on my forehead grew deeper with every message I read. My month away had left a gigantic mess at home and I had a lot of cleaning up to do. I started by calling up Khan.

"Magni, is that you?" His voice came through loud and clear, sounding frantic.

"Yeah, it's me."

"Tell me where you are."

"I'm in Alaska, just like I told you I would be."

"You need to come home, right now!" He sounded desperate. "I'll give you anything you want, as long as you come back to work."

"You sound tired. Are you okay?"

"No, I'm not fucking okay. I haven't slept for a month and everything is in chaos."

"I'm sorry to hear it. I truly thought you and your new co-ruler would be better off without me as the third wheel."

Khan groaned. "Don't start, Magni. Pearl can never replace you and you know it. She and I are strong strategists, but your expertise is in controlling the soldiers. No one does that better than you, and the men are loyal to you."

"I'm not interested in coming back to work, if Pearl is going to outrank me."

"That won't happen for at least ten years."

"Good, then you have plenty of time to find a solution without me."

"Magni, for fuck's sake, just come back and help me get things under control. We'll figure out a solution once we get there. Pearl had an idea although it's a really bad one."

"Tell me anyway." I scrolled down and grew nervous when I counted at least twenty calls from the school. "Is Mila okay?"

"Yes, Mila is fine. She just misses you a lot."

"And Laura?"

"Everyone is fine. And we all want you to come back home."

"I'm waiting to hear Pearl's idea."

He groaned as if it was painful to say it out loud. "She suggested we'd make a Council to include you as an equal to both her and me."

"Pearl said that?" I lowered my wristband and looked out the window over the snow-covered trees beneath me.

"Yeah, but I told her 'no' of course."

"Why?"

"Because it's a fucking bad idea, Magni. The only reason to make Pearl a co-ruler in the first place is to honor the demand from the Motherlands Council that equality will go both ways. Setting up a Council in the Northlands with only three people won't offer equality since it will still be you and me outweighing Pearl as the only female."

"I see."

"We would need at least four members in the Council and two of them would need to be female."

"Hmm."

"Now you see why it's such a bad idea? Pearl is opinionated enough – we don't need another strong woman like her to complicate things further. She's already threatening not to sleep with me if I don't release the Huntsmen."

I froze and lowered my voice. "What are you talking about?"

"Franklin and seven of the Huntsmen were convinced that I was holding you prisoner, and they came to rescue you. The fucking fools held Pearl, Laura, and me locked in my office demanding to know if I had killed you."

"Why didn't you tell them to fuck off?"

"Because they were holding a gun to my head and wouldn't listen to reason. Laura fought one of them, and I thought he might kill her."

"Who?"

"Did he hurt her?" My voice rose as my heart pounded in my chest.

"No, at the time I was afraid he would, but looking back I can see that it was never his intention. She hit him hard with my marble cube when he tried to restrain her."

I whistled. "Good for her. The Huntsmen must've known they were risking everything."

"They said you would've done the same for them."

"Hmm."

"Anyway, it was Pearl who finally convinced them that we were as concerned about you as they were. After that, they let us go."

"What did you do with them?"

"What do you think? They were waving a gun close to my pregnant wife's face. I want to hang every one of them."

"You didn't tell me that Pearl was pregnant." My tone softened. "Congratulations."

"I would've told you if you had been around. But you don't have to act surprised. You knew about it before I did."

"Ahh, you two really tell each other everything, don't you?"

"Pretty much."

"It sucks that she won't sleep with you. Maybe you should give her what she wants."

"You're only saying that because the Huntsmen were fighting to get to you."

"You're right about that. It's nice to know that some people are still loyal to me."

"I guess. Not sure you deserve it, though."

I lowered my chin. "Why not?"

"You're not exactly showing much loyalty yourself, are you? You left the Huntsmen not knowing what had happened to you, and you left your wife to fend for herself, not even appointing a new protector for her."

"Boulder was there, I knew he would protect her."

"He already has Christina to protect, and I'm busy enough trying to keep together the pieces of this country. Finn lives in the Motherlands now, and Archer has a school to run with a pregnant wife to protect. Do you realize what that means?"

My jaw hardened. "What are you saying?"

"I'm saying that the only male available to be Laura's protector was Marco."

"You made an unmarried man her protector?" My voice was frosty.

"You didn't give me much choice and with you choosing to leave there's the question of your divorce and Laura's future with another husband."

"Another husband." My heart almost stopped. "Did she sleep with Marco?"

"All I know is that she has slept here in your suite most nights. The other night she has slept at the school."

"With him?"

"I can't confirm or deny it, but I was told that Laura isn't sleeping alone."

"Where. Is. Laura?" The three words were pressed out through my teeth."

"She wasn't here for breakfast, so I assume that she is at the school."

My nostrils flared and fear burned in my chest. Marco was handsome, charming, and easy-going like Finn. I had always thought of him as nothing but a big boy, but he and Laura were the same age. Boulder and Finn had both married the women they protected, and I was no fool. Laura was lonely and felt rejected by me. I'd left her open and vulnerable for Marco to seduce.

"So, are you coming back or what?" Khan asked.

"Yes, I'm coming back. In the meantime, do as Pearl told you to and release my men. I'll deal with them later after I've dealt with Laura."

"These are truly troubling times if you and Pearl team up against me," Khan muttered and ended the call.

I pushed accelerate and was grateful that I had the fastest hybrid in the Northlands.

CHAPTER 35
Fight Training

Laura

Despite being only fourteen years old, Solomon was half a head taller than me and toned with muscles.

"Solo, you'll be training with Laura today," Archer told the boy, whose face stiffened. "What's wrong?"

"No offense, but I'm a great fighter and I don't need her to teach me."

"You idiot," Archer smacked the back of his head, with a grin. "You're going to teach Laura."

"Oh." Solomon straightened up and squared his chest. "I'd be honored to."

"Don't underestimate her. She's fast and a very intelligent fighter."

Solomon nodded and smiled at me. "This is going to be fun."

"Marco will be up at the new gym teaching the beginners, while I'll train the Nboys outside." Archer looked around the large schoolroom. "I figured you two could push the tables aside and train in here."

"Sure." Solomon was already clearing an area in the middle, and I helped him.

"Are you okay being alone with Solo?" Archer asked me.

"No problem." I grinned at the boy. "If he does something I don't like, I'll just beat him up."

"You have my permission," Archer said with a laugh on his way out.

Solomon moved with grace, was a superior fighter, and was very serious about his training.

"Again," he demanded for the seventh time when he wanted me to perfect a kick.

"Jesus, you're just like Magni," I complained and dried away sweat from my forehead.

"I'm *not*." The boy looked away with a frown.

I stopped in front of him, and leaned my head back to look into his blue eyes. "You could've been his younger brother. You two look so much alike with your size, eyes, and fighter skills."

Solomon pressed his lips together.

"What's wrong?"

"You are not the first to compare me to him, but I'm nothing like him. I would *never* leave my wife."

Lowering my head, I bit my lip. "Solo, it wasn't Magni's fault. You don't know the whole story and you shouldn't judge him. Magni is a good and honorable man."

"He left you."

"Technically, I left him first."

Solomon folded his hands into fists and kept them close to his thighs. "When I marry Willow, nothing is going to make me want to leave her."

"You plan to marry Willow? That's nice."

"You think I'm not serious," Solomon said and began arguing. "Just because we are young doesn't mean we don't know how we feel. I love her."

His words knocked my breath from me. "You love her?"

He nodded with determination.

"Did you tell Willow that?"

Solo turned around and took up his fighter position. "Yes, I did, and when she's old enough to marry, we'll make it official."

I chewed on my lip, unable to speak.

"Let's try that kick again," Solo instructed and waited for me to get into position before he attacked.

The thought that two children had no problem declaring their love for each other was humbling to me. They were twelve and fourteen but not afraid to say such powerful words.

Magni and I were adults and married. We had no excuses, so why hadn't I told Magni how I felt about him when I had the chance?

Solomon's attack took me by surprise and I landed on my ass. My mind had been occupied with blaming myself for pushing Magni away and I hadn't been concentrating. Annoyed with myself, I cursed low and took Solomon's hand when he pulled me up. "Thank you."

"You got to clear your mind and focus."

Loud screams from the outside made me look out the window, and I saw a flash of red appear for a second.

"What the fuck?" Solomon breathed behind me. "He's going to crash at that speed."

I ran to the window, my fingers almost boring into the frame, and my heart speeding with fear. It was Magni and he was coming in much too fast. Something had to be wrong with his hybrid.

The thought that I was about to watch the man I loved crash and burn made me stiff with fear. My eyes locked on the red drone in the sky.

"Get back, get back," Archer screamed outside and the Nboys ran for cover.

Magni was always careful with his hybrid, but this time it came down so fast that it slid over the ground and made scratching sounds.

When the door opened, Magni didn't step out. He jumped out and ran straight for the school, shouting at Archer and the boys. "Where is Marco?"

Disappointment filled me. "Marco?" I turned to look at Solomon, my eyes blinking in confusion. Why hadn't Magni asked for me or maybe Mila? Why Marco?"

Solomon lifted both hands as if to say that he had no clue but was wondering the same thing. "We'd better find out what's going on – come on, Laura."

Solomon ran, while I walked, trying to get my emotions under control.

I saw Magni enter the gym and a second later, Marco came sprinting out with Magni and all the children on his heels.

"What's going on?" I asked when Marco ran past me.

He didn't stop to explain, so instead I stepped in front of Magni with both hands outstretched, shouting for him to stop. It was a matter of trampling me down or stopping, and thank God, Magni chose the latter. Towering over me, his face was scrunched up in anger.

"Why are you chasing Marco?" I demanded to know.

Magni looked past me to Marco, who had stopped a little further away. All the children were gathering to see the action. Lifting his hand, Magni pointed at Marco. "You wouldn't be running if you hadn't done something you shouldn't."

"I didn't do anything," Marco called back with confusion on his face. "Of course I'm running when you look like you're about to kill me."

"What is this about?" I asked low enough for only Magni to hear.

He looked down at me, his right eyebrow raised in a perfect arch. "Did you sleep with him?"

The sweetest feeling of relief hit me right in my chest. Magni was back and he still cared about me. I closed my eyes and sighed, but Magni misunderstood and took it as a sign of guilt.

"You did, didn't you?" Magni growled low.

I was just about to protest and clear up the misunderstanding when Solomon heroically pushed me back and got between me and Magni.

"I won't let you touch her."

307

Both Magni and I warned him to stay out of it.

"I'll fight you if I have to, but I won't let you put a finger on Laura."

"You would fight *me*?" Magni pushed forward. "Are you kidding me?"

"Solo, no!" The fear in Willow's voice was real.

"I've been wanting to kick your arrogant little ass for a long time," Magni hissed at the teenager. "But I don't have time right now. *Move* the fuck away from my wife."

Archer moved closer. "Solo, do as he says. Don't meddle in things you don't understand."

"I understand that Laura has been sad and that he's not treating his wife right," Solo shouted back to Archer.

"What did you say?" Magni grabbed the boy's collar. In reflex, Solo pushed back with a hand to Magni's shoulder.

"Hey, hey, stop." Marco came back. "Whatever you're angry about, don't take it out on the boy. If you want to fight someone, you can fight me."

Magni changed his focus from Solomon to Marco. "Oh yeah? Those are big words coming from a man who ran like a coward just a minute ago."

"Marco isn't the coward. You are!" Solomon accused my husband. "You *left* Laura."

A warning growl came from Magni, and Archer scolded Solomon. "You're way out of order, boy. You're coming with me to my office, right now."

"Solo, I don't need you to protect me," I assured the young man, but he wouldn't budge and held his stance between me and Magni.

"It's okay, Laura, I can take him in a fight." Solo didn't get a chance to finish his sentence before he got knocked out cold by Magni.

Willow screamed as if Solo had been killed and ran to throw herself on top of his body.

"Magni, no. He's just a kid." Kya came running too, and I bent down, shaking his shoulder. "Solo, open your eyes."

"He's going to be fine," Magni said when Willow looked up at him with tears in her eyes.

Solo's eyes blinked open after Kya had slapped his cheeks a few times.

"What happened?" he asked with confusion on his face.

"Magni hit you," Willow explained and took Solo's hand.

"Be happy I only put him to sleep for a second instead of knocking his teeth out. I bet you wouldn't find him so pretty with short hair and no teeth."

Willow opened her mouth to speak, but Archer was quick to put his hand on her shoulder. "Magni had every right to hit Solo. If he'd come between me and Kya like that, I'd have done much worse."

Willow defended her boyfriend. "He was just trying to protect, Laura."

"Laura was never in danger," Archer argued. "And if she had been, Marco and I would have handled it."

"Willow, Archer is right," I told the girl. "Magni would never hurt me."

I turned to Magni. "Why did you chase Marco like that?"

Magni pointed at Marco, who was now only about ten feet away. "Keep your hands off my wife."

"What are you talking about? I never touched Laura."

Magni was stabbing his finger in Marco's direction. "You're not her protector. *I am!*"

Marco and I exchanged a glance of confusion.

"Don't look like you don't know what I'm talking about. Khan told me how he made you her protector and that you two sleep together."

Marco held up both his palms in a sign of peace. "There must be some misunderstanding. I'm not Laura's protector and I've never slept with her."

"Are you saying Lord Khan is lying?"

"No – I don't know." Marco looked to me for help and I stepped away from Solo, who was now sitting up with a hand to his head.

"You must have heard wrong, Magni. That's all," I said.

"Laura." Magni stepped so close that his chest touched my arm. "What is going on between you and Marco?"

I closed my eyes, calling for patience.

"Laura, look at me. Tell me that you aren't fucking him."

As if someone had turned on a laser beam inside of me, I opened my eyes and pinned Magni with such intensity that he jerked back a little. "This is absurd. You and I are going to talk, right now." In long strides, I walked to the cabin, trusting that my temperamental husband would follow me. I held the door and closed it when he was inside.

"What the hell was that?" I scolded. "I haven't seen you for a month and then you come back here acting like a jealous lunatic."

"What was I supposed to do?"

"You were supposed to talk to me about it. If you had asked me, I could've told you that there is nothing between me and Marco."

Magni was pacing the room. "Why would Khan tell me that he's your protector, if he's not?"

"You'll have to ask Khan about that."

"So there's nothing going on between you and Marco?"

I rubbed my face. "How many times do I have to tell you? There's *nothing going on* between us. He's far too young for me anyway."

"You're the same age, Laura."

"Yes, but he's not *you*."

Magni stopped pacing and turned to look at me. "Say that again?"

We stood three feet apart with loaded energy between us.

310

My voice softened as the joy that he was back caught up with me. "He's not you."

Magni shifted his weight from one leg to the other. "So you're not going to divorce me?"

"No." I took a step closer. The words that I'd wanted to tell him for so long were right on my tongue, and my heart felt like it was exploding.

Magni stepped closer too, pulling me into a tight hug and saying the words that I wanted to hear. "I love you."

"What?" I whispered, as if I hadn't heard right.

"I love you, Laura." Magni released me from the hug, his blue eyes looking into mine with a new sense of vulnerability.

"I love you too. I always have," I whispered back.

His face lit up and we laughed together when he visibly released a deep breath. "Are you sure?" he asked.

"Yes. I love you, Magni," I repeated with a rush of relief that the words were finally out.

"Even though I'm a jealous lunatic?"

I tilted my head, still grinning. "I never thought you would admit it."

He nuzzled against my neck and buried his hands in my hair. "Shit, I missed you."

"I missed you too, but you really shouldn't have knocked out Solo."

"I would knock out anyone who came between me and you." Magni leaned down to kiss me.

I placed a hand over his mouth. "No. If we start kissing, we'll be having sex in a second, and what we need to do is talk about our relationship."

I expected Magni to roll his eyes, but he nodded and sat down on the bed and listened.

"Things are changing fast in the Northlands, and I want to be part of that. I'm working with Pearl on building more experimental schools, and the first couples will be matched soon. I like that Pearl involves me and listens to my ideas."

"I understand."

I stood for a second, waiting for him to object to what I had just said. When he didn't, I walked over to stand between his legs, gently touching his hair. "I know it's hard for you to not be in control all the time, but I would never do anything stupid or reckless."

He looked up at me. "Like fighting a large Huntsman?"

"Khan told you?"

"Yes. What were you thinking, Laura?"

"Khan shouldn't have mentioned that."

"I'm glad he did. Khan said he was terrified that they'd shoot you." Magni closed his eyes and looked like he was trying to keep his emotions under control. "The thought alone makes me want to scream."

"Nothing happened." I slid down on his lap and placed my arms around his neck.

Magni leaned his forehead against my hair and held onto me. "I could have lost you, Laura."

"You didn't," I whispered. "I'm right here."

Looking deep into my eyes he repeated my new favorite words. "I love you so much."

"Why didn't you ever tell me?"

"Because I'm a proud fool."

"What happened to you in Alaska? The Magni I know would never admit that."

"Nothing happened, and that was the problem. I had too much fucking time to think."

"And you concluded that you're a proud fool?"

"Yes."

I smiled and kissed him. "I could have saved you the trip and told you that."

He squeezed me tighter. "It was one of those things I had to discover for myself."

I kissed him again.

"Laura, I'm truly sorry for storming off like I did. I know I blow up and get angry too often for my own good, and I want to change it."

"Wow, I'm impressed. Does that mean you can live with my being both a Motlander and a Northlander?"

"As long as you stay with me." He placed his head against my neck and breathed me in. "Laura, I wish I could use words like Finn or Khan, but I'm not that kind of man."

I stroked the back of his hand that rested on my hip.

"I know how to talk about other things, but I'm lost when it comes to expressing how I feel about you."

"Try."

Magni looked pained when he straightened up, and his chest rose and fell. "Okay, you know how much it hurts when you get shot or stabbed?"

"No."

He bit his lip. "No, of course not. But did you ever break a bone or something?"

"I twisted my ankle once and it got all swollen."

"Right." He nodded with a thoughtful expression. "I think the same happened to my heart when you left me. It was so swollen that there was no room for it to beat and it hurt worse than the time I broke three of my ribs." He placed his hand on his chest. "I consider myself tough when it comes to physical pain, but this was way worse than anything I've gone through in the past. With a physical injury, you can take painkillers and keep still until it heals. When we were apart, the pain in my heart was constant, and I couldn't breathe."

I looked down. "I'm sorry, Magni."

"Did your heart hurt too?" he asked me.

"Yes, but more like a slow ache that grew stronger. I missed you a lot."

He gave me a sad smile and kissed my nose. "I know I'm terrible at explaining it, but my feelings for you,

Laura…" He sighed. "I would do anything for you. You know that, don't you?"

The edges around my moist eyes softened in a smile. "Your words were perfect."

"Yeah?"

"Yeah."

"And you don't think me a weak man because I couldn't breathe when I thought I'd lost you?"

"No. I don't think anyone would ever accuse you of being weak. And if they did, I'd punch their nose in."

"I didn't see you punching Solo when he accused me of being a coward."

"Because he's too young to understand that things aren't black or white. He's got this conviction about marrying Willow, but soon he'll leave this school and most likely they'll never see each other again."

"So, he's naïve. That doesn't give him the right to say shit like that to my face."

"Can't you cut Solo some slack? He looked up to you and you disappointed him."

"Why should I? He didn't call you a coward when you came back after *six* months, I was only gone for *one* month."

"At least give him credit for being brave enough to stand up to you and defend me."

Magni rubbed the bridge of his nose. "There's that. The boy has serious balls. If only he had brains too."

"He's not stupid."

"You don't think picking a fight with me was stupid?"

"I would call it foolish."

"Same thing, Laura." Magni played with my hair. "But to be fair, I was the same way at his age. Always thinking I was invincible and immortal."

"And now?"

"Now I know that I have a big weakness. I don't fear rebels or warriors, but I fear you."

314

"Because I've learned to fight?" I winked at him.

He smiled and leaned in to plant a slow kiss on my lips. "What I meant was that I fear losing you."

I held up my thumb and index finger, letting them almost touch. "Aren't you just a *little bit* scared of fighting me?"

He laughed. "I'm terrified of fighting you."

"Aww, that's so sweet of you to say."

"Imagine if I hurt you by accident; that would be unforgivable."

I pretended to be offended and tried to get up from his lap, but Magni held on to me and his low chuckle made me soft inside.

"Where do you think you're going? We did the talking." His eyes fell to the bed with an insinuating smile.

"You want make-up sex?"

He nodded and slid his hand up my leg. "It's been a month and I've thought about you non-stop."

Nuzzling the hair on his nape, I whispered, "I thought about you too. I regretted that I didn't tell you how much I loved and admired you."

"Admired, huh?"

"Magni, when your Huntsmen came to find you, one of them told us a story about how you took his place as a hostage last year."

"Hmm. And you want to know why I didn't tell you about it. There was no need to worry you."

"I want to know how you got away from those men."

Magni shrugged. "Laura, sweetie, most rebels are disgruntled men who have no military background. They talk a big talk, but have little to back it up."

"But they had tortured your men."

"True, and that's why I showed the rebels no mercy. It was supposed to be an easy assignment so I sent a team of new guys to take care of it. They were too green; it was my fault that I hadn't sent a more experienced group to deal with it."

"But the rebels had weapons and you volunteered to be a hostage. How did you get out of that situation?"

"With your training you should know that a warrior like me doesn't need weapons to defend myself. They were amateurs who overestimated the threat of a gun to my face."

"They held a gun to your face?"

"Not for long."

"But how did you unarm them?"

"I'll show you some other time, but right now I want to make love to you."

I angled my head with a curious smile. "Not fuck me?"

"I'll do that in round two." Magni was kissing me and pushing me back on the bed when a knock sounded on the door.

"Not now," he shouted.

"Magni?"

We both raised our heads and looked to the door at the sound of Mila's voice.

With some speed, Magni got up to open the door. Mila had turned around and was running away with her head lowered.

"Mila honey," he called and ran after her.

She turned her head and still looked sad when Magni kneeled in front of her. I couldn't hear what he told her, but he was holding her hands and had his head close to hers looking apologetic.

Mila listened and when he was done talking, she lifted her hand and placed it on his cheek.

They looked at each other and he said a few more words waiting for her reply. I was no great lip reader, but it looked like Mila spoke the words "I forgive you."

Magni hugged her and rose up from the ground with Mila still in his arms. Her feet dangled over the ground and her arms were gripping fiercely around his neck. When he turned to me, I saw tears in his eyes. Magni had never looked more attractive to me than he did at that moment.

CHAPTER 36
Farewell Party

Magni

After being isolated in Alaska for more than a month, it was overwhelming to be back at the school. Boulder, Christina, Pearl, Khan, Laura, and I had all been invited to join the twenty children and their four teachers for a Christmas party. The celebration served as a farewell party as well. Some of the Motlander children were going home to family members for Christmas in a few days, and Shelly was leaving to start her psychology degree back in the Motherlands.

"I can't tell you how grateful we are for all your help capturing the Nmen who crossed the border unauthorized." Isobel was holding Laura's hands and smiling at her.

"It was the least I could do after everything you've done for me."

Isobel looked up when Hunter and Willow came up carrying plates and cutlery. "Can I help with anything?"

"No, Kya says that you're the guest of honor and she just wants you to sit down and enjoy yourself."

"That's very kind of her, thank you, Willow." Isobel leaned back when Hunter placed a plate in front of her. "Aren't you excited that you have found your twin?"

The young man stopped and looked down at Isobel with his beautiful green eyes that matched his sister's. "That depends on which day you ask me. Most of the time Willow is great, but she can be pretty moody too. Kya says it's because she's gone into puberty and that it's all hormones."

Isobel looked over at Willow, who was setting out knives and forks. "Willow dear, rolling your eyes is a bad habit and considered rude."

"I'm sorry, Councilwoman, I didn't mean for you to see that."

I chuckled at the fact that Willow hadn't regretted doing it, only that she'd been caught.

Pearl, who sat close to the girl, touched her elbow. "I remember going through puberty, Willow. Sometimes you can laugh and cry within the same minute and not know why. It will get better." Her head turned to Hunter. "You will understand when it happens to you."

The boy scoffed. "As long as my voice doesn't crack like Solo's."

Shelly, who had just entered the room with a bowl of food, set it down on the table and looked to Hunter. "So you would rather have a boy's voice for the rest of your life than go through the changes to have a man's voice?"

"That's not what I said."

"You shouldn't stress about it, Hunter, it's natural and happens because of the rapid growth of the larynx and vocal cords. Think of your vocal cords as a harp that just grew in length. Now your brain has to learn how to play the new instrument, and the longer cords give off a deeper sound. It takes a little practice, but a cracking voice is merely proof that an adolescent boy's brain hasn't become completely proficient at coordinating its careful monitoring of the sounds coming from the vocal cords."

"Geez, Shelly, I didn't ask for a lecture." Hunter shook his head. "You're like a walking ancyclopedium."

"I think you mean an encyclopedia," she called after him when he walked off.

"There's nothing wrong with being smart," Isobel told Shelly. "We're all excited to see what you'll do with that brain of yours."

Shelly looked after Hunter and bit her lip. "I'm hoping that studying psychology will make me less awkward."

"You're not awkward," Isobel said and I wondered if she meant it or was trying to comfort Shelly. The girl was sweet and brighter than most adults, but fuck yeah, she was awkward.

I might be a hothead, but Shelly had her own quirks and would give random lectures about useless facts that no one asked for. She didn't have the same level of empathy as most of the other Motlanders, and although she was never intentionally cruel she would call out people and humiliate them without wanting to.

"It's okay, I know I am." Shelly gave Isobel a smile. "But as I said, a degree in psychology should be helpful in understanding people better. After that I can focus on what I'm really interested in."

"Which is?"

"Optimizing functionality and design."

Isobel frowned. "Oh, I see. That's a wide-open description; do you know what you want to do more specifically?"

"Yes, I'll take a degree in engineering and help make machines fit the human experience better.

"What kind of machines," Hunter asked with mischief in his eyes. "Are you talking about sex-bots?"

Shelly didn't seem to get that he was teasing. "I'm curious about machines designed to serve a purpose in human lives. Sex-bots are per definition included in that category."

Hunter laughed and called out to Plato and Solo. "Hey, can you believe Shelly is going to use her brains to improve sex-bots?"

The white noise from all the people in the room went silent.

320

"She's not," I said, feeling a little sorry for the teenage girl who flashed red when she saw everyone staring at her.

"I hope you do," Hunter told her. "Marco says he might be able to get me in as a tester for the new models when I'm old enough to use them. He's been in contact with Charlie, you know, the owner of the factory we visited in the Motherlands."

The children continued their conversation but I was distracted when I heard Isobel mention Devlin's name.

"I was disturbed to read the report. What an awful man, and to think that he signed up to be matched with a woman again. He even requested to be paired with the poor woman he held hostage."

"Julia?" Laura set her elbows on the table leaning closer to Isobel, who sat on the opposite side from us.

Isobel nodded. "Yes – Julia."

Laura shook her head. "Devlin didn't hold Julia hostage. She was at the border when the wall crumbled and when he came across, she thought it would be a good idea to hide him in her house."

Isobel wrinkled her nose. "That's not what I heard."

Laura asked to see the report and when Isobel let her see the file on her wristband, I saw her eyes move from side to side as she read what it said. "Hans wrote this?" she asked.

I read to myself.

The owner of the house, Julia, had red-rimmed eyes and was shaking when she let us in to her house.

As the most skilled mediator on site, I made sure to go first when we entered the hallway and confronted the suspect in the living room. He was verbally aggressive and the atmosphere was tense, which is why I asked Laura to stay behind me at all times.

When we informed Devlin that he would be shipped back, the situation escalated and I had to use my superior negotiator skills to calm him down. I avoided a physical altercation only because I outsmarted him and made him see that he had a lot to be sorry about. He refused to apologize to Julia and threatened that he'd see her again in the future. Julia seemed terrified of him and was crying a lot.

"What the fuck is this?" I pointed to the file. "That's nothing like you explained it to me, Laura."

Laura's eyes were narrowed and her voice was trembling with indignation. "That's because it's pure fiction."

"What do you mean?" Isobel asked with a look of concern.

"That report is made up to make Hans look good, but it wasn't like that at all."

For minutes, Laura explained her version of things to Isobel. The older woman's eyes grew bigger and her face paler. "I can't believe it. Why would Hans lie to us?"

I cleared my throat. "When Finn heard that Laura was working with Hans, he indicated to me that Hans wasn't to be trusted."

"This is most shocking." Isobel's eyes were glazed over and her fingers played with her necklace.

"I'm sorry, but Hans is no hero. He kept hiding behind me and did nothing to soothe the situation in that house. Julia and Devlin were in love and Hans was disgusted by it."

With resolution, Isobel stood up. "If you'll excuse me, I'll go make a few calls. I have to get to the bottom of this."

Boulder and Khan came in as Isobel walked out.

"What is wrong with Isobel?"

I shrugged. "She just found out that one of her mediators is a fraud and a liar."

Boulder sat down a large jug of beer.

"Isn't that the same thing?"

Picking up the jug I poured beer into glasses. "I don't know. Why don't you ask Khan? He's got experience with lying."

Khan plopped himself down on a chair at the end of the table not far from me. He looked tired. "When are you gonna let it go?"

"You told me Marco was Laura's protector and that they slept together."

"I said I'd heard that she didn't sleep alone, which was true."

"You knew that I was sleeping with Mila because she asked me to," Laura pointed out.

"Yes." Khan took the glass I handed him. "But I was desperate to make Magni come home so I catered to his jealousy. Kind of genius when you think about it."

"Marco could have been killed," Boulder complained.

Khan scoffed. "No. Archer would have never allowed it."

"What wouldn't I have allowed?" Archer called from the doorway."

"For Magni to kill Marco."

"Of course not. But a good fight would have been entertaining."

Pearl came in with Kya, and the children began taking their seats.

"We shouldn't talk about it," Khan warned. "Pearl is still upset that you knocked out a child."

I scoffed. "Solo is no child. He's a young man and he'd be offended if I'd spared him. He was out of line and he fucking knows it."

"No doubt, but you know how the women are; they dislike violence in general and are overprotective when it comes to the students."

Boulder, Khan, Archer, and I all turned our heads to look at Solo, who stood brooding at the other end of the table with a big black eye.

"How is the eye doing?" Boulder called out.

"What part of *let's not talk about it* didn't you get?" Khan hissed.

Boulder didn't seem to care and chuckled. "Just a warning, young Solo. If you ever see me and Christina having an argument, I suggest you stay out of it. I won't be as nice about it as Magni was."

Solo's pride was hurt and he gave a sideways glance to Willow before he sat down at the table.

"You're being jerks," Laura whispered to us. "If you can't see that Solo is a fine Nman then you're blind."

We men exchanged a glance and Khan gave a small eye-roll before he called out in a voice loud enough for everyone to hear. "Tell you what, Solo. If I get a report of a husband abusing his wife, I'll let you come with the team that investigates. No man is allowed to abuse a woman in this country. I believe you have a good heart and the courage to confront anyone who doesn't understand that."

Solo straightened in his seat. "Yes, Lord Khan. That would be an honor."

Laura whispered a "thank you," low enough for only us men to hear.

"Let's hope it will never be relevant," Khan muttered.

"It might, with all the new brides coming in. There will be a cultural clash," Laura said in a low voice. "A Motlander woman might accuse her husband of abuse if he gives her a simple ass spanking."

"What are you whispering about down there?" Pearl asked from the other end of the table.

"Nothing, dear." Khan gave her a smile.

"I can tell you're up to no good. Are you saying bad things about the food? The children spent a lot of time preparing it."

"It looks delicious," I said and grabbed for the large bowl of salad that was being passed around.

"What the fuck, Magni, did you convert or something?" Boulder asked with a deep voice when he saw me fill half my plate with salad.

"Convert?"

"You're not a vegan now, are you?"

I laughed. "Hell no, I just didn't eat much green stuff in Alaska. I missed all the crunchiness of a good salad."

"I keep telling you," Mila said and pointed her fork in my direction. "You don't need meat. Salad and greens are delicious."

I smiled at her as white noise filled the room when the bowls and plates with food were passed around.

"Let's have a toast," Pearl exclaimed and raised her glass. "Wait a minute, where's my mom?"

"Isobel had to make a call," Laura informed her.

"Okay, but cheers to the rest of us."

I looked around the large table where we sat squeezed together to fit. Everyone was raising their glasses, clinking them together in the air. A few of the kids were hanging over the table to reach a friend on the other side.

"Nicki, Rochelle, Victoria, and Paysey, you're getting your long hair in the food, please sit back in your seats," Kya reprimanded. "And Willow, would you please pass the meat."

Willow picked up the tray as if it was the most disgusting thing in the world.

"I didn't ask you to eat it, just to pass it along."

Hunter stabbed his fork into a large piece of chicken breast and dangled it in front of Willow's face. "Wanna try? It's really good."

"Stop it, Hunter," Solo ordered from a few seats away. I chewed on my salad and studied the young man for a second. He did have clear leadership skills and an authority that was unusual for his age. I'd seen him fight and knew he was outstanding. The fingers on my right hand began tapping the tabletop. My logic was telling me he would be worth keeping an eye on and someone I should pick for my elite Huntsmen unit. Yet, there was resistance in me – I'd never liked Solo.

Why?

William and Nero quarreled a little and right away Solo scowled at them and told them to shut up. My hand stopped tapping when I accepted what I'd known from the beginning. I didn't like Solo because he was too similar to me. Seeing him was like seeing what I didn't like about myself.

"That boy looks and acts a lot like me," I told Laura.

She swallowed a mouthful and raised her glass, looking at Solo before she leaned against me. "Don't tell him that. I mentioned it and he got offended."

"He *what?*" My words came out louder than planned and made the people around us look up at me.

Laura waited for them to resume eating before she spoke again. "You saw it yourself. He's not a fan anymore."

I threw the fork down on my plate and leaned back thinking hard. It wasn't that my ego was depending on a fourteen-year-old schoolboy to respect me, but it still bothered me that he'd called me a coward.

"What's wrong?" Khan asked.

"I'm not a coward."

"I never said you were."

"Solo said it."

Boulder, who sat next to me, elbowed me. "Don't worry about it. The boy doesn't know half of what you've done for this country or the people you love. If he's lucky enough to do a tenth, people will call him a hero."

"He sees things as black and white," I muttered.

"Didn't we all when we were his age?" Boulder asked.

Khan lifted his glass and looked thoughtful. "Pearl says that I still do."

"I'm starting to think Pearl is right about a lot of things," I said with a raised eyebrow.

"Told you." Khan laughed.

I kept looking at Solo with my eyebrows drawn close.

"Solo, come here for a second," Khan called to the young man. Four children had to get off the bench for Solo to get out, but he came to stand next to our end of the table, his head bowed down in respect for his ruler. "Lord Khan."

"About what I said before." Khan pushed his plate away and leaned his forearms on the table. "Laura just pointed out to me that we should expect cultural clashes between the Motlander brides and the Nmen. Archer tells me you want to become a warrior, and that you'll be going into the army when you're done here. Is that true?"

"Yes, Lord."

"You still have six months left at this school and in that time I'd like you to have a private mentor to take full advantage of your potential. With training you could become the greatest warrior this country has ever seen."

Solo's eyes flew to me. "Greater than Magni?"

"I doubt it!" I said dryly and was annoyed with Khan for putting thoughts like that into the head of the young man.

"That depends on Magni." Khan shifted his focus to me. "Could you train Solo to become better than you?"

"I'm already as good as Marco," Solo interjected. "Soon I can take Archer too."

"Yes, I heard." Khan had that mischievous look in his eye that meant he'd already made up his mind about something. "That's why I would like Magni to be your mentor. If he thinks you're good enough, he might pick you for his Huntsmen."

I snorted and crossed my arms. "The boy doesn't have what it takes. He's too arrogant and self-absorbed."

With his black eye narrowed in determination, Solo turned to me. "I'm prepared to work hard and do whatever it takes."

"You think I'd be your mentor after you insulted me in front of my wife?"

Laura's hand squeezed my thigh under the table, but I wasn't done grilling Solo. "Being part of the Huntsmen requires deep loyalty and extraordinary fighting skills. We only pick the fiercest, bravest, and most intelligent warriors."

"I know, sir."

"No, you don't know, Solo! You think it's a glorious job, but it's dangerous and scary."

"I'm not afraid." The young man fisted his hands and looked straight into my eyes.

"You'd have to go on secret missions, sometimes without warning to the people you love. Sometimes you'd be gone for a month."

Solo frowned and his eyes glanced over to Willow, Hunter, and some of the other children who were all following the situation.

"Was that where you were, sir, on a secret mission?"

"What I do and where I go is none of your business."

Solo licked his lips and centered himself again. "I would like nothing more than to be part of the Huntsmen, sir, and I'd be deeply honored to have you as my mentor."

I took so long before I spoke that sweat showed on his forehead. Being part of the Huntsmen was a dream for many boys and young men. Few were as perfect for it as Solo. "Let me think about it for a few days. Maybe I can run you through some tests next week and see how tough you are, but I'm warning you." I held up an index finger. "I don't tolerate whiners."

"Understood."

"You can return to your seat," Khan told him and a minute later I watched his face split in a grin when he hurried to tell his friends about what had just happened.

"So, you were on a secret mission, were you?" Laura asked next to me.

Leaning close to her, I whispered into her ear. "Sounds better than being lovesick."

"Mom, what's wrong?" Pearl got up when Isobel returned. "What happened?"

Isobel headed for our end of the table and Pearl followed her. "Mom, you don't look so well."

Boulder was quick to get out of his seat and let Isobel sit down.

"I checked up on Hans' references," Isobel started and brushed her hair back with hands that were trembling. "I don't know how to tell you this, but we've been duped."

"By *we*, you mean you and the Council," Khan clarified as to emphasize that he hadn't been fooled.

"Hans made up his credentials. He's fresh out of mediator training."

"Who's Hans?" Sultan, one of the youngest boys, who'd been eavesdropping, asked.

"This is an adult conversation," Boulder told him and of course that piqued the interest of all the children.

"I can't believe we fell for his lies," Isobel said in a shaky voice. "Such unbelievable betrayal and deceit." She shook her head as if she still couldn't believe it.

Khan leaned in. "I'm sorry, Isobel, but before you start concluding that Hans' behavior is due to his male gender, it's not. Both men and women have lied as long as people have been around on this planet. Nothing new or special about that."

"I didn't say it was because he was a man," Isobel objected.

Pearl tapped her lip. "Hmm, I wonder what his motive for lying was?"

Isobel nodded. "That's what I can't figure out, either."

"Maybe you should ask him," I suggested. "I'm an expert at interrogating people. If you want me to, I could get him to talk."

Isobel held up a hand. "No thank you, Commander, I don't trust your methods. From what I've heard, they violate a number of fundamental human rights."

"I didn't offer to torture him, just question him."

"His motive is obvious." Khan had a self-satisfied gleam in his eyes, like he was a genius among slow thinkers. "Hans' deceit is nothing but a silent rebellion against the tyranny of women. You've stripped men of power and he's one of the few who won't stand for it. What options did you leave him with except to work the system to his advantage?"

"But to lie like that?" Isobel was fiddling with her earlobe.

Khan laughed. "I'm sure he's not the only one who tells you what you want to hear. In this country, the rebels plan to assassinate me to gain power. Do you think he was planning to kill the Council?"

"Oh, Mother Nature, no," Isobel exclaimed.

"Then you're fine. Don't worry about it, it's much worse when the fuckers collude and plot against..."

Pearl cut Khan off with a discreet nod to the children. "Khan, let's not get into an argument about politics. This is supposed to be a celebration."

"What are you going to do to Hans?" Laura asked.

Isobel took a sip of water from the glass Pearl handed her. "I'll recommend he spends some time in a place of reflection to find his mental balance again. He's been making some very poor choices."

"In other words, prison," I muttered.

"It's not a prison."

I angled my head and raised an eyebrow. "Can he leave?"

"Yes, of course, as soon as he's well again."

"Funny how you talk about human rights, when you fucking mind-control your people. We might lock our people up for criminal actions, but we stay out of their heads."

Isobel looked at me. "I don't know what you're talking about. We only try to help people feel better."

"No one is questioning your good intentions, Mother," Pearl said. "It's just that sometimes good intentions can lead to bad situations. Just because you don't understand or condone people's behavior doesn't mean you should lock them up until they agree to see things your way."

"No, it's much easier to kill them," I said to break the heavy atmosphere.

"What?" Isobel gaped at me.

"When some stupid-ass rebel wants to attack Khan and Pearl, I tell them to change their minds or die."

"He's kidding, Mom," Pearl told Isobel with a smile while Khan refilled her glass of water. "It's just Magni's strange humor." Pearl gave me the stink-eye and shook her head as to say, *It's not funny.*

I shrugged and leaned against Laura, whispering into her ear. "Looks like Isobel would rather hear lies than the truth after all."

CHAPTER 37
Matching Couples

Laura

Isobel folded her hands in front of her. "As I've mentioned before, letting Nmen with a criminal past take part in the matching program would be unwise. We should exclude those individuals."

Pearl's hands were folded on the table in front of her. "Mother, I understand and appreciate your concern. Khan and Magni, however, have made a strong point that any man who has served his sentence shall not be further punished by his past. I tend to agree with them."

Isobel's cheeks were growing redder as the two women battled in what Motlanders would consider a fierce argument. They even resembled each other in body posture.

"This is something I'd need to discuss with the Council. Allowing such matches would be upsetting to many of the members." Isobel lifted her hands to massage her temples. "As it is, this matchmaking program is causing great distress for many of us. To include men with violent pasts would increase our concerns further. If something were to happen to any of these women, it would be on us. We allowed it."

I leaned forward. "With all due respect, Chairwoman, there is such a thing as a free choice. These women aren't children and they understand they're taking a risk. If something happens to them it's on *them*, not you."

"But our role is to keep our people safe."

"I get that. Councilwomen are like overprotective moms, but you're suffocating your people with your love.

The applicants aren't children and they don't need you to limit their options by excluding men who might be their perfect match. Let them make that decision for themselves." My speech was more to the point than Isobel was used to, and her eyes darted to Pearl, as well as to Christina and Erika, who were both in the room too.

All morning we'd been working on finalizing the matching process. Khan hadn't been able to join us since he was with Magni dealing with urgent matters.

Pearl was looking over the deadlines for the project. "We'll need your approval before tomorrow night, Mother. Every woman will receive her top ten matches tomorrow night and she'll have two days to decide which five candidates she wishes to meet in person."

"Erika made an excellent suggestion that Khan agreed to." Pearl smiled at our mother-in-law. "Why don't you tell it yourself?"

Erika gave a small smile and looked at Isobel when she spoke. "As you might have heard, some of the most wealthy and influential men in the Northlands were charged with conspiracy to overthrow my son. As a result, their assets were confiscated, and Khan has approved some of that wealth being used to fund new experimental schools and initiatives to support the Motlander women's integration into our society."

"That's wonderful." Isobel smiled.

Erika nodded and angled her head. "Yes, and fitting if you think about it. Those men held a very low opinion of women. They considered us intellectually impaired. This money can support women getting to work here and keep them safe from men who might feel threatened by them." Erika paused and looked around at Christina, Pearl, and Isobel. "I have to say that being part of this project has been nothing short of amazing."

I rubbed Erika's back. "It's empowering to see women make decisions, isn't it? I used to think you were the strongest woman I knew because I saw you stand up to both Khan and Magni at times. Now I know that we can give the men a run for their money. We are going to bring the Northlands up to a new standard that will benefit everyone living here."

"On that note," Pearl said and pulled up some images of drones. "I've visited some of the mining towns and it was disturbing to see how poor some of the Nmen are. I believe that one of the reasons is the lack of mobility. There's no public transportation in this country. Either you're rich enough to have a drone or you have no money and you're stuck. Many of the drones that fly around are a safety concern. They fly too fast like Magni's or they're too old and should be scrapped."

"What do you suggest?" I asked.

"We need to establish a public transportation system."

"But it's possible to hire a drone already," Erika pointed out.

"Yes, but we need to give the people a more affordable option. One that will allow people to commute to a job. Right now, they are geographically bound and that's not serving the people."

I whistled. "Sounds ambitious, Pearl."

Pearl gave me a confident smile. "Oh, we're just getting started. I'm planning to improve the health care system, establish more food banks, and provide free education."

"Education *is* free."

"Yes, but I'm talking about adults. Too long the Northlands have been the rich man's dream and the poor man's nightmare. I want to help everyone live at their full potential. Education is a key part of that."

"You have a good heart, Pearl." I meant every word. "I'm sorry that Magni doesn't like you much. I wish I could do something to change it."

Pearl and Isobel exchanged a glance and then Pearl spoke in a serious tone. "There is something you can do."

I sighed and gave an apologetic smile. "I already tried talking sense with him, but Magni is skeptical by nature."

"Mila asked Magni to adopt her." This time it was Isobel who spoke. "God knows why, but the child loves him."

I frowned. "So do I, and if you knew him better, you'd understand."

"That's right," Erika chimed in.

"Mila wrote me and Pearl a letter asking for the Council to approve Magni's becoming her official father. It was decorated with nice drawings of her in the middle and you and Magni on each side."

"I didn't know that," I whispered and swallowed the lump in my throat when Isobel handed me the letter. "What are those?" I pointed to some smaller creatures next to the three of us in the picture.

"Those are all the pets Mila is wishing for."

"There's at least fifteen."

"Yes, I believe they are mostly dogs, cats, and a pet pig. The seven small ones I think are rabbits and guinea pigs."

"You spoke to her about the drawings?" I asked.

"I did," Pearl said in a soft voice. "I explained to her why Magni can't adopt her. Only Motlanders can do that, which is when she asked if *you* could adopt her."

"Me? When was this?" I could feel my heart race with the possibilities opening up to me.

"Last week," Pearl responded. "With you being an official Motlander, Isobel is willing to approve the adoption since it's Mila's highest wish."

I gaped. "You'll let me adopt Mila?"

"Yes." She smiled. "When Christina adopted Raven we allowed Boulder to become her adopted father. It made sense since he was the spouse of Christina and would function as Raven's father. He signed some conditions about her rights, one of them being that she can't be auctioned off in a tournament unless she chooses so herself."

"Okay." I nodded my head with excitement pressing inside my chest.

Pearl handed me some documents. "These are the adoption papers. What do you think, Laura? Will Magni like me better when he learns that I helped fulfill Mila's biggest wish?"

I got up to hug her. "I can't speak for him, but I love you for it."

We sat for a while, talking about ways to break the news to Magni and Mila. After settling on a simple plan, we walked down the hallway to Khan's office.

"It's an invasion of women," Khan joked when the five of us entered at the same time.

Boulder came over to kiss Christina and his hand stroked her belly. "Did you ladies get some work done?" he asked with a smile.

"Yes, we did."

"So did we," Khan said and looked at Pearl and Isobel. "You'll be happy to hear that I pardoned the Huntsmen."

When Isobel frowned, Pearl explained. "The soldiers who held us against our will thinking that we were hiding Magni."

"Oh, I see."

Pearl elaborated, "Khan and I have been in a disagreement about what consequences they should face for their actions."

"I didn't spare them because of our arguments," Khan emphasized. "It was Magni's condition for getting back to work."

Magni shrugged. "I trained those men to be the best warriors in the Northlands and they're loyal to me. I can't do my job without them and since you're asking me to return to my job, it's a package deal."

"Thank you Magni, for making Khan do the right thing." Pearl spoke the words in a soft and melodic voice and her smile was genuine when she walked over and snaked her arm around Khan's waist, leaning against him. "We are going to the school and would like you to come and help us send off Isobel, Shelly, and the others."

"Would you mind if I stayed here? I'm drowning in work," Khan excused himself.

Pearl blinked, and I could tell her mind was spinning to come up with a plausible excuse that wouldn't make Magni suspicious or reveal the surprise about the adoption.

"It's just that you said you're announcing my pregnancy to the country in your speech tonight. I'd like the children at the school to hear it from us first."

Khan lowered his head and thought about it. "You think it would mean a lot to them?"

"Yes, I do. Please, Khan, it means a lot to me too."

"All right, then I'll come." He shuffled some papers around on his desk and gave a short order to Magni. "Go talk to your men. They'll be glad to get out of the prison cell they're in."

"No," I shrieked.

Boulder, Khan, and Magni all looked at me with concern. "What's wrong, Laura?"

I'd never been good at coming up with lies on the spot. "It's just that Mila called me before and one of the boys has been teasing her. She was asking for you."

"Who teased her?" Magni took a step closer to me. "Is she okay?"

"She wouldn't say who, but she asked for you."

As expected, Mila's needing him did the trick and Magni left with the rest of us. Pearl's eyes bulged at me when Magni muttered about all the ways he'd teach the boys not to mess with Mila.

I was biting my lip, worried that he'd storm into the school and cause havoc in his quest to protect Mila from all harm. Pearl saw me sweating and came to my rescue.

"Magni, I know I'm asking a lot, but would you allow me and Khan to make our announcement before you interrogate Mila about who teased her?"

Magni nodded in agreement. "Sure."

He kept his promise and didn't say a word when Khan and Pearl gathered everyone in the schoolroom and told the good news.

The children were congratulating Pearl and Khan. Mila, Rochelle, Paysey, Nicki, and some of the others offered to play with the baby and babysit if ever needed.

Magni's eyes roamed the room, shooting silent questions at the boys to see if any of them would crack just from his scowling at them.

I walked over and pulled him to a corner. "You know I love you, right?"

"Yes. I know." He angled his head. "You don't need to worry, I'm not going to throw a tantrum. I've decided I'm going to stay in control when I learn who did it."

"About that..." I called Mila over. "Sweetie, would you please go to Pearl. She has something for Magni to see."

Mila hurried and was given a folder that she brought back to us. "Here you go." She handed it to Magni. "What is it?"

Magni opened the folder and read the title, before his eyes flew to me. "What is this?"

My face softened and I couldn't hold back the tears in my eyes. "Mila, why don't you help Magni read it?"

Mila moved closer to him and looked down at the folder. "I can't read that first word."

Magni caressed her hair. "It says certificate."

Mila read slowly. "Certificate of adop..." Her eyes grew wide.

"Certificate of adoption," I finished for her.

Both Mila's hands flew to her mouth and she kept looking from me to Magni and back again as if waiting for us to confirm that it was true.

"If Magni signs this paper, you'll officially be our daughter," I said and lowered my forehead to Mila's temple. "See, I already signed."

The folder in Magni's hands was shaking and his Adam's apple jumped as he kept blinking his moist eyes while looking into Mila's.

"Do you want him to sign?"

Mila's head nodded up and down and the heels of her palms dried tears from her eyes. "Yes," she cried.

I handed Magni a pen, and using his thigh as support under the folder, he signed the papers with his hand trembling with emotion. As soon as it was done, he picked up Mila and held her with one arm while pulling me into his other arm. Mila and I were crying happy tears and Magni was laughing and planting kisses on our faces and hair. "My girls," he kept saying.

"What's going on?" Raven asked and I looked up to see that we'd attracted an audience.

Khan took the initiative. "I'm happy to announce that I'm not the only one who's growing his family. My brother and his wife Laura have adopted Mila as their daughter."

The joy was like waves of happiness running through the crowd, and everyone wanted to congratulate us.

"I showed Magni the letter that Mila had sent to Pearl and told him it had been Mila's idea for me to adopt her."

Magni laughed. "Who would have known that you being a Motlander would end up being a good thing?"

"You need to thank Pearl. She was the one who argued our case with the Council and without her none of this would have been possible."

I watched as Magni pulled Pearl to the side and thanked her. They spoke for a while and ended up smiling.

"What did you say to her?" I asked with curiosity.

"That I was grateful for her help."

"And?"

"And I apologized for the times I've given her shit."

"No way. You *apologized* to Pearl?"

Magni met my eyes. "Do you think less of me for apologizing to her?"

"No, why would I? I'm impressed with you." I leaned in and kissed him just as Kya stood up on a chair.

"Can I have your attention?"

"Look, Kya looks like a grown-up now," one of the boys teased. Compared to the women in the Motherlands, Kya was average in height, but with the Nmen being way above six feet, she looked petite next to them.

"We can't all be tall as you Nmen," Kya retorted and pointed to the boys. "It's like with everything in nature. We all grow until we're perfect. I just reached perfection a lot sooner than the rest of you."

"That's right, you have the perfect height for Archer to lean his arm on your head when he's tired," Plato joked.

"And you have the perfect height to keep quiet while I give my speech." Kya lifted her finger to underline that she wanted him to listen. "Today we're saying goodbye to our beloved Shelly, who is leaving to go to college. Shelly, step forward dear."

The teenager took a small step forward, and pulled her sleeves over her hands, like she always did.

"Shelly, you've been an amazing help to all of us and we're going to miss you *so* much. The children have made you a farewell present to remember us by." Rochelle and Nicki both carried a box to Shelly. "You'll find letters and drawings from the children in the box, and some artwork that they made for you."

"Hey, I made one of the presents for you too," Marco piped up. "It's in the box."

"What is it?" Solomon asked. "A poem?"

340

Marco scoffed. "As if. No. The children were painting on stones, so I decided to paint a portrait of you."

"I wanna see it," Raven said and grinned.

Shelly opened the box and took out a stone that fit inside her palm.

Raven frowned after studying the stone. "It doesn't look like Shelly at all, it looks like you painted popcorn or something."

"That's because the stone was too small to paint all of Shelly. There was only room for her gigantic brain."

"Ahh." Raven nodded. "You painted a brain on the stone. Now I see it."

"Thank you very much for your thoughtful gifts. I've loved being here at the school and I hope to get the chance to come back and visit some time," Shelly announced.

I watched the quirky girl get hugged by the Motlander children as she moved around the room. From the first time I met Shelly, I'd always felt the need to give her a makeover. My hands were tingling to see what kind of swan hid inside the ugly duckling. I would love to help her get rid of her severe acne and trim those bushy eyebrows.

"I have a gift for you as well," Shelly said to Marco when she reached him. "Yesterday, the children told me you had painted a stone for me, and I thought I'd give you something too." She held out her hand. "I didn't have time to wrap it, and it's not as fancy as your fine portrait of me. But of course you set the bar impossibly high with that gift."

Marco laughed. "I know."

"It's just a small reminder for you of the time we've had together."

Marco looked down at Shelly's palm as she opened it. "A seashell," he said and picked it up. "Thank you."

"I picked this up on the beach we went to, do you remember?"

"The one in the Motherlands, sure."

"A seashell is symbolic in a way," Shelly said and with the box from the children still in her hand, she crossed her free arm over her chest to scratch her neck, which had changed to a crimson color.

Marco brushed back his shoulder-length curly brown hair and looked closer at the seashell. "Symbolic of what?"

"Of you. The animal who lived inside that shell was soft and vulnerable on the inside and needed a hard shell too."

Marco laughed in his untroubled charming way. "Very funny, but I'm as tough as they come, and you know it."

Shelly shrugged. "If you say so."

"I'll treasure this shell. If people ask me I'll tell them it's a wonderful reminder of a genius girl who was wicked smart but needed to learn to shut up once in a while. You know, like a clam or an oyster."

Shelly leaned her head to one side and furrowed her bushy eyebrows. "And I'll show people your gift and say it's a reminder of a young man who had stones for brains."

"You do that." Marco looked down at the seashell again. "I hope you'll come back to visit us."

I didn't tell Marco at that moment that soon Pearl and I were going to offer him a position as a mentor at one of the new experimental schools. Even if Shelly came back to visit, Marco wouldn't be here. The chance of the two of them ever meeting again was slim.

"Can I give you a farewell hug?" Shelly asked and Marco leaned back, his eyes widening. Men didn't touch females. Here at the school there were exceptions to that rule since they massaged each other as part of Kya's curriculum. But a back or foot rub was one thing. A hug, however, was a very intimate thing and Magni shifted his balance next to me.

"Can't you just shake Marco's hand?" he asked Shelly.

A ghost of insecurity flashed on her face before she steeled herself. "No, I would like to give Marco a hug. He's been my friend and I'll miss him."

"Okay," Magni said and pinned the young man with his gaze. "But keep your hands where I can see them."

I elbowed Magni. "You're making it awkward. Stop."

But the damage was already done and Marco was stiff when Shelly rose up on her toes to hug him. The hug lasted less than three seconds and the whole time Marco was looking at Magni to make sure my husband wasn't going to jump him.

"What's going on?" Khan called out across the room.

Magni held up a hand. "Marco touched her with my permission."

Khan came over with a serious expression on his face. "Since when do you approve of young men touching females? You almost killed Solo for the same thing."

"I caught Solo kissing Willow. Not the same thing."

"Who would have known you two were lovebirds?" Khan clapped a hand on Marco's shoulder.

"We're *not* love birds," Marco insisted. "She's just a kid."

The men were so preoccupied that they missed the way Shelly's face fell. I had been fifteen once and knew what it was like to have a crush on someone older who didn't see me as anything but a child.

"Besides, Shelly is a Motlander and I'm going to win my bride in a tournament," Marco stated. "I want the million dollars."

"You sound like the money is more important than the woman," I said in a disapproving tone.

"I didn't mean it like that. It's just that I want a really nice hybrid like Magni has and they're expensive."

"Maybe I'll let you fly mine someday," Magni said.

Marco looked like Christmas had come early. "That would be amazing. How fast can it go?"

The men began a boring conversation about drones and with a kiss to Magni's cheek, I moved away with Shelly.

"I feel so clueless when they talk about engine power and all that shit," I told her. "I'd much rather talk about beauty products."

"Beauty products?" Shelly wrinkled her nose. "I prefer talk about engines over beauty products any day."

I chuckled. "Someday that might change; you never know."

Shelly gave a sideways glance in Marco's direction. "Maybe."

"There are products that would help clean your skin, and if you trimmed your eyebrows, and treated your hair with some silk oil, I'll bet you'd be the prettiest girl in the room."

Shelly bit her lip. "Beauty is superficial. I'm not a vain person."

"Okay."

She stood for a second, shooting glances in Marco's direction. "You really think I'd be the prettiest girl in the room."

"I'm not saying it to be polite. You should know by now that's not the Northlander way. All I'm saying is that you have a secret weapon, if you ever decide you want a man's attention."

Shelly gave a quirky giggle that reminded me the girl was truly just a teenager.

We all gathered outside the school to send off Isobel, Shelly, and the Motlander children who were going home for Christmas.

Mila stood between Magni and me when we waved to the drone. "I would like to sleep at the school tonight," she said and looked up at me.

"Sure."

"It's just that Nicki is sad about everyone leaving and I promised I'd sleep with her."

"You're a good friend, Mila, and you don't have to go home with us every night. You can do like Raven does and go home on the weekends," I explained.

"We'll come by the school all the time," Magni added and bent down to her height. "And if any of the boys messes with you, I want you to tell me, okay?"

Mila gave him a small smile. "I think a lot of them are jealous of me."

"Why?"

"Because I have the coolest parents."

Magni looked over to the group of Nboys. "You think so?"

"I heard Storm say it's unfair that only the girls get adopted, and that Solo is lucky he might get to train with you. They don't have families to go home to on the weekends or for Christmas."

Magni straightened up to his full height and stood for a second, looking thoughtful. "Maybe we should do something about that."

CHAPTER 38
Insatiable

Magni

Laura and I had always been very physical, but these past days since I returned from Alaska, we were making up for lost time and couldn't get enough of each other.

Every surface in our suite had been used and I kept thinking Laura would ask me to take a break and stop bothering her, but she seemed as insatiable as me.

"I missed you." Laura flew into my arms when I walked into our suite.

I managed to catch her and grinned when she wrapped her legs around my waist like a monkey.

"You missed me *a lot*, didn't you?"

Laura's energy was playful, and she unbuttoned the top of my uniform jacket and licked my neck up to my jaw.

"If I get this welcome every time I come home, you'll have me home earlier and earlier every day."

She bit my earlobe and whispered, "More time to play."

"You want to play?" I carried her to the bed and threw her down. "Let's play then."

While I got rid of my shoes, jacket, and shirt, Laura got up on her knees on the bed and did a little strip show, pulling off her dress in an erotic way.

Eager to feel her, I reached forward but she moved back and laughed. "If you want me, you'll have to catch me."

With a groan, I chased her with only my pants still on. She was running over the bed and furniture with incredible speed and agility, and it brought out the hunter in me.

"I'll catch you and when I do, I'll spank your ass so hard, Laura."

She laughed and turned around, mocking me by letting me get close before she ran again.

"I'm bigger and stronger than you are."

"But I'm faster."

"Sure you are." My laugh felt as refreshing as an open window letting in fresh spring air to my soul. Like a sly wolf chasing down a delicious deer, I cornered her. "Did you think you stood a chance?"

"Did you?" she said, her chest rising and falling as she panted from all the running.

Her answer confused me but I didn't have time to think before she attacked me. Her hands were in my hair, pulling my head down, and she was kissing me, hard and demanding, her teeth biting into my lower lip. With her body she pushed me to walk backward until I stumbled into a chair.

Laura had never been this aggressive with me before and I wasn't sure what to make of it. "What are you doing?" I asked.

She pulled her head back enough to lock eyes with me. "I'm taking what's mine."

The lust in her eyes made chills run down my spine in the most satisfying way. I'd never felt this desired in my life and it was a fucking rush. Laura's hands opened my pants and when she squatted down, I moaned with anticipation. "Oh shit, Laura."

Her beautiful long ginger hair framed her pretty face when she looked up at me with a mischievous smile. She had sucked me before but it was the way she did it – like she was running the show. It should make me feel like less of a man, but it was fucking amazing to feel the power radiating from her. If someone had told me from the beginning that letting Laura take charge a little would make her ten times as fun in bed, I would have done it sooner.

I was as hypnotized when her hands freed my cock and spread the pre-cum up and down my shaft.

"Fuck, this is so hot, Laura." My lips opened in a moan when Laura looked straight into my eyes and opened her mouth, sticking out her tongue and licking up and down my shaft. I had to close my eyes for a second to make sure it was real. She was still sucking my cock when I opened them again. Her technique was impeccable, and she had me almost losing my mind with the way her head bobbed and the sounds she made.

"I want to fuck you." I pulled her up and carried her to the couch, turning her around and spreading her legs. It was a magnificent sight of female perfection with her long red hair cascading down her back and her round ass sticking out to entice me.

"Yes," She gave a deep moan when I entered her from behind. "It feels so good."

"I fucking missed you too," I panted.

"Harder," she moaned as I took her on the couch.

"What did you say?" I smacked her ass. "Who told you I take orders?"

Laura turned her head and looked at me with hooded eyes full of lust. "What's the matter, you don't like it when I beg you to take me harder?"

With a low growl, I pressed my fingers into her hips and fucked her harder, my heart racing and my eyes feasting on her creamy skin.

"Yes, that's it." Laura's body was rocking back and forth and her tits were swaying from the movements. The sight alone made my sack harden.

"I want you to fill me with your cum, Magni."

"As if you had a choice." I growled and pulled her up to bite her shoulder in a sign of dominance. "I'm going to fuck you every day until your belly starts bulging with my kid."

"Do you promise?" Her laugh was sexy and I kept taking her, pushing us both closer to a climax.

"Yes. Yes. Yes." Laura's voice was high-pitched and she threw her head back on my shoulder screaming my name in her euphoria. "Yes, Magni, Yes."

All the loneliness I had suffered was gone. With Laura's insides cramping around my cock as if she would never let me pull out of her, we were as connected as we could ever be. I pushed in deeper and stilled for a second as I shot my load of semen inside her with deep moans.

Laura remained in her position, waiting for me to move.

"You. Are. Mine." The statement came out low and strained as every part of my body was recovering from the intense sex. I didn't move until she confirmed it.

"That's right. I'm all yours."

A deep sigh of satisfaction sounded from me as I pulled back and walked to the bathroom to clean up.

Laura followed me and sat down on the toilet to press out the semen.

"Don't do that. Go lie down on the bed with your feet in the air. I want a child with you."

She took some paper and dried herself, before doing as I had told her to.

"We had a meeting with the Nboys today," I said when I joined her in the bed a few seconds later.

"Who did?"

"Me, Archer, Marco, and Boulder."

"Wow, sounds serious. What was the meeting about?"

"We told them that we consider them *our* boys."

Laura reached for another pillow to get her head up higher. "*Your* boys?"

"Yeah, you know, that even though they don't have a father they can count on us if they need guidance or help with anything."

"You told them that?"

"It was the thing Mila said about them being jealous that she had parents. I had a father myself and to be honest, I always envied the boys who didn't because my father was a pain in the ass. I asked Boulder, Archer, and Marco, who grew up without parents, and they said that they never felt that they were missing out on anything.

"I guess it's a case of you don't miss what you don't know about. The problem is that our boys at the school are exposed to Motlander children talking about growing up in family units and having parents. Plus, they saw Raven and Mila getting adopted."

"So you figured you men could give them a sense of family?"

I gave a slow nod. "Yeah, or maybe just express in words what we've never told them."

Laura's eyebrows rose and she smiled. "Magni Aurelius, are you turning into a sensitive man of words?"

"Fuck no. I left the talking to Boulder and Archer."

"Did you say *anything*?"

"Yeah, I said that I expected great things from them and that I'd whip their asses if they didn't perform their best."

"Hmm. That sounds more like threats to me."

"Hey, they wanted fathers, that's how fathers are."

"No, Magni, that's how *your* father was. Maybe you need to redefine what a good father is and build them up instead of making them insecure."

I protested. "They aren't insecure. They are cocky arrogant bastards just like we were at their age."

Laura laughed. "You're still arrogant and cocky, but I love you."

Laura looked edible at that moment, and I pulled her into position and rolled on top of her, her body warm and welcoming. "Show me how much you love me."

Laura was smiling when I kissed her and our teeth banged against each other a little. Her hands nuzzled my nape and shoulders, our tongues twirling against each others in a slow dance. When she lifted her legs to wrap them around me, I didn't care that we'd just had sex. My cock grew hard again and I wanted her.

Her eyes widened a little when I slid inside her.

"But we just..."

"So?" This time I moved slow and deep, taking all the time in the world. Leaning my weight onto my elbow next to her head gave me one hand free to tuck her hair behind her ear, and cup her face. "You're fucking gorgeous, do you know that?"

She moved her head and caught my thumb between her lips, nibbling at me like she wanted to eat me up. "This feels different," she whispered and the softness in her eyes mirrored the state I was in. In a gentle movement, I pulled my thumb out and kissed Laura again, my hips rotating and pushing in and out of her at a slow pace.

A deep moan escaped Laura and I felt butterflies take off in my stomach. "I think the difference is that we aren't fucking but making love," she whispered into my mouth.

She was right.

Laura and I had always had fiery sex with lots of positions, and sweaty bodies. What we had just finished ten minutes ago had been just that. This was something else.

"I love you," I whispered and trailed soft kisses down her jaw. "I love you, I love you, I love you."

Laura's small laugh was the sound of pure joy, and she pulled me back in for a kiss that tasted salty.

"What is it, babe?"

Laura didn't dry away her tears. "I'm just so happy."

A smile grew on my face. My wife was crying with happiness, and I'd never felt like a bigger man.

We made slow love and when Laura came in my arms I felt like the richest man in the universe. I had a family now and my wife was as mad about me as I was about her.

"Maybe making love twice that close together will give us twins," Laura joked when we lay naked together, her head on my chest and her fingers playing with my wedding band.

"That would be a bonus. What was it you wanted to name our child if it's a daughter?" I asked.

"Aubri if it's a girl, and you wanted Mason if it's a boy, right?"

"Uh-huh. And what if we have more than two?"

"We'll let Mila come up with a name. It's her younger siblings after all."

I turned my head and placed a kiss on Laura's soft hair. "Thank you for adopting Mila with me."

"I would adopt Mila any day. She's the kindest girl in the world."

"Yeah. She's almost too kind and pacifistic," I pondered out loud. "Good thing she has us as parents now. We'll have to toughen her up a little."

Laura lifted her hand and looked at me. "I don't think we should try and change Mila. It would break my heart to see someone as pure and innocent as her grow cynical."

I nodded. "All right. That's true. But we'll have to make sure she marries someone as fierce and strong as me. Someone who can protect her."

Laura grinned. "That's a given, Magni. With you as her father no young man is going to look at her unless he's either stupid or very brave."

"That's what I'm hoping for, but we should still keep an eye on the boys at the school. Which reminds me, now with Shelly gone they need an assistant teacher to Kya. I hope you don't mind, but I suggested that you could stand in until they find one."

Laura looked stunned. "Does that mean you're okay with me working for real?"

"Isn't that what you wanted?"

"Yes."

"Well." I let my finger trail over her collarbone. "Kill me if I sound like a Motlander, but I've been thinking."

"About what?"

"About how miserable we were when we tried to mold each other into what we thought we wanted. I wanted you to be an obedient and submissive wife, and you wanted me to be a Momsiman who worships you.

Laura laughed. "I never said that I wanted you to be a Momsiman."

"The point is that I've changed my mind. I see the strength in you and I don't want you to play small, Laura. I want Mila to have a role model in you. She should trust her own instinct and not follow some foolish boy onto a slippery roof."

"I want that for her too, but you do understand that it means I might say no to you at times."

"You *should* say no to me if I'm being unreasonable."

"You *unreasonable*!" She laughed. "*Never*."

I tickled her. "Hey, I can still spank your ass if you're being naughty."

"Ooh, then I'll think of ways to say no to you in naughty ways.

The playful energy between us was back and it made me laugh.

Laura smiled and cupped my face. "I love it when you smile and laugh, Magni. You never used to do that, and it makes you even more handsome and sexy."

"How could I not laugh and smile after the sex we just had. You're turning into a fucking sex goddess, Laura."

She kissed me, letting her tongue slide over the rim of my teeth, and climbed up to straddle me.

With my hands planted firmly on her ass, I squeezed her cheeks.

Laura leaned down and locked eyes with me. "Are you sure you can handle the new Laura?"

I responded with a confident smile. "If anyone can handle you, honey, it's me. Don't forget that I'm still the strongest warrior in the world."

Laura raised her eyebrows in a mischievous smile. "Are you, though? I would say that *I'm* the strongest warrior. After all, I'm the one on top here."

"I can't argue with that." I laughed, and when her hands reached for my hands and we intertwined our fingers, it might as well have been our hearts reaching for each other. "Every warrior has a weakness," I said with emotion in my throat. "You're mine, Laura."

Her blue eyes melted in a beaming smile. "That's only fair, since you've always been my weakness as well."

EPILOGUE
Toddlers

Laura

"Throw me another beer, will you?" Magni called out to Khan, who stood closest to the large tub where the ice cubes meant to keep the drinks cool had melted long ago.

We were all gathered to celebrate our twins' fourth birthday, a tradition that we had adopted from the Motlanders.

"Mila, go tell Mason he has to share the sword with Aubri."

Mila, who was close to fifteen, flashed her dimples in a grin. "I told him to share it three times already, but he keeps saying that swords are for boys."

I was tempted to go talk to my son myself, but being nine months pregnant, getting up from my chair felt like an exhausting project in this heat.

"We've got too many kids," I muttered to Christina, who sat next to me with her baby in her arms.

She laughed. "I know, I was just telling Boulder that three is enough for us. I feel like I've been pregnant non-stop for the last five years."

"I think the men think it's a competition to see who can have the most children," Athena laughed. "Finn is obsessed with having a daughter."

"But he adores the boys," I said and looked over to the soccer field where Finn, Archer, and Boulder were playing with the children. The students had changed since I'd first visited the school. What had started as an experiment had become a permanent school. Mila, Tommy, Victoria, and William were the only students left from the first batch of kids. At the end of the summer they would be moving on to their new schools, and it would be an adjustment not to have Mila around as much.

"Yes, he adores the boys." Athena smiled and chuckled when Finn picked up his two-year-old and four-year-old sons and ran with them under his arms to get to the ball quicker. "How could he not, they are copies of him and laugh at his jokes."

"You laugh at his jokes too," I pointed out.

"I have to. I'm trying to bring wisdom into my boy's heads and he sabotages me by making funny faces behind me. Either I get mad or I laugh with them."

"I wish Freya would laugh a little more," Pearl said and nodded her head in her daughter's direction. Rather than playing herself, the girl stood next to the soccer field and gave instructions to the others. "I mean her speech is advanced for her age, but she's too serious and all she wants to do is play chess or the piano. That's not normal for a four-year-old."

Christina, Athena, Kya, and I laughed. "What did you expect with you and Khan as parents?"

Pearl stroked her belly and smiled. "I'm hoping this one will be a more fun-loving member of our family, and get Freya to play a little."

We all took a second to look at Freya, who watched the others play with a serious expression. The contrast between her parents' dark and light colors had resulted in a beautiful child with olive skin, soft brown curls, and piercing green eyes.

Pearl looked at Christina. "I would have loved Freya to be a bit more like Raven. That girl doesn't take no for an answer, and she's so driven."

Christina nodded. "That's Raven for you, but Freya is strong too in her own way. Besides, I worry about Raven. She wants to be a police officer."

"She would be great at it, don't you think?" Pearl asked.

Christina bit her lip. "Being the first woman in the police force will be challenging. I don't want her to deal with all that. It would be much easier if she chose a different profession."

"I'll bet being the first at it is part of why Raven wants to do it," I said. "She has that strength to go first everywhere."

Christina nodded. "Boulder and she train together every time she's home. He says she's become a strong fighter."

"She's very strong. I trained with her a few months back, and she might be only sixteen but she's incredible." I tilted my head. "Mila could learn a little from Raven. She can't fight for shit."

Kya placed a hand on my shoulder. "Mila is a lover, not a fighter. You should be proud of her."

"I am." I smiled at Kya and looked back at all the children playing with the schoolchildren and some of our men. "You do realize, Kya, that soon we'll have enough children between us to fill your entire school, right?"

Pearl counted. "Boulder and Christina have three, Khan and I will have two soon. Finn and Athena have two and are working on number three, and Laura and Magni have the third coming. With your own two kids, that makes for around thirteen kids."

Kya looked up at Khan and Boulder, who were talking behind us. "We'll need to extend the school soon."

"Why?"

We women laughed. "Because you men won't stop breeding babies and we want our children to stay together."

Athena raised a hand. "Not me. Finn and I are staying in the Motherlands."

357

"Why? Wouldn't you love your boys to go to this school?" Kya asked and threw her hands up. "Look at this place. It's lush, tranquil, and it has amazing teachers. What's not to like?"

Athena laughed. "I'd miss my job too much. But you're right – this place is wonderful, which is why we come often."

"What about Tristan, how is he doing?" Christina asked Athena.

Athena lit up. "Didn't I tell you Tristan designed his first drone?"

We all made sounds of excitement. "Two years into his apprenticeship and he's already designing a drone." I whistled, impressed.

"I doubt he did it all by himself, but Mr. Wrestler is very pleased with him." Athena was beaming with pride when a loud scream made us all look to the soccer field, where Mason had decided to combine sword fighting with soccer playing and was using his soft play-sword to fight off the other children for the ball.

"That's unfair," Freya shouted from the sidelines. "It's against the rules." With her hands on her hips she gave a pout of indignation and complained to Finn. "Mason should be dispolified."

"It's called disqualified, honey," Pearl corrected her daughter.

"Hey, Freya, he's your cousin. Show some loyalty," Magni called to his niece.

Freya came stomping over. "Uncle Magni, Mason needs to learn the rules."

Magni laughed. "He's a rule-breaker like his father." Squatting down, Magni waved Freya over and pulled her up on his lap. "One day you'll be older and Mason is going to use all that feistiness to defend you against bad Nmen."

"What bad Nmen?"

"The ones that want to take the power away from your dad and me. They are confused men who are fueled by petty anger. Mason will grow up to punish them and keep you safe."

Freya looked like a wise old woman when she tilted her head. "People shouldn't be punished for their anger. They will be punished *by* their anger."

One of Magni's eyebrows rose up, and he sat Freya back down on the ground and stood to his full height looking at Khan. "That's what you get from marrying a Councilwoman."

Khan grinned. "I still have time to influence her." His eyes found Mason and Aubri, who were on the ground in a fight over the sword again. "At least my nephew and niece are descended from two warriors; I trust that they'll keep my chess player safe when the time comes."

"You're not thinking about changing the law and making Freya the next ruler, are you?" Magni asked in a low voice.

"You don't need to whisper," Pearl teased. "It's a good question and I think we're all dying to know the answer."

"No, I'm not going to change the law. I'm hoping Pearl gives birth to a son next and then he'll be the first-born son."

"What if he doesn't want to be ruler?" Pearl asked. "A Council is a great way to distribute the heavy responsibility. For you too."

Magni emptied his beer and went for another one, handing Khan one at the same time.

"The Northlands aren't ready for a female ruler."

"That's right." Magni opened his beer and lifted it to Khan. "We're the last free men and we'll stay that way."

"For now," Pearl said low beside me.

I smiled and enjoyed the sounds of children playing and friends talking.

When Finn came over to join us and get something to drink, he brought a following of the children with him.

"Seems you're very popular," I remarked.

"Of course I am. They don't see me as often as they see the rest of you scoundrels and whales."

I stuck out my tongue. "This whale would get up to kick you, if my belly wasn't too heavy."

"Bring it on. I would just have to tip you over and you wouldn't be able to get up again." He laughed.

My index finger waved in warning. "I might be down like a turtle, but my scoundrel of a husband could still kick you for me."

"Don't mind Finn calling us whales," Athena said. "He's just teasing. He's told me plenty of times that women are beautiful when they're pregnant."

Finn blew Athena a kiss. "You're always beautiful."

Aubri wanted to sit on Finn's lap and so he opened his arms to her. She was the perfect mix between Magni and me with her strawberry blond hair and blue eyes. "And you, my warrior princess, you're my new spirit animal." Finn squeezed her from behind and turned his head to his sons. "Did you see how Aubri outran all of us before? You've got to watch out or she'll be tougher than you."

Finn's two sons weren't happy sharing their dad, and the two-year-old climbed up his back while the four-year-old ran to Athena with a pout.

"Hey, Aubri, come to Mommy," I called and she came running into my arms. "Are you going to be tougher than the boys?"

Aubri had the cutest freckles across her nose; she nodded with enthusiasm.

Magni came over and placed a kiss on her head. "Are you going to find a big strong warrior like your dad when you grow up?"

"Yes."

"Good." Magni smiled at me. "And Aubri, will you remind him that even though you're smaller than him, it doesn't mean you're weak?"

She nodded to her father again and I placed a kiss on her chin. "And will you remember that even though your strong warrior might not express his emotions much, he still feels as deeply as you do?"

Aubri had no patience for our adult talk and wriggled out of my arms, to run back to her brother.

Christina chuckled. "I don't think Aubri got any of that."

I smiled. "That's okay. It took us a while to figure out as well."

This concludes Men of the North #5 – The Warrior

A message from Elin Peer:
Before I tell you about the next book in the series, called *The Genius*, I want to thank my daughter Pearl for letting me use her poems "Generations of Mirrors" that Mila read out to Laura, and "Truth," that Solomon read out at the poetry night.

In January 2018, "Generation of Mirrors," won Pearl a first prize in a literary contest for middle schoolers. Yes, I'm bursting with pride for her.

If you liked Magni's and Laura's story, I would be forever grateful if you'll take a second to leave a review on Amazon. I can't tell you how much it means to me and how it motivates me to keep writing books for your entertainment.

Want more?
In the next book we'll jump ten years ahead and follow Shelly, the genius that you've come to know as Kya's

assistant teacher. Now twenty-five and still smart as a whip, Shelly's curiosity makes her do the craziest thing.

The Genius – Men of the North #6

With three degrees and the highest measured IQ in the Motherlands, Shelly Summers knows that she's socially awkward. It doesn't bother her since as the head engineer for Advances Technologies she has little time for social interactions anyway.

When she learns that one of the testers for the sex-bots her company manufactures is her old crush, Marco, she's curious to see if he'll recognize her now that she's ten years older and no longer has bushy eyebrows and a bad case of acne.

A normal person would have said something when Marco doesn't recognize her from his past. A normal person would definitely have said something when he mistakes her for an advanced sex robot and thinks his job is to do a test run.

Things are about to get very awkward for this genius...

The Genius is the sixth book in the series *Men of the North* that has readers raving about its perfect mix of love, action, wisdom, and humor.

Check out my website elinpeer.com for an overview of my other books and make sure you sign up for my newsletter to be alerted when I release new books.

Want to connect with me? Great – I LOVE to hear from my readers.

Find me on facebook.com/AuthorElinPeer
Or connect with me on Goodreads, Amazon, Bookbub or
simply send an email to elin@elinpeer.com.

ABOUT THE AUTHOR

Elin is curious by nature. She likes to explore and can tell you about riding elephants through the Asian jungle, watching the sunset in the Sahara Desert from the back of a camel, sailing down the Nile in Egypt, kayaking in Alaska, and flying over Greenland in helicopters.

She can also testify that the most interesting people aren't always kings, queens, presidents, and celebrities, because she has met many of them in person.

After traveling the world and living in different countries, Elin is currently residing outside Seattle in the US with her husband, daughters, and her black Labrador, Lucky, which follows her everywhere.

Elin is the kind of person you end up telling your darkest and deepest secrets to, even though you never intended to. Maybe that's where she gets her inspiration for her books. One thing is for sure: Elin is not afraid to provoke, shock, touch, and excite you when she writes about unwanted desire, forbidden passion, and all those damn emotions in between.

Want to connect with Elin? Great – she loves to hear from her readers.

Find her on Facebook: facebook.com/AuthorElinPeer
Or look her up on Goodreads, Amazon, Bookbub or simply go to www.elinpeer.com.

ABOUT THE AUTHOR

Made in the USA
Monee, IL
08 August 2020

37686090R00207